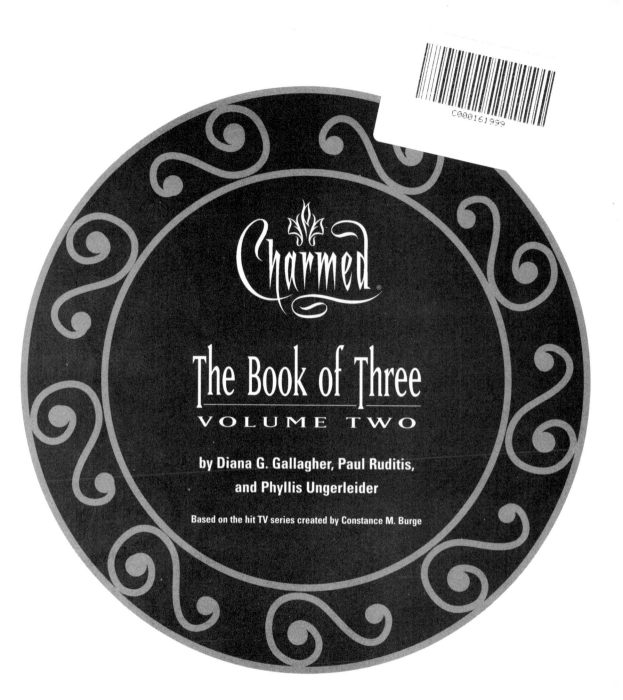

Charmed

The Book of Three
VOLUME TWO

by Diana G. Gallagher, Paul Ruditis,
and Phyllis Ungerleider

Based on the hit TV series created by Constance M. Burge

New York London Toronto Sydney

SIMON SPOTLIGHT ENTERTAINMENT
An imprint of Simon & Schuster Children's Publishing Division
1230 Avenue of the Americas, New York, New York 10020

SIMON SPOTLIGHT ENTERTAINMENT and related logo are trademarks of Simon & Schuster, Inc.
Designed by Lili Schwartz
Manufactured in the United States of America
First Edition 10 9 8 7 6 5 4 3 2 1
Library of Congress Control Number 2006925837
ISBN-13: 978-1-4169-2530-9
ISBN-10: 1-4169-2530-9

Dedication

The demonic line of evil known as Swarm Demons are pack hunters of the Underworld. The Swarm Drones follow the orders of their King without question and often sacrifice themselves for the good of the collective body.

In memory of

AARON SPELLING

Thank you for
keeping us entertained

Acknowledgments

E. Duke Vincent, Brad Kern, Jim Conway, Jon Paré, Jennifer Rees, Sheila Cavanaugh, and the entire cast and crew of *Charmed* for all of their help in bringing this book together.

Additional thanks to everyone at Spelling Entertainment, CBS, Viacom, and Simon Spotlight Entertainment, beginning with our wonderful editors, Terra Chalberg and Beth Bracken, as well as Risa Kessler, Paula Block, John Van Citters, Christina Hahni, Jonathan Levin, Renate Kamer, Mitch Haddad, and the incomparable Nan Sumski.

Table of Contents

Aaron Spelling

1923—2006

When we first started out on *Charmed*, the show was picked up for a full season after only two airings; that's never happened to us before! Eight years later, *Charmed* has become the longest-running series in the history of television featuring all female leads. That's a milestone of which we can all be proud. With the power of our three good witches Piper, Phoebe, and Paige—we are truly "Charmed."

Foreword

*P*eople ask me all the time, "What's the secret to keeping a show on the air for so long?" As if somehow I, having survived eight seasons of *Charmed,* have been made privy to the exclusive club of show runners who alone know the highly classified, secret ingredient. The truth is: I don't have the slightest idea. It's obviously many factors, of course, with luck being at the top of the list. But luck is also the product of hard work, and the one common denominator that links all of the writers, producers, cast, and crew who I've been privileged to work with over these many years is exactly that: hard work. If you're a fan of the show (and I assume you are, otherwise why are you even reading this?), you have all of those wonderful people to thank for the show you have been so loyal to. Most people don't realize how much effort goes into making twenty-two mini movies every year, especially a show like *Charmed,* which requires so much mythology and magic. The first show runner I ever worked for, Michael Gleason, my mentor, once told me that if, out of twenty-two episodes, you can make four great ones, suffer through only four turkeys, and make the rest better than average, then you've had a successful season. Well, I like to think that these last three seasons of *Charmed* have done better than that. In fact, I can't think of even one turkey in that span, although I'm, admittedly, partial. I've spent eight years of my life dedicated to this show and am honored to have been a part of it. But we wouldn't even have made it out of the starting gate if it weren't for you, the fans. So, on behalf of all of us at *Charmed,* thank you for allowing us to have been a part of your lives for so long. We hope we were able to bring a little magic into your world.

Blessed be.

Brad Kern
Los Angeles, California

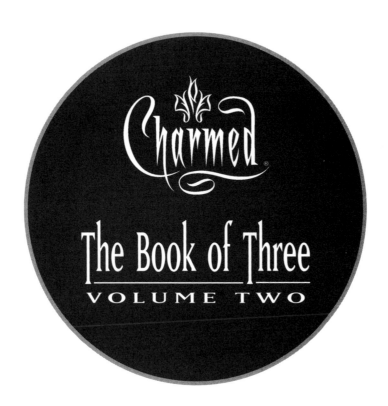

Charmed

The Book of Three

VOLUME TWO

Book of Three

CHARMED CHARACTERS

PIPER HALLIWELL

Devastated when Leo leaves for a higher calling, Piper is determined to have the normal life she's always wanted. She dates other men, but being a Charmed One and the mother of a mischievous toddler witch makes romance and an ordinary existence impossible. Although fate seems determined to keep her and Leo apart, she knows he's the only man she'll ever love. The warm relationship that develops with adult Chris helps Piper through the rough times. His birth provides a new beginning for Piper, Leo, and their family.

However, after Gideon tries to kill Wyatt, Piper is haunted by the prospect of losing people she loves. Wyatt and Chris have protective powers, but Leo is plagued by self-doubt and threats. After living without him, Piper will not give him up again—not to preserve the Avatar's demon-free world nor to appease the Elders. Her love is so strong she dies, touching Leo's heart despite the Elders' influence. With a new identity following her faked death, Piper looks forward to life without demon attacks and growing old with her husband.

Piper's demon-free existence as "Jenny" is marred by guilt for the Innocents she's not helping and a sense of loss for who she is: a witch, Leo's wife, Wyatt's mommy, and the owner of P3. Juggling so many responsibilities is hectic, but she's relieved to be herself again. After weathering a few marital bumps, Piper settles into a familiar routine that takes a cruel twist: Leo is frozen and will not be revived unless the Charmed Ones prevail in the Ultimate Battle. When the battle goes badly, Piper refuses to accept her sisters' deaths. Stubborn and undaunted, she changes the past to fix the future and save the present—as well as saving Leo, Phoebe, and Paige.

PHOEBE HALLIWELL

With Cole behind her and a career as an advice columnist established, Phoebe adapts to her new empathic power. The loss of Jason Dean undermines her faith that she'll find true love and have a family. However, when a vision quest reveals a daughter in her future, she dates intensely to find the father. Phoebe's use of magic for personal gain prompts the Tribunal to strip her powers, but having to rely on her wits and wisdom strengthens her as a Charmed One.

Historically, Halliwell women have never held on to their men, and Phoebe believes she's no different. Jason rejected her magic, and Leslie chose his career. Her vision power is returned when she's willing to die for an Innocent, and her neglected Charmed identity is revived. However, the promise of a daughter is a persistent influence. She helps the Avatars to realize her dream and then risks her dream to make the world right again for everyone. Unaware that Cole sent Drake to save her from a loveless life, she cautiously considers the possibility of love. Her faked death clears the way to follow her dreams as a woman—not a witch.

Phoebe as "Julie" doesn't have time to miss her old life: "Signs" lead her back to her column and solving Charmed problems. After loving and losing Dex Lawson, who also rejects her magical identity, Phoebe's desperate attempts to conceive make her realize that some things can't be forced to happen. The vision daughter is real, and eventually, she'll fall in love with the child's father. In the meantime, she moves out of the Manor to establish an individual life. Victim then victor in the Ultimate Battle that defeats the Triad, she finally finds everything she ever wanted—true love with Coop.

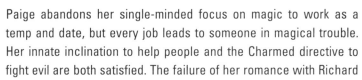

Paige abandons her single-minded focus on magic to work as a temp and date, but every job leads to someone in magical trouble. Her innate inclination to help people and the Charmed directive to fight evil are both satisfied. The failure of her romance with Richard Montana shakes her faith in her ability to carry out the Charmed mission. However, forced to act alone at Magic School, she regains her magical confidence and discovers a talent for teaching. As a result, a subconscious yearning to be independent of her sisters emerges.

Paige saves Magic School and throws herself into running it with dedicated determination. Her affinity for righting wrongs draws her to Agent Kyle Brody, who appreciates magic. Believing

in the Avatars' Better Way, Paige blames herself when an Avatar kills Kyle. Although rattled by the mistake, she trusts her instincts and turns Magic School over to Leo. Becoming a full-fledged Whitelighter is a shock, but her whole life has been spent helping others. She embraces a calling independent of the Power of Three and the new possibilities that open when she "dies" and becomes someone else.

Paige resents giving up magic for safety, and she soon realizes that she can't find true love as "Jo" or build a new magical or mortal life on a lie. However, being Paige again solves only part of her identity problem. Guiding Billie and saving Innocents fulfills her as a witch. Henry Mitchell, a parole officer with a good heart who embraces her magical nature, satisfies her as a woman. However, the essence of Paige isn't complete until she embraces her inner Whitelighter.

LEO WYATT

Although Leo tries to accept his responsibilities as an Elder, he can't deny his love for Piper. He resists moving Up There until his presence threatens his family. However, when he tries to fulfill his new destiny, a paternal imperative drives him back to the mortal world to protect Wyatt and pursue a second chance with Chris. To save his sons and restore balance in the universe, he kills Gideon.

Tricked into killing another Elder, Leo loses faith in himself and the powers of good. He has always put the safety of his family first, even when that meant staying away. Torn between his love for Piper and the greater good, he has tried and failed to have both. After his misguided union with the Avatars, the Elders erase his memory to help him find his way again. His true path is true love, and a human Leo returns to his wife and sons. His powers are gone, but his knowledge of magic is an invaluable asset to the Charmed Ones. When the sisters pretend to die, he welcomes the chance to start over.

Leo tries to make the new life work, but he hates living a lie and gladly reverts to his true identity. Still, the adjustment to being human is not easy. The household witches respect him as a source of wisdom, but he resents being taken for granted as an errand boy and handyman. After those issues are resolved, he realizes that Piper needs and depends on him as much as always—just in different ways. Then destiny marks him to die. Frozen in a demon's lair, he awaits his ultimate fate—a long and happy life with Piper when the Charmed Ones prevail in the Ultimate Battle.

WYATT MATTHEW HALLIWELL

At ten months, Wyatt's powers begin to develop beyond the protective shield he uses when threatened. He learns that he can influence situations with magic and uses "orb eyes" to scare away his mother's dates. However, as the Ultimate Power on Earth, he's prized and feared by friend and foe. He's comfortable at Magic School but unaware that the enemy lurks within the protected halls. Adept at protecting himself, he eludes Gideon's attempts to kill him and escapes events that turned him evil when his father kills Gideon.

Wyatt's magical nature complicates his responses to events in his life—having a younger brother and missing his father. Leo's here-again-gone-again status is upsetting, but Piper, his devoted aunts, and Magic School help him cope. The Terrible Twos are not without hazards, however. Unable to articulate his worries, he acts out: turning his parents into dollhouse people to protect them, orbing without permission, and trusting a manipulative demon that tries to turn him evil. Still, raised among people who cherish and love him, his development is normal despite his unusual abilities.

Wyatt weathers the confusion caused by his parents' many faces, new identities he doesn't perceive, and their eventual return, and he settles into ordinary routines at home and preschool. Although crafty evil can still manipulate the three-year-old, the bond of trust with Leo is forever stronger. Still, when Dad leaves, Wyatt is old enough to wonder if he caused the problems. An understanding more mature than his years emerges when he advises Piper to act as "Daddy would." Raised in a loving home, his good heart is never perverted by his immense power.

CHRIS PERRY

Chris Perry, a Whitelighter from a dark future, journeys back in time to protect Wyatt from turning evil. Assigned as the Charmed Ones' Whitelighter, he keeps his mission and his identity as Leo and Piper's second son secret. When that truth becomes known, other truths emerge. He's hostile toward Leo, the father who was never around while he was growing up, and remote from Piper, the beloved mother who died when he turned fourteen. However, since his presence has altered the past and the future is fluid, these things could change. The man who dies in a false supersweet reality is born to grow up in a different, but normal, world with loving parents and an older brother who wields his power for good.

BILLIE

An athletic, fearless, and teleki-netic young witch, Billie becomes Paige's primary charge and the Charmed Ones' protégée. Wise and willful, she reminds the Charmed Ones that they alone can protect the world from demons run amok, and the sisters reemerge as the Halliwells. When Billie remembers that her sister was kid-napped by a demon fifteen years before, her determination to find Christy becomes a reckless obsession that endangers her and the Charmed Ones. After Christy is rescued, Billie is blind to her sister's evil agenda and susceptible to her manipulations, which turn her against the Charmed Ones. When she finally faces the truth, the Charmed Ones give her a chance to redeem herself. Killing Christy to save her friends is devastating, but she survives with the Charmed Ones' help and forgiveness.

DARRYL MORRIS

Darryl, a police officer and the Halliwells' mortal confidant, has never hesitated when called to help in a magical crisis. However, the relationship is damaged when the Cleaners erase evidence of Charmed magic during a crime. He's convicted of murder and almost executed, and he retains the memory when history reverts. His decision to stop covering for the sisters is thwarted by Inspector Sheridan's suspicions about their involvement in many unsolved crimes, Kyle Brody's theories about magic, and Sheridan's disappearance. The danger-ous association threatens his marriage, but his profound respect for truth and justice puts him forever on the side of good and the Charmed Ones. His loyalty is repaid when the Charmed Ones "die," and the ultimate cover-up frees him to move on to a new life with his family on the East Coast.

VICTOR BENNETT

Absent from his daughters' younger lives, the father of the Charmed Ones steps up whenever they need him as adults. He's stunned to learn that he has a second grandson and easily settles into a rapport he and Chris developed over years together in the future. Overwhelmed by his first orbing experience, he apparently learns to love it. An active member of the family now, he helps his magical daughters cope with the demonic dangers that plague their Charmed lives. He is there, without question, to care for Wyatt and Chris when the sisters "die" and to help them begin new lives as his nieces. When an Elder wants to take the boys and a demon wants to kill him, he is steadfast and committed to keeping his family intact and safe. After his daughters return to life as themselves, he remains a valuable source of advice and a trustworthy babysitter. Wise in the ways of magic, he weathers the confusion of Charmed chaos and uses his wits to protect those he loves.

PENELOPE "GRAMS" HALLIWELL

Even in spirit form, Grams is candid and demanding when it comes to the safety of her granddaughters and great-grandson. Her wrath knows no limits if they are threatened. She's as annoyed with the Charmed Ones for living apart as she is dismissive of Chris's competence and Leo's common sense. Surprised to learn that Chris is her second great-grandson, she counsels Piper on the difficulties of raising magical children and presides over Chris's Wiccaning. Displeased when the sisters fake their deaths and abandon their Charmed legacy, she is bluntly honest: Just because they want to live normal lives doesn't mean they can. However, she is always there when they need her, whether she approves or not.

PATRICIA HALLIWELL

Always the calm voice of reason, Patty's logical advice helps Piper understand and deal with Wyatt. As strong and protective of her daughters as Grams was of her, she has no problem overriding her mother's dictates and opinions when necessary. Even though they are divorced, she and Victor share a parental bond that endures.

SAM WILDER

A once fallen Whitelighter redeemed by his daughter, Sam returns to ask Paige's help saving a lost charge. He stayed away for three years out of deference to her adopted father, an absence that hurt her without her knowing. When Paige almost loses him to the demon Vaklav, she realizes there's room in her heart for two fathers. Sam helps Paige embrace her Whitelighter destiny, and he welcomes the overdue reconciliation.

ELISE ROTHMAN

Editor of the *Bay Mirror*, Elise is Phoebe's friend as well as her boss. Thrilled with Phoebe's talent and insights as an advice columnist, she cautions Phoebe not to forsake love and family to pursue a successful career. She made that choice and regrets it, although she doesn't regret leaving her shmuck husband, James L. Connors. Understanding and accommodating, especially regarding Phoebe's frequent family emergencies, she is Phoebe's source of professional and romantic advice. Elise trusts Phoebe to take the newspaper to press while she takes a family emergency day off—at P3 with Richard Dillard. When Phoebe "dies," Elise realizes she thought of her as "the daughter I never had."

SHELIA MORRIS

Darryl's wife and the mother of Darryl Junior and Michael, Shelia becomes invaluable to the Charmed Ones as a babysitter for Wyatt. Her acceptance of the sisters' mission to eradicate evil makes life easier for Darryl. She doesn't know about his close encounter with death, and she's upset when he pushes the sisters away. They're like family. However, when Sheridan makes it clear that Darryl could lose his job or go to prison because of the Halliwells, Shelia gives him an ultimatum—them or his family. However, when the sisters need his help one last time, she accepts Darryl's determination to do the right thing.

MANY MEN AND JOBS

LEO: Leo will always be the love of her life, but Piper must repeatedly deal with losing him for one reason or another. As an Elder, he must sever his family ties and live Up There. When he accidentally kills an Elder, she could lose him to recycling—starting over from birth. To resolve the conflict that made him become an Avatar, the Elders erase his memory and send him out to find his own path. Piper dies to bring him back, a psychic shock that Leo cannot ignore. As a human without magical powers, he is confident and capable despite Piper's overprotective worry. Through new identities and old, he's with Piper where he belongs—until destiny demands his death. Nothing must distract Piper from a threat graver than anything the Charmed Ones have encountered before. Frozen instead, Leo waits in limbo while his family faces the Ultimate Power. A Charmed victory frees him to live the life he and Piper always dreamed of having.

DAVID, AKA MR. RIGHT: Paige and Phoebe conjure the perfect man as a birthday present for Piper in "Prince Charmed." Gorgeous, sensitive, and charming, David knows Piper's every need and desire and convinces her not to give up on love before his twenty-four-hour lifespan ends.

GREG THE FIREFIGHTER: Tall and good-looking, Greg takes Piper on a fourth date in "Chris-Crossed." Released from her reservations by an Inhibition Spell, Piper almost makes love to him on top of a fire truck. Since raising and protecting Wyatt is a full-time job, she decides not to see him again in "Prince Charmed." Although she gives Greg another chance in "I Dream of Phoebe," Chris makes sure the handsome fireman understands that Leo is the man she loves. Piper runs into Greg's car, which provides an opportunity for them to get back together in "The Last Temptation of Christy," but Piper won't betray Leo.

RYAN AND BRETT: The handsome young men are open to dating a woman with a small child, until Wyatt scares them away with his "orb eyes" in "Soul Survivor."

SETH: A gorgeous, divorced, single dad, he calls Piper for a second date after Chris interrupts the first in "Love's a Witch."

COOP: A cupid sent by the Elders to help Phoebe find love in "Engaged and Confused," he discovers that her heart is blocking her ability to love ("Generation Hex"). In the process of finding her a match, he falls in love with Phoebe in "The Torn Identity." She discovers she feels the same about him in a dream in "The Jung and the Restless," and pursues the relationship under the influence of an obsession spell in "Gone with the Witches." Coop faces being left out of the Charmed loop when Phoebe has to fight the Ultimate Battle ("Kill Billie: Vol. 2"), but nothing can make him forsake the woman he loves ("Forever Charmed").

CROSS, TIM: A graduate student in Dr. Rousseau's psychology class with Phoebe, Tim asks her out while he's changing her flat tire in "Death Becomes Them." Killed by a Raptor demon, he's turned into a zombie and terrorizes Phoebe as part of Zankou's plan to shake the Charmed Ones' confidence.

DEAN, JASON: The owner of the *Bay Mirror*, Jason has a professional interest in Phoebe as a successful columnist and a romantic interest that goes beyond the physical attraction unleashed in "Valhalley of the Dolls" and "Power of Three Blondes." Phoebe finally embraces their mutual affection in "My Three Witches," but Jason is unnerved by her uncanny ability to know how he feels before he does in "Little Monsters." After many close calls, Jason learns that Phoebe is a witch when she's possessed by Mata Hari's karma ("Used Karma"). Unable to accept her magical nature or the chaos it creates, he walks away.

DRAKE: A demon-turned-human with only two weeks left to live, Drake has an unbridled enthusiasm for life and love that Phoebe can't resist ("Carpe Demon"). Intrigued by the prospect of a whirlwind romance in "Show Ghouls," Phoebe allows herself to fall in love with him in "The Seven Year Witch." Drake's death hurts, but she realizes that life without love is hollow and worse than the pain of love lost—a message Drake carried from Cole.

HANGIN' CHAD: A DJ for KQSF in "Valhalley of the Dolls," Chad is attracted to and intimidated by successful women. He makes a lunch date with Phoebe and then stands her up.

LAWSON, DEX: A man Phoebe saw but never met in the elevator at work, Dex comes to her funeral in "Still Charmed and Kicking." A sculptor, he's attracted to "Julie," whose perky personality and insight remind him of her cousin ("Malice in Wonderland"). Thrown together in an earthquake that "Julie" foretold, they share an intimate moment when love is ignited in "Run, Piper, Run." Thanks to Paige's meddling, Phoebe learns that Dex broke all ties with his old girlfriend two months before in "Desperate Housewitches." However, when "Julie," whom he married under a spell, turns out to be Phoebe ("Rewitched"), he can't cope. With the marriage annulled and questioning how they really feel in "Kill Billie: Vol. 1," Dex and Phoebe agree that too much happened too fast, and the relationship won't work.

MARK, MIKE, MITCH, AND RON: A few alphabetical dates in Phoebe's quest to find the father of the child she foresaw in her vision quest. As illustrated on a lunch date with Mitch ("Spin City"), she can find out if the man of the day is the right man with a single touch. None of them are.

MARKS, TODD: An old boyfriend from Phoebe's senior year at Baker High, he is still a little infatuated at their "Hyde School Reunion." Phoebe resents his wife's jealous insults but avoids a scene. However, a flashback teen Phoebe picks up where she and Todd left off—until the spell wears off and everyone reverts to their normal lives.

MICHAEL: The style editor at the *Bay Mirror*, he has asked Phoebe out and been rejected before ("The Torn Identity"). Coop convinces him to try again and acts as Michael's Cyrano, which convinces Phoebe to accept a date. Coop's words, not roses and candy, made the difference. She dates him once in "The Jung and the Restless."

ST. CLAIRE, LESLIE: Phoebe feels an immediate and overwhelming attraction to Leslie, the man Elise hires to write "Ask Phoebe" while Phoebe takes a couple of months off in "A Call to Arms." Finally convinced he can write her column ("The Bare Witch Project"), she's a little jealous when he wins the Reader's Choice Award for a column he wrote

in "Cheaper by the Coven." They both give in to the mutual attraction in "Charrrmed," but Phoebe isn't ready for a relationship ("Styx Feet Under"). Unwilling to carry on a long-distance romance, Leslie leaves in "Once in a Blue Moon." However, their signs are compatible, and Phoebe wonders if they might have a second chance later.

TURNER, COLE: Doomed to an eternal existence between life and death in "The Seven Year Witch," Cole knows that Phoebe is giving up on love. He arranges for the sorcerer to make Drake human, hoping that Phoebe will fall in love with the effervescent ex-demon and escape her loveless life. The plan works, but Cole will spend forever missing the woman he loves.

PAIGE'S MEN

BEN: Twenty-one and a grad student at Magic School, he's infatuated with Paige and receptive when a twelve-year-old version of her kisses him in "Cheaper by the Coven."

BOB: The time-consuming aspects of minding Billie drive Paige to an online dating site. She meets Bob for coffee and finds out he's a boring, self-absorbed market research expert, blah, blah ("Desperate Housewitches").

BRODY, KYLE: An agent with Homeland Security, Brody is intent on proving his theories that magic exists ("Charrrmed"). He doesn't want to harm the sisters ("Styx Feet Under") and creates a cover story for resurrected Piper in exchange for a future favor. In "Once in a Blue Moon," Brody tells Paige he became a cop to find the unknown evil that murdered his parents. He accepts her magic, and she trusts him in "Someone to Witch Over Me." Solving a Magic School mystery in "Charmed Noir" ends with a kiss, but Paige loses patience with his Avatar obsession in "There's Something About Leo." Love clouds her judgment regarding his treatment of Inspector Sheridan ("Witchness Protection"), but she helps him face some hard truths in his past in "Ordinary Witches." Although demons killed his mother and father, Brody's instincts tell him that the Avatars are evil. He dies trying to stop them from remaking the world in "Extreme Makeover: World Edition." He returns as a Whitelighter to kiss Paige goodbye in "Charmageddon" and hints that they might meet again.

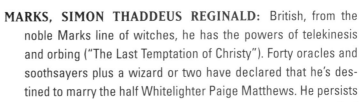

MARKS, SIMON THADDEUS REGINALD: British, from the noble Marks line of witches, he has the powers of telekinesis and orbing ("The Last Temptation of Christy"). Forty oracles and soothsayers plus a wizard or two have declared that he's destined to marry the half Whitelighter Paige Matthews. He persists despite Paige's rejections and Henry Mitchell's belief that he himself can meet any magical challenge. Simon gives up when Henry points out that he doesn't care enough about Paige to learn anything about her and just wants a trophy witch to enhance his power.

MITCHELL, HENRY: A parole officer with a sincere desire to help people, Henry appreciates Paige's understanding of human nature, especially when she stops him from mistakenly ruining a young man's life in "Battle of the Hexes." He uses a baby's missing father as an excuse to see her again ("Hulkus Pocus") and finally invites her to lunch in "Vaya Con Leos." Henry comforts her—no questions asked—when Leo is frozen. He was raised in foster homes, and his lack of trust prevents him from getting close to people ("Mr. & Mrs. Witch"). Paige realizes she's fallen in love with him when she heals a gunshot wound that threatens his life in "Payback's a Witch." Henry isn't afraid when Paige reveals her magical powers ("Repo Manor"). He loves that she uses her abilities to help the world ("12 Angry Zen"), and he loves her. After he survives a fireball injury and a duel with Simon Marks, he asks Paige to marry him in "The Last Temptation of Christy." Their engagement party becomes their wedding night. He and Paige marry at the Manor in "Engaged and Confused" and honeymoon in Tahiti in "Generation Hex." He experiences being Paige when Coop puts her in his head to resolve Paige's identity problem ("The Torn Identity"), but nothing can destroy their happily ever after ("Forever Charmed").

MONTANA, RICHARD: A handsome, twenty-something witch on the rebound in "Love's a Witch," Richard meets Paige a year after his fiancée is killed in a family feud. He attracts more than Paige's do-gooder attention. After his family leaves town, he supports Paige's calling to help people using magic in "Soul Survivor." Paige defends Richard's renewed use of magic and her right to pursue a relationship without being

hounded when Phoebe worries that she's falling too fast in "Sword and the City." However, when Richard swears off magic in "Witchstock," Paige refrains from using her powers in his presence as a demonstration of support. Convinced that he has his family's bad karma ("Used Karma"), he resorts to magic to cleanse himself, then to fix the unintended consequences of the spell. Richard refuses when Paige offers to bind his powers in "I Dream of Phoebe," but he must ultimately accept that magic will ruin his life. Paige ends the relationship for his sake when Richard takes a power-stripping potion.

MR. RIGHT/VINCENT, AKA MR. WRONG: Repeatedly conjured by Paige, the good and evil versions of her Mr. Right know her every desire. Mr. Right becomes a flesh-and-blood man as a result of helping the Charmed Ones destroy Vincent and his evil influence over Paige ("A Wrong Day's Journey into Right").

OSCAR: In "Valhalley of the Dolls" Paige breaks a spell that turned Oscar, a handsome millionaire, into an English bulldog and then accepts a dinner date.

TRAINING INSTRUCTOR: Paige engages in a brief dalliance with the training instructor at the police academy in "Malice in Wonderland."

WHIT: Paige as "Jo" meets the gracious and gorgeous young man at P3's first speed-dating event ("Rewitched"). The instant chemistry with Whit fizzles when Paige realizes that a romance won't be real because her identity isn't real.

LEO'S LADY

EVE: An attractive mom in Wyatt's playgroup, Eve makes a play for "Louis." Eve's jealous husband, Carl, punches Leo/Louis, which prompts Piper to create a new identity who is married to "Louis" ("Run, Piper, Run").

▲ Walking dogs (**"VALHALLEY OF THE DOLLS"**)

▲ Receptionist (**"FORGET ME . . . NOT"**)

▲ Fruit packer (**"POWER OF THREE BLONDES"**)

▲ Companion/nursemaid (**"LOVE'S A WITCH"**)

▲ Retirement home/magician's assistant (**"MY THREE WITCHES"**)

▲ Law firm secretary (**"SOUL SURVIVOR"**)

▲ Desk manager/Phoebe's assistant (**"SWORD AND THE CITY"**)

▲ Filling in at P3 during Piper's pregnancy (**"SPIN CITY"**)

▲ Nanny duties after Chris is born (**"A CALL TO ARMS"**)

▲ Headmistress, Magic School (**"THE BARE WITCH PROJECT"**)

▲ Whitelighter (**"LITTLE BOX OF HORRORS"**)

▲ Cop-for-an-hour (**"MALICE IN WONDERLAND"**)

PAIGE'S CHARGES

MITCHELL HAINES: reluctant speedy guy (**"FREAKY PHOEBE"**)

A MAN IN NEW ZEALAND: not shown (**"IMAGINARY FIENDS"**)

JOANNA: future Whitelighter, killed by Zankou (**"DEATH BECOMES THEM"**)

BILLIE: A telekinetic witch (**introduced in "STILL CHARMED AND KICKING"**)

SPEED: Eighteen, parolee, future Whitelighter going straight (**"BATTLE OF THE HEXES"**)

MIKELLE: Twenty with tattoos and piercings, she dies and saves Paige (**"THE JUNG AND THE RESTLESS"**)

CHRONOLOGICAL FAMILY HISTORY
PART TWO

The **Warren** line of witches and the **Marks** line of witches worked together during the Salem Witch Trials of 1692.

The Summer of Love in 1967 ended tragically for flower child **Penny Halliwell**. **Allen**, her first husband and daughter **Patricia**'s father, was not magical, but he had a poet's talent and soul. When an evil witch posing as Penny's best friend killed him, the shocking loss changed Penny into a formidable demon hunter with a primal determination to protect her family. Consequently, the Charmed Ones' survival is a direct result of Allen's death. **Leo Wyatt**, a young Whitelighter with a roving eye and the ability to manipulate orbs for entertainment, was in Penny's circle of magical friends.

Piper was a small child when **Victor** and **Patty** separated. She blamed herself and suffered from night terrors.

Paige returned to New York City on December 28, 1981, with **Kyle Brody**. Posing as five-year-old Kyle's imaginary friends, they witnessed the murder of his parents, **Jack** and **Ruth**, in an airport warehouse at 7:52 p.m. Demons, not Avatars, were responsible.

Phoebe began eavesdropping on **Piper**'s bedroom from the bathroom and hall in the fourth or fifth grade.

Phoebe dated **Jake Singer** in tenth grade at Baker High School. In her senior year she was a troublemaker who hung out with a wild crowd. Memorialized in the yearbooks as "The most likely to do . . . time!" she was guilty of shoplifting, ditching class, lying, and stealing boyfriends. Her nickname was Freebie.

Paige's first love was a boy named **Vincent**, who wanted to give her the world.

In 2003 **Piper** and **Leo** were forced to separate when Leo became an Elder, but they remained connected by their son,

Wyatt. Piper began to date, then stopped when she became pregnant with *Chris*.

Phoebe loved her job as an advice columnist for the *Bay Mirror,* and she loved the paper's owner, **Jason Dean**, until her magic drove him away. Her powers were stripped when she used them to find the future father of her child.

Paige embarked on a series of temp jobs and fell in love with a nonpracticing witch, **Richard Montana**, a relationship that was doomed by his addiction to magic.

Whitelighter **Chris Perry** traveled back in time to save *Wyatt* and the future from an unknown evil. The younger son of *Piper* and *Leo*, he arrived before his conception date and almost ceased to exist before his birth was assured. Future Chris died just before he was born into a better world.

Shortly before his first birthday, February 16, 2004, *Wyatt's* identity as the Ultimate Power on Earth was revealed. **Mordaunt**, who tried to steal Excalibur, was "baby's first demon vanquish." Too young to accept mortal constraints, he flourished at Magic School.

Paige took over Magic School in the fall of 2004. She relinquished the post a few months later, shortly after she became a full-fledged Whitelighter.

Suddenly human in early 2005, *Leo* moved back with his family permanently. A "walking Book of Shadows," he took over running Magic School until the school was abandoned to protect the sisters.

Phoebe returned to college for a graduate degree in psychology and took classes from **Professor Slotkin**. *Wyatt* returned to mortal preschool. His teacher was **Miss Henderson**.

The Halliwell sisters and Leo "died" in an explosion at the Manor in the spring of 2005 and emerged as their "cousins" on Victor's side of the family, **Jenny, Julie,** and **Jo Bennett**. When Jenny was mistaken for a famous model accused of murder, Piper became another cousin, **Jamie**, who was married to **Louis** aka Louie. After a few weeks, it became obvious that the sisters couldn't deny their magical destiny or forsake their true selves. The sisters reemerged as the Halliwells with the help of a Homeland Security cover story.

Paige reconciled her relationship with her biological father, **Sam Wilder**, in the fall of 2005, and then she met Henry and fell in love. They married with a ceremony in the Manor in the winter of 2006 and honeymooned in Tahiti.

Leo was frozen, an alternative to death, to give **Piper** and her sisters a fighting edge when they face a grave, final danger. **Wyatt** blamed himself for his father's absence, a misconception Piper corrected on his third birthday. Leo is reunited with his family, never to leave again, after the Charmed Ones win the Ultimate Battle.

The Charmed Ones reclaim Magic School, and **Leo** begins teaching again, a career he maintains until he retires. **Piper** sells P3 and opens a restaurant. Their daughter, **Melinda**, is born when **Chris** is three.

The Angel of Destiny marries **Phoebe** and **Coop** at Magic School. They have three daughters, two and four years apart, and **Billie Jenkins** is their trusted babysitter. Phoebe writes a best selling book titled *Finding Love*.

Paige passes on her knowledge to future witches and Whitelighters. She and **Henry** have twin girls and a boy, **Junior**, who is two years younger.

In the bright future of 2026, created when **Chris** saves **Wyatt** from turning evil, Chris marries **Bianca**, a Phoenix Coven assassin turned to good by his love.

By 2050, **Piper** and **Leo** will have nine grandchildren aged four to fourteen. **Matthew**, their first grandson, attends Magic School and orbs. A granddaughter is telekinetic. The elderly Piper and Leo pass the time playing a Charmed version of Scrabble.

Alternate Histories and Realities

Alternate History 1 ("FORGET ME . . . NOT")

A: Wyatt brings a fire-breathing TV dragon to life, and the beast ravages San Francisco. The exposure of magic is so massive the Cleaners are compelled to intervene. Wyatt is too powerful and uncontrollable to remain in the real world. The Cleaners take him and erase all evidence and memory of his existence. However, the sisters' inability to recall events of the previous day, including a fistfight Phoebe started at the *Bay Mirror*, prompts the Charmed Ones to write a memory restoration spell. Although Wyatt destroys the dragon to save Piper, the Cleaners arrive to take him anyway. This time, the Charmed "Fill in the Blanks" spell prevents erasure of the witches' memories.

B: After the Cleaners erase all evidence of Wyatt's existence, they are startled to learn that the Charmed Ones remember everything. The Cleaners cannot erase the witches, since that would tip the balance of power to evil. However, they refuse to return Wyatt. The Charmed Ones use magic on local TV to demonstrate that they can and will keep the Cleaners busy cleaning up after them for the next fifty years unless Wyatt is returned. The Cleaners comply and erase the *Bay Mirror* riot to appease Phoebe.

Alternate Reality 1 ("MY THREE WITCHES")

The Charmed Ones face death in pocket realms created by the demon Gith from their own unfulfilled desires.

PHOEBE/JASON: Confronted with instant TV stardom and a penthouse, Phoebe quickly deduces that the world isn't real, but was fashioned from Jason Dean's desire to give her everything he thinks she wants. Since the construct is Jason's, he's mortally wounded by a gunshot. Phoebe joins Paige when Chris combines their pocket realms.

PAIGE: In a world where magic is accepted and practiced openly, Paige learns there's a downside. Mad Max demons hunt and kill Innocents, and she can't possibly save them all. She and Phoebe pool their desire to be with Piper to escape.

PIPER: A normal world with no magic leaves Wyatt susceptible to a potentially fatal fever and

Piper vulnerable to a car accident on the way to the hospital. Powerless in the absence of magic, Gith dies in a gasoline explosion, and the pocket realms are dissolved.

Alternate History 2 ("CHRIS-CROSSED")

Chris Perry came back from 2026, where Wyatt's enormous power has created a future of death and destruction. San Francisco lies in smoking ruins, and the Manor has become the Halliwell Memorial Museum. The tourist attraction is a tribute to the legendary Charmed Ones, who vanquished a thousand demons before they were vanquished. In his twenties, with long, tangled hair and brooding eyes, the future Wyatt believes nothing—neither good nor evil—has meaning except power. He wields his magic with contempt for everyone, including Chris, whom he cannot forgive for betraying him. Chris, however, is committed to saving him.

Alternate History 3 ("WITCHSTOCK")

Transported back to 1967 in Grams's red go-go boots, Paige saves her grandfather, Allen, when an evil witch tries to kill him. He was supposed to die, a historical fact known to the visiting twenty-first-century Charmed Ones. To restore the future and save themselves, they do not interfere when a warlock kills Allen instead. Contrary to expectations, Penny does not make the transition from pacifist flower child to deadly demon hunter until the warlock threatens her granddaughters. The future is restored when she experiences a protective rage and kills the warlock.

ADDITIONAL ALTERED EVENT A: In the altered future, Grams reverts to her 1960s flower child mentality and is almost consumed by the slimy green blob creature known as the Demon with No Name.

ADDITIONAL ALTERED EVENT B: Prior to 1967 changes in events surrounding Allen's death, the Charmed Ones vanquished the blob creature later, in Chris's original future, rather than in 2003.

Alternate Reality 2 ("THE COURTSHIP OF WYATT'S FATHER")

The Ghostly Plane is a gray realm of inanimate mortal-world basics—buildings and streets, but no cars or trees. Damien, a Darklighter, draws Leo and Piper into this limbo between life and death through a portal Gideon provides. No powers work here, giving Damien an advantage he loses when the portal is reversed.

Alternate History 4 ("THE COURTSHIP OF WYATT'S FATHER," "HYDE SCHOOL REUNION," AND "SPIN CITY")

In Chris's original future, before he returns from the future to save Wyatt, Leo isn't around much. His letters are an inadequate substitute, and Chris grows up resenting a father who had time for everyone but him. Piper dies from unknown causes when Chris turns fourteen. There are indications that Victor suffers medical problems caused by smoking cigars. Wyatt is turned evil slowly, as a result of having to protect himself from Gideon, who tries incessantly but cannot kill him.

Alternate Reality 3 ("IT'S A BAD, BAD, BAD, BAD WORLD, PART 1")

To distract the sisters, Gideon opens a portal into an opposite world where evil prevails. The mirror realities of good and evil allow the universe to maintain balance. Good and evil Charmed Ones are forced to cooperate to save their good and evil Wyatts.

Alternate Reality 4 ("IT'S A BAD, BAD, BAD, BAD WORLD, PART 2")

A supersweet reality is created when too much good in the opposite evil world throws off the balance in the Grand Design. All rules must be obeyed, and all infractions are met with extreme measures. Leo, Chris, Paige, and Phoebe are unaffected by the transition, which occurred as they were coming back from the opposite evil world. Since only an act of great evil will restore the universal balance, Leo kills Gideon, the Elder who tries to murder Wyatt for "the greater good."

Alternate History 5 ("THE BARE WITCH PROJECT")

When a stronger Lord Dyson returns to the eleventh century with Lady Godiva, he kills her instead of being starved out of existence. As a result, men rule with absolute authority, and women never achieve equality. Twenty-first-century women wear black and are flogged for talking in public. Phoebe is married to advice columnist Leslie St. Claire and they have children. Magic is not used, demons hide, and magical children live in fear. The original time line is restored when the Charmed Ones recall Lady Godiva and vanquish Lord Dyson before she goes back to finish her ride.

Alternate Reality 5 ("CHARMED NOIR")

Dan and Eddie Mullen, Magic School students, write a 1930s novel, *Crossed, Double-Crossed,* that draws the reader into the book. Whatever happens in the story happens for real: Dan dies, and Kyle Brody is shot. Although Phoebe and Piper can add handwritten plot twists from outside, they can't write Paige, Brody, or Eddie a means of escape. The only way out is for Eddie to find the Burmese Falcon.

Alternate History 6 ("THERE'S SOMETHING ABOUT LEO")

The Avatars allow Leo to tell Piper about his changed status, which launches a disastrous series of events. Piper loses an Innocent because her sisters are distracted trying to "save" Leo. Driven by his intense hatred of Avatars, Kyle Brody threatens Leo. Leo kills Brody, but not before Brody attacks him with a potion that kills Avatars. Dying Leo and the Avatars turn time back to the moment before Leo told Piper that he was an Avatar.

Alternate History 7 ("WITCHNESS PROTECTION," "EXTREME MAKEOVER: WORLD EDITION," AND "CHARMAGEDDON")

Kira the Seer gives Phoebe a glimpse of her unborn daughter and the Avatars' utopian future with no demons. The sisters embrace the changed world without demons, where everything flows smoothly—until the Avatars "remove" Leo for creating conflict. Forced to remember the pain of loss, the Charmed Ones work

with Zankou. With their powers diminished, the Avatars can resurrect Brody or change the world back. The sisters choose the world. Everyone the Avatars "removed" is returned, including Leo.

Alternate History 8 ("IMAGINARY FIENDS")

Vicus, a demon that preys on children, gains young Wyatt's trust and curses Wuvey, his teddy bear. The curse turns Wyatt evil slowly over the years, but Future Wyatt, a wonderful son at twenty-five, is instantly transformed. When young Wyatt trusts Leo enough to give him Wuvey, the curse is broken and the good future Wyatt is restored.

Alternate History 9 ("KILL BILLIE: VOL. 2" AND "FOREVER CHARMED")

Empowered by the Hollow, the Charmed Ones permanently vanquish the Triad Spirit. Then Billie and Christy Jenkins, also empowered, and the Charmed Ones exchange energy-ball fire, destroying the Manor. Phoebe, Paige, and Christy are killed, but Leo is returned. Unwilling to accept her sisters' deaths, Piper uses Coop's cupid ring to go back in time. She gathers a young Patty from 1975 and Grams from 1982 to form another version of the Power of Three in 2006. Together they send the Hollow back into containment before the energy balls collide, which nullifies the original time line.

Alternate History 10 ("FOREVER CHARMED")

Although Piper, Patty, and Grams contain the Hollow, Chris and Wyatt's future is altered. In this history, Wyatt is exposed to the Hollow, and his powers are lost. The Angel of Destiny takes Leo back, but Billie realizes that Dumain has been using her and Christy. Going back to before Wyatt is taken, Billie and the Charmed Ones intercept Dumain and Christy warning the Triad. The Spirit of the Triad is vanquished again, with Charmed potions, and Dumain and Christy are killed. Wyatt's powers are restored and the Ultimate Battle ends the way it is supposed to—with all the Charmed Ones alive.

Alternate Identities ("STILL CHARMED AND KICKING," "MALICE IN WONDERLAND," "RUN, PIPER, RUN," "DESPERATE HOUSEWITCHES," AND "REWITCHED")

PIPER, AKA JENNY BENNETT: Although she's always wanted a demon-free, normal life, Piper has trouble adjusting to extreme change and her new identity. Leo and her children keep her from feeling alone, but she still feels lost. A job interview leads to her arrest as Maya

Holmes, a local model accused of murdering her photographer boyfriend. When Maya is cleared, Piper abandons the look to become someone else—again.

PIPER, AKA JAMIE BENNETT: "Jamie" is married to "Louis," but no one at preschool knows Wyatt's cousin is his mother. Her insecurities in part enable a Possessor demon to temporarily win Wyatt's trust. The strain of living as someone else makes Piper realize she'll only be happy being herself, a feeling her sisters share.

PHOEBE, AKA JULIE BENNETT: Now that she's "dead" and living as someone else, Phoebe learns that Elise loves her like a daughter and Dex Lawson, the handsome man in the elevator at work, secretly admires her. After Dex drops some hints, Elise hires "Julie" to write Phoebe's column, but it's difficult to maintain the facade in familiar surroundings. Dex is reluctant to believe she's psychic, but he's not reluctant to pursue their romance. Annoyed with Paige for meddling, Phoebe forgives her when Paige turns out to be wrong about Dex's affair. Dex admits he ended a casual affair with an ex-girlfriend, Sylvia, when he met "Julie." When a spell prompts Dex and "Julie" to get married, Phoebe wants to make it work. She also realizes that she and her sisters can't abandon their Charmed destiny or identities. Too many Innocents are being hurt. Dex is shocked to find out that "Julie" is Phoebe, and the fast-track romance hits a dead end.

PAIGE, AKA JO BENNETT: Paige isn't happy about giving up magic to be safe from demons, and the "new charge jingling" won't let her ignore her Whitelighter calling. Tutoring Billie keeps her within the realm of magic, but "Jo" can't actively participate, which is frustrating. When a cool guy at P3's speed-dating debut falls for "Jo," Paige can't pursue a relationship based on a lie.

LEO, AKA LOUIS OR LOUIE: Still married to Piper/Jenny, Leo tries to adapt to a magic-free existence, but he knows Victor's assessment is right: They can't stop being the powerful, magical people they are. Louis continues taking care of the children, including attending the mothers' playgroup as an unmarried cousin Eve finds attractive. When Leo announces that he liked Piper's "Jenny" alias better than "Jamie," it's a clue to both that they just want to be themselves.

MISCELLANEOUS FAMILY FACTS

▲ The large stone holding Excalibur for Wyatt is stored in the attic. **("SWORD AND THE CITY")**

▲ In the 1960s Penny Halliwell cast a "Return to Owner" spell on her possessions, including red go-go boots, earrings, and a ring. **("WITCHSTOCK")**

▲ Wyatt inherits the Peace Blanket his great-grandmother, Penny "Grams" Halliwell, owned in 1967. **("WITCHSTOCK")**

▲ Prue lost the charm bracelet their mother, Patricia Halliwell, gave Piper when she was a child. Leo finds it and gives it to Piper for her birthday in 2003. **("PRINCE CHARMED")**

▲ Leo still has his grandmother's red quilt. **("USED KARMA")**

▲ Christopher was Leo's father's name. **("IT'S A BAD, BAD, BAD, BAD WORLD, PART 2")**

▲ A Halliwell ancestor, Beatrice Warren, had one leg. **("THERE'S SOMETHING ABOUT LEO")**

▲ Grams made the dollhouse replica of the Manor when the sisters were children. **("SCRY HARD")**

▲ Wyatt's teddy bear is named Wuvey. **("LITTLE BOX OF HORRORS")**

▲ Paige's adoptive father was a firefighter. **("THE LOST PICTURE SHOW")**

▲ Leo's grandfather gave him a 1941 Chevy pickup sixty years ago. **("VAYA CON LEOS")**

▲ Wyatt plays "Candy Land" with his grandfather. **("KILL BILLIE: VOL. 2")**

Book of
White Magic

The Charmed Powers

GENERAL FACTS ABOUT THE CHARMED POWERS

▲ The Charmed Ones are the most powerful witches the world has ever known, the fulfillment of Melinda Warren's magical decree that each generation in the Warren line would be stronger than the last.

▲ Charmed magic is emotion based.

▲ The Charmed Ones protect the Innocent and follow the *Wiccan Rede*, "And it harm none, do as ye will."

▲ New powers manifest without warning and must be mastered with practice.

▲ A trigger may be required to use a new or unfamiliar power.

▲ The powers grow stronger with time.

▲ The powers must not be used for personal gain.

▲ A spell cannot backfire if there's no personal gain.

▲ The powers do not work on good witches.

▲ If possessed by another, the powers will be attracted to the Charmed witch of origin.

▲ The powers do not work prior to the time of birth, as technically they do not exist.

▲ The Power of Three bond is severed if the Charmed powers are used against each other. The powers are lost until the personal and magical rift is repaired.

▲ Charmed magic can be used to reverse the effects of evil magic without consequences.

▲ Centuries of good karma protect the Charmed Ones.

   ▲ Their bodies are the vessels that hold their powers, but their minds retain the knowledge to use them.

PIPER

PRIMARY POWER: to slow or speed up molecules.

▲ Learns to astral project **("SOMETHING WICCA THIS WAY GOES . . . ?")**

PHOEBE

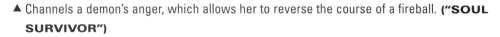

PRIMARY POWERS: precognition and levitation.

▲ Develops the empathic ability to feel other people's emotions. **("VALHALLEY OF THE DOLLS")**

▲ Senses intense emotions of population over distance. **("FORGET ME . . . NOT")**

▲ Channels a demon's anger, which allows her to reverse the course of a fireball. **("SOUL SURVIVOR")**

▲ Will know/sense if one of her sisters dies. **("THE COURTSHIP OF WYATT'S FATHER")**

▲ The Tribunal strips Phoebe's powers, which she used for personal gain **("CRIMES AND WITCH-DEMEANORS")**. She remains a witch who can mix potions and cast spells.

▲ Power of premonition is restored when Phoebe is willing to die to protect an Innocent. **("STYX FEET UNDER")**

▲ Learns to astral project. **("SOMETHING WICCA THIS WAY GOES . . . ?")**

▲ Phoebe's premonitions always work out, just not always how she thinks they will. **("KILL BILLIE: VOL. 1")**

▲ Talks to herself in the "future daughter" vision. **("HULKUS POCUS")**

PAIGE

PRIMARY POWERS OF THE WHITELIGHTER: to orb, sense and locate, assist in healing.

▲ Employs glamours to alter her appearance. **("FORGET ME . . . NOT" AND "SHOW GHOULS")**

▲ Becomes a full-fledged Whitelighter. **("LITTLE BOX OF HORRORS")**

▲ Learns to astral project. **("SOMETHING WICCA THIS WAY GOES . . . ?")**

▲ Completely integrates being a Whitelighter. **("THE LOST PICTURE SHOW")**

▲ Heals without assistance. **("PAYBACK'S A WITCH")**

WYATT

PRIMARY POWERS: to generate a protective shield and orb himself to the location of a loved one.

▲ Orbs an object: pacifier. **("VALHALLEY OF THE DOLLS")**

▲ Changes TV channels with a blink. **("FORGET ME . . . NOT")**

▲ Conjures a real being, a dragon, from a fantasy TV image. **("FORGET ME . . . NOT")**

▲ Uses his magic, "orb eyes," to influence the actions of others. **("SOUL SURVIVOR")**

▲ As the ultimate power on Earth, commands Excalibur with telekinesis. **("SWORD AND THE CITY")**

▲ Orbs to save himself from Gideon. **("IT'S A BAD, BAD, BAD, BAD WORLD, PART 2")**

▲ Vanquishes a threat with a blink. **("IT'S A BAD, BAD, BAD, BAD WORLD, PART 2")**

▲ Senses and orbs to his father's location. **("THE BARE WITCH PROJECT")**

▲ His intense feelings manifest in real beings. **("CHEAPER BY THE COVEN")**

▲ His power to heal emerges to save Piper when she dies from Thorn demon poison. **("THE SEVEN YEAR WITCH")**

▲ Reduces his parents to six inches tall and locks them in the dollhouse to protect them. **("SCRY HARD")**

▲ Levitates his toys. **("LITTLE BOX OF HORRORS")**

▲ Manifests his feelings in action figures he brings to full-size life. **("PAYBACK'S A WITCH")**

CHRIS PERRY

PRIMARY POWERS OF THE WHITELIGHTER: to orb and use telekinesis.

▲ As a witch, he's immune to Piper's freeze power. (**"CHRIS-CROSSED"**)

▲ He can put calls from charges on mute. (**"I DREAM OF PHOEBE"**)

▲ He begins to orb objects at eighteen months. (**"KILL BILLIE: VOL. 2"**)

BILLIE:
THE CHARMED ONES' PROTÉGÉE

●**PRIMARY POWER:** telekinesis.

▲ Enhanced human traits of resourcefulness and athletic prowess. (**"STILL CHARMED AND KICKING"**)

▲ Utilization of modern technology, computer, and GPS to scry. (**"MALICE IN WONDERLAND"**)

▲ Adept at nunchaks (enhanced by telekinesis) and produces a transport potion. (**"DESPERATE HOUSEWITCHES"**)

▲ Studies the Book of Shadows and utilizes Charmed spells and potions. (**"DESPERATE HOUSEWITCHES," "REWITCHED," AND "KILL BILLIE: VOL. 1"**)

▲ Develops the rare power of projection, the ability to transform objects and beings with an emotional thought or word, no spell or potion required. (**"MR. & MRS. WITCH"**)

▲ Learns to control and use projection. (**"12 ANGRY ZEN"**)

▲ Channels Christy's power to amplify her own. (**"THE TORN IDENTITY"**)

WHITE MAGIC PRACTITIONERS

WHITELIGHTERS

The guardian angels of good witches, Whitelighters guide and advise their charges to use their powers to save Innocents.

Abilities:

▲ Are always in contact with (within "hearing" of) their charge.

▲ Orb through the Neutral Plane to transport themselves or others from one earthly or mystical location to another.

▲ Power to heal, with exceptions (see Limitations).

▲ Possess a powder that enhances the power of suggestion, which allows memories to be erased.

▲ Automatically fluent in the language of their charges and the Whitelighter "clackety-clack" language.

▲ Glamour, to appear as someone else.

▲ Telekinesis.

▲ Hear the Elders' Global Alerts regarding impending threats.

▲ Have an automatic connection to a new charge.

▲ Can hear charges even when they call on a subliminal level, without knowing.

▲ Can sense an Innocent's pain.

Limitations:

▲ Healing exceptions:
Cannot heal dead people, animals, themselves, or self-inflicted wounds.
Can only heal mortals injured by evil.
Cannot heal demons; trying invites an attack of black magic energy.

▲ Cannot sense a charge if one is in the mortal world and one is in the Underworld.

▲ The bond with a charge takes time to form.

▲ Clipped wings render a Whitelighter mortal and susceptible to sickness, aging, and death.

▲ Committing evil acts results in the Whitelighter being recycled: beginning the life cycle over from birth.

SPECIFIC WHITELIGHTERS

The Warren Witch Line

MATTHEWS, PAIGE: An incessant ringing in her ears heralds her emergence as a full-fledged Whitelighter ("Little Box of Horrors"). Despite her animosity toward the Elders, she can't deny her destiny or desire to help people. She convinces her first charge, Mitchell Haines, to embrace his powers and use them to save Innocents ("Freaky Phoebe"). Losing Joanna to Zankou is devastating ("Death Becomes Them"), but she copes. She can change her name and appearance, but she can't stop being a Whitelighter when a new charge calls ("Still Charmed and Kicking"). She is forced to take on her new charge, Billie, in "Malice in Wonderland." Her Whitelighter abilities are not completely activated until she wholeheartedly embraces her status ("The Lost Picture Show"). Her ability to heal without help is activated when Henry almost dies ("Payback's a Witch").

HALLIWELL, WYATT: Half Whitelighter with enormous powers, his abilities to orb ("Valhalley of the Dolls") and heal ("The Seven Year Witch") emerge while he's a toddler. For his sake, Piper will use his healing power only in extreme circumstances ("Scry Hard"). Paige teaches him to be a Whitelighter in "Imaginary Fiends."

PERRY, CHRIS: Leo and Piper's second son, he cannot heal ("Valhalley of the Dolls"), but he has the power of telekinesis, which he uses to combine Phoebe and Paige's pocket realms in "My Three Witches." His orb power manifests when he's eighteen months old ("Kill Billie: Vol. 2").

WYATT, MATTHEW: Leo and Piper's first grandson ("Forever Charmed").

OTHER WHITELIGHTERS

BRODY, KYLE: Killed by an Avatar when he tries to stop them from changing the world in "Extreme Makeover: World Edition," the Elders reward him for dedicating his mortal life to fighting evil and

make him a Whitelighter ("Charmageddon"). See also: "Paige's Men" in the chapter "Many Men and Jobs."

DANNY: Assigned to the Charmed Ones because the Elders suspect that Leo killed Zola, an innocent Elder ("Once in a Blue Moon"), he is mauled by the Charmed Beasts.

JOANNA: A future Whitelighter and one of Paige's charges, she's killed by the demon Zankou to undermine Paige's confidence ("Death Becomes Them").

MARCUS: Volunteer bait for the beasts that mauled Whitelighter No. 1 ("Once in a Blue Moon"), he is injured by the Charmed Beasts. However, he captures the sisters in the crystal cage trap.

MIKELLE: A punk, Mikelle is captured and killed by Salek, a Darklighter, while Paige is preoccupied in a dream ("The Jung and the Restless"). She returns as a Whitelighter to heal Paige.

SPEED: Eighteen and a parolee, his future as a Whitelighter is threatened when he's pressured to help rob a liquor store in "Battle of the Hexes." Speed refuses, and Paige's belief in him convinces Henry to give the boy another chance.

WILDER, SAM: Once Patricia Halliwell's Whitelighter, he became her lover and fathered Paige. Reinstated as a Whitelighter with his daughter's help, he needs Paige's help again—to save a future Whitelighter he lost fifty years ago ("The Lost Picture Show"). Father and daughter resolve their differences while dealing with the demon Vaklav.

WILLIAMS, JONATHAN DAVID, AKA JD: A future Whitelighter in Sam's charge, JD, is captured by Vaklav's camera and held in photographic limbo for fifty years, until his father—his last grieving relative—dies. Released so Vaklav can replace him with another subject who will provide pain, JD sacrifices himself to save Sam and Paige, which establishes his worthiness to become a Whitelighter ("The Lost Picture Show").

ELDERS

A higher level of Whitelighter, they control the ranks of the guardian angels and track the good witches they protect.

Abilities:

▲ Can listen to anyone at will, but are discerning.

▲ Can transport witches through time.

▲ Catalog knowledge of all things supernatural.

▲ Maintain limited contact with evil.

▲ Will know when a Charmed One dies.

▲ Age is irrelevant.

▲ Employ invisibility shields.

▲ Command of lightninglike electrical energies as weapons.

Limitations:

▲ Are not all-knowing.

▲ Are not aware of events in the plane between life and death.

▲ Cannot see the mortal realm during an eclipse.

▲ Cannot control witches after death.

▲ Cannot counter or penetrate all Upper-Level demon magic.

▲ An Elder who kills is recycled, to begin the life cycle over from birth.

▲ Can't fix aging.

SPECIFIC ELDERS

WYATT, LEO: A World War II medic, he was killed at Guadalcanal and was immediately given Whitelighter status. When he empowered the Charmed Ones as goddesses to defeat the Titans, his actions altered his destiny, and he became an Elder. Convinced that his presence on Earth endangers his family ("The Courtship of Wyatt's Father"), he goes Up There to stay as an Elder.

Six months later he returns wearing an Elder's golden robes, which he abandons when he stays to protect his family. Killing Gideon is justified ("It's a Bad, Bad, Bad, Bad World, Part 2"), but when he's tricked into killing Zola, an innocent Elder, in "A Call to Arms," the Elders suspect him ("The Bare Witch Project") and bar him from Up There.

ADAIR: One of two Elders on the Tribunal ("Crimes and Witch-demeanors").

ANDREA: Answering Piper's call, Andrea explains that the Elders only suspect that Billie and Christy are the Ultimate Power that Piper must defeat to free Leo ("The Jung and the Restless").

ARAMIS: One of two Elders on the Tribunal ("Crimes and Witch-demeanors").

GIDEON: Leo's mentor and the founder of Magic School ("The Legend of Sleepy Halliwell"). But Gideon's goodness is corrupted. One of the most powerful Elders ("It's a Bad, Bad, Bad, Bad World, Part 1"), he tries to kill Wyatt for the "greater good," unaware that his attempts are why the boy turned evil ("It's a Bad, Bad, Bad, Bad World, Part 2"). See also: Book of Black Magic and Magic School sections.

JONAH: Believing that the Charmed Ones are dead, Jonah tries and fails to convince Victor to let the Elders raise Wyatt and Chris ("Still Charmed and Kicking"). Plagued by reporters on the trail of a sensational story in "Kill Billie: Vol. 1," Paige turns to the Elders in desperation. Jonah explains that the problem is human, not magical, and advises her to demonstrate that the Halliwells are ordinary and not newsworthy. Piper contacts him about the Hulk virus, which threatens to wipe out all magical beings ("Hulkus Pocus"), and gives him the cure.

KHEEL: After meeting with Zankou, who reveals that Leo is an Avatar ("Ordinary Witches"), Kheel combines his powers with other Elders to kill Leo, an effort that fails. He believes the Elders have been too lenient with Leo ("Carpe Demon").

ODIN: A member of the Magic School Board of Elders ("The Bare Witch Project"), he is also an Elder with authority ("Once in a Blue Moon"). Since the Charmed Ones are needed to counter an impending, unknown threat, he allows Leo to remain at large. After sharing Phoebe's vision of the Avatars' future with no demons in "Witchness Protection," he remains slightly skeptical. In order to retain Leo as an Elder without the constant threat of losing him to Piper,

Odin orchestrates a scenario to identify Leo's true preference ("The Seven Year Witch"). He cheats to make Leo choose Up There, but he gives up and restores Leo's mortality when Piper's love proves stronger.

SANDRA: A female, she warns Leo that a great, unknown threat is coming in "The Bare Witch Project." She explains that Zola is missing, and Leo is a suspect. After warning Leo that the Avatars may be making their move ("There's Something About Leo"), she reiterates that the Elders need him on their side. After learning that Leo is an Avatar ("Ordinary Witches"), she joins other Elders, who try but fail to kill him. She defends Leo and his motives for joining the Avatars to the other Elders ("Carpe Demon"), but warns Leo to stay out of magical affairs. She works with Odin, erasing Leo's memory to help him choose between the Elders and Piper ("The Seven Year Witch"). However, she also "tells" the Charmed Ones that they should actively look for him. Sandra counsels Paige regarding her new status as a full-fledged Whitelighter in "Little Box of Horrors." She heals Piper and tells the sisters about the spell to destroy the Nexus, or Suxen ("Something Wicca This Way Goes . . . ?"). However, the Elders will isolate themselves from the Charmed Ones to protect themselves.

UNNAMED ELDER #1: A female on the Magic School Board of Elders in "The Bare Witch Project," she breaks up a fight between Simon and Duncan.

UNNAMED ELDER #2: Summoned to save Leo from the Angel of Death in "Vaya Con Leos," he and an Avatar provide hints that lead Piper to an Angel of Destiny.

URBAN: He warns Leo not to move against Gideon ("It's a Bad, Bad, Bad, Bad World, Part 2"), but to protect the "greater good." Although Gideon's actions are not condoned, others share his fear of Wyatt. Note: Saving Wyatt from Gideon prevented an evil Wyatt from emerging, which protected the "greater good." Urban agrees to let Leo help find missing witches ("Charrrmed") and admits that the Elders will need Leo back because of the gathering storm of power. He tries to bolster Piper's spirits regarding frozen Leo in "Payback's a Witch."

ZOLA: A friend of Leo's, he tries to keep Leo focused on the right path ("A Call to Arms"). Tricked by Barbas, Leo kills Zola in a fit of irrational rage.

ANGELS OF DESTINY

Possessing knowledge of all things, they are more powerful and higher in the hierarchy of good than Elders, but not the pinnacle.

ANGEL OF DESTINY: She perceives multiple futures based on various actions ("Vaya Con Leos"), including the Charmed Ones' greatest challenge. Since it won't affect the outcome, she agrees to let Leo be frozen rather than die. Although the Ultimate Battle does not go as she anticipated in "Kill Billie: Vol. 2," she returns Leo as promised. She temporarily takes him back in "Forever Charmed," but she returns him again when the Charmed Ones vanquish the Triad a second time. She presides at Phoebe and Coop's wedding.

GOOD WITCHES

JENKINS, BILLIE: Young and fearless, she employs telekinesis and her athletic prowess to attack her first demon, Elkin, in "Still Charmed and Kicking." Although she's failing college metaphysics, she teaches herself to scry with a computer and GPS ("Malice in Wonderland"). She and the Charmed Ones agree to help each other, and her "demon-inspired" idea saves an Innocent in "Run, Piper, Run." She discovers that evil has taken over Magic School ("Desperate Housewitches") and pushes the Charmed Ones to be themselves ("Rewitched"). When she remembers that her sister was kidnapped by a demon ("Kill Billie: Vol. 1"), she becomes obsessed with finding her ("The Lost Picture Show") and is stunned to learn that her parents had never given up looking

("Mr. & Mrs. Witch"). Her overzealous efforts almost get Henry killed in "Payback's a Witch." She learns to project at will and "sees" a young, scared Christy imprisoned in a cave ("12 Angry Zen"). Christy is the "key to the Ultimate Power" ("The Last Temptation of Christy"), and Billie is the Ultimate Power ("Engaged and Confused"). Manipulated into turning on the sisters, she unites her power with Christy's in "The Torn Identity," and the Ultimate Power emerges. She reluctantly accepts Christy's premise that the Charmed Ones are no longer working for the greater good ("The Jung and the Restless") and helps turn the magical community against them ("Gone with the Witches"). Completely in Christy's thrall, Billie joins her sister to call the Hollow and kill the Charmed Ones ("Kill Billie: Vol. 2"), but Christy dies. After she realizes that Dumain used and lied to her ("Forever Charmed"), the Charmed Ones give Billie a second chance. She proves her loyalty to the Halliwells and the greater good when she vanquishes her evil sister to save them.

CALLAWAY FAMILY: Locked in a generational feud with the Montanas, the remaining family members are: James Callaway, the patriarch; Grandma, his mother; and two sons, Roy and Burt. Olivia Callaway, fiancée of Richard Montana, was killed in energy-ball cross fire in 2002 and freed from her quest for vengeance in "Love's a Witch." The original cause of the feud has been long forgotten.

CASTILLO, BRENDA: Kidnapped by Captain Black Jack Cutting, this young practitioner dies of rapid aging when the pirate cuts her with a cursed athame in "Charrrmed."

HAINES, MITCHELL: Paige's first charge as a Whitelighter, he blames himself for his fiancée's death and balks at using his hyperspeed power to help people ("Freaky Phoebe"). Paige convinces him that they can't fix everything, but they can save some. He helps the Charmed Ones defeat the sorceress Imara.

MARKS, SIMON THADDEUS REGINALD: A telekinetic witch with the ability to orb, he believes he's destined to marry a half Whitelighter, Paige ("The Last Temptation of Christy"). He's obsessed with his family's powerful history and determined to carry on the tradition with a powerful marriage. A resident of Sussex, England, he returns there when Paige and Henry make it clear she's not interested.

MONTANA FAMILY: Locked in a generational feud with the Callaways, the remaining family members are Benjamin, the kind, battle-hardened patriarch; Steve, the younger, hotheaded brother; Rosaline, the attractive, fifty-year-old matriarch; two uncles, and Richard. Benjamin is killed when the yearlong truce ends in "Love's a Witch." No one knows what caused the hostilities with the Callaways.

MONTANA, RICHARD: Trapped in the family feud with the Callaways, he gives up magic to avoid being cursed in "Love's a Witch." He assists Paige in summoning a ghost and demon ("Soul Survivor"), saves Phoebe and Paige from an explosive potion, and begins using magic again in "Sword and the City."

MONTANA, STEVE: Steve accidentally kills Olivia Callaway, his brother Richard's fiancée in "Love's a Witch." To atone, he becomes a pro bono lawyer ("Used Karma") and forsakes magic, but he gives Richard their father's spell to banish spirits.

NATALIE: Leo assigns Chris to be Natalie's Whitelighter in "Forget Me . . . Not" to assess what he can handle. Chris rejects the assignment to concentrate on protecting Wyatt and the sisters.

TALI: A target in the demonic reality TV show *Witch Wars*, Tali is killed during the game.

OTHER BENEVOLENT BEINGS

BARBAS, AKA THE DEMON OF HOPE: The opposite of the evil demon Barbas, good Barbas resides in an evil mirror reality ("It's a Bad, Bad, Bad, Bad World, Part 1").

CHINESE ZODIAC: Twelve Zodiacs protect Buddha's mystical staff and the eternal cycle ("12 Angry Zen"). The staff passes from one Zodiac to the next at the New Year. Only six out of the twelve are seen—Dog, Rooster, Dragon, Tiger, Rat, and Snake.

CLARENCE, AN ANGEL OF DEATH: Sent to help Chris cease to exist, an unusual circumstance, his services are not required when Chris is conceived ("The Courtship of Wyatt's Father").

COOP: The Elders assign Coop as Phoebe's exclusive Cupid, hoping he will get her love life back on track ("Engaged and Confused"). To cure Phoebe's resistance to love ("Generation Hex"), he takes her on a tour of past loves, all of which ended badly. The block is shattered when she remembers the spark of new love. Even so, finding the right man for her remains a seemingly impossible assignment. Coop's feelings for Phoebe emerge, but the rules prevent him from wooing her ("The Torn Identity"). He takes advantage of an it's-only-a-dream loophole to kiss Phoebe in "The Jung and the Restless,"

and she gives in to her own feelings ("Gone with the Witches"). He loves Phoebe but is hurt when she excludes him to fight the Ultimate Battle in "Kill Billie: Vol. 2." Chris and Wyatt explain that the Elders intended for Coop and Phoebe to fall in love ("Forever Charmed"). The romance is not forbidden, and Phoebe marries Coop.

DWARF: In "Sword and the City," the head dwarf brags he has connections and can acquire valuable objects, such as armor and castles. Super speed, cunning, and wit are the primary defense mechanisms.

ENOLA, A SHAMAN: Nineteen and an old soul, Enola guides Phoebe on a vision quest to face her inner demons and future in "The Legend of Sleepy Halliwell."

FAIRY: Grateful when Paige kills the Wicked Witch ("Spin City"), breaking the spell that turned her into an old woman, the fairy helps Paige defeat the Spider demon and save Piper. Paige asks the Fairy to return Henry's things ("Repo Manor"). A fairy is killed when Piper, under an obsession hex, refuses to help repel an Assassin demon attack in "Gone with the Witches."

GNOME: Represented by Mr. Monkeyshines, a professor at Magic School in "Charmed Noir," gnomes have no natural enemies but do have an uncanny capacity to annoy and anger people.

GUARDIANS, ANGEL: The inner voice, conscience, and instincts within that protect everyone from harm ("Someone to Witch Over Me"), also known as guardian angels. Some guardians are stronger than others, the Charmed Ones' guardians being the strongest.

GUARDIANS OF PANDORA'S BOX: Every generation, one girl from a lineage of magical beings is designated to guard Pandora's Box ("Little Box of Horrors"). They have the power of telekinesis, and the older guardian trains the new one. Immune to the ills of the world stored in the box, they alone can release and retrieve them. Piper cannot freeze them.

HOPE: An eighteen-year-old college student at U.C. Berkeley, she becomes the new guardian of Pandora's Box when Nina, the old guardian, dies ("Little Box of Horrors").

THE LADY OF THE LAKE: The legendary keeper of Excalibur, she dwells in the pond in Harding Park ("Sword and the City") and entrusts the sword to the Charmed Ones.

LIAM: A young leprechaun working with O'Brien ("Gone with the Witches"), he is killed by an Assassin demon.

LO PAN: Keeper of the Secret Garden, he is a servant of the Chinese Zodiac that protect Buddha's mystical staff ("12 Angry Zen"). He helps Billie learn to control her projection power and Piper

to be patient. At the new year, when the staff passes from one Zodiac to the next, he is elevated to the Zodiac as the new Rooster.

MUSE: To prevent Henry from canceling their dinner date, Paige asks Henry's muse to inspire his letter writing ("Repo Manor").

MYSTICAL BEINGS COLLECTIVELY: All the mystical entities help the Charmed Ones fight Zankou ("Something Wicca This Way Goes . . . ?") As part of the Triad's bid for power, they are beaten and slaughtered in a demon attack and become convinced that the Charmed Ones no longer care what happens to them ("Gone with the Witches").

NINA: The guardian of Pandora's Box ("Little Box of Horrors"), she is killed by Katya, a shapeshifter.

O'BRIEN: Paige calls on this leprechaun to bring Henry good luck ("Repo Manor"). When Paige asks him to check out the mysterious platform at Magic School ("Gone with the Witches"), he is duped by Dumain, Billie, and Christy into thinking the Charmed Ones are using him for selfish reasons. When the hexed Paige brushes him off during a demon attack, he believes the Charmed Ones are now the bad guys and helps convince the rest of the magical community.

OGRE: Tall and unkempt with bulbous ears, ogres smell bad ("Sword and the City"). When the Wicked Witch turns the ogre into a wimpy little man, Paige kills the witch and breaks the spell ("Spin City"). The ogre squishes the Spider demon to help Paige save Piper. An ogre defends the Charmed Ones ("Gone with the Witches") and is killed in the demon attack.

RATHMERE: A powerful wizard who created more than five hundred potions and spells before the Spider demon began a century-long feast on his magic in 1904 ("Spin City").

RILEY: Brother to Shamus as all leprechauns are ("Spin City"), he gives Paige a shillelagh for luck when she reverses the Wicked Witch's spell that made him tall.

SATYR: Crankier than their appearance suggests in "Sword and the City," satyrs have small horns, wear homespun, and carry a panpipe.

SOOTHSAYER: A gardener who counsels magical people, the soothsayer helps Piper and Leo understand each other's problems by switching them into each other's lives ("The Lost Picture Show").

WOOD NYMPH: Paige reverses the Wicked Witch's spell that changed the nymph into a cranky man ("Spin City"). The wood nymph helps Paige defeat the Spider demon. Taking the Charmed Ones' side when O'Brien accuses them in "Gone with the Witches," the wood nymph is stunned when Phoebe, under a spell, won't help save the magic people.

MORTALS PAST AND PRESENT

DENISE: A jilted housewife, she plots to kill her unfaithful husband after she accidentally gets Piper's power ("Ordinary Witches"). She gives the power back after Zankou attacks.

DRAKE: A demon who makes a deal with a sorcerer to become human for a year ("Carpe Demon"), he spends his limited time learning and living. Tricked into using the demonic powers he has retained, he loses them to the sorcerer. When the Charmed Ones vanquish the sorcerer, Drake is rescued from purgatory to become a teacher at Magic School—for two weeks.

FLOWERS, CAROL: A source for Seth Parra's article on the mob; he blames himself for her death ("Kill Billie: Vol. 1"). When the *Bay Mirror* reporter refuses to back off the story of the Halliwells' mysterious ties to Homeland Security, Paige pretends to be Carol's ghost to frighten him off.

GEORGE AND MARIE: A bartender and a waitress in 1899, these ill-fated lovers are doomed to be burned to death forever in Cabaret Fantome because the owner, Count Roget, made a deal with a demon to escape purgatory. In a desperate attempt to find help, George's spirit possesses Darryl's old friend Mike ("Show Ghouls").

HOLMES, MAYA: After leaving Assistant District Attorney Walter Nance for a young photographer, Curtis, Maya is falsely accused of murdering her new boyfriend. She's also the model Piper uses for a new identity in "Run, Piper, Run." When the Charmed Ones scare Nance into confessing that he killed Curtis, Maya is cleared—and Piper needs a new false face.

JENKINS, MR. AND MRS.: Once a happy, loving couple, Billie's parents settled into robot and wallflower personas after their oldest daughter was kidnapped in 1990. Billie accidentally turns them into "cold-blooded assassins" with her projection power ("Mr. & Mrs. Witch") and reverses the transformation with an emotional appeal after she finds out they never stopped looking for

Christy. Billie's mother explains that her grandmother was a witch, and the power skipped a generation. They return to see Christy ("Generation Hex") and are murdered by Noxon demons, a plot instigated by Candor, one of the Triad demons, to keep their oldest daughter bound to evil.

KEYES, AGENT: A Homeland Security agent, he is aware that the Halliwells are linked to the paranormal ("Something Wicca This Way Goes . . . ?"). He is not convinced the sisters died when the Nexus exploded, but he knows they won't surface if he stays in town ("Still Charmed and Kicking").

LADY GODIVA: Conjured from a history book by a Magic School student, she rode naked in the eleventh century to protest her husband's unjust taxes ("The Bare Witch Project"). This event was a milestone in the struggle for women's equality and rights.

LEO: Choosing Piper over the Elders, Leo becomes human in "The Seven Year Witch." He has no powers and no charges.

MANDI: An annoying supermom at Wyatt's preschool, she's possessed by a demon that kidnaps Wyatt ("Desperate Housewitches"). She survives the dispossession.

MIKE: A security guard who helped Darryl get onto the police force, Mike is possessed by the spirit of George until the Charmed Ones free the lost souls trapped in Cabaret Fantome ("Show Ghouls").

MITCHELL, HENRY: When Cupid puts Paige in Henry's head ("The Torn Identity"), he experiences her orb power. See also: "Paige's Men" in the chapter "Many Men and Jobs."

MURPHY, RUSS: A Homeland Security agent, he is assigned to watch and wait for the "dead" Halliwell sisters to show themselves ("Still Charmed and Kicking"). He maintains surveillance on Billie and the Manor ("Rewitched") and provides a cover story for the sisters' reemergence in exchange for their help on occasional cases. He is exposed to demons, fireballs, Whitelighters, and orbing when he helps Paige and Sam locate Vaklav, a demon photographer who is responsible for several missing people over many decades ("The Lost Picture Show"). He asks the sisters to inspect cold case files with a para-7 suspicion or higher in "Battle of the Hexes." However, the Charmed Ones confront him when Billie is infected with a virus the government created using a captured demon ("Hulkus Pocus"). The target of the witches' powers and wrath, he decides that Homeland Security no longer needs their services.

NICK: A veteran and ex-con, he robs a bank when Henry and Paige fail to help him get a loan in "Payback's a Witch." He's possessed by a Possessor demon, who tries to force Paige to expose magic.

NORMAND, JOHN: The owner of a phone company that's ripping off its customers ("Carpe Demon"), Normand decides to return his ill-gotten gains after an encounter with Drake/Robin Hood and a near-death experience.

RONNIE: A construction worker, he learns that his wife is sleeping around when he accidentally acquires Phoebe's power of premonition ("Ordinary Witches"). He agrees to give the power back when he glimpses the Avatars' idyllic future.

RYAN, INSPECTOR: Volunteers to help Inspector Sheridan when a judge and city councilman go missing in "Freaky Phoebe."

SHERIDAN, INSPECTOR: A mortal, this aggressive detective is possessed by a phantasm, which Barbas controls ("Crimes and Witch-demeanors"), and her mission to expose Darryl and bring the Charmed Ones to "justice" begins. She's an undercover cop/dancer in the evil universe ("It's a Bad, Bad, Bad, Bad World, Part 1"). Injured by Leo, she suffers some memory loss while searching the Manor in "A Call to Arms." Her pursuit of the Charmed Ones is thwarted when Agent Brody shoots her with a tranquilizer dart in "Charrrmed." Darryl suspects that Brody is responsible for Sheridan's mysterious disappearance ("There's Something About Leo"). With Kira the Seer's help, Phoebe and Darryl find Sheridan in a mental hospital ("Witchness Protection"). Brody caused her persistent comatose state, which he reverses after he becomes a Whitelighter. She returns to the police department to work as Darryl's partner ("Carpe Demon"). When a city councilman and a judge disappear, the sisters are implicated, and Sheridan's suspicions are renewed ("Freaky Phoebe"). Convinced that the sisters are criminals, she tries to get to Darryl through Shelia ("Death Becomes Them"). Darryl tells her that the  Halliwells are above reproach and she should not mess with them. Ignoring his advice, she assists Agent Keyes and is killed by Zankou when she enters the Manor to spy in "Something Wicca This Way Goes . . . ?"

TOULOUSE: The bouncer at Cabaret Fantome ("Show Ghouls"), he was trapped in Count Roget's endlessly repeating fire with other Innocents.

THE NOT NECESSARILY EVIL

ANGEL OF DEATH: He collects the souls of the dead ("Styx Feet Under"). People must die in order according to his List to preserve the cosmic balance in the Grand Design. He maintains that death gives life meaning, since it forces people to *live*. Coming for Leo is hard ("Vaya Con Leos"), because the Angel of Death has gotten to know him and the sisters. This influences him to help Piper find out why Leo must die. See also: Clarence, another Angel of Death, in "Other Benevolent Beings."

BEAST, THE: Derek, a human used by a Manticore to sire a hybrid child in "Little Monsters," uses demonic potions to change himself into an entity powerful enough to rescue his son from the Manticore pack.

BIANCA: A witch born into the Phoenix Coven of assassins, Bianca falls in love with Chris Perry in 2026 in "Chris-Crossed." She uses her magic to help Chris prevent events that turn Wyatt evil. Although killed by evil in Wyatt's dark future, she may live to marry Chris if he succeeds.

CALLAWAY, OLIVIA (THE GHOST OF): Olivia was killed in the family feud in 2002, but her spirit lingers with a need for vengeance and a desire to be with Richard Montana in "Love's a Witch." She crosses over when she forsakes vengeance to embrace forgiveness.

CHARMED BEASTS, THE: The Charmed Ones are transformed into beasts, manifestations of their anger toward everyone Up There ("Once in a Blue Moon"). This event occurs only once every fifty years, when there are two blue moons in one year.

THE CLEANERS: Empowered to protect magic by good and evil, these neutral men in white suits are not listed in the Book of Shadows. As depicted in "Forget Me . . . Not," they have the ability to erase evidence and reset history whenever magic is exposed. In "Crimes and Witch-demeanors," their actions almost cause Darryl's execution for murder.

GREMLINS: Blue-gray imps standing twelve inches tall, gremlins chuckle incessantly and move with lightning speed. While their destructive mischief can be harmful, they will mind their manners and assist good to avoid being vanquished, as they did for Paige in "Power of Three Blondes." A gremlin appears with other magical beings in "Sword and the City."

HYBRID MANTICORE: Wyatt does not sense inherent evil in the baby son of a human and Manticore in "Little Monsters," confirming Paige's theory that even demon genetics can be overcome in the right parental environment.

LEO, THE AVATAR: He becomes an Avatar to heal Piper and Phoebe, who have died, and he believes that ending the conflict between good and evil will create a better, safer world ("Someone to Witch Over Me"). He uses the powers of the Avatars to woo Piper, his only reason for wanting to be an Avatar ("Charmed Noir"). He questions an Elder's assumption that the Avatars are malevolent and learns to control the emotional outbursts that trigger his new powers ("There's Something About Leo"). Leo finally confides in Piper ("Witchness Protection") and convinces her that the Avatars' new world will be good ("Ordinary Witches"). His power helps the Avatars and the sisters implement the change in "Extreme Makeover: World Edition," but then he realizes the new world is a mistake. The Avatars "remove" people to control conflict, and Leo sacrifices himself, hoping the Charmed Ones will change everything back ("Charmageddon").

LEO THE DEMON: Created by Wyatt as a response to conflict; he blames himself for his father's absence ("Cheaper by the Coven").

SHAKTI: The Hindu goddess of creation, she created all things with her lover, Shiva. If they consummate their love again, all things will be obliterated. Considered the ultimate lovers, the couple is called upon at Hindu weddings ("A Call to Arms").

SHIVA: The Hindu god of destruction ("A Call to Arms"), he is the co-creator of all things; see Shakti.

SIGMUND: A teacher at Magic School ("The Legend of Sleepy Halliwell"), he aids Gideon in the belief that killing Wyatt is for the greater good ("Spin City"). He assists in Piper's efforts to identify the threat in "A Wrong Day's Journey into Right" and is killed by Gideon when he decides to tell the sisters about the plot ("Witch Wars").

SORCERER: The sorcerer uses demonic ingredients in his spells but provides magical remedies for good. In "Love's a Witch," he cooperates with Leo, an Elder, when Chris asks for a potion to protect secrets.

TRIBUNAL, THE: Composed of two Elders and two demons, this council monitors magic to protect it from exposure ("Crimes and Witch-demeanors"). The only things about which good and evil agree are keeping magic unexposed and keeping the Hollow contained. The Tribunal created the Cleaners.

TURNER, COLE: Doomed to spend a loveless eternity in a cosmic void between life and death, Cole launches dual scenarios to help Phoebe regain her belief in love ("The Seven Year Witch"). He arranges for Piper to die of Thorn demon poison. The psychic shock brings Leo back after Phoebe defends the power of his and Piper's true love to Odin, an Elder. Cole also arranged Drake's human adventure, hoping that Phoebe would fall in love with the ex-demon and embrace love again. Both ploys work.

VALKYRIES: From the Book of Shadows, "A powerful race of demigoddesses who scout battlegrounds for dying warriors, then take their souls to Valhalla, where they prepare them for the final world battle." The island of the Valkyries is located in the Indian Ocean and is magically camouflaged. In "Valhalley of the Dolls," Freyja, Mist, Leysa, and Kara are pitted against the Charmed Ones when, at Chris's instigation, they hide Leo and accept Piper as a Valkyrie.

WONDER WITCH: Billie is transformed into a superhero with great speed and strength when she dons the Golden Belt of Gaea ("Battle of the Hexes"). She uses the powers to save Innocents and kill demons before the belt exerts its ultimate imperative to destroy all men.

WHITE MAGIC ENTITIES, OBJECTS, AND RITUALS

ENTITIES AND OBJECTS

ASTRAL PLANE: A realm of spirit and energy ("Power of Three Blondes"). Time does not move forward in the Astral Plane ("Generation Hex"), where the unvanquishable Rondok, a Noxon demon, is sent in a state of partial vanquish that will be eternal.

BOOK: A 1930s novel titled *Crossed, Double-Crossed*, designed by Dan Mullen to build his brother Eddie's confidence, physically draws readers into its pages and plot ("Charmed Noir"). When Eddie solves the mystery and ends the story, the book becomes inert.

BUDDHA'S MYSTICAL STAFF: Protected by twelve Chinese Zodiacs, it passes from one Zodiac to the next at the New Year ("12 Angry Zen"). If it falls into demonic hands, the obsessive influence it exerts will be evil.

CHESS SET: One half of the playing board exists in the reality of good, the other half in the world of evil, allowing both Magic School headmasters to play. Captured pieces are vanquished ("It's a Bad, Bad, Bad, Bad World, Part 1").

COSMIC VOID: Oblivion between life and death, Cole Turner's eternal destination ("The Seven Year Witch").

CRYSTAL BALL: In addition to its fortune-telling properties, a crystal ball can be used as a remote eavesdropping and visual monitoring device ("Witch Wars").

CUPID'S RING: It enables people to travel in time to see people they have truly loved ("Forever Charmed").

DEATH'S LIST: People must die in order on the List to maintain cosmic balance, but circumstances can change the order ("Styx Feet Under").

DOLLHOUSE: Designed and furnished by Grams as a replica of the Manor; Leo finds it when he cleans the attic. Wyatt miniaturizes and installs his parents in the house for safekeeping ("Scry Hard"). The Charmed Ones are placed in the dollhouse again when the demons Phoenix, Patra, and Pilar channel the Power of Three to destroy the Slave King ("Repo Manor"). A spell switches the evil three into the dollhouse, which Piper blows up.

DREAMWORLD: A person's dreams, accessed by a potion where truth can be found ("The Jung and the Restless"). Dreamworld is neutral territory, neither good nor evil.

EXCALIBUR: Whoever possesses the legendary sword with the golden hilt will be invincible ("Sword and the City") and will desire to rule. The sword is bound to the Ultimate Power on Earth or the Chosen One, Wyatt.

GHOSTLY PLANE: The way station between death and crossing over, where a Darklighter traps Leo and Piper in "The Courtship of Wyatt's Father." Phoebe's soul has a brief sojourn in the Ghostly Plane when Imara's body is destroyed ("Freaky Phoebe").

GOLDEN BELT OF GAEA: Fashioned by goddesses for the Greek queen Hippolyta, who wanted men and women to be equal, the belt transforms the wearer into a being with superhero strength and speed ("Battle of the Hexes"). Found in a cold case file at Homeland Security, the belt compels the wearer to use its powers to rid the world of men, and it will drive the wearer mad before she dies. It can be removed only with the goddesses' spell and destroys evil entities that dare wear it.

GRAND DESIGN: The universe maintains a balance between good and evil ("It's a Bad, Bad, Bad, Bad World, Part 1"). Tinkering with the Grand Design can alter the balance ("It's a Bad, Bad, Bad, Bad World, Part 2"). People must die in order according to the Angel of Death's List to maintain the cosmic balance of the Grand Design ("Styx Feet Under"). The Avatars claim that eliminating the duality of good and evil will reinstall the original Design ("Extreme Makeover: World Edition"). A primary precept of the Grand Design is that everything happens for a reason ("Vaya Con Leos").

KARMA: The "great cosmic justice system," karma keeps good and evil in balance. It accumulates to be passed on through generations of a family, and unfinished karma waits to complete its cycle ("Used Karma").

LOST SOULS: Spirits of the dead who are unable to move on due to confusion. The souls of good people who die violently in a group are sometimes held back by the bad souls among them.

MANOR, THE: The Halliwell family home for generations, it becomes the symbolic seat of power after the sisters "die." A demon that controls the Manor will rise to power in the Underworld ("Still Charmed and Kicking"). The Manor is destroyed during the Ultimate Battle between Billie and Christy Jenkins and the Charmed Ones ("Kill Billie: Vol. 2"). It remains intact when history is altered and the destructive event is prevented in "Charmed Forever."

MYSTICAL BLUE MOON: A blue moon, two full moons in one calendar month, occurs roughly once every two and a half years. The Mystical Blue Moon occurs once every fifty years, when there are two blue moons in one year.

PLASMA: The only source is the Ghostly Plane. Ghosts use plasma balls as weapons ("Love's a Witch").

PYRITE CRYSTALS: The crystals resonate a harmonic tone in the presence of evil; used as a demonic alarm.

SPIRIT BOARD: Trapped in the dollhouse, the sisters get a message to Billie through the Halliwell family spirit board ("Repo Manor").

SHADOW: The power within the Spiritual Nexus, it is drawn to the dominant force in proximity to it, good or evil. Confused by the presence of the evil Zankou and the good Charmed Ones, it possesses Leo, a neutral ("Scry Hard"). A Charmed spell sends it back into the Nexus.

SPIRITUAL NEXUS: A concentration of power beneath the land upon which the Manor was built in 1906, the Nexus can be either good or evil, depending on the nature of the magic that controls the Manor ("Scry Hard"). Strengthened by stolen Charmed powers, Zankou successfully absorbs the Nexus in "Something Wicca This Way Goes . . . ?" He is vanquished by the Power of Three spell that destroys ancient power.

TAROT: An ancient form of fortune-telling using a deck of twenty-two pictorial cards of allegorical figures. Note: Chris Perry's Judgment card is spelled Judement ("Spin City").

TIME PORTALS: Creating a portal is not an exact science, as Chris and Leo find out in "Soul Survivor," when they are cast into a prehistoric era and the Civil War. A spell can be used to create a one-way door back to a specific point in time. Leo uses the Avatars' power to send Paige and Kyle Brody back to 1981 through a time portal in "Ordinary Witches."

WOLF: A projection of Phoebe's inner self, a wolf guides her to Enola, a shaman at Magic School, where she embarks on a vision quest to face the truth about her future ("The Legend of Sleepy Halliwell").

WUVEY: Wyatt's favorite stuffed bear is cursed by the demon Vicus to turn Wyatt evil in "Imaginary Fiends," but Wyatt's trust in Leo removes the curse. Phoebe animates Wuvey to find out what's bothering Wyatt ("Payback's a Witch").

WYATT'S ACTION FIGURES: On his third birthday, Wyatt animates his toy soldier, Indian chief, and sheriff and instills them with his own personality to express his questions and confusion about Leo's absence ("Payback's a Witch").

RITUALS

VISION QUEST: Enola teaches Phoebe to make the vision quest potion, which the subject drinks. The person on the quest cannot be brought back until they've seen what they are meant to see. Phoebe sees her future as a mother ("The Legend of Sleepy Halliwell"). With Chris as his spirit guide, Leo learns he's meant to return to his family ("Someone to Witch Over Me").

WICCANING: The ancestral blessing bestowed by the magical members of the family, living and dead, that sets a witch's compass for good ("Cheaper by the Coven").

Miscellaneous Magical Lore

▲ Dogs bark when there is intense magic in the air. **("VALHALLEY OF THE DOLLS")**

▲ Magic requires the presence of people to use it and doesn't exist in prehistoric times. **("SOUL SURVIVOR")**

▲ Karma cannot be cleansed, even with a spell. **("USED KARMA")**

▲ Ghosts require years of practice to cross over into the mortal realm, and they need a connection to a living person. **("THE COURTSHIP OF WYATT'S FATHER")**

▲ Magic can be used to influence the world but must not take over free will. **("CRIMES AND WITCH-DEMEANORS")**

▲ The universe maintains a balance between good and evil called the Grand Design. **("IT'S A BAD, BAD, BAD, BAD WORLD, PART 1")**

▲ Burdock root is difficult to find. **("IT'S A BAD, BAD, BAD, BAD WORLD, PART 1")**

▲ Herbal tea with castor root dulls the senses. **("LITTLE BOX OF HORRORS")**

▲ Add mandrake root to shapeshifter vanquishing potions. **("IMAGINARY FIENDS")**

▲ How curses come about is often more important than the magic that created them. **("IMAGINARY FIENDS")**

▲ Using magic will alert and attract demons. **("STILL CHARMED AND KICKING")**

▲ Signs always lead you where you belong. **("MALICE IN WONDERLAND")**

▲ Magic can't erase fears. **("KILL BILLIE: VOL. 1")**

Trok Demon

Vanishing
Spell

Let the Object
of Objection
Become but
a Dream
As I cause
the Seen
To be Unseen

Book of Shadows

...candles in a loose circle on the
...at the candles and then Chant:

...RDS
...CRY
...n the
...ER Side
...me to Me I
...Summon thee

...all the
...ɑllwell
Matriarchs

The Warren line **Book of Shadows** is a leather-bound volume of spells, magical lore, and family history dating back to 1693. Locked and unlocked by the Triquetra embossed on the dusty cover and the first page, the book binds and guides the Power of Three.

Penned by the powerful line of Warren witches, the Book of Shadows is the most powerful of magical tomes, and possession of it is, therefore, sought by all evil beings. It is an extension of the Charmed Ones and reflects their nature—good or evil.

NOTE: Most witches create a Book of Shadows to be passed down through the generations.

PRECEPTS AND RULES

THE WARREN LINE BOOK OF SHADOWS:

▲ Cannot be touched by evil, with these exceptions:

The Charmed Ones become evil ("Bride and Gloom").

Charmed blood is used to disguise evil ("A Witch in Time").

The Charmed identities are stolen ("Power of Three Blondes").

▲ Cannot be removed from the Manor except by a Charmed One.

▲ Is a source of information regarding evil magical entities, but not evil mortals.

▲ Changes as needed, often by the hand of a Warren ancestor.

▲ Contains no references to fairies, elves, or trolls, which can be seen only by Innocent eyes, mostly children.

▲ Cannot be photocopied.

▲ Opens to appropriate pages to facilitate research.

▲ Has color-coded pages designated by Paige:

Red: demons and warlocks

White: benevolent beings

Green: nature

SPELLS AND POTIONS

To Vanquish a Trok Demon
("VALHALLEY OF THE DOLLS")

Upon summoning the Trok demon, freezing is recommended to avoid the sonic blast of its roar.

From other worlds far and near,
Let's get him, the Trok, out of here.

RESULT: Instead of freezing, Piper blows up one of the Trok's two heads. The spell vanquishes the demon in flames.

The Memory Spell
("VALHALLEY OF THE DOLLS")

To restore Piper's memory and negate the ultrachipper personality created by Leo's pain removal spell.

Powers and emotion tied,
A witch's heart is where it hides.
Help her through her agony,
Bless her with her memory.

RESULT: The spell erases Piper's memory of everything.

To Reverse Oscar's Curse
("VALHALLEY OF THE DOLLS")

I call upon the Halliwells,
I call our powers to undo this spell.
Make right again, that we must,
Reverse the curse that made this mutt.

RESULT: Oscar the bulldog is transformed back into a man.

To Reverse the Memory Spell
("VALHALLEY OF THE DOLLS")

Spell was cast,
Now make it pass.
Remove it now,
Don't ask me how.

RESULT: The spell restores Piper's memory,
but she remains cut off from her pain.

To Reveal Piper's Heart
("VALHALLEY OF THE DOLLS")

Rewritten version of "To Reveal Phoebe's Heart" from
"A Witch's Tail, Part Two," Volume I

Open Piper's heart to reveal
That part which only Phoebe feels.
Send it back from whence it came,
But don't protect her from the pain.

RESULT: Phoebe feels Piper's pain and hurls it back,
forcing Piper to confront and deal with her emotions.

To Fill in the Blanks
("FORGET ME . . . NOT")

Written by Paige and Phoebe when they do not
remember events of the previous day;
cast by Paige:

Moments lost make witches wonder,
Warlock's plot or demon's plunder?
If this is not a prank,
Help us to fill in the blanks.

The spell takes them back a day with their
memories of what will happen intact.
When the Cleaners attempt to erase their
memories in the do-over, the spell
protects them.

Memory Spell

To fill in the blanks

Moments lost
Make witches wonder

Warlock's plot or
Demon's plunder

if this is
not a prank
help us to
Fill in the Blanks

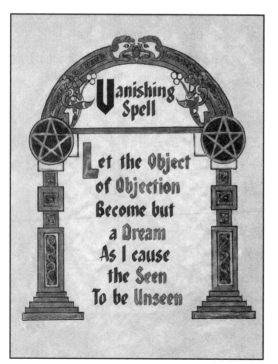

Vanishing Spell

Let the Object
of Objection
Become but
a Dream
As I cause
the Seen
To be Unseen

The Vanishing Spell
(VOLUME 1: "HELL HATH NO FURY" AND "CHARMED AND DANGEROUS"; VOLUME 2: "FORGET ME . . . NOT" AND "MY THREE WITCHES")

Let the object of objection
Become but a dream,
As I cause the seen
To be unseen.

Piper eliminates the Golden Gate Bridge to
convince the Cleaners to return Wyatt. Paige
uses this spell to clean up a mess.

To Call a Witch's Power
(VOLUME 1: "HOW TO MAKE A QUILT OUT OF AMERICANS"
AND "CHARMED AND DANGEROUS")

aka To Call a Lost Witch
(VOLUME 1: "CHARMED AGAIN PART ONE" AND "HELL HATH NO
FURY"; VOLUME 2: "POWER OF THREE BLONDES," "BATTLE OF THE
HEXES," AND "ENGAGED AND CONFUSED"; mentioned but not recited:
"MR. & MRS. WITCH," "REPO MANOR," "12 ANGRY ZEN," AND
"THE LAST TEMPTATION OF CHRISTY")

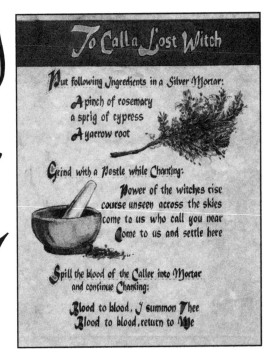

aka To Call a Lost Sister
("SOUL SURVIVOR")

After they steal the Charmed identities, the
Stillman Sisters use this Warren spell to take
the Charmed powers.

Power of the witches rise,
Course unseen across the skies.
Come to us who call you near,
Come to us and settle here.

RESULT: The evil witches gain the
Charmed powers, but they lose the
Power of Three when they turn the
powers on each other.

The Charmed Ones use the spell to revive the
Power of Three and regain their abilities.

To Locate Paige
("LOVE'S A WITCH")

Phoebe uses a cloth soaked with Paige's blood
to find her sister and learn the cause of her injury.

Lead me back from whence this came,
Help me help my sister's pain.

To Identify Source of Injury
("LOVE'S A WITCH")

Piper heats the shirt soaked in Paige's blood in a simmering potion
to identify the source of the injury. The shirt whitens,
indicating the source was a plasma ball.

How to Perform a Séance
Variation No. 3: Ceremony to Contact the Dead
("LOVE'S A WITCH")

Variation No. 1: Volume 1
("PRE WITCHED")

Variation No. 2: Volume 1
("TRIAL BY MAGIC")

Light five candles arranged in a circle. Join hands during the incantation,
and do not break the circle until the Spirit moves on.

Unknown spirit we call to thee,
Those who wish to set you free.
Cross on over so we may help,
Come to us, reveal yourself.

To Vanquish a Ghost
(VOLUME 1: "RECKLESS ABANDON"; VOLUME 2: "LOVE'S A WITCH")

Option No. 1: Boil a mandrake-root potion and pour over the ghost's bones.
Option No. 2: Destroy the object of its obsession.

To Find a Blood Relative
(VARIATION OF "TO BRING AN ANCESTOR BACK"—
VOLUME 1: "THE WITCH IS BACK")

Blood to blood, I summon thee.
Blood to blood, return to me.

Empathic Power Immunity Spell
("LOVE'S A WITCH")

Written by Phoebe to block her sisters' emotions.

In the name of the Halliwell line,
Bar my sisters from this power of mine.

RESULT: This spell and all other variations fail.

To Summon Zahn
("SOUL SURVIVOR")

We call upon the ancient powers
To summon one to save a soul.

To Bestow Power on a Mortal
("LITTLE MONSTERS")

Written by Paige to help Darryl resolve a hostage situation.

Blessed with powers from my destiny,
I bless this hero with invincibility.

RESULT: Bullets bounce off Darryl, but he destroys everything he touches with his superhuman strength.

To Call the Book of Shadows
("CHRIS-CROSSED")

I call upon the Ancient Power
To help us in this darkest hour.
Let the Book return to this place,
Claim refuge in its rightful space.

To Go Back in Time
("CHRIS-CROSSED")

Draw a large Triquetra on the wall and then recite:

Hear these words, hear the rhyme,
Heed the hope within my mind.
Send me back to where I'll find,
What I wish in place and time.

RESULT: A portal of blue light opens within the Triquetra.

WARNING: This spell allows only one-way travel back in time.

NOTES:

▲ In alternate 2026, Evil Wyatt devises a variation that permits two-way travel to the past and future.

▲ Chris tears the spell page from the Book of Shadows when he returns to 2003 the second time.

▲ The Charmed Ones devise a potion that works, but it is blocked by Gideon ("It's a Bad, Bad, Bad, Bad World, Part 1").

To Restore Lost Powers
("CHRIS-CROSSED")

Powers of the witches rise,
Come to me across the skies.
Return my magic, give me back
All that was taken in the attack.

NOTE: This is another variation of the spell "To Call a Lost Witch or Sister."

To Summon the Dead

**(VOLUME 1: "CHARMED AGAIN, PARTS ONE AND TWO"
AND "NECROMANCING THE STONE")**

Variation No. 1 of the séance ritual
("WITCHSTOCK"):

Hear these words, hear my cry,
Spirit from the other side.
Come to me, I summon thee,
Cross now the great divide.

Variation No. 2 of the séance ritual
("THE COURTSHIP OF WYATT'S FATHER"):

Sister spirit, we call to thee,
Cross on over so we may see.

Variation No. 3 of the séance ritual; shortened to call Grams
("CHEAPER BY THE COVEN"):

Hear these words, hear my cry,
Spirit from the other side,
Cross now the great divide.

RESULT: Rather than creating a conduit
for Piper to cross over, the spell sends
Chris to the Ghostly Plane.

To Summon the Dead

Place five candles in a loose circle on the floor, light the candles and then Chant:

Hear these words
hear my cry
Spirit from the
Other Side
Come to Me I
Summon thee
Cross now the Great divide.

To Disarm a Cop
("WITCHSTOCK")

Written by Penny Halliwell, 1967

They have no right,
They have no power.
Turn their hate sticks
Into flowers.

To Attract a Cop
("WITCHSTOCK")

Written by Piper to escape jail in 1967

Come this way and be seduced,
I have a girl to introduce.
Fall for her, you can't resist her,
Trust me, mister, she's my sister.

NOTE: In 1967 the Charmed Ones are still witches,
but without powers, which do not yet exist.

To Disarm an Evil Entity
("WITCHSTOCK")

May peace and love
From the moon above
Flow through your heart
On the wings of a dove.

RESULT: Penny Halliwell's 1967 hippie spell has no effect on the warlock Nigel.
NOTE: The spell has no effect on the Demon with No Name blob creature
when hippie Grams uses it in an alternate 2003.

To Vanquish a Warlock
("WITCHSTOCK")

Written by Penny Halliwell, 1967

Snuff this warlock
His days are done,
But make him good
For the ecosystem.

To Vanquish the Demon with No Name and Other Miscellaneous Evil Creatures
("WITCHSTOCK")

Drawing on the Power of Three,
Destroy this evil entity.

To Create the Perfect Man
("PRINCE CHARMED")

Write desired personality trait on paper. Drop the papers into the bubbling potion base.
Add pheromones to individual taste.

A perfect man we summon now.
Another way, we don't know how.
To make our sister see the light,
Somewhere out there is Mr. Right.

RESULT: Formed from golden orbs, the product has a built-in lifespan of twenty-four hours.
NOTE: Phoebe added the "hot Latin type" ingredient to the formula to create
David for Piper's birthday.

Variation No. 1, using candles to recall the man created by an original spell:

The perfect man I summon now.
Another way I don't know how.
Bring him now into the light,
Come back to me, Mr. Right.

ABERRATION: Paige's original spell created good and evil versions of her
Perfect Man ("A Wrong Day's Journey into Right").
NOTE: The potion to make Mr. Right/Mr. Wrong
real requires the subject's own blood.

Instant Dinner Party
("PRINCE CHARMED")

On Piper's day, set this table
With all the food that you are able.

To Cleanse an Aura
("USED KARMA")

Modified by Richard Callaway to cleanse karma.

I call to thee, pure witches' fire
Through vortex flow the heavenly mire.
Cleanse brackish (karma) of debris,
From dark to light sweep history.

RESULT: The spell captures Mata Hari's unfinished karma and injects it into Phoebe. Richard's karma is unaffected.

Aura Cleanse

I call to thee, pure Witches fire, Through vortex flow the heavenly mire, Cleanse brackish aura of debrise, From dark to light sweep history...

To Vanquish the Swarm King
("USED KARMA")

Demon Swarm that serves as One
Vanquish him from which they come.

To Vanquish the Headless Horseman
("THE LEGEND OF SLEEPY HALLIWELL")

Power of Three unite,
To end this grisly fright,
Reverse the roles
And make us whole.

NOTE: The identity of the entity that cast the spell must be known to reverse it.

Swarm Demons

Distant relatives of Razis and Vampires

The demonic line of evil known as Swarm Demons are pack hunters of the Underworld. The Swarm Drones follow the orders of their King without question and often sacrifice themselves for the good of the collective body.

The Crystal Cage to Trap Demons

**(VOLUME 1: "SIGHT UNSEEN," "CHARMED AND DANGEROUS,"
"DREAM SPELL," AND "BABY'S FIRST DEMON"; VOLUME 2: "I DREAM
OF PHOEBE," "WITCH WARS," "IT'S A BAD, BAD, BAD, BAD WORLD,
PART 1," "ONCE IN A BLUE MOON," AND "BATTLE OF THE HEXES")**

A demon caught within the sphere of empowered crystals will be rendered helpless and trapped by the energies its presence triggers. The trap may be kept opened to lure a demon and completed by placing the last crystal once it's inside. An overcharged cage can be lethal.

NOTE: Billie as Wonder Witch, wearing the Golden Belt of Gaea, breaks free of the crystals and wrecks the attic.

Teenage Vengeance Wish
("HYDE SCHOOL REUNION")

Written in Phoebe's handwriting in the back of her Baker High School yearbook as a senior.

*Those who mock who I am
Let them always remember when.*

RESULT: Empowered by adult Phoebe's magic, the spell triggers a flashback morph effect. The effect is triggered by anger and turns Phoebe into a teenage version of herself.
NOTE: The spell is voided when adult reason reasserts itself.

To Curse a Rival
("HYDE SCHOOL REUNION")

Spontaneous spell cast by flash-morphed Teen Phoebe.

*I'd rather be rich
Than a bitch.*

RESULT: The rival, Todd's wife Paula, turns into a dog.
NOTE: Paige reverses the adolescent spell.

To Re-Create the Past
("HYDE SCHOOL REUNION")

The past is the future,
And the future's the past.
Let's welcome back
The senior class.

RESULT: With a wave of teen Phoebe's hands, the ballroom is transformed into a nineties motif. While her old classmates remain physically unchanged, they revert to teenage behavior.
NOTE: Paige reverses the adolescent spell.

To Foil Rick's Robbery
("HYDE SCHOOL REUNION")

Make them see what cannot be,
Flames that leap to make them flee . . .

To Foil Rick's Robbery, Part II
("HYDE SCHOOL REUNION")

. . . make him hear what isn't there,
His deepest worry come to bear.

A New Face for Rick
("HYDE SCHOOL REUNION")

Who you were, you're now another,
Take the face of Wyatt's brother.

RESULT: As soon as Rick Gittridge changes to look like Chris, three Scabber demons shimmer in and dissolve him with acid.

To Reverse a Spell Cast by the Wicked Witch of the Enchanted Forest
("SPIN CITY")

You who found me at this bar
Turn back to who you really are.

RESULT: Riley the leprechaun becomes short again.
NOTE: Paige vanquishes the classic Wicked Witch with an unknown spell.

To Vanquish a Spider Demon
("SPIN CITY")

The vanquishing potion must be blessed with the blood of all three Charmed Ones.

NOTE: An antidote for the Spider demon's venom is available.

To Cause Chaos
("CRIMES AND WITCH-DEMEANORS")

Cast to call the Cleaners.

Flowers that bring desire,
Make them turn to fire.

To Vanquish Gideon
("IT'S A BAD, BAD, BAD, BAD WORLD, PART 1")

A Power of Four spell by good and evil Paige and Phoebe.

We call upon the ancient lore,
To punish with the Power of Four.
Strike down this threat from both there and here,
Make him suffer, then—disappear.

RESULT: Gideon's skin blisters, but the Elder orbs out before the spell is complete.

To Make Paige and Phoebe Happy
("IT'S A BAD, BAD, BAD, BAD WORLD, PART 2")

Cast by Piper in an alternate, supersweet reality.

Call now the powers Blessed be,
To make my sisters happ, happ-ee!

NOTE: The spell is nullified by the necessity of saving family lives.

To Dispossess
("A CALL TO ARMS")

We call upon the mortal ways
And Gods who guide but may not stay,
We seek those of divinity
To separate from and set them free.

To Send Lady Godiva Back
("THE BARE WITCH PROJECT")

From lands afar in time and space,
Take her now from this our place.
One that dwells so must remain,
Send her back to her domain.

RESULT: Lord Dyson was conjured with Lady Godiva and must return with her.

To Call Lord Dyson
("THE BARE WITCH PROJECT")

We look to find the evil set free,
Bring this demon before us three.

Variation of the Godiva Spell
("THE BARE WITCH PROJECT")

From lands afar in time and space,
Take them now from this our place.
Two that dwell so must remain,
Send them back to their domain.

RESULT: A stronger Lord Dyson returned and killed Lady Godiva, which altered history.

To Summon the Matriarchs
(VOLUME 1: "NECROMANCING THE STONE"; VOLUME 2: "CHEAPER BY THE COVEN")

I call forth from time and space
Matriarchs from the Halliwell line,
Mothers, daughters, sisters, friends,
Our family's spirit without end.

To Counter Sarpedon's Time-Stop
("SOMEONE TO WITCH OVER ME")

Show me what the evil sees,
Even if at lightning speeds.

To Switch a Power
("ORDINARY WITCHES")

What's mine is yours,
What's yours is mine.
I offer up my gift to share,
Switch our powers through the air.

Variation: To Switch a Power
("REPO MANOR")

What's theirs is yours,
What's yours is theirs.
I offer up this gift to share,
Switch the bodies through the air.

To Break the Avatars' Spell
("CHARMAGEDDON")

Following Leo's advice, Phoebe touches the Book of Shadows to induce a vision of everyone she's lost. The memory of her grief breaks the "Better Place" daze.

To Summon a Sorcerer
("CARPE DEMON")

Sorcerer of darkness, demon of fright,
I call you now into my sight.

NOTE: The sorcerer has his lair protected, and the spell fails to work.

To Vanquish a Sorcerer
("CARPE DEMON")

Evil blasts we cannot use,
The Power of Three now lights their fuse.

Tips for Future Whitelighters
("SHOW GHOULS" AND "THE SEVEN YEAR WITCH")

Added to the Book of Shadows for Wyatt and Chris by Leo in case he's not around to advise them. Leo wrote, "To my sons, Wyatt and Chris . . . Love, Dad."

NOTE: Alerted by the information on this page, Drake has Wyatt use his power to heal to save Piper.

To Confine the Shadow Demon
(VOLUME 1: "IS THERE A WOOGY IN THE HOUSE?" AND "THE IMPORTANCE OF BEING PHOEBE"; VOLUME 2: "SCRY HARD")

I am light,
I am one too strong to fight.
Return to dark where shadows dwell,
You cannot have this Halliwell.

To Swap Souls
("FREAKY PHOEBE")

To reverse Imara's soul-swapping spell, recite the incantation,
then drop a lock of the subject's hair into the potion.

Lock of hair completes our goal,
To help us reclaim our sister's soul.
Banish this demon, spare no pain,
Bring Phoebe back from the Ghostly Plane.

To Communicate with Wyatt
("IMAGINARY FIENDS")

Help this mother understand,
The thoughts inside her little man.
Though his mouth be quiet,
Let us hear the inner Wyatt.

RESULT: Written to help Piper understand toddler Wyatt, the spell brings
adult Wyatt back from the future.

To Remove the Curse on Wuvey
("IMAGINARY FIENDS")

Evil taints what was once held dear,
Remove this curse away from here.

RESULT: This spell and several others fail.
Love, the best magic always and forever, works.

To Return Wyatt to the Future
("IMAGINARY FIENDS")

A son in the future, a son in the past,
Seeing anew what once has past.
Return him to now to whence he came,
Right when he left, all now the same.

To Transform Zankou into a Pig
("SOMETHING WICCA THIS WAY GOES . . . ?")

Something wicked in our midst,
In our home where he exists.

NOTE: The protective wards are weakened when the Charmed Ones lose confidence, which allows Zankou to steal the Book of Shadows ("Death Becomes Them"). The Charmed Ones reclaim it with the Power of Three spell ("Something Wicca This Way Goes . . . ?").

How to Banish a Suxen
("SOMETHING WICCA THIS WAY GOES . . . ?")

From ancient time this power came,
For all to have, but none to reign.
Take it now. Show no mercy,
For this power can no longer be.

RESULT: The Nexus and Zankou experience an explosive end in the Manor basement.

To Hide True Identities
("STILL CHARMED AND KICKING")

I call upon the Ancient Powers,
To mask us now and in future hours.
Hide us well and thoroughly,
But not from those we call family.

NOTE: To complete the identity change, new names are written on paper and added to a potion that is triggered by an herb.

75

To Make a Lover's Dream Come True
("REWITCHED")

Cast by Billie so Phoebe won't cancel a getaway with Dex.

Hear these words, hear my rhyme,
Bless these two in this time.
Bring them both into the fold,
Help them now cross love's threshold.

RESULT: Phoebe and Dex get married but don't remember anything when they cross the threshold to enter the Manor, and the spell is broken.

To Vanquish Antosis
("REWITCHED")

Hear us now, the witches call,
He who makes the Samaritans fall,
We speak as one the Sisters Three
And banish you to eternity.

To Regain True Identities
("REWITCHED")

I call upon the Ancient Powers
To unmask us now and in future hours.
Show us well and thoroughly,
Reveal ourselves so the world can see.

To Erase Painful Memories
("KILL BILLIE: VOL. 1")

After this cruel memory is seen and said,
Erase these thoughts from my heart and head.

To Hide Leo from Death
("VAYA CON LEOS")

Hide him from sight
So I might fight,
Ignore which leaves bereft
My husband from the Angel of Death.

To Call the Angel of Destiny
("VAYA CON LEOS")

Power of Three we summon thee,
And call to us the Angel of Destiny.

To Animate Wuvey
("PAYBACK'S A WITCH")

Little boy's bear,
Show me how you care,
Tell me how you'd feel,
If you were real.

To Find Pator
("THE TORN IDENTITY")

Ancient powers, we summon thee,
We, the Power of Three,
And seek your help in finding
The demon who is hiding.

To *Release* the Hollow
("KILL BILLIE: VOL. 2")

Nos dico super inconcessus vox.
Bonus quod malum
Ultirusque a profugus,
Addo is hic, addo is iam.

To *Return* the Hollow
("FOREVER CHARMED")

Iam is addo, hic is addo,
Malum quod bonus,
Vox inconcessus super dico nos.

GRAMS'S LITTLE BLACK BOOK

(an appendix to the Book of Shadows)

Sibling Rivalry
("CHEAPER BY THE COVEN")

Cast your petty jealousies
To darkest night.
Let these feuding siblings
No longer fight.

RESULT: The rivalry is removed from Chris and Wyatt and absorbed by Paige, Phoebe, and Piper, regressing them to twelve-year-old mentalities.

To Silence a Chatty Child
("CHEAPER BY THE COVEN")

Let this girl
Quick as a sneeze,
Stop this snit
And promptly freeze.

NOTE: The subject thaws in a minute.

To Reverse Spells in the Little Black Book
("CHEAPER BY THE COVEN")

Made up by Patty when she was nine.

Reverse the spell from the book,
And please restore what was took.

SPELLS FROM NON-CHARMED SOURCES

To Protect Secrets
("LOVE'S A WITCH")

A potion brewed by the sorcerer, commissioned by Chris. The potion requires
a rare Kotochul egg, which can be found in the Swampland. When the textured shell
is broken and the contents added to a cauldron of simmering red liquid
and leaf stalks, the potion flares.

WARNING: Ingestion may cause violent illness or other unpleasant side effects.
Ingested by Piper and Paige to block their emotions from Phoebe. The potion works without ill
effect. Ingested by Chris to prevent Leo from learning that he sent the Elder to Valhalla.

To Banish Spirits
("USED KARMA")

Richard Montana brews the potion to rid Phoebe of Mata Hari's bad karma.
The recipe, however, remains a family secret.

Everything You Always Wanted to Know About Portals But Were Afraid to Ask
("THE COURTSHIP OF WYATT'S FATHER")

The title of a chapter in a text Gideon gives
Paige and Phoebe as an aid to reverse
the portal into the Ghostly Plane.

To Bestow Luck

**(VOLUME 1: "LUCKY CHARMED";
VOLUME 2: "SPIN CITY" AND "REPO MANOR")**

A leprechaun blessing: Luck to you!

Slainte is tainte!

NOTE: The luck may be good or bad.

To Call the Tribunal
("CRIMES AND WITCH-DEMEANORS")

*Di! Ecce hora!
Uxar mea me necabit!*

Duncan's Spell to Conjure Lady Godiva
("THE BARE WITCH PROJECT")

*Where royals once lived,
So did she.
Bring forth the naked babe,
From the eleventh century.*

Duncan's Spell to Return Lady Godiva
("THE BARE WITCH PROJECT")

*A time for everything,
And everything in place,
Return what's been moved
Through time and space.*

Protection Spell
("STYX FEET UNDER")

Paige uses a graduate student's spell to protect an Innocent. However, as usually happens with protection spells, it backfires. Army Chaplain Arthur does not die of a mortal wound, which suspends all death.

Avatar Vanquishing Potion
("CHARMAGEDDON")

Zankou translates the instructions for making the Avatar vanquishing potion from the hieroglyphs in an ancient Egyptian tomb. The Charmed Ones, however, must make it.

To Go Back in Time
("SHOW GHOULS")

Used by Drake to temporarily return to 1899.

Free our souls from their shells,
See where the lost spirits dwell,
Long enough to find their pain,
Quick enough to return again.

Escape from the Ordinary
("SHOW GHOULS")

Phoebe finds this spell in the Cabaret Fantome fortune teller's book, *Portals and Immortals: A Mystical Journey*. She uses it and Tarot to return her soul to 2004.

Vita brevis abaraxis!

To Remove the Golden Belt of Gaea
("BATTLE OF THE HEXES")

For all the world to work as one
In harmony, it must be undone.

NOTE: Written by the goddesses who made the belt, found in a Magic School history book.

To Call the Rainbow Road

(VOLUME 1: "LUCKY CHARMED"; VOLUME 2: "REPO MANOR")

Go n-eirian bothar leat.

To Send a Demon to the Astral Plane

("GENERATION HEX" AND "THE TORN IDENTITY")

Chanted by Magic School students Ryan and Jen, who learned the spell from Leo.

Demon of fire, demon of pain,
We banish you to the Astral Plane.

THE FINAL ENTRIES

PHOEBE

So much has happened over the past eight years, so much has been gained and lost. . . . In some ways I felt like my life was just beginning . . . and it was. For, though I had loved before, I'd never really known love until I met Coop. . . . A man with whom I shared the special little girl I had long ago foreseen but thought I might never have, along with two other special little girls I had not foreseen, who all taught me much about life, not the least of which was . . . forgiveness. And all along, I kept trying to help people, though not just with advice . . . but with love, thanks to Coop . . .

PAIGE

—Phoebe has become somewhat of an expert on the subject . . . As for me, life without demons opened up similar avenues. Henry continued to help people, of course—even if they didn't necessarily want to be helped—while still helping me with the twins and Junior . . . which allowed me the time to finally embrace my inner Whitelighter and help the next generation of witches come into their own . . .

PIPER

—so that Paige could pass on all that she'd learned, not just to her own children or to mine or to Phoebe's, but to all the future witches and Whitelighters-to-be . . . which was important because there was a gap between when we were doing the fighting and when our kids would take over. . . . Allowing me time to go back to my roots and cook something other than potions for once . . . and then sell P3 and open the restaurant I'd always dreamed of having . . . As for Leo, after we reclaimed Magic School, he went back to teaching . . . which he continued to do until it was time to retire. And though we certainly had our struggles and heartaches over the years, there's no question in my mind . . . that our lives have absolutely been Charmed.

Book of
Black Magic

BLACK MAGIC PRACTITIONERS

AVATARS

A force of power that isn't restrained by concepts of good and evil, they exist outside of time and space and possess enormous power. A battle was fought with the Avatars to determine the future of the world five thousand years ago, and vials of an ancient Avatar vanquishing potion survived ("There's Something About Leo"). **NOTE:** Cole was elevated to Avatar in "Centennial Charmed," but he was killed in an alternate history he created.

ALPHA: An older male, he believes the endless battle between good and evil is pointless and the world will be better without the conflict. He reveals himself and this "truth" to Leo in the Elder's vision quest and convinces Leo to become an Avatar by offering the power to bring Phoebe and Piper back from the dead ("Someone to Witch Over Me"). He helps Leo woo Piper and save Paige with Avatar powers but urges Leo to embrace his existence as an Avatar ("Charmed Noir"). To stop Leo's power spikes, he agrees to let Leo tell Piper he's an Avatar, a decision that ultimately requires reversing time to correct the mistake ("There's Something About Leo"). With the consent of Beta and Gamma, he uses Kira the Seer to show Phoebe their Utopian future in "Witchness Protection." He allows Leo to send Kyle Brody back in time to end his hatred of Avatars ("Ordinary Witches"). When his hopes for a Better Way are dashed by the Charmed Ones in "Charmageddon," he changes the world back and leaves.

BETA: The female Avatar, she urges Leo to bring the Charmed Ones into the fold ("Charmed Noir") as part of the plan to end the conflict between good and evil. She warns Leo that reversing time drains the Collective ("There's Something About Leo" and "Ordinary Witches"). She kills Brody to protect herself, but the ancient Avatar-vanquishing potion kills her anyway ("Extreme Makeover: World Edition").

GAMMA: The younger male Avatar, who harasses Leo as a Creature head in "Someone to Witch Over Me." He works closely with Alpha but recognizes that twenty-first-century people aren't ready for Avatars or the Change ("Charmageddon").

CREATURE HEAD: An Avatar appears as a ghostly, disembodied head in "A Call to Arms" and sets Leo and Barbas against each other with the power of suggestion. The head returns in "The Bare Witch Project" and "Charrrmed" to shake Leo's trust in his beliefs, the Elders, and himself. The head tells Leo he's a danger to his family and kills a Possessor demon with energy bolts from its eyes ("Once in a Blue Moon"). The Charmed Ones see it and know for sure that Leo is being set up so the Elders won't trust him. But the head continues to harass Leo ("Someone to Witch Over Me").

THE COLLECTIVE: Avatars, all capable of appearing as floating heads, enlist a Possessor demon to separate Leo from his family ("Once in a Blue Moon"). They require more power to remake the world without good and evil—the Change—and need Leo's strength to complete the Collective. The Avatars' power is not inexhaustible, but it can be strengthened with the addition of new power ("There's Something About Leo"). An Avatar's use of power drains power from the whole Collective. The Collective—Alpha, Gamma, Leo, and ten others—monitor the new world for conflict and remove offenders in their Star Chamber ("Charmageddon"). When confronted with the ancient vanquishing potion, they change everything back and leave.

UNNAMED FEMALE AVATAR: Summoned to save Leo in "Vaya Con Leos," she cooperates with an Elder to help Piper find the Angel of Destiny.

DARKLIGHTERS

DAMIEN: Hired by Gideon to kill Leo ("The Courtship of Wyatt's Father"), Damien wounds the Elder in the Ghostly Plane. He is vanquished by his own lieutenant.

LIEUTENANT: Damien's longtime associate ("The Courtship of Wyatt's Father"), the lieutenant sacrifices his friend to protect Gideon's secret complicity in the plot to kill Leo.

SALEK: A Darklighter leader, he plots to kill the Charmed Ones by targeting Paige's charge, Mikelle ("The Jung and the Restless"). However, killing the future Whitelighter foils the plan. Mikelle returns to save Paige from Darklighter poison.

SID: An underling of Salek's, he fails to kill Mikelle ("The Jung and the Restless").

UNNAMED DARKLIGHTER: Kills the witch Tali in "Witch Wars," before the Gamemaster kills him.

DEMONS

UPPER-LEVEL DEMONS:

▲ Have human form and bleed red.

▲ Vanquish with a potion using their flesh.

▲ Throw fire—an upper-level power.

▲ Do not dream.

LOWER-LEVEL DEMONS:

▲ Bleed green.

▲ Do not dream.

ACOLYTES OF THE ORDER: Committed to bringing the cult's vanquished leader back, the acolytes sacrifice themselves to help the Dark Priest, the high priest of the Order, turn Wyatt evil in "Prince Charmed." They have the ability to appear as someone else.

AKU: Wiser and stronger than other Celerity demons he teaches ("Someone to Witch Over Me"), Aku warns about the Avatar threat and tests the protective power of Sarpedon's stolen guardians. He is one of three Celerity demons who kill Kyle Brody's parents in 1981 while trying to acquire vials of an ancient Avatar vanquishing potion ("Ordinary Witches").

ANTOSIS: Staking out his territory aboveground, Antosis employs the Imp Master and imps to kill Good Samaritans in "Rewitched." Identified by Billie, he's vanquished by a Power of Three spell.

ASSASSIN DEMONS: A horde is instructed by the Triad and Dumain to attack the magical community, a ploy to remove good beings as the Charmed Ones' helpful allies ("Gone with the Witches").

BARBAS, AKA THE DEMON OF FEAR: Barbas is granted permanent resurrection by the Tribunal when he wins a portion of his case against the Charmed

Ones ("Crimes and Witch-demeanors"). He joins Gideon's plot to kill Wyatt ("It's a Bad, Bad, Bad, Bad World, Part 2") in order to have the balance between good and evil restored in the universe. After he tricks Leo into killing an Elder, Paige and Phoebe vanquish him with a potion ("A Call to Arms"). **NOTE:** Barbas has been the most resilient and persistent demonic threat to the sisters since they regained their powers and became the Charmed Ones in 1998. He's the inspiration for Billie's idea to bring Walter Nance to justice ("Run, Piper, Run").

BENZOR: An Upper-Level demon allied with Zankou, he works aboveground disguised as Judge Thomas Hendricks ("Freaky Phoebe"). Imara, in Phoebe's body, vanquishes him.

BLACK HEART: A female demon, she works with Haas to drive young Innocents crazy with a "Malice in Wonderland" waking nightmare. They succeed in bringing the Charmed Ones out of hiding and are vanquished for their trouble.

BOSK: A low-level demon with minimal powers, Bosk attempts to find the lost city of Zanbar and acquire its powers in "I Dream of Phoebe." He's vanquished by the evil Jinny in the bottle.

BOUNTY HUNTERS: Rathbone and Flynn work with the sorcerer who made a deal with Drake in "Carpe Demon." Flynn captures Miss Donovan, the librarian at Magic School, when she goes to the Underworld to get information about Drake.

BRUTE: An entry in the Book of Shadows reads: "An Upper-Level demon with overwhelming physical strength. They work alone, generally crushing their victims' skulls." One participates and dies in "Witch Wars."

BURKE: A bounty hunter, he tracks demons for hire who don't follow instructions ("Vaya Con Leos"), and keeps his prey in frozen stasis. When Billie and the Charmed Ones discover Reinhardt frozen in Burke's lair, the unknown entity that employs Burke is angered. The entity destroys Burke with a mysterious wind and blows up Reinhardt.

CAPED SHADOW DEMON: A mysterious entity with a tattooed forehead and talons, he kidnapped Christy, Billie's sister, on Halloween when they were children ("Kill Billie: Vol. 1").

CELERITY DEMONS: As defined in the Book of Shadows ("Someone to Witch Over Me"), they "are powerful beings who can move at the speed of light and live off lesser demons." They appear in "Ordinary Witches" and "Extreme Makeover: World Edition."

CIRIL: A lesser demon employed by Xar ("Engaged and Confused"), he attacks Piper after warning her that the Triad is back. Christy vanquishes him.

COMMON FIENDS: Horned demon and Slime Devil, mentioned but not depicted in "My Three Witches." A Fierce demon speaks for the demonic horde that Barbas enlists to neutralize Leo as the Charmed Ones' protector ("A Call to Arms").

CRAVEN: Leader of the Tribe demons, he works with Zankou to access the power of the Shadow in the Nexus ("Scry Hard").

CREO: A knowledgeable demon who knows and fears the entities that kidnapped Christy, "Payback's a Witch." Aware of the Triad's plan, he seems to serve Christy when the entities are gone ("The Torn Identity"). He remains a loyal instrument of the Triad ("Gone with the Witches") and commits suicide by fellow demon, Goon, rather than give the sisters information.

CRILL: One of two demon members of the Tribunal ("Crimes and Witch-demeanors").

DALEEK: An Upper-Level demon allied with Zankou, he works aboveground undercover as City Councilman Wexler ("Freaky Phoebe"). Piper and Imara, in Phoebe's body, vanquish him.

DARK KNIGHT: A "mad paladin of destruction," according to the Book of Shadows in "Sword and the City," the Dark Knight shimmers and conjures weapons from thin air. Mordaunt kills him when his services are no longer needed to secure the power of Excalibur.

DARK PRIEST: His Eminence is the high priest of the Order, an ancient cult that was once all-powerful. Convinced that Wyatt is the cult's reincarnated leader in "Prince Charmed," he reverses the boy's morality with a scepter and turns him evil. The Dark Priest is vanquished by his own magic when Chris intervenes to save Wyatt.

THE DEMON WITH NO NAME: A blob of green slime, this evil creature is attracted to and feeds off magic, growing more massive as it consumes. Although electricity can hurt it, nothing can kill it except the Power of Three ("Witchstock").

DEMONATRIXES: Blond, leather-clad assassins with a preference for throwing stars, which can be used to vanquish them ("A Wrong Day's Journey into Right").

DEMONIC HEALER: A common fiend, he heals Barbas ("A Call to Arms"), and then Barbas kills him.

THE DOGON: Masked on one side of his face, this ambitious demon kills and absorbs other demons' powers with his talon ("Kill Billie: Vol. 1"). His attempt to become leader of the Underworld is thwarted by Billie, who vanquishes him with her wits and a potion tossed into his open mouth.

DOMINAX: A goth-type female demon that wants to get Billie before Billie gets her ("Payback's a Witch").

DOPPELGANGERS: Phoenix, Patra, and Pilar, members of an enslaved demonic race, practice for years to replicate the Charmed Ones and their powers ("Repo Manor"). They channel the Power of Three and use a Charmed potion to vanquish the Slave King before the Charmed Ones vanquish them.

DREYLOCK: The leader of the Scather demon clan, he is vanquished by Christy, who was once their captive ("The Last Temptation of Christy").

DUMAIN: A demon with aspirations to join the Triad, Dumain concocts the plan to use Billie and Christy Jenkins to kill the Charmed Ones in "Gone with the Witches." He appeared to the girls as their childhood imaginary friend and returns to make sure they fulfill the Evil destiny he devised. He provides a vision of Evil Wyatt's alternate future to convince them that the Charmed Ones must be stopped. After trying to expose Wyatt to the Hollow, he escapes harm when the Charmed Ones, empowered by the Hollow, permanently vanquish the Triad ("Kill Billie: Vol. 2"). He tries to trick Billie into saving the Triad in "Forever Charmed." After the Charmed Ones permanently vanquish the Triad in the second time line, Piper vanquishes Dumain.

ELKIN: A new-generation demon, Elkin scares his victims to death by magnifying their fears ("Still Charmed and Kicking"). He is vanquished by Piper, who is posing as Wyatt.

EMRICK: Unaware that he's been infected by the Hulk virus, Emrick attacks Billie. She quickly gets the upper hand and threatens to kill him if he doesn't help her get information about her sister ("Hulkus Pocus"). Emrick eventually "hulks out" and dies of the virus.

EXECUTIONER DEMONS: "Minions of a low cadre," as defined in the Book of Shadows, they are "incapable of thoughts or deed. Usually found in the employ of higher-level demons or mortals proficient in the dark arts." They can be vanquished with their own weapons or with a variety of potions. The head Executioner demon in "Sword and the City" sought to improve his station by helping the Dark Knight.

GAMEMASTERS CORR AND CLEA: The producers of the demonic reality TV show *Witch Wars*, this demonic couple uses the game to entice other demons to wager their powers, which they accumulate with a power-sucking athame. They are vanquished by a demonically empowered Phoebe.

GITH: This demon feeds off the energies people expend wanting things they may never get. His victims are sent through a vortex into pocket realms or alternate realities created from their desires, where they will die. Venturing into Piper's fantasy magic-free world, he dies in a gasoline fire in "My Three Witches."

GOON: A minion of the Triad, he dies in a voluntary fireball exchange with Creo ("Gone with the Witches").

HAAS, PAUL: Haas plans to assume control of the Underworld by controlling the Manor, the symbolic seat of power now that the Charmed Ones are dead ("Still Charmed and Kicking"). A real estate agent aboveground, he plans to buy the Manor from the Halliwell estate after he kills Victor. Failing that, he lures the Charmed Ones out of hiding using Innocents as bait ("Malice in Wonderland"), and they vanquish him.

IMP MASTER: This demon carries a swarm of imps that kill with slashing teeth ("Rewitched"). Billie vanquishes him and the swarm with a potion.

JAVA: A member of the Scather demon clan, he performs the ritual to call the Triad in "The Last Temptation of Christy."

JONDAR: A grungy bottom-feeder who lives in a smoky labyrinth of caves with a pet Tentacle ("The Torn Identity"), he captures Pator. The Noxon kills him in a steam vent.

KAAL: Mentioned by Nomed and presumed killed by the Charmed Ones ("Kill Billie: Vol. 2).

KAHN: Counsel to Zankou, his sensible advice regarding the Nexus is rewarded with death ("Something Wicca This Way Goes . . . ?").

KAM: A brutish demon among those who take over Magic School, he is killed by the Possessor demon when he questions her plan ("Desperate Housewitches").

KAZL: One of three Celerity demons who kill Ruth and Jack Brody in 1981 ("Ordinary Witches"). Zankou kills him, exacting revenge for Brody so the agent will work with him to stop the Avatars in "Extreme Makeover: World Edition."

KIMOTO DEMON: Killed by a Demonatrix, but unseen ("A Wrong Day's Journey into Right").

KRYCHEK: These Lower-Level demons have a spiral tattoo on their neck ("Hulkus Pocus"). Homeland Security captures one and uses it to create a "powers" serum, an experiment that fails, creating instead a fatal virus. The Krychek demon, the primary carrier of the Hulk virus, spreads the infection before the disease kills him.

LANTOS: Imara's chief minion ("Freaky Phoebe"), his loyalty to the sorceress is repaid with death when she sacrifices him to maintain her cover as Phoebe.

LAYGAN: A small but politically adept demon, he questions Zankou's plans for surviving the Avatars ("Ordinary Witches") and continues to advise him through the Avatar crisis ("Extreme Makeover: World Edition" and "Charmageddon").

LORD DYSON: A Repressor demon who feeds off repressed emotion ("The Bare Witch Project"), which makes him stronger and unleashes the emotions in his victims. Starved by Lady Godiva's act of defiance in the original eleventh century, he becomes too strong to vanquish until he becomes the target of Leo's rage.

LUCIUS: Shape-shifter Katya's outspoken minion, he is vanquished by Piper ("Little Box of Horrors").

MAD MAX DEMONS: Residents of Paige's pocket realm in "My Three Witches," they resemble post-holocaust-film thugs and attack Innocents with fireballs.

MAGNUS: Minion of Novak and keeper of his crypt ("12 Angry Zen").

MALVOC: An Enoch demon, Malvoc stakes out feeding grounds according to "ancient rules etched in brimstone" by killing Innocents located at the points of a pentagram. He frames a rival gang, the Sokols, for the deaths so Piper will stop protecting the fifth Innocent. Leo vanquishes him in two time lines ("There's Something About Leo").

MANTICORE: Listed in the Book of Shadows as "vicious demons with supernatural strength and venomous claws, Manticores communicate in high-pitched cries and tend to travel in packs." As depicted in "Little Monsters," these yellow-blooded, lizard-type demons feed off fresh demon kill, possess super speed, and are immune to Piper's power. There is no vanquishing potion until the Charmed Ones develop one to save a human/Manticore hybrid baby.

MARGOYLE: An ambitious overlord, he wants to use the Hulk virus to gain control of the Underworld ("Hulkus Pocus"). He is forced to cure infected demons before all evil magical beings are eradicated.

MASKED DEMONS: Aztec and Chinese False Face demons ("Cheaper by the Coven"), they have not appeared for centuries.

MERCURY DEMONS: They command thermal blasts that can take down ten demons, and they can alter their appearance and dress with a snap of their fingers ("Carpe Demon"). Drake was a Mercury demon before he became human.

NANTA: She switches babies at birth so Dalvos will be raised in the powerful Pelham family ("Mr. & Mrs. Witch"), and her evil influence molds the boy as he grows up. However, when the Charmed Ones expose Dalvos as a murderer, her demonic plan to gain mortal corporate power is ruined.

NOMED: Once mentored by the Triad ("Kill Billie: Vol. 2"), he knows the new generation of demons can never assume power over the Underworld as long as the Triad keeps coming back. He helps the Charmed Ones permanently vanquish the Triad.

NOVAK: Leader of six demons who try to steal Buddha's mystical staff when it changes Zodiac hands every year ("12 Angry Zen"). He hibernates to conserve his strength but is vanquished by Billie and the Charmed Ones through the staff.

NOXON DEMONS: Experimented on by other demons and made unvanquishable ("Generation Hex").

PATOR: A Noxon demon who can't be vanquished, he was tortured by Magic School students in Advanced Combat class, ("Generation Hex"). He and his brother, Rondok, begin killing the students for revenge, but in a final battle with the surviving students, Rondok is sent to the Astral Plane, while Pator walks away from the battle and lives. However, he had earlier helped Rondok murder Mr. and Mrs. Jenkins, Billie and Christy's parents. Pator survives to be chased by the Charmed Ones, who want to know what he knows, and Christy and Billie, who want to kill him ("The Torn Identity"). United as the Ultimate Power, Billie and Christy vanquish the unvanquishable demon for good.

PHINKS: A minion of Barbas ("Crimes and Witch-demeanors").

POSSESSOR DEMON: When this demon invades and takes over the body of another being, it retains the use of that being's powers. Leo is taken over by a Possessor demon ("Once in a Blue Moon"), and a Charmed potion separates the demon from him. A female Possessor demon uses the body of Mandi, a mother at Wyatt's preschool, to kidnap Wyatt and raise The Source ("Desperate Housewitches"). She's vanquished by the Charmed Ones, who are not as dead as she presumed.

RAHL: A minion of Creo, he objects to following the dead Triad's plan ("The Torn Identity"), and Creo kills him.

RAPTOR DEMON: A hired assassin, this snarling demon in a black mask attacks and kills with a three-pronged claw ("Death Becomes Them").

REINHARDT: Tattooed on his face, he is hired by entities unknown to kidnap Billie's sister, Christy ("Vaya Con Leos"). He is frozen by Burke and destroyed by a swirling wind.

ROHTUL: A Possessor demon, Rohtul targets Billie, who tortured him for information about her sister in "Payback's a Witch." He's separated from Henry's parolee, Nick, before Billie vanquishes him with a potion.

RONDOK: A Noxon demon driven by revenge for the pain and humiliation of being a Magic School test subject ("Generation Hex"), he kills three of the five students who are responsible. The survivors, Ryan and Jen, send him to the Astral Plane in a state of permanent vanquish with Piper's help. Prior to that, he and his brother Pator murdered Mr. and Mrs. Jenkins, Billie and Christy's parents.

SALKO: One of Zankou's demonic minions, he survives Zankou's attempt to command the Nexus, "Something Wicca This Way Goes . . . ?"

SARGON: Trader of souls who preys on the afterlife, he signed a deal with Count Roget in 1899. Trapped in a repeating, endless loop of the fire in Cabaret Fantome, the count was saved from going to purgatory, and many good souls were prevented from moving on ("Show Ghouls"). The Charmed Ones vanquished Sargon in 1999.

SAVARD: A member of an enslaved demonic race, Savard trains the Doppelgangers to replicate the Charmed Ones ("Repo Manor") and traps the sisters in the dollhouse. The Charmed Ones use their wits to enhance their diminished powers, vanquishing him with a telekinetic shove and a stalagmite.

SCABBER DEMONS: Tall and thin with a preference for overcoats, Scabber demons spew yellow acid that dissolves whatever it touches. Piper's power and bullets cannot stop them ("Hyde School Reunion"), but their own acid kills them.

SCATHER DEMON CLAN: Clawed demons hired by the Triad to kidnap and hold Christy Jenkins ("The Last Temptation of Christy"). Christy vanquishes them with fire.

SCOUTER DEMON: Mentioned but not depicted in "The Bare Witch Project," it can be found in a swamp.

SHOUTER DEMON: A representative urges the demon mob to release Zankou ("Witchness Protection").

SIRK, AKA KEVIN: Half human with a demon father, Sirk attempts to kill all his human blood relatives in order to become all demon ("Styx Feet Under"). When the Charmed Ones vanquish his demon half, he becomes completely human instead and dies with a soul.

SMOKER DEMONS: These smoky demons surface when Mercury is in retrograde ("A Wrong Day's Journey into Right"), and their smoky forms are shrouded in black robes.

SOKOLS: The rival gang of Enoch demons vying for control of territory Malvoc attempts to secure by ancient rules in "There's Something About Leo."

SOLLAL: Second to Zira, he helps the sorceress manipulate Billie and the power of the Golden Belt of Gaea to gain power over male demons ("Battle of the Hexes"). Billie vanquishes him on Zira's command.

SOUL-BLASTER DEMON: This demon hurls energy bolts that separate souls from their bodies. One is enlisted by Mordaunt and Piper in "Sword and the City" to join the Round Table.

SPIDER DEMON: According to the Book of Shadows, this vamped-out female demon is an "evil creature that emerges from its hidden lair every one hundred years to feed off the most magical being it can detect." Venom from its fangs and nails changes other beings into Spider demons that are subservient to the original ("Spin City"). The small spider form it uses as an escape mechanism enables a helpful ogre to squash it.

SWARM DEMONS; KING: Tall, humanlike demons with a hive mentality, they are distant relatives of Kazis and vampires ("Used Karma"). Whenever one drone is killed, two drones replace it. Vanquishing the Swarm King destroys the hive. A Swarm King leads a demon mob against the Charmed Ones and is vanquished by Leo ("Witchness Protection").

TAI: An arrogant male demon who uses Zira's powers of sorcery ("Battle of the Hexes"). Zira directs Billie, who is under the influence of Gaea's belt, to vanquish him.

TAKAR: Xar's minion ("Engaged and Confused"), he's vanquished by Christy when she escapes Xar's dark crystal cage.

TAM: Working with the "Mandi" Possessor demon at Magic School, he's the only one who knows how to bring someone back from the Wasteland, or demonic limbo ("Desperate Housewitches").

THOR: Vanquishes a shorter demon for shushing him during a viewing of the demonic TV show *Witch Wars*.

THORN DEMON: Muscular, agile, and tattooed, male Thorn demons use fireballs ("The Seven Year Witch"). Females fire poisonous thorns, which can be fatal.

THRASK: One of two demon members of the Tribunal ("Crimes and Witch-demeanors").

THRULL DEMON: A Thrull demon is vanquished by a Swarm King when he suggests releasing Zankou, "Witchness Protection."

TOMAR: A new-generation demon, he is second to the Dogon ("Kill Billie: Vol. 1").

TRACKER: This demon specializes in tracking good and evil entities ("Hulkus Pocus"). Rohtul uses a Tracker to keep tabs on Billie in "Payback's a Witch."

TRIBE DEMONS: Marked by a crescent-shaped tribal scar on their faces ("Scry Hard"), they wield crescent weapons that resemble boomerangs.

TROK: A demon with one good eye in each of its two heads and a powerful roar, the Trok strikes in advance of a major demonic move against Wyatt. After Piper blows up one of its heads in "Valhalley of the Dolls," the demon is vanquished with a spell.

VAKLAV: A demon that feeds off the pain of his victims and those who grieve for them, Vaklav captures people's lives with a camera. He holds them in a collage photograph until the last mourner dies, eliminating the source of pain he requires ("The Lost Picture Show"). Victims are released, killed, and replaced until Paige frees Sam and Vaklav's twelve other captives. Then she captures Vaklav with his own camera.

VASSEN: An Enoch demon in Malvoc's gang ("There's Something About Leo").

VICUS: Invisible to everyone except his victim, he fades out in increments—body, followed by head, followed by eyes ("Imaginary Fiends"). He preys on young children with powers, cursing beloved objects that will turn them evil slowly over time. Evil Wyatt from the future betrays him, and the Charmed Ones vanquish him.

VULTURE DEMONS: Cave dwellers that devour their prey ("Cheaper by the Coven"). A female Vulture demon objects to releasing Zankou in "Witchness Protection," but Zankou spares her life for being honest.

XAMO: A creepy new-generation demon that fears Billie ("Payback's a Witch").

ZAHN: A Lower-Level demon, Zahn improved his status by auctioning souls to Underworld collectors, eaters, and traders, who paid Zahn with powers. His accumulated powers are lost and the souls freed when the Charmed Ones destroy the contracts in "Soul Survivor."

ZANKOU: The most powerful demon in the Underworld, Zankou was banished and imprisoned by The Source. A demon mob frees him to fight the Avatars ("Witchness Protection"). He decides to stop the Avatars by killing the Charmed Ones, which will prevent the Collective from gaining their powers ("Ordinary Witches"). When killing the sisters fails, he enlists Brody's help to stop the Avatars ("Extreme Makeover: World Edition") and then turns to Leo and the Charmed Ones ("Charmageddon"). With the Avatars gone, Zankou plans to take over the Underworld with the power of the Shadow in the Spiritual Nexus ("Scry Hard"). To defeat the Charmed Ones, he steals the Book of Shadows ("Death Becomes Them"). He steals Charmed powers and successfully unites with the Nexus, just before the Charmed Ones destroy the ancient power, which vanquishes him, too ("Something Wicca This Way Goes . . .?").

ZOHAR: A minion of Nomed ("Kill Billie: Vol. 2"), he is sacrificed so the Hollow-empowered Charmed Ones will have his ability to fire energy balls.

ZYKE: One of three Celerity demons who kill Jack and Ruth Brody in 1981 ("Ordinary Witches"). Zankou kills him to convince Brody to work with him against the Avatars ("Extreme Makeover: World Edition").

GOOD GUYS GONE BAD

FORGOTTEN ONES: Evil entities who were born good but were turned evil by Vicus, a demon that preys on and curses children ("Imaginary Fiends").

GIDEON: An Elder, Gideon mentored Leo when he became a Whitelighter, supported Leo and Piper's wish to marry, and started Magic School to instruct generations of good magical beings. Posing as a concerned friend, he reveals the existence of Magic School in "The Legend of Sleepy Halliwell." His plot to kill Wyatt for the "greater good" is advanced when he convinces Leo to leave his family and live as an Elder ("The Courtship of Wyatt's Father"), and Piper moves into

Magic School with Wyatt for protection ("Spin City"). He defends the Charmed Ones before the Tribunal in "Crimes and Witch-demeanors," where Barbas learns of his plot to kill Wyatt. Gideon kills Sigmund before he confesses to the Charmed Ones, who are close to uncovering the plot ("Witch Wars"). His first attempt on Wyatt's life is thwarted by good and evil Paige and Phoebe in "It's a Bad, Bad, Bad, Bad World, Part 1." Gideon is unaware that his failed but persistent attempts to kill Wyatt cause the boy to turn evil ("It's a Bad, Bad, Bad, Bad World, Part 2"). Although he believes he's acting for the "greater good," Gideon's willingness to embrace evil and kill makes him—by definition—an evil being. Leo kills him, an act of great evil that restores balance in the universe.

VINCENT: An evil version of Paige's Mr. Right ("A Wrong Day's Journey into Night"), he uses his enormous influence to turn Paige to the dark side.

INANIMATE OBJECTS

AMULET: The amulet catches and stores guardians, providing whoever possesses it with the protective power of those guardians ("Someone to Witch Over Me"). Sarpedon benefits from the amulet's power until Phoebe takes it.

BLOOD-RED CRYSTAL: Given to Billie by Christy to help her enter and leave the Charmed Ones' dreams ("The Jung and the Restless").

CATTLE PRODS: Demonic variety used by Pator and Rondok to hurt Magic School students who tortured them ("Generation Hex").

CRYSTAL OF KAZIMAR: The intensity and frequency of this artifact's emissions will be apparent when its dormant power is activated ("Battle of the Hexes").

CURSED ATHAME: Cursed by a witch, anyone who is cut with the blade ages rapidly and dies ("Charrrmed").

DARK CRYSTAL CAGE: Used by Xar to hold Christy ("Engaged and Confused"). She breaks out.

DARKLIGHTER ARROW: Tipped with Darklighter poison and used to kill Whitelighters. The poison is fatal to Whitelighters and Darklighters. Chris was shot by Gith in "My Three Witches" and healed by Leo.

EYE OF AGHBAR: An amulet that protects against a witch's power ("I Dream of Phoebe").

FAUSTIAN DEAL: A contract Larry Henderson signed with the demon Zahn in "Soul Survivor," agreeing to exchange his soul for wealth and success; it contains a protection clause: Paragraph 5, subsection 6, line 3. "All souls in my possession will burn in eternal flames upon my untimely demise." The contract is null and void if the paper is destroyed.

FOUNTAIN OF YOUTH: In the possession of Captain Black Jack Cutting, Aphrodite's fountain produces rejuvenating water when turned on by a Golden Chalice ("Charrrmed"). Piper destroys it.

GENIE BOTTLE: Passed from demon to demon for centuries, the bottle is inscribed with a warning in Arabic: Whoever wishes Jinny free will take her place ("I Dream of Phoebe").

GOLDEN CHALICE: Stolen from a museum, the chalice turns on the Fountain of Youth ("Charrrmed").

THE HOLLOW: A force with the power to consume all magic, all life, and the world, it was contained thirty-five hundred years ago with the cooperation of good and evil. The Charmed Ones and the Jenkins sisters both summon and absorb the Hollow in order to defeat one another in the Ultimate Battle ("Kill Billie: Vol. 2"). Piper, Patty from 1975, and Grams from 1982 form a new Power of Three to contain the Hollow in "Forever Charmed," which prevents the destruction of the Manor and the deaths of Paige and Phoebe.

MYSTICAL FOG: Ghost pirates can return only when the mystical fog rolls in ("Charrrmed").

PANDORA'S BOX: According to myth, the box containing all the ills of the world—sorrow, pestilence, war, death, and plague—was a gift from the gods to Prometheus ("Little Box of Horrors"). Black with silver edging, the six sides are decorated with crossed bones. It exists solely to tempt and whispers to prod the curious to open it. The evils are released as streams of black smoke. The first wave is sorrow, and when all the ills have fled, only hope remains.

PARANOIA CRYSTAL: A touch of the crystal, given to Brody by Zankou, infects witches with paranoia. The affliction can be transmitted from witch to witch ("Extreme Makeover: World Edition"). Breaking the crystal reverses the effects.

PENDANT: The symbol in Christy's diary, crafted into a necklace she is given to wear by her captors ("12 Angry Zen").

POCKET REALM: A deadly alternate reality created from a victim's desires ("My Three Witches").

POOL: A bubbling, metallic pool, controlled by a seer, that reveals truths and never lies ("Cheaper by the Coven").

POWER-SUCKING ATHAME: Absorbs and transfers the powers of a victim into the person who wields it ("Witch Wars").

ROUND TABLE: Inlaid with a pentagram and demonic runes in "Sword and the City," the table is a conduit for the transfer of power from four beings to the entity seated in the primary position. The transfer is triggered by a spell.

RUBY CRYSTAL: Predates the crystal ball as a means of magical voyeurism ("Witch Wars").

SAI DAGGER: A slim knife easily hidden in boots and clothing, it is Katya's weapon of choice ("Little Box of Horrors").

SCEPTER OF THE ORDER: A jeweled wand, the scepter reads and alters morality through the eyes. In "Prince Charmed," the Dark Priest uses the scepter to turn Wyatt evil. Piper uses it to make Wyatt good again.

TRIAD PLATFORM: The Spirit of the Triad manifests in this hovering white disk ("Gone with the Witches" and "Kill Billie: Vol. 2").

VORTEX OF DEADLY DESIRES: A gateway controlled by Gith in "My Three Witches," through which his victims are cast into pocket realms created from their own empty desires.

WASTELAND: The demonic limbo between life and oblivion ("Desperate Housewitches" and "Engaged and Confused").

WHITE RABBIT: A form taken by Black Heart to lure Innocents into a nightmare scenario ("Malice in Wonderland").

ZANBAR: Once guarded by hounds, this seat of power for an ancient evil empire was buried in the Arabian desert ("I Dream of Phoebe"). Whoever sits on the throne controls the city's power.

MALEVOLENT MORTALS

COUNT ROGET: In 1899 he made a deal with the demon Sargon. To escape going to purgatory, he and many good souls were trapped in an eternal fire at Cabaret Fantome ("Show Ghouls"). His soul escaped into Drake, but the Charmed Ones vanquished him, and he was pulled into eternal fire below.

DALVOS: Switched at birth to infiltrate the Pelham family, Dalvos is raised by Nanta to assume control of the multinational Pelham Corporation ("Mr. & Mrs. Witch"). Outwitted by the Charmed Ones, Dalvos "confesses" to killing his cousin, Grant Pelham, and the demonic plan to gain a power base in the mortal world is set back thirty years.

NANCE, WALTER: An assistant district attorney with a deep fear of growing old, he's enraged when Maya leaves him for a younger man. He kills the new boyfriend and frames Maya for the murder ("Run, Piper, Run"). The Charmed Ones scare a confession out of him, bringing Nance to justice and saving Maya.

MISCELLANEOUS EVIL ENTITIES

ALCHEMIST: Obsessed with death, he helps Zankou upset the sisters by turning Innocents they didn't save into zombies ("Death Becomes Them"). Zankou kills him when he's no longer needed.

CROSS, TIM: A student who wants to date Phoebe. The alchemist turns him into a zombie to terrorize her ("Death Becomes Them").

DAVIDSON, INSPECTOR REECE: Killed by the Seekers while investigating Cole Turner's disappearance ("Death Takes a Halliwell"), he is reanimated by Zankou's alchemist to torment Phoebe ("Death Becomes Them").

DAVIS, INSPECTOR: A fictional corrupt cop ("Charmed Noir").

GRIMLOCK EGGS: Destroyed (not depicted) in the run-up to the Avatars' changed world ("Extreme Makeover: World Edition").

IMPS: Nastier than gremlins, imps maim and kill with slashing and are carried by an Imp Master ("Rewitched"). These tiny guns-for-hire and the master are vanquished with a potion.

JOHNNY THE GENT: A fictional villain in the Mullen brothers' novel, he murdered Dan Mullen ("Charmed Noir").

LIPS: One of Johnny the Gent's henchmen in a 1930s-style novel ("Charmed Noir").

PARROT: A ghost of Captain Cutting's parrot is freed with the pirate crew ("Charrrmed").

PHANTASMS: Nebulous creatures that only possess bad beings ("Crimes and Witchdemeanors"), they can move between the mortal world and hell. A phantasm must be removed from a subject with a potion and captured in a wand to vanquish it.

SNYDER, LIEUTENANT: A fictional corrupt cop ("Charmed Noir").

TENTACLE: An underground creature that holds a being's powers when it holds the being ("The Torn Identity"). Kept as Jondar's pet, it dies when he dies.

ZOMBIES: To weaken the Charmed Ones, Zankou's alchemist turns many of the Innocents they lost into zombies in "Death Becomes Them."

MYTHICAL MANIFESTATIONS

DRAGON: Dragons predate the Book of Shadows. The dragon conjured by Wyatt from TV breathes fire, flies, rains destruction on the city of San Francisco, and builds a nest from the wreckage. In "Forget Me . . . Not," Wyatt wills the dragon out of existence when it attacks Piper.

THE HEADLESS HORSEMAN: Conjured by Zachary, a Magic School student, to get revenge on teachers, the Headless Horseman in "The Legend of Sleepy Halliwell" is vanquished by a Power of Three spell.

SEERS AND SOOTHSAYERS

EVIL SOOTHSAYER: A soothsayer warns Emrick to beware of Margoyle ("Hulkus Pocus"). Margoyle kills the soothsayer for not getting information fast enough.

KIRA: A cunning and crafty seer, she uses a metallic pool to reveal truth ("Cheaper by the Coven"). She aids Sirk with visions of the future ("Styx Feet Under") but warns that premonitions don't come with guarantees. After showing Phoebe the Avatars' utopian future, she is vanquished by Zankou before she becomes human ("Witchness Protection").

SHAPE-SHIFTERS

ABET: A shape-shifter who lurks in aboveground alleys, Abet is killed by the Dogon ("Kill Billie: Vol. 1").

KATYA: A shape-shifter, she once worked for the Dark Lords of the Underworld

("Little Box of Horrors"). Aspiring to a position of power and hoping to impress Zankou, she kills Nina, the guardian of Pandora's Box, and releases the ills of the world. Paige vanquishes her with a potion.

OTHER SHAPE-SHIFTERS: One participates as a contestant on the demonic TV show in "Witch Wars," assuming the appearance of Kyle, a crime reporter with the *Bay Mirror.* Zankou kills a shape-shifter to gain his power ("Witchness Protection").

SORCERERS AND SORCE

IMARA: Smart and ruthless, this sorceress reported to The Source, but she will not be subservient to his successor ("Freaky Phoebe"). She swaps souls with Phoebe, tricks her sisters into eliminating Zankou's allies, and helps Piper vanquish her ugly body. A Charmed spell recovers Phoebe's soul, and Imara's essence is cast out and taken below.

JINNY: An ancient sorcerer condemned Jinny to an eternal existence as a genie when she refused to marry him ("I Dream of Phoebe"). Freed by Phoebe, she kills Bosk before Richard Montana wishes her back into the bottle.

SORCERER: With aspirations to take the throne and rule the Underworld, he needs Drake's powers to fight Zankou. He makes Drake human for a year with a catch: If Drake uses his destructive power, he forfeits the power to the sorcerer and is sent to purgatory ("Carpe Demon"). The Charmed Ones vanquish the sorcerer.

ZIRA: A sorceress, Zira plots to conquer or kill male demons, allowing females to rule the Underworld ("Battle of the Hexes"). She is vanquished by the Golden Belt of Gaea, which destroys evil entities that wear it. Paige orbs the belt around Zira's waist.

THE SOURCE

The Source of all evil, he is betrayed when a seer convinces Cole to become the Hollow and uses The Source's energy balls to weaken him. The Source is vanquished with a Power of Three spell that calls on the power of the entire Warren line. He is brought back from the Wasteland in "Desperate Housewitches," with the combined power of Tam's pentagon, the "Mandi" Possessor demon's spell, and Wyatt's magic. The Charmed Ones vanquish the Possessor demon, and since she conjured The Source, he is vanquished with her.

SPIRITS

CAPTAIN BLACK JACK CUTTING: He tricked a witch to gain immortality ("Charrrmed"). He kills her after she cuts him with her cursed athame. Now, three hundred years later, he looks his age. Bound to Captain Cutting by the pirate captain's oath—an iron-clad point of honor—the crew cannot escape his curse. When Cutting breaks his oath not to harm the Charmed Ones, the crew mutinies, killing him and freeing themselves to die at long last. A pirate captain's word is a point of honor.

FIRST MATE REZNOR: When Captain Cutting goes back on his word, Reznor kills him, freeing the souls of the pirate's captive crew ("Charrrmed").

MATA HARI: In "Used Karma," the unfinished bad karma of the infamous Dutch-born World War I double agent possesses Phoebe, who has been duplicitous and leading a double life with Jason. Mata Hari's spirit is banished with a Montana family potion.

TRIAD

A council of three powerful demons that sent other demons to kill the Charmed Ones for two years after the Power of Three was activated (Volume 1). Believed vanquished by Cole, they return when Billie rescues Christy, the witch they hired the Scather demon clan to kidnap and imprison ("The Last Temptation of Christy"). After the Charmed Ones vanquish Asmodeus and Baliel in "Engaged and Confused," Candor tells Christy they've taught her everything they know to help her save Billie—the Ultimate Power. To keep Christy bound to evil, Candor hires the Noxon demons to kill her parents ("Generation Hex"). Enraged, Christy plunges a fatal fist through Candor's body, vanquishing him.

XAR: Banished from the Triad, he tries to stop them from getting the Ultimate Power ("Engaged and Confused"). The Triad vanquishes him, which he believes is a better fate than having to answer to them.

SPIRIT OF THE TRIAD

The spirits of Asmodeus, Baliel, and Candor return through a hovering white disk to supervise the final stages of their plan to kill the Charmed Ones ("Gone with the Witches"). When all the witches—the Charmed Ones and the Jenkins sisters—are dead, the balance of power will tip to evil, and they will be able to return—again. The Charmed Ones, aided by Nomed and the Hollow, permanently vanquish them in "Kill Billie: Vol. 2." After the original time line is altered to save Paige and Phoebe ("Forever Charmed"), Billie projects the sisters back in time to permanently vanquish them again with potions.

THE ULTIMATE POWER

The identity of the Ultimate Power, Billie Jenkins, is revealed by Candor of the Triad ("Engaged and Confused"). Her sister, Christy, seals her fate as the key to the Ultimate Power when she vanquishes Candor, who hired Rondok and Pator to kill their parents ("Generation Hex"). Lies enable Christy to turn Billie against the Charmed Ones, and the Ultimate Power emerges when they unite to vanquish the unvanquishable Pator in "The Torn Identity." Playing their predetermined roles in the Triad's plan, they turn the magical community against the Charmed Ones ("Gone with the Witches"). Billie and Christy try to kill the sisters, but the Charmed Ones retreat to the Underworld with the Book of Shadows. The Jenkins sisters and the Charmed Ones summon and split the Hollow to fight the Ultimate Battle at the Manor ("Kill Billie: Vol. 2"), but it doesn't turn out as the Angel of Destiny expected. Paige and Phoebe die. When Piper, a young Patty, and Grams alter the first time line and save Paige and Phoebe ("Forever Charmed"), Billie uses her Ultimate Power of projection to help the Charmed Ones defeat the Triad again—forever.

VAMPIRES

VAMPIRE QUEEN: She agrees to help the Charmed Ones vanquish Zankou, then double-crosses them because Zankou got to her first ("Something Wicca This Way Goes . . . ?").

VAMPIRES

Immortal demons of the night, vampires are repelled by direct sunlight, crucifixes, garlic and holy water. Vampires are immune to witch's powers, but most can be destroyed with a wooden stake driven through the chest. The Power of Three, however, is needed to vanquish a Vampire Queen, an act that will destroy all of her vampire spawn as well. Gifted with the ability to transform into bats, vampires also have the power to change their victims into vampires instead of killing them, but this transformation isn't complete until the new vampire feeds on human blood.

WARLOCKS

▲ Kill to steal a witch's powers.

▲ Move with super speed as in "the blink of an eye" or "to blink."

▲ Do not bleed.

▲ Cannot hide their actions from Upper-Level beings.

▲ Blinding or strobe light prevents them from blinking.

NOTE: A rivalry exists between demons and warlocks.

NIGEL: In 1967 this blond warlock plots with the evil witch Robin to kill and steal the powers of several covens at a flower-power gathering at Penny Halliwell's Manor ("Witchstock"). When Nigel attacks her time-traveling grand-daughters, Penny summons the rage to kill him.

UNNAMED WARLOCK: A contestant on the demonic TV show in "Witch Wars."

EVIL WITCHES

▲ Kill to steal a witch's powers.

CHARMED ONES IN BLACK: The exact opposites of the Charmed Ones in an evil reality, which is necessary for universal balance ("It's a Bad, Bad, Bad, Bad World, Part 1").

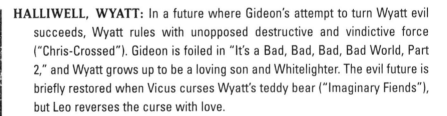

HALLIWELL, WYATT: In a future where Gideon's attempt to turn Wyatt evil succeeds, Wyatt rules with unopposed destructive and vindictive force ("Chris-Crossed"). Gideon is foiled in "It's a Bad, Bad, Bad, Bad World, Part 2," and Wyatt grows up to be a loving son and Whitelighter. The evil future is briefly restored when Vicus curses Wyatt's teddy bear ("Imaginary Fiends"), but Leo reverses the curse with love.

HUGO: Vicus turned this young male witch evil at a young age ("Imaginary Fiends"). He wields an energy whip and is vanquished with powerful blasts by good Future Wyatt.

JENKINS, CHRISTY: Billie realizes that her older sister must have powers too, a hypothesis that's supported when she learns that her grandmother was a witch ("Mr. & Mrs. Witch"). Christy was kept in a cave by unknown evil entities ("12 Angry Zen") and is rescued by Billie. Her abilities as a telepathic firestarter are revealed in "The Last Temptation of Christy," and she vanquishes the

Scather demons with fire. A protégée of the Triad ("Engaged and Confused"), the last survivor of the triad, Candor, assures her that she will unite with her sister, the Ultimate Power. When her parents are killed, she kills Candor in a vengeful rage ("Generation Hex"), sealing her destiny as an evil force. After turning Billie against the Charmed Ones with lies, she unites with her sister, and the Ultimate Power emerges ("The Torn Identity"). To sever the bond between Billie and the Charmed Ones, Christy sways Billie into believing that the sisters are using their powers for selfish ends and must be stopped ("The Jung and the Restless"). She finally convinces Billie to take action against the Charmed Ones ("Gone with the Witches"), but the sisters escape to the Underworld before they are killed. Undeterred by Billie's reservations, Christy follows Dumain's advice to summon the Hollow ("Kill Billie: Vol. 2") for the Ultimate Battle with the Charmed Ones. Her conversion to evil is absolute ("Forever Charmed"), and Billie vanquishes Christy with her own fireball to save the Charmed Ones.

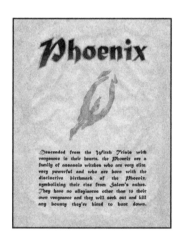

PHOENIX COVEN: Elite assassins, they have a phoenix birthmark on their inner wrists, which symbolizes the rise from the ashes of Salem ("Chris-Crossed"). Powerful and tenacious, these hired guns drain powers by plunging a fist into the victim's body. Interrupting the process leaves the victim with a lethal open wound. Immune to Piper's explosive power, Phoenix witches can reconstitute their black ash remains. They shimmer.

ROBIN: Posing as a good witch and Penny Halliwell's best friend in "Witchstock," Robin is killed by her own energy ball when Paige saves her grandfather, Allen.

STILLMAN SISTERS: Mabel, Mitzy, and Margo are defined in the Book of Shadows as "common witches known for their small-time hustles and cons. Not worth vanquishing." After their plot to become the Charmed Ones fails in "Power of Three Blondes," they are arrested for murdering a door-to-door salesman.

WICKED WITCH OF THE ENCHANTED FOREST: A classic wicked witch, with a pointed black hat, warts, and a large bubbling cauldron ("Spin City"), she's vanquished by Paige after turning benign magical beings into opposites of their normal selves.

WIZARDS

WIZARD: An old wizard recites the incantation to release Zankou ("Witchness Protection").

ZAKAL: Old and well connected, he used to work for The Source ("Repo Manor"). Claiming that his visions aren't reliable, he refuses to give Piper information about Leo. Phoebe's doppelganger vanquishes him.

bLack magic spells and rituals

Identity Spell
("POWER OF THREE BLONDES")

Used by the Stillman sisters to steal the Charmed identities.

Blinking faces, blank ho-hum,
We are they, and they are no one.
Grant to us the Power of Three,
And turn them into nobody.

Dark Knight Vanquishing Potion
("SWORD AND THE CITY")

Suggested by Mordaunt to kill the Dark Knight.

Wereboar tusk *1 pinch*
Nymph hair *1 lock*
Wraith essence *3 drops*
Black poppy *1 level tsp.*
Arrow leaf *2 leaves*
Dwarf lotus *3 petals*
Aged pixie tea *1 cup*
Loggerhead *3 drops*
Turtle scales
Kudrin tree oil *1 drop*

NOTES :

▲ Richard Montana supplied the rare ingredients, which his family had been collecting for generations.

▲ Mordaunt intended the potion to kill whoever made it.

WARNING: Black poppy mixed with wraith essence explodes.

Round Table Power Transfer
("SWORD AND THE CITY")

All entities seated at the table place an extremity in one of five slots. The Receiver recites:

Bexaxis . . . cotrah . . . mierrahh!
Supreme demonic powers,
Leave your hosts and find a new home
In this willing heart.

After the powers flow through the table into the Receiver, the donors explode.

Inhibition Spell
("CHRIS-CROSSED")

This spell to remove inhibitions can be found in the Phoenix Coven's Grimoire,
but it is a carefully guarded secret.

Chant to Revive the Leader of the Order
("PRINCE CHARMED")

. . . sentio aliquos
togatos contra me conspirare . . .

Blessing the Acolytes of the Order
("PRINCE CHARMED")

As they embark on missions to revive the ancient leader.

THE DARK PRIEST:
He led us long ago,
And once he returns,
He will lead us again.
And He will reward you
For your unwavering faith.

ACOLYTES:
Denando y sentio.

THE DARK PRIEST:
Help us cleanse Him
Of the poison
That corrupted Him.
Turn Him so that
He may lower his guard,
So that we may return Him
To the fold,
To his destiny.

NOTE: Most acolytes do not survive their tasks, whether practicing with the Wyatt model or attempting to penetrate the real Wyatt's protective force shield.

Chant to Welcome Him/Wyatt to the Order
("PRINCE CHARMED")

THE DARK PRIEST:
Nihil curo de ista tua sulta . . .

ACOLYTES:
Radix lecti . . .

THE DARK PRIEST:
Behold, He has returned to us,
To his rightful place,
To one day lead us back to . . .

Mata Hari's Curse
("USED KARMA")

Mata Hari, possessing Phoebe, waves and releases a scarf to ruin Jason Dean's business dealings with the French.

Curses on this merger!

RESULT: A geyser of champagne erupts, frog legs and escargots return to life, and pigeons fly out of a chafing dish.

To Kill a Demonatrix
("A WRONG DAY'S JOURNEY INTO RIGHT")

What once resided in this place
Shall soon be gone with no haste.
Make this girl age in time,
As punishment for her heinous crime.

RESULT: Instant aging, death to dust.

To Activate the Ruby Crystal
("WITCH WARS")

Mallock cormon alli-tas.

Portal to Opposite Reality
("IT'S A BAD, BAD, BAD, BAD WORLD, PART 1")

Written by Gideon using a Triquetra drawn on a wall.

In the place and in this hour,
We call upon the ancient powers.
Open the door through time and space,
Create a path to another space.

NOTE: The Charmed Ones believed this spell would return Chris to the future.

To Pierce Wyatt's Shield
("IT'S A BAD, BAD, BAD, BAD WORLD, PART 1")

An athame is empowered to penetrate the shield.

Wanton powers in this blade yield,
Penetrate that which would shield.

NOTE: Once pierced, the shield stays down when Gideon
faces Wyatt again ("It's a Bad, Bad, Bad, Bad World, Part 2").

To Free Zankou
("WITCHNESS PROTECTION")

Lexonero bestia. Lexonero!

To Free the Shadow
("SCRY HARD" AND "SOMETHING WICCA THIS WAY GOES . . . ?")

Natum adai necral—
Daya intay layok

NOTE: When Zankou casts the spell, it fails because Piper is still in the Manor. The Power of Three is strong enough to negate the presence of good and evil.

To Swap Souls
("FREAKY PHOEBE")

Recite the incantation, then drop a lock of the subject's hair into the potion.

Ekat ym lous,
Ekat a demrahc eno,
Edart meht won!

To Reverse the Charmed Pig Spell
("SOMETHING WICCA THIS WAY GOES . . . ?")

Reverse this spell
From whence I fell.

To Bring Back The Source
("DESPERATE HOUSEWITCHES")

We call to you that away was torn,
Return master of all evil born!

NOTE: Wyatt's touch activates the potion that recalls The Source. However, since the Possessor demon chanted the spell, The Source is vanquished when she is.

DEMONIC POWER PLAYS

In the absence of an all-powerful evil force, many ambitious demons try to take control of the Underworld.

THE CAMELOT GAMBIT

▲ Mordaunt accumulates enough demonic power to wrest control of Excalibur from Piper, Wyatt's proxy.

▲ Wyatt, the Chosen One who rightfully commands Excalibur, kills Mordaunt with the sword.

THE ORDER REVIVAL

▲ An ancient cult called the Order, believing Wyatt is the reincarnation of their vanquished leader, reverses his morality from good to evil with a scepter.

▲ The Charmed Ones vanquish the Order's acolytes.

▲ The Dark Priest dies by his own magic.

▲ Wyatt's morality is changed back to good with the scepter.

AN ARABIAN EMPIRE

▲ Whoever sits on the throne of the lost city of Zanbar, seat of power for an ancient evil empire, will be all-powerful.

▲ Bosk and Jinny's attempts to raise the buried city and secure its power are thwarted by a genie wish.

THE TRAITOR TRAP

▲ Gideon, founder and headmaster of Magic School, regrets that the Elders allowed Wyatt to be born. The concentration of so much power in one being threatens the forces of evil and good, and he vows to correct the mistake.

▲ Evil forces enlisted to carry out the plot:
1. Darklighters Damien and his Lieutenant attempt to kill Leo, which will leave Wyatt vulnerable.
2. The gamemasters, Corr and Clea, are used to distract the Charmed Ones; see Witch Wars Gamble.
3. Barbas is to distract the Charmed Ones.

▲ Rules and considerations:
1. The Charmed Ones must not be harmed.
2. Innocents must not be harmed.
3. Gideon abandons both rules in "Witch Wars."

▲ Leo kills Gideon to save Wyatt and restore universal balance.

THE CHARMED CHAMPION

▲ Vincent, Mr. Right's evil twin, tries to turn Paige evil, making her the most powerful entity in the Underworld.

▲ Having an irresistible influence over Paige, he plans to become real and rule by proxy over her demonic realm.

▲ Vincent and his influence are destroyed by Piper's power with Mr. Right's selfless assistance.

THE *WITCH WARS* GAMBLE

▲ Gamemasters Corr and Clea create a demonic TV reality show.

▲ Contestants on *Witch Wars* wager their powers, hoping to acquire glory and the powers of the witches they kill.

▲ Corr and Clea hope to accumulate enough Upper-Level demonic power to rule the Underworld.

▲ Demonically empowered, Phoebe vanquishes Corr and Clea, and the show is cancelled.

ANCIENT POWER CLASH

THE AVATARS:

▲ The Collective hopes to create a world beyond good and evil.

▲ Leo's power as an Avatar and the power of the Charmed Ones are required to implement the Change.

▲ After the Change, the Avatars monitor conflict from a Star Chamber and "remove" anyone who disrupts the flow.

▲ Confronted by the Charmed Ones and the ancient vanquishing potion, they change the world back and leave people who aren't ready for them yet.

ZANKOU AND THE UNDERWORLD:

▲ Zankou organizes the Underworld to save demons from annihilation by the Avatars.

▲ Killing the Charmed Ones will deprive the Collective of the power needed to implement the Change.

▲ He enlists Brody to stop the Avatars, but Brody's last vial of potion only kills Beta.

▲ With the Collective weakened, he enlists Leo and the Charmed Ones to make the ancient Egyptian vanquishing potion, which forces the Avatars to restore the Grand Design of good versus evil.

THE ELDERS:

▲ Their position of power will be lost in the Avatars' future.

▲ They attempt and fail to kill Leo, and then trick him into leaving Piper to rejoin them Up There.

▲ Leo's love for Piper is stronger than his calling, and the Elders give him up—forever.

THE SHADOW SHOWDOWN

ZANKOU PLOTS TO ACQUIRE THE ULTIMATE POWER OF THE SHADOW:

▲ Tribe demons attempt to remove the sisters and take over the Manor so the Shadow will be drawn to Zankou's evil presence. The presence of the Charmed Ones thwarts the plan twice.

▲ Zankou weakens the Charmed Ones, steals the Book of Shadows, steals Piper and Phoebe's powers, and absorbs the ancient power of the Nexus.

SUBPLOTS TO JOIN OR THWART ZANKOU:

▲ The shape-shifter Katya once worked for the Dark Lords and wants a position of power. She releases the evils from Pandora's Box to impress Zankou. Vanquished by the Charmed Ones.

▲ Imara, a sorceress, reported to The Source but wants to rule now. She soul-naps

Phoebe's body to weaken Zankou by vanquishing his Upper-Level demon allies. Daleek and Benzor are killed, but Linson is spared when Imara is vanquished.

▲ After Zankou unites with the Nexus, the Charmed Ones destroy both with a Power of Three spell.

DEMONS AND WITCHES AND BEARS OH MY!

▲ Vicus curses Wuvey to make Wyatt evil so his power can be added to a Collective of good beings turned bad.

▲ Evil Wyatt can't kill his father, and young Wyatt trusts Leo, reversing the curse and its evil effects.

OUT SOURCE AGAIN

▲ A female Possessor demon brings back The Source so they can be Mommy and Daddy to Wyatt, the beginning of an evil dynasty to replace the Charmed Ones.

▲ The Charmed Ones—not dead—vanquish both wannabe parents.

TERRITORIAL DESIGNS

With no Charmed Ones to threaten them, demons stake out territory aboveground:

▲ **ANTOSIS:** Uses imps to kill Good Samaritans to place his mark across entire neighborhoods.

▲ **THE DOGON:** Determined to lead the Underworld, he kills other demons to gain their powers and territories.

▲ **MARGOYLE:** Wants to create a superdemon force with the Hulk virus before another Underworld overlord acquires the power.

▲ **THE SORCERESS ZIRA:** Attempts to overthrow male domination of the Underworld to install female rule.

THE CORPORATE TAKEOVER

▲ To gain a powerful foothold aboveground, Nanta raises the human Dalvos to assume control of the Pelham Corporation.

▲ Since the Charmed Ones cannot vanquish a human, Piper poses as Dalvos, who confesses to killing his cousin and rival.

THE TRIAD TRIES AGAIN

▲ For fifteen years the Triad exerts an evil influence over Christy Jenkins, the key to the Ultimate Power—Billie.

▲ The Charmed Ones trick Asmodeus and Baliel into vanquishing themselves.

▲ Christy vanquishes Candor with a fist through his body.

▲ The Spirit of the Triad continues to oversee the last phases of the plan to kill the Charmed Ones.

▲ They are vanquished by the Hollow-empowered Charmed Ones in one time line and by Charmed potions in a subsequent time line.

THE ULTIMATE POWER PLAY

▲ Dumain, a demon who aspires to join the Triad, provides the Triad with the plan to kill the Charmed Ones.

▲ Dumain appears as Billie and Christy's imaginary friend to put the process in motion.

▲ The Triad hires the Scather clan to kidnap and imprison Christy.

▲ Christy is raised to unite with the Ultimate Power, Billie, to fulfill her destiny: taking out the Charmed Ones.

▲ Billie's determination to find Christy, after her powers manifest as an adult, is part of the plan.

▲ After Billie turns on the Charmed Ones, she and Christy link their powers and accomplish the impossible, vanquishing an unvanquishable demon.

▲ Billie's ties to the Charmed Ones are broken.

▲ Convinced they are saving the world from Evil Wyatt, Billie and Christy try to kill the Charmed Ones, but they escape.

- ▲ Both sets of sisters absorb part of the Hollow to fight the Ultimate Battle, which destroys the Manor and kills Christy, Paige, and Phoebe.

- ▲ When the time line is altered, Billie uses her power of projection to help the Charmed Ones vanquish the Triad so they cannot resurrect—ever.

- ▲ Christy, as evil as the Triad intended, is killed by Billie with her own energy ball.

- ▲ Evil loses Billie and her Ultimate Power to good.

A NEW GENERATION

- ▲ A new generation of young demons will gain power over the coming decades.

- ▲ Eventually, they will fill the power vacuum left by the Triad and challenge another generation of Charmed Warren Witches.

MISCELLANEOUS EVIL MALADIES

POSSESSIONS

▲ The ghost of Olivia Callaway possesses Paige to be near Richard Montana (**"LOVE'S A WITCH"**).

▲ Mata Hari's karma possesses Phoebe (**"USED KARMA"**).

▲ A phantasm possesses Inspector Sheridan (**"CRIMES AND WITCH-DEMEANORS"**).

▲ Shakti and Shiva, the Hindu goddess of creation and god of destruction, possess Leo and Piper (**"A CALL TO ARMS"**). Although they are not evil, another consummation of their love will destroy all things.

▲ A Possessor demon invades Leo (**"ONCE IN A BLUE MOON"**).

▲ George's spirit possesses Darryl's friend Mike, a security guard, to escape unending death by fire (**"SHOW GHOULS"**).

▲ Human and neutral, Leo is possessed by the Shadow from the Nexus (**"SCRY HARD"**).

▲ Imara swaps souls with Phoebe to inhabit Phoebe's body (**"FREAKY PHOEBE"**).

▲ A Possessor demon uses Mandi, a preschool mom, to kidnap Wyatt (**"DESPERATE HOUSEWITCHES"**).

INFECTIONS

▲ Chris is infected with Spider demon venom (**"SPIN CITY"**).

▲ Paige is infected with an aging curse (**"CHARRRMED"**).

▲ Billie is infected with the Hulk virus (**"HULKUS POCUS"**).

Magic School

MAGIC SCHOOL

was established by the Elders when they realized that untrained young magic can lead to disaster. With Gideon in charge, Magic School provided an environment protected from evil where new generations of magical beings could develop their social skills and powers.

Fearing that the protections Gideon guaranteed could not be maintained, the Elders decided to close the school following the headmaster's death. Paige won the fight to keep it open, but she had to run it safely. She succeeded, but she felt confined by the mundane minutiae and gladly relinquished the job to Leo.

Magic School's protective wards were breached when Zankou used the Charmed Ones' stolen powers to enter. The school was abandoned to protect the lie about the Charmed Ones' deaths. Evil moved in and stayed—until the Charmed Ones won the Ultimate Battle and reclaimed it.

The Rules

▲ Within the walls of Magic School, not everyone sees the same things, only what they are meant to see.

The Campus

▲ A door exists on the front stairs landing into the Manor.

▲ Tall, massive, arched double doors lead into the Great Hall, the spiritual center of Magic School. Marble pillars support a high ceiling, and stacks of magical texts line the walls.

▲ Classrooms and other facilities are accessed from an Endless Hallway.

▲ The headmaster has a study equipped with a crystal ball and a window into an evil, opposite reality.

The Headmaster

GIDEON: Founder and Leo's old mentor ("The Legend of Sleepy Halliwell"), Gideon uses his position of trust in an evil plot to kill Wyatt ("The Courtship of Wyatt's Father"). He serves as headmaster until his death ("It's a Bad, Bad, Bad, Bad World, Part 2"). See also the Book of Black Magic section.

WYATT, LEO: Human, with no powers but a vast knowledge of magic, Leo accepts the position as headmaster of Magic School ("Scry Hard"). A natural administrator, he easily manages running a school and being Paige's Whitelighter adviser. When the school is reclaimed for good after the Ultimate Battle, Leo resumes his duties as headmaster and teacher.

The Headmistress

MATTHEWS, PAIGE: Paige is appointed as the new headmistress after she convinces the Elders to keep the school open ("The Bare Witch Project"). Her duties include ordering supplies and writing student progress reports ("Cheaper by the Coven"). She also serves as peacekeeper and policy maker ("Charmed Noir") and undertakes the tedious task of giving applicants and their parents tours of the facilities ("Show Ghouls"). Feeling cooped up by the requirements of the job, she happily lets Leo take over ("Scry Hard").

The Magic School Board of Elders

ODIN: Although worried about safety, Odin agrees to keep Magic School open and appoints Paige as the new headmistress ("The Bare Witch Project"). He returns to Magic School in his capacity as an Elder to heal mauled Whitelighters ("Once in a Blue Moon"). He shares Phoebe's vision of the Avatars' utopian future ("Witchness Protection").

The Teachers

BEN: Twenty-one and a grad student, he teaches classes of younger students ("Cheaper by the Coven").

DONOVAN, MISS: The librarian, she's a suspect when Mr. Monkeyshines is murdered following an argument about banning books. Agent Brody exonerates her with a gunpowder test in "Charmed Noir." She wants to replace the gnome as the new literature professor ("Carpe Demon") but becomes Drake's TA instead. Mrs. Winterbourne taught her to astral project.

DRAKE: Hatched as a demon, Drake aspires to be human after a lifetime of reading books that taught him the value of feelings ("Carpe Demon"). He wishes to spend his last two weeks of life passing on what he's learned as the new literature professor. He teaches a class on advanced musical composition with a dancing troll ("Show Ghouls"). After a short, whirlwind romance with Phoebe, he spends his final moments in Magic School with Cole ("The Seven Year Witch"). Cole arranged for Drake's adventure to save Phoebe from a life without love.

FEENEY, MR. (not shown): Runs the after-school program ("Freaky Phoebe").

LAWRENCE: Young, teaches the corporealizing class, his specialty ("Freaky Phoebe").

SIGMUND: A small man in his forties with the power to levitate, he instructs teenagers and temporarily loses his head in "The Legend of Sleepy Halliwell." His complicity in Gideon's plans to kill Wyatt is revealed in "Spin City." However, he believes the foul plot is for the greater good. Despite this, he helps Piper track down the threat ("A Wrong Day's Journey into Right"). When he decides to tell the sisters the truth, Gideon murders him ("Witch Wars"). See also the Book of White Magic section, subheading "Not Necessarily Evil."

MONKEYSHINES, MR.: A professor, he's convinced that novels and other books are a bad influence on the students and tries to get some banned. He's shot to death when he's drawn into the Mullen brothers' novel, *Crossed, Double-Crossed*.

WINTERBOURNE, MRS.: Blond and kind, she has the ability to astral project and runs the nursery, where Wyatt instantly adapts, in "The Legend of Sleepy Halliwell." She remains cheerful and tolerant of Piper's extreme concerns about Wyatt's interactions with other toddlers ("Witch Wars"). Mrs. Winterbourne cares for Piper when she goes into labor ("It's a Bad, Bad, Bad, Bad World, Part 1"). She informs Paige that the Elders are closing the school ("A Call to Arms"). Miss Donovan mentions that Mrs. Winterbourne has gone on sabbatical ("Carpe Demon"). The Spirit of the Triad platform hovers in her old classroom in "Gone with the Witches."

The Students

"THE LEGEND OF SLEEPY HALLIWELL"

HERMAN: A conjurer and shy, at sixteen he is well-versed in the history and exploits of the Charmed Ones.

QUENTIN: Seventeen, he's a good kid and a Sleepy Hollow buff.

SLICK: Seventeen and a shape-shifter, this bully with a bad attitude learns a lesson when Piper turns him into a frog.

ZACHARY: Sixteen and telepathic, he is mercilessly bullied and resents being separated from his family. Wanting revenge on the teachers, he taps into the powers of others to create the Headless Horseman. Unhappy and not inherently evil, he is allowed to return home.

"THE COURTSHIP OF WYATT'S FATHER"

SARA: Fourteen, with the power of telekinesis, she's reprimanded by Gideon for using her power to shelve ancient texts.

"WITCH WARS"

EMILY (mentioned only): Age two and psychic, she takes one-year-old Wyatt's modeling dough.

"THE BARE WITCH PROJECT"

DUNCAN: Fifteen and a conjurer, Duncan casts a spell that calls Lady Godiva out of a history book. He resents being picked on but doesn't stand up for himself. With Paige's guidance, he gains confidence to "step up and be a man."

SIMON: Fifteen, he picks on Duncan.

"CHEAPER BY THE COVEN"

BEN: Twenty-one and a grad student; See Teachers.

"CHARMED NOIR"

MULLEN, DAN: Coauthor of *Crossed, Double-Crossed,* he dies of gunshot wounds at Magic School in 1984. His missing brother, Eddie, is presumed to be the killer by everyone except their parents.

MULLEN, EDDIE: Coauthor of *Crossed, Double-Crossed,* he is still living within the pages of the magical novel, where only one day has passed since his brother was shot by Johnny the Gent. Eddie, Paige, and Brody escape the book alive when he destroys the Burmese Falcon.

"SHOW GHOULS"

APRIL: Age twelve, applying for admission, she tours the facilities with her father.

"GENERATION HEX"

JEN: She and Ryan are the only two out of five members of the Advanced Combat class left alive. She helps Ryan and Piper send Rondok, a Noxon demon to the Astral Plane.

RYAN: Nineteen and a witch, he is hunted by Rondok, a Noxon demon he tortured in Advanced Combat class. Using Leo's lessons, he and Jen find a viable plan to vanquish the unvanquishable demon.

"FOREVER CHARMED"

WYATT, MATTHEW: Six, with the power to orb, he's Leo's first grandson.

Charmed Events Within the Magical Halls

▲ The Charmed Ones must identify the student who created the Headless Horseman and remove the threat (**"THE LEGEND OF SLEEPY HALLIWELL"**).

▲ Gideon's help is sought to extract Leo and Piper from the Ghostly Plane (**"THE COURTSHIP OF WYATT'S FATHER"**).

▲ Pregnant Piper and Wyatt move into Magic School for protection (**"SPIN CITY"**).

▲ The Great Hall is utilized for library reference and family meetings (**"A WRONG DAY'S JOURNEY INTO RIGHT" AND "WITCH WARS"**).

▲ Good and evil members of the Charmed family infiltrate mirror realities (**"IT'S A BAD, BAD, BAD, BAD WORLD, PART 1"**).

▲ Gideon kidnaps Wyatt when Piper leaves for the hospital to have Chris (**"IT'S A BAD, BAD, BAD, BAD WORLD, PART 2"**).

▲ Paige fights to keep the school open (**"A CALL TO ARMS" AND "THE BARE WITCH PROJECT"**) and becomes the headmistress.

▲ A masked manifestation of Wyatt's guilt about his parents fights Leo (**"CHEAPER BY THE COVEN"**).

▲ Paige uses a graduate student's protection spell, which backfires (**"STYX FEET UNDER"**).

▲ Elders heal two Whitelighters attacked by the Charmed Ones (**"ONCE IN A BLUE MOON"**).

▲ Paige and Agent Kyle Brody are drawn into the Mullen brothers' novel, *Crossed, Double-Crossed*, and become the characters Lana and the Fed (**"CHARMED NOIR"**).

▲ Leo and Piper exchange heated words about Wyatt and Chris spending more time at Magic School than at home (**"WITCHNESS PROTECTION"**).

▲ Paige announces that Magic School has satellite TV (**"CARPE DEMON"**).

▲ Paige retires, and Leo becomes headmaster (**"SCRY HARD"**).

▲ Paige and Piper use the library to research Pandora's Box (**"LITTLE BOX OF HORRORS"**).

▲ Magic School becomes the Charmed Ones' base of operations to stop Zankou from acquiring the power of the Nexus (**"SOMETHING WICCA THIS WAY GOES . . . ?"**).

▲ Leo and Billie discover that demons have taken over the school (**"DESPERATE HOUSEWITCHES"**).

▲ Billie locates Reinhardt, the demon who kidnapped her sister (**"VAYA CON LEOS"**).

▲ The Charmed Ones attack the Triad and vanquish two of them (**"ENGAGED AND CONFUSED"**).

▲ The Charmed Ones, empowered by the Hollow, vanquish the Spirit of the Triad so the Triad cannot return (**"KILL BILLIE: VOL. 2"**).

▲ The Charmed Ones use potions to permanently vanquish the Triad again when history is altered (**"FOREVER CHARMED"**).

▲ Phoebe and Coop get married in the Great Hall with the Angel of Destiny presiding (**"FOREVER CHARMED"**).

Demonic Events Within the Magical Halls

▲ Paul Haas and Black Heart discover that the Charmed Ones are no longer protecting the school and that the magic within is available for evil (**"MALICE IN WONDERLAND"**).

▲ A Possessor demon posing as the human Mandi kidnaps Wyatt and conjures The Source to help raise the Charmed boy (**"DESPERATE HOUSEWITCHES"**).

▲ Antosis operates out of Magic School while trying to stake out territory aboveground (**"REWITCHED"**).

▲ The Dogon moves in while he's killing other demons and absorbing their powers in his bid to become the leader of the Underworld (**"KILL BILLIE: VOL. 1"**).

▲ The sorceress Zira plots to overthrow male demon domination of the Underworld (**"BATTLE OF THE HEXES"**).

▲ Margoyle tries to harness the Hulk virus (**"HULKUS POCUS"**) but cures the infection before demons are wiped out.

▲ Phoenix, Patra, and Pilar practice being the Charmed Ones and using the sisters' powers under the supervision of Savard (**"REPO MANOR"**).

▲ The annual opening of Novak's crypt occurs (**"12 ANGRY ZEN"**).

▲ The Triad moves in after Christy is in position in the Manor (**"THE LAST TEMPTATION OF CHRISTY"**).

▲ Noxon demons Rondok and Pator hunt and kill the students who tortured them (**"GENERATION HEX"**).

▲ Christy vanquishes Candor after he has her parents murdered (**"GENERATION HEX"**).

▲ Christy's minion, Creo, inhabits the school, where she can find him (**"THE TORN IDENTITY"**).

▲ Christy and Billie set up shop (**"THE TORN IDENTITY" AND "THE JUNG AND THE RESTLESS"**).

> ▲ The Spirit of the Triad manifests in a classroom (**"GONE WITH THE WITCHES"**), where it oversees the planned destruction of the Charmed Ones.

> ▲ Piper kills Dumain and Billie kills Christy with her own fireball, ending evil's reign at the school (**"FOREVER CHARMED"**).

Specific Library Books

EVERYTHING YOU WANTED TO KNOW BUT WERE AFRAID TO ASK
Gideon refers to the chapter on portals to rescue Leo and Piper from the Ghostly Plane (**"THE COURTSHIP OF WYATT'S FATHER"**).

GREAT WOMEN OF HISTORY
A student conjurer brings an illustration of Lady Godiva to life (**"THE BARE WITCH PROJECT"**).

CROSSED, DOUBLE-CROSSED
A novel written by the Mullen brothers in 1984, it ceases to pull people into the plot when the story is finished in 2004 (**"CHARMED NOIR"**).

POSSESSIONS, CONFESSIONS, AND GHOSTLY OBSESSIONS: A DEMON'S GUIDE TO EVERYTHING MAGICAL
Drake refers to the passage on lost souls, spirits that die violent deaths and are prevented from moving on by confusion (**"SHOW GHOULS"**). The book is equipped with three-dimensional metaphorical illustrations, for example, a knotted rope.
NOTE: Drake sold this book lair-to-lair in the Underworld when he was still a Mercury demon.

FAIRY TALES
After he moves into Magic School (**"MALICE IN WONDERLAND"**), Haas refers to a fairy tale in the dusty volume titled "How Cinderella Nearly Turned the Charmed Ones into Pumpkins."

EPISODE GUIDE

Season Six

INTRODUCTION

Charmed premiered in the United states on October 7, 1998, with Alyssa Milano, Holly Marie Combs, and Shannen Doherty as Phoebe, Piper, and Prue Halliwell, three sisters who learned that they were witches possessing the Ultimate Power of good in the Power of Three. The Halliwells were charged with protecting the Innocent while they learned to use their new magical abilities. But they were not alone in their battle. A guardian angel in the form of Whitelighter Leo Wyatt (Brian Krause) was watching over them.

The Charmed Ones quickly learned the price they would have to pay in their war against evil when Prue's on-again, off-again love Andy Trudeau (T. W. King) died at the end of the first season. The tragedy did ultimately provide them with an ally in the form of Andy's partner, Inspector Darryl Morris (Dorian Gregory).

Over the course of three seasons, the Charmed Ones continued to grow into their powers and fight the good fight. But nothing could prepare them for the death of Prue when Shannen Doherty left the show at the end of Season Three. This paved the way for the entrance of an unknown half sister (and half Whitelighter) named Paige—played by Rose McGowan—to enter the picture.

The Power of Three was reborn, and the sisters continued to battle the forces of evil with their magical and mortal compatriots. But all was not death and destruction. Over the years the Charmed Ones found love. Piper and Leo married and gave birth to a son named Wyatt; and Phoebe fell in love with a demon named Cole (Julian McMahon), though that relationship ultimately met a tragic end.

At the close of the fifth season a new mystery man, a Whitelighter from the future named Chris (Drew Fuller), came into the Charmed Ones' lives. Though he claimed to be on their side, his true intentions were unclear, especially when he ended the season by making Leo disappear.

In those five seasons, *Charmed* was bounced around the schedule on the WB. The audience showed their devotion to the series by following it in every new time slot, even when up against the then-difficult Thursday night "Must See TV" lineup on NBC. Throughout the episode guide that follows, interviews with the cast and crew will highlight the challenges and rewards of working on the popular series. The interviews in the book were conducted in the eighth and final season, allowing all involved the chance to look over the experience as a whole and comment on the amazing ride it has been.

BRAD KERN (EXECUTIVE PRODUCER): I remember when I first got hired, Jonathan Levin, the president of the studio, came to me on a very difficult day—I think we were on the third episode, and I was exhausted then and overwhelmed, because we didn't really know what the show was early on in the season, or at least what the series would be. He said, "Do you think you've got five years in you on this show?" And I said, "No way." And to this day, when I see him he always teases me about that.

Now it was three years ago that my five years would have ended. I must be a masochist. . . . No. It's great. I never imagined we'd be here. I don't think you can ever start a show and imagine it would last this long, especially in this day and age, with so much competition and so many channels to compete with for the audience's eyes. I'm just thrilled.

AARON SPELLING (EXECUTIVE PRODUCER): Working with the WB has been wonderful. They've been so supportive of us, and it really means a lot to me. In fact, *Charmed* has always been "charmed." When the original Phoebe (Lori Rom) left the show for personal reasons, we got Alyssa Milano, and several years later, Rose McGowan came in. Now we've added Kaley Cuoco to the series and these three ladies, along with Holly Marie Combs—who's been with us from the beginning—are simply wonderful and beautiful actresses. These ladies are why the show has such longevity.

It's important to also note how creative our show runner, Brad Kern, and his staff are at keeping the stories so unique and inventive. I can't tell you how much I love this show. We've never done anything like it, and it's been a truly magical experience.

E. DUKE VINCENT (EXECUTIVE PRODUCER): We're very fortunate to have two great shows. We got Brenda Hampton on *Seventh Heaven* and we've got Brad Kern on *Charmed*. And they've both been there since the beginning. Without them I don't think we'd be on all this time. And of course, the girls. We've got three stars on the one show. As you know, we started out with a little bit of a different mix. In the fourth year we got Rose. It's worked out very well. A lot of people thought it wouldn't work if you lose one of the key players in a show like this. But it did, in fact, work. And I consider our show very fortunate from that point, that it did work. But it's been a great run.

We've had some changes in the writing staff along the way, but it's been super. I have taken the attitude of, if it's not broken, don't fix it. So I just leave Brad alone and let him do his thing. I told him, "If you get in trouble, call me. Otherwise I don't want to hear from you." If they have a problem, my phone rings. Recently it hasn't rung very often. Early on it rang all the time. But now it doesn't ring.

THE EPISODES

"VALHALLEY OF THE DOLLS"
Original air date September 23, 2003

WRITTEN BY BRAD KERN | DIRECTED BY JAMES L. CONWAY

In the months since the Charmed Ones saved the world (again), Phoebe has been given the power of empathy, and Paige has started temping because she decided that she needs a life away from her sisters and magic. Piper doesn't seem to mind that Leo is now Up There with his fellow Elders. In fact, she's positively chipper about it, and everything else—incessantly, annoyingly, and very un-Piperly chipper.

Phoebe and Paige decide that a memory spell will help Piper deal with recent events so that she can work through them. Unfortunately, it backfires, and Piper can't remember anything—including who and what she is. It's time to find Leo and get him to undo whatever it was he did to make Piper forget her pain. Only, Leo's not with the other Elders. Paige and Phoebe eventually find him on the magical island of Valhalla—where he had been sent (unbeknownst to the Charmed Ones or Leo) by Chris. The sisters need to become Valkyries to enter Valhalla undetected so that they can rescue the Elder.

Their mission is easily accomplished with three pendants obtained by Chris, and a warrior's spirit "borrowed" from Darryl Morris. When Piper sees Leo in the gladiator ring, her memory—and her pain—come flooding back. Although she still doesn't voice her feelings, they pour out through empath Phoebe. When the diatribe is done, there is very little left of the old Piper. Leo is rescued from Valhalla, but Piper decides that she is a Valkyrie and remains. Just to make things a little more interesting, three warriors follow Phoebe, Paige, Leo, and Darryl through the portal back to San Francisco.

The Valkyries are led by Piper when they go to "the City" to retrieve their warriors. At least that puts her back on home turf, and her sisters should have an advantage. Phoebe believes Piper has chosen to be a Valkyrie because it is too painful for her to be herself. They need to reverse the memory spell they put on her, even if it is hard for her to deal with things, or they won't get her back. They track down Piper and her fellow Valkyries and the warriors. But the reversal doesn't work, and Piper returns to Valhalla.

Time to come up with a Plan B. Leo has seen his fellow Elders, who believe that Phoebe has been given the empathy power at this time so that she'll be able to save Piper. Chris remembers a spell in the Book of Shadows that makes someone else feel what you are feeling. Phoebe has already experienced Piper's emotions. If she can project those back onto Piper with the spell, they will hopefully get their sister back. The plan works, and when Piper is flooded with all of her conflicting emotions, she becomes Piper again. She promises the Valkyries that she and her sisters will keep the secret of Valhalla, and the Charmed Ones return home.

Once Piper's settled back into the Manor, Leo tells her that the Elders want him to hang around to make sure that she and her sisters aren't being targeted. But Piper asks him to leave so that she can move on with her life. She can't get over him if he's always there. Leo regretfully grants her request.

Meanwhile, Phoebe's empathic powers have had her channeling Jason's hots for her—and reciprocating his emotions. But she's not sure if his attraction is purely physical, so she asks to slow things down a bit.

And Paige's first temp job as a dog walker yields some unexpected results. It turns out that Oscar, one of the pooches she's been walking, is really a man who has been cursed by an evil witch. Paige was obviously given this particular job to help Oscar by reversing the curse. And she's glad she does, when the hunky human version of Oscar asks her out.

"Where exactly are you trying to find Leo . . . Jupiter?" **PHOEBE HALLIWELL**

"Banish a guy to an island of beautiful women and he complains? You just can't win."

CHRIS PERRY

BEHIND THE SCENES

JIM CONWAY (CO-EXECUTIVE PRODUCER/DIRECTOR): That episode was a lot of fun. It was a huge episode. This was where we did all of the sword fighting and we had the little arena. Those gals were terrific in those great outfits. That was a lot of fun for us. We went out and spent four days at the Los Angeles arboretum. That's where we did all the exterior work. They've got these great tropical areas there that we used. The sword fighting with Brian was great. He learned how to do it, and he did most of that himself.

PAUL STAHELI (PRODUCTION DESIGNER): We turned the cave into a miniature coliseum where Brian did combat. We put a cage in there and little bleacher seats for the Valkyries. I took the motif from where we started when the Valkyries were racing about outside. We shot that at the Los Angeles arboretum in groves of bamboo. So I just made everything of bamboo as it tied them out there with them inside.

CELEST RAY (MUSIC COORDINATOR): With Smash Mouth, one thing I remember is we went back and forth with the label on who was going to deliver the equipment. We want the actual equipment. It has to be real. If the drummer is signed to a particular drum kit, we have to make sure that we have that drum kit. Or we have to blank out the name on the drum kit.

On this episode there was an issue that we couldn't deliver the equipment the day before because we were on a beach. So then there's the fear of our call time being six thirty in the morning. So how do we get the equipment there and make sure that it's there in time for the shoot? There are those sorts of issues.

Other issues that I've dealt with are hair and makeup. You can understand where the artist wants to have their own hair and makeup, but we have a union show. We have to have our union people on set. So we try to accommodate them the best that we can.

KEN MILLER (EXECUTIVE IN CHARGE OF POSTPRODUCTION): We make it good for [the bands]. We try to make it real comfortable for them as we would for our actors. We just try to make it as good as we can. We always have a contract person on the set. If there are any problems, you know . . . we'll put Evian water out for them. It's the same as dealing with actors and actresses. You want to make it comfortable so the record company and the band have a good experience. And they usually do. We hear from the groups.

DREW FULLER (CHRIS) ON JOINING *CHARMED* IN THE FIFTH AND SIXTH SEASONS: If anything, it was a blessing. Didn't have to worry about ratings. Didn't have to worry about finding an audience. Didn't have to worry about finding a good night. A lot of people fret during pilot season, "Oh, is my pilot going to be picked up? And if it gets picked up, are they going to keep me? And if they keep me, are we going to get on a good night? Are we going to get Friday at ten?" There are so many worries that go into it. To come into a show where that initial legwork has already been taken care of, it allows you just to focus on the acting and having the fun of it.

"FORGET ME . . . NOT"
Original air date October 5, 2003

WRITTEN BY HENRY ALONSO MYERS | DIRECTED BY JOHN KRETCHMER

Wyatt orbs a dragon out of the television and onto the streets of San Francisco. Although it is the innocent act of a toddler, it exposes some very powerful magic, and it brings out the Cleaners—a neutral entity that exists only to protect magic. The Charmed Ones are helpless against the Cleaners, who take Wyatt and erase everyone's memory. The sisters don't remember the baby or what happened the previous day.

Loss of memory does not sit well with three powerful witches. They cast a "fill in the blanks" spell, and it rewinds time. They can now relive the day they've forgotten and look for clues to the missing pieces. Since everything is as it was the previous day, Piper finds her baby right where he belongs. Phoebe finds that her empathic powers caused her to channel a coworker's rage at Elise, and she started an all-out brawl at the *Bay Mirror*! And Paige finds that someone at her current

temp job thinks he saw a dragon fly by the high-rise building's window. The truth is confirmed when Wyatt orbs Piper to the dragon because he wants to play with his new "friend."

Enter the Cleaners. Given the Charmed Ones' record of covering their own magic, the Cleaners offer them one chance to make things right. If they fail, the Cleaners will take over and then take Wyatt, and all memory of him will be erased. The sisters—with Wyatt in tow—go after the dragon, but they cannot take a scale off it to make their vanquishing potion work. Faced with losing her son, Piper goes for broke. She remembers Leo's advice that the way to fix things may be maternal rather than magical, and she boldly approaches the dragon. Her gamble pays off when Wyatt vanquishes the dragon as it moves to attack his mommy.

The dragon is gone, but the Cleaners determine that the Charmed Ones cannot successfully clean up its aftermath. Making good on their threat, they take Wyatt and erase everyone's memory. But the "fill in the blanks" spell the sisters cast earlier is still working, and their memories are not erased this time. They flush out the Cleaners by exposing their magic on television. Piper threatens that they will keep it up until her son is returned. The Cleaners can keep erasing their magic, but they cannot erase the Charmed Ones, as that would tip the balance from good to evil. The Cleaners know this is true and give in to Piper, who promises to keep Wyatt in check. And, as long as they're there, Phoebe also asks the Cleaners to erase the riot at the *Bay Mirror* so she can keep her job.

"Well, at least now we know what happened—too bad we won't remember any of it."

PAIGE MATTHEWS

"Come on, you fire-breathing lizard. Come and get me."   **PIPER HALLIWELL**

BEHIND THE SCENES

PETER CHOMSKY (PRODUCER): When I first read the script, I was thinking, "Wow." I had seen the outline and knew we were going to have a dragon, but until you get the script, you really don't know what you're facing. Fortunately we had a director—John Kretchmer—who sees that he knows what he's going to shoot. He sees the film before he shoots the film, which most directors do, but he's got it down. He's got a complete shot list. He knows exactly, every single shot he's going to make.

Working with somebody who is that organized helps us tremendously to be able to get him the shots that he envisions, because we know these are the shots he's going to give us. He's not going to be changing it. Then we can budget it properly. We can prepare for it properly. We can work very closely with Steve Lebed, our visual effects supervisor, and he can get these shots where they need to be when we're going to need them to get on the air.

Knowing that, they modeled the complete dragon. They were able to provide a wire-frame model of the dragon for the editors to work with so that we could figure out the timing and the placement. From there we were able to lock the show, lock the cuts, and get Steve working to get those shots done. It turned out great.

STEPHEN LEBED (VISUAL EFFECTS SUPERVISOR): I started early with Brad Kern coming up with the designs; talking about the shape of the dragon, the kind of action the dragon will play into. When we finally got our script, we broke it down to just the few shots where we'd see the dragon. The idea was that the dragon was only going to play in just a few scenes, and we'd try to get the most bang for our buck.

Originally we had planned on doing thirteen original shots of the dragon in that particular episode. By the time the show was cut together, we had thirty-three. It got up quite a bit. But it was fun. John Kretchmer was the director of that episode, and he's really great to work with. He had worked on *Jurassic Park* [as first assistant director], so he was used to the complexities of doing computer-generated creatures and timing it to live action.

We just staged our shots in such a way so that we could feature the dragon as much as possible and tie real elements into the scene, like when the dragon is flying out of a tunnel. Randy Cabral, the special effects coordinator, would set off live explosions within the tunnel, and we'd have a car driving out on fire and smoke billowing out. Later on we would take that shot and create our own layer of smoke in front of the dragon so that it looked like the dragon was emerging from the smoke and flying out toward the lens and blowing fire. It was quite a challenge. It was a lot of work in a short amount of time.

RANDY CABRAL (SPECIAL EFFECTS COORDINATOR): This was a pretty fun episode. It was a good mix of visual effects and special effects. When we had the dragon flying through the tunnel, that was a potential fiasco because I had this fireball that had to come out of the mouth of the tunnel. I looked at it with the fire marshal and he said to me, "You know, there's all kinds of dry brush up there. What are you going to do?" I said, "I'll wet down the hillside on this side. I'll have a fire truck on this side and a fire truck on that side. So if anything goes awry, at least we'll be able to knock it down before it goes." He said, "Well, if the winds get faster than fifteen miles an hour, I'm pulling the plug on the whole deal." So we were all a little nervous that morning. But when we showed up and the winds were lying down, it was like, "Okay, let's get this gag." And it worked flawlessly.

"POWER OF THREE BLONDES"

Original air date October 12, 2003

WRITTEN BY DANIEL CERONE | DIRECTED BY JOHN BEHRING

The Stillman sisters, Mabel, Mitzy, and Margo, are described in the Book of Shadows as "common witches known for their small-time hustles and cons—not worth vanquishing." Unfortunately for the Charmed Ones, the blond Stillman sisters manage to perform an identity theft spell and make the world—and the Book of Shadows—believe that they are truly Piper, Phoebe, and Paige. The Blond Ones then say the spell "To Call a Witch's Powers" and finish their transformation into the Charmed Ones. But since Paige's orbing power is from her Whitelighter side, it is not susceptible to the spell, and she is able to orb her sisters and herself to safety after Mabel tries out Piper's firepower.

Our good sisters know that the only way to put things back to normal is to convince Chris who's who, so they devise a standoff between Charmed Ones and Blond Ones at midnight. By that time, though, Margo has written and chanted an anti-orb spell. It doesn't give her orbing power, but it prevents Paige from using it. It looks like the "common witches" may wind up the winners, but Chris senses that something is not quite right. He causes the Blond Ones to bicker, which breaks their Power of Three. The true Charmed Ones are then able to defeat their nemeses with three well-placed punches. They recite the spell to call their powers back to themselves, and all is right with our world again.

During all of this, Leo has floated a rumor Up There that he knows who scattered his orbs to Valhalla. When Chris is the only one who seems interested in this development, it confirms to Leo that Chris was the perpetrator. And he lets Chris know that when he has enough evidence to prove it, everyone will know.

"Everyone in the world thinks we're trashy blondes. I do have to hand it to them, though . . . they've taken identity theft to a whole new level." **PAIGE MATTHEWS**

"We are charmed and dangerous." **MITZY STILLMAN**

BEHIND THE SCENES

AARON SPELLING (EXECUTIVE PRODUCER): There is such a fine line between comedy and drama, and *Charmed* walks it so beautifully, thanks to the creative writing of Brad Kern and his staff and to our three beautiful stars. That's the thing about Holly, Alyssa, and Rose—they can act both comedy and drama masterfully and make the balance so believable to the television audience. For any project that we do, it's important to straddle the line of comedy and drama to help insure that the audience is entertained.

JIM CONWAY (CO-EXECUTIVE PRODUCER): "The Power of Three Blondes" was fun because we had these three gorgeous girls who were trying to be our girls. I've always loved the ones that had a lot of humor in it.

"LOVE'S A WITCH"
Original air date October 19, 2003

WRITTEN BY JEANNINE RENSHAW | DIRECTED BY STUART GILLARD

Paige is trying hard to make her own path in life away from her sisters and magic, but it doesn't seem to be working. Every temp job she gets has magical overtones, and the latest one—a home helper to an elderly woman—has magic in spades. When Paige is hit with what appears to be an energy ball launched from across the street, she finds herself in the middle of a centuries-old feud between two witch families—the Callaways and the Montanas.

The energy ball turns out to be a plasma ball, which was launched by the ghost of Olivia Callaway, former fiancée of Richard Montana. She was accidentally killed in the cross fire a year ago, and her death led Richard to give up magic because of what it's done to his family and his love. The Charmed Ones hold a séance and miraculously get the surviving members of both clans to attend. Olivia admits orchestrating the most recent attacks on both the Montana family and her own because her death was not avenged. Both families stomp out in a renewed rage. Paige goes after Richard, but her body is taken over by Olivia before she reaches him. As Paige, Olivia goads Richard into returning to magic and the feud. He reluctantly enters the fray and is struck by an energy ball from Olivia's father. Olivia is initially stunned, but then she realizes that if she can't have him in life, she will in death. Still in Paige's body, she taps into her Whitelighter powers and orbs Richard—and Paige—to her crypt.

Seeing the futility of their ways, Richard's mother and Olivia's father go to Piper and Phoebe to put an end to the fight. They lead the sisters to Olivia's tomb, Piper blasts it open, and the specter rises out of Paige. The youngest Charmed One is unharmed and pleads with Olivia to give up her vengeance. She knows that Olivia had been a loving person and asks her to find that love within herself again. If she lets Richard live, she will be able to move on—and more importantly, end the feud with life rather than death. Olivia knows that Paige is right. She asks for forgiveness and ascends to the heavens.

Meanwhile, Phoebe's empathy powers are putting

everyone on edge, especially Chris, who's afraid she'll figure out that he was the one who sent Leo to Valhalla. The young Whitelighter gets a potion from an old sorcerer that will block people's thoughts so that Phoebe can't tap into them. It works, and the sisters are one big, happy, private family again. And Chris is safe—for now.

It's also time for Piper to start dating again, which leads to her asking Leo for a formal divorce.

PIPER: *"I mean, I was married to an angel, for crying out loud. Who is gonna compare to that?"*

PHOEBE: *"I know, but you also dated a demon, a warlock, and a ghost. You know, that's what you should be scared of."*

BEHIND THE SCENES

RANDY CABRAL (SPECIAL EFFECTS COORDINATOR): There was a lot of stuff in that episode. In that respect we relied on Stephen Lebed, our visual effects supervisor, who probably is one of the greatest. He's got great ideas and great plans, and we're able to do it with no ego. I say, "Steve, I got an idea about this." And he says, "Hey, that's great. I'll mix it with mine." So between the two of us, we can mix a little physical with a little bit of his magical, and it comes out really good. In that respect we're fortunate that we've got him onboard. I think it pays off.

STEPHEN LEBED (VISUAL EFFECTS SUPERVISOR): Whenever possible, my approach is one where we want to tie as much reality into it as we can. Sometimes we'll have to paint in our own [computer-generated effect] explosions, or we'll have to paint in fire effects simply because of the proximity of an actor to an effect, or safety issues, or sometimes it's because of time. In that particular episode, because it was essentially the Hatfields and the McCoys, we knew going in that there were going to be lots of flames and lots of explosions. Randy and his guys had the time to go through it and actually place all the squibs and hits and all the explosions and fire effects. It really made everything that we did that much better, because now when we added our fireball or added whatever the effect was, Randy was always tied into it and always gave us a much more beautiful image, a much more striking image.

"MY THREE WITCHES"
Original air date October 26, 2003

WRITTEN BY SCOTT LIPSEY & WHIP LIPSEY I DIRECTED BY JOEL J. FEIGENBAUM

The Charmed Ones are happily living their individual lives, so when a demon opens a vortex in the floor of the Manor, Piper has to vanquish him by herself. She has no problem with it, but it upsets Chris that the sisters still won't listen to him. He decides to teach them a lesson.

Chris finds Gith, a demon who feeds on desires, and hands him a spell to get the Charmed Ones. Gith determines the sisters' desires and sucks each of them into an alternate reality that manifests

those wishes. Piper lives in a "normal" world without magic, and Paige lives in a world where magic is normal. Unaware that Phoebe is an empath, Gith reads her channeling Jason's desires for her, and he creates that world. The sisters soon realize that they are in some sort of alternate reality, but they don't know how to get out.

Gith watches all of the events unfold in a cauldron in his lair. When Chris orbs in to put an end to the game, Gith shoots the Whitelighter with a Darklighter's crossbow. The demon sensed that Chris didn't really desire to kill the Charmed Ones, but since that is Gith's greatest desire, he doesn't want anything interfering with his plan. As Chris fights for his life, he manages to magically move Phoebe into Paige's alternate reality. They believe they can put an end to whatever's happening—but they'll need the Power of Three. Since the pocket realms they are in are fueled by desire, they combine their desire to find Piper. They get there just as Gith is about to kill their sister. A very normal car accident in Piper's realm causes an explosion that vanquishes Gith and blows the sisters out of the alternate reality and into the demon's lair. They call for Leo, who heals a sick Wyatt and the injured Chris.

Piper hails Chris as their hero, thinking that he had gone to Gith's lair to save them. Leo suspects otherwise, but Piper's gratitude softens the Elder, and he gives Chris another chance.

"Call me butter, 'cause I'm on a roll."   **PAIGE MATTHEWS**

"Whitelighters don't kill, or did you not read the manual?"   **LEO WYATT**

BEHIND THE SCENES

ROSE MCGOWAN (PAIGE): Some of the jobs were quite nonsensical. I couldn't really understand, you know, 'cause I was, like, "Wait a second. If I was a social worker, I clearly went to college. I quit being a social worker to be a temp worker so I could help people?" Looking back on that—which I don't know why that didn't occur to me at the time—I was, like, what the hell is that? A social worker *is* helping people. Why would I go be a temp worker? To me that was kind of absurd.

And then, I guess, I wanted to be a social worker again [in Season Eight], but I don't know what happened with that, because I'm clearly not a social worker now. So Paige has had all sorts of jobs. At this point it would be just funny if she went and worked at a Kmart. I think that would be more of a hoot, helping people with finding the proper bra size. I could be of service to humanity that way.

The Power of Three

PIPER

PHOEBE

PAIGE

BILLIE

Family Album

The Charmed Ones
& Their Men

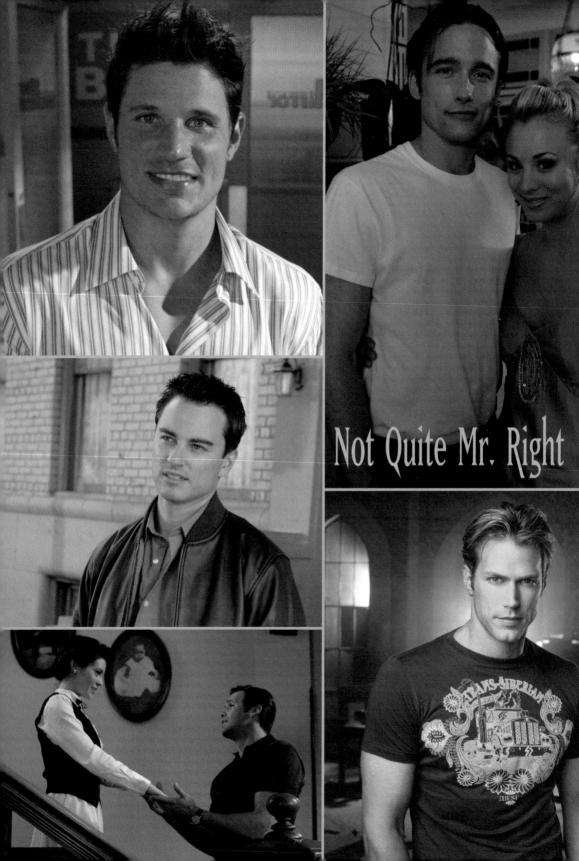

Not Quite Mr. Right

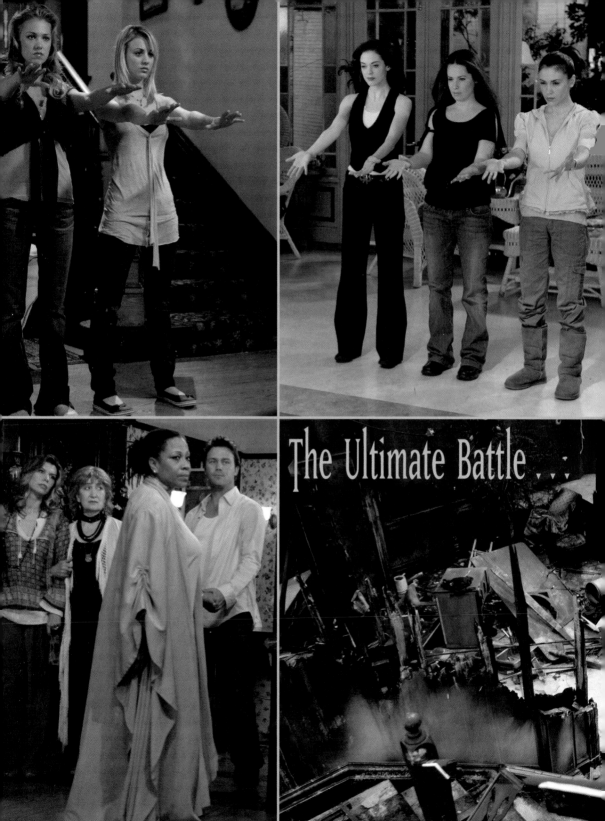

The Ultimate Battle . . .

...Rewound

And They
All Lived Happily
Ever After

The Power of Four

"SOUL SURVIVOR"

Original air date November 2, 2003

WRITTEN BY CURTIS KHEEL | DIRECTED BY MEL DAMSKI

Paige's latest temp job has her working for Larry Henderson, a very nice man who is giving away money to worthy causes left and right. The reason he's doing this is because Larry knows he's going to die at midnight. He'd made a Faustian deal with a demon named Zahn five years earlier, when life wasn't treating him so well, and it's time to pay up. Zahn was a Lower-Level demon until he started his business of auctioning souls for powers. By the time the Charmed Ones try to get rid of him for what he did to Larry, they find he's gained so much strength that they'll need a potion to vanquish the demon.

Despite the fact that it was Larry's choice to deal with Zahn, Paige feels responsible for losing an Innocent. When her sisters don't share her fervor to save Larry's soul, she turns to Richard Montana. Richard is supportive of Paige's feelings, and he encourages her to do what she thinks is right. Paige offers Zahn her soul in place of Larry's. After all, a Charmed One is much more valuable than a mere mortal. Her plan is to get to the vault where Zahn keeps the contracts of all the souls he's collected. Every contract contains a clause that all souls in his possession will burn in eternal flames upon the demon's demise. Paige knows her sisters are working on a potion to vanquish Zahn, and she can't let those souls be lost.

Before she headed Down There to deal with Zahn, Paige had asked Richard to go to her sisters and tell them to reverse the "To Call a Lost Witch" spell, which will take them to her in Zahn's lair. She knows that even if they are angry with her, they won't let her die. Paige destroys the vault, freeing the souls to move on; Piper and Phoebe vanquish Zahn with their potion; and the Charmed Ones settle their differences—for now.

While all this is going on, the sisters can't find either their Whitelighter or family Elder. That's because Chris and Leo are lost in a time portal created by Chris to be able to go back to the future to see if it's changed. Unfortunately, time portals are very hard to control, and the guys wind up running from dinosaurs and somehow explaining their way out of the Civil War. It's unclear just how they make it home safe and sound—but they do.

And if that's not enough to keep the Charmed Ones busy, Piper is testing her suitors' reactions to her being a single mom by introducing them to Wyatt on the first date. It seems to go well each time until, unbeknownst to Piper, Wyatt shows the men his powers, and they beat a hasty retreat.

Meanwhile . . . Phoebe has to contend with the slimy columnist Spencer Ricks again when Elise hires him at the *Bay Mirror*. When he proves himself to still be a pig, Phoebe turns him into a four-legged version—at least for a little while.

"I think we have to talk to Paige, because this whole Power of One kick of hers is getting out of control." **PIPER HALLIWELL**

"Bitch later, vanquish now." **PAIGE MATTHEWS**

"I love watching lawyers explode." **PHOEBE HALLIWELL**

BEHIND THE SCENES

STEPHEN LEBED (VISUAL EFFECTS SUPERVISOR): The thing about the T-Rex was, because everybody has seen *Jurassic Park*, everybody now has a certain expectation of what a dinosaur should look like. So our challenge was to at least meet those expectations as much as we could. With *Jurassic Park* they had a lot of time. They had a year, and they had artists working on it around the clock for months to perfect each shot. We had two weeks.

Early on we took an existing T-Rex model that we had and I had my artists clean up the model. Then I had a really great texture artist go through and paint very detailed texture maps of a T-Rex that basically gave it more wrinkles and more texture. We felt that if we could at least give it a lot of texture, a lot of interest, that—plus the animation—would hopefully fool the audience into thinking that it's real. That was the approach we took.

Mel Damski was really great. He directed that particular episode. He gave us a lot of freedom. We discussed all the shots and the challenges. Whereas the dragon took place at night or in the rain or very subdued lighting, the T-Rex was in broad daylight. That was a real challenge to make it feel like it was a part of the scene and have it integrated into the shot to make it feel like they were actually running from something real.

"SWORD AND THE CITY" *Original air date November 9, 2003*
WRITTEN BY DAVID SIMKINS | DIRECTED BY DEREK JOHANSEN

Camelot comes to Halliwell Manor when the Lady of the Lake appears to Piper in a clogged sink. The Charmed Ones follow the Lady and witness Executioner demons kill her for Excalibur—the legendary magical sword. Before she can explain, she is gone. And, just like the legend, the sword is once again firmly implanted in the stone.

Paige orbs the sword and the stone back to the Manor's conservatory, and magical creatures of every size and shape line up to try their luck. Having had enough of her house and her life being interrupted by a legend (and fairies, and ogres, and dwarves), Piper cuts into the line and easily pulls the sword from the stone, bringing Mordaunt to the Manor. He says he is but a "humble teacher," there to instruct Piper how to use the sword, now that it has chosen her to be the new queen of

Camelot. In reality, he is an evil being who is trying to get the Ultimate Power of the sword for himself.

Even though Piper initially rejects being chosen by the sword, its spell soon overtakes her. She quickly learns how to wield the weapon, and as Mordaunt had hoped, becomes one with it. Piper now craves the power she once denied. But Phoebe and Paige figure out Mordaunt's game when a potion recipe he gives them almost kills them. They realize that he is just using Piper to get the sword and will dispose of all of them once he has the power it affords. Unfortunately, Piper is too far gone by now and doesn't believe her sisters' warnings. She leaves with Mordaunt for Camelot.

Piper amasses the knights for her Round Table—all creatures of the Underworld—and things are going according to plan for her evil manipulator. Mordaunt vanquishes the demonic knights and steals all of their powers. This gives him enough strength to take the sword away from Piper. He stabs her with it so he can get to his ultimate goal—the one for whom the sword was truly meant, the being with the Ultimate Power on Earth: Wyatt. Mordaunt leaves the wounded Piper where she can be found by her family, reasoning that they will leave Wyatt alone in the house and come to save her. But he doesn't count on Leo, Phoebe, and Paige figuring out his plan. He goes to the Manor to kill Wyatt, only to stab an innocent teddy bear and find the baby safely tucked in his aunt Paige's arms. Leo, Phoebe, and a healed (and back to normal) Piper orb in, then Piper takes Wyatt and has him call for the sword. It leaves Mordaunt and readily comes to its rightful owner. Wyatt telekinetically flips it around and vanquishes Mordaunt with the object he so coveted. Piper decides to leave Excalibur back in the stone until Wyatt is older and ready to assume his responsibility.

While they are not dealing with magical swords and demons, Phoebe and Paige are at odds about Paige's growing relationship with Richard. And Paige's latest temp job is as Phoebe's assistant at the *Bay Mirror*!

"Hey, the Lady of the Lake came to the Charmed Ones for help, I'm not messing with that."
LEO WYATT

"Is it me, or does it still smell like ogre in here?"
PHOEBE HALLIWELL

"I bet you didn't expect this when you got up this morning."
MORDAUNT

BEHIND THE SCENES

RANDY CABRAL (SPECIAL EFFECTS COORDINATOR): That was quite a challenge. We built all those swords. We hand-machined and hand-tooled all of the swords, so it was really a custom type of build. We had to make a lightweight one for Holly because she had to actually practice with it and flip it around. That was a really great episode. We went out and filmed on the Grossman property out in Hidden Valley. It was just awesome. We used the pond. Vinnie [Borgese] and I donned scuba gear so we could put our bubble gags out in his pond for the Lady in the Lake part. It was really a lot of fun.

NOON ORSATTI (STUNT COORDINATOR): Holly has got a great ability for retention. She was able to figure out the fight extremely quick. And she was pregnant on top of it. At that point, I don't know if it was public news. She told very few people at first. We didn't want to do anything that hurt her. But what an ability to learn and learn quickly. For that matter, all the girls have a great ability to do that.

For the sword fighting, I brought in a sword master. He luckily got cast as the Dark Knight. So that worked out perfectly. So while I'm over here rigging something to throw somebody around, he's helping to choreograph and come up with a nice fight. We worked out all the neater moves with Nancy Thurston, Holly's double on that. It was actually probably two or three days of rehearsals and then putting Holly in the mix. She just lit up and nailed it. Those giant swords are no light, easy-to-wield things. Then throw a set of chain mail on you and you've got yourself a task. But she did fantastic. That was a really fun episode.

HOLLY MARIE COMBS (PIPER): That's actually one of my favorite episodes. It was funny—well, it wasn't so funny, but it was kind of creepy—that we did that episode while I was pregnant, even though I got stabbed in the gut. It was one that I'll always remember for that. But that one was fun and our guest star, Edward Atterton [Mordaunt], was really, really good, which makes our jobs so much easier than they are.

"LITTLE MONSTERS"
Original air date November 16, 2003

WRITTEN BY JULIE HESS | DIRECTED BY JAMES L. CONWAY

The Charmed Ones encounter Manticores for the first time when they vanquish one, only to find that it's left a baby behind. The adorable tot looks perfectly normal—and human—except for a serpent-like tongue that he joyfully flicks in and out. When the sisters bring him home, Wyatt immediately becomes attached to his new playmate. He especially delights in playing peek-a-boo. Wyatt doesn't have to cover his eyes to make his buddy disappear, because the little guy actually disappears and reappears right in front of him.

Chris warns that the sisters must get rid of the demon baby, but they refuse. They do acknowledge that the Manticores will be looking for the infant, though, and they have to be prepared. The Charmed Ones devise a potion that they hope will work. The baby's cries attract the Manticores, and thankfully, the potion does the trick on some of them. The rest are vanquished by a Beast who also answered the "call." When the Beast cannot get to the baby, he takes Piper hostage instead.

Piper soon realizes that this is no ordinary Beast. For one thing, she's being held hostage in

the suburbs, not the Underworld. The Beast turns out to be the baby's father. He explains that Manticores mate with humans to create hybrids, so they can blend in and hide in plain sight. The demons usually kill their mates after conception, but the man—who is now the Beast—got away. He took any kind of potions he could steal from the Manticores to give himself enough power to defeat them and reclaim his son, and the result is the beastly creature that stands before Piper. The only way he can turn back into a mortal is to die, and he is willing to do so to save his child. New mother Piper completely understands this father's emotions and offers to help the Beast.

Unfortunately, at the same time, her sisters are making a deal with the Manticores—they will help the demons get the baby so they can get their sister back. Once Phoebe and Piper hear the entire story, they turn on their new allies to rescue the baby. Since the little guy is half-Manticore, they need to make sure he's not around when they start throwing vanquishing potions. Piper gets him to play peek-a-boo. He shimmers out, the sisters vanquish the demons, and the baby shimmers back in, safe and sound. He is reunited with his father, who had almost been killed by the Manticore attack orchestrated by Phoebe and Paige. The Beast was wounded severely enough to return to his human state, and the man, Derek, was then healed by Leo. Derek can now raise his son for good rather than evil.

In between fighting the Manticores, Paige jumps at the chance to help Darryl with a hostage situation. The youngest Charmed One casts a spell on the cop to make him invincible and accidentally turns him into a superman!

And Phoebe's empathic powers get her into a bind when she channels Jason's feelings and blurts out, "I love you, too," before he has the chance to express himself. The couple goes through the classic male/female dance when the L word is spoken, but in the end, Jason finally gets to tell Phoebe, "I love you, too"—all on his own.

"So wait, you told him that he loves you before he told you that he loves you?"

PIPER HALLIWELL

"This is my raison d'être."

PAIGE MATTHEWS

BEHIND THE SCENES

TODD TUCKER (SPECIAL EFFECTS MAKEUP): That was probably the heaviest episode we have done. We had three people in complete creature makeups. The Manticore characters not only had face and hands but they also had arms and feet. So other than from the waist down to the knees everything was a makeup. . . . And there were two of them. So those were pretty involved makeups. The Beast character had hands, head, and a muscle suit. And they all shot at the same time. So it was a pretty involved makeup trailer. A lot of people in the trailer that day.

Everything was pretty big. But those guys were really good. They played the parts really well. I took the Manticore guys aside and worked with their walks and their body motions so that they could create a certain feeling that was the same for both of them so they were both from the same creature tribe. And they got it really well. They pulled it off.

The Beast character had a lot of lines and had to really emote through this makeup and through this suit. The actor who played the part, Seth Peterson, did a great job. It's hard sometimes for actors to be put in that heavy of a makeup and then still perform. It just takes your concentration away. So when I get an actor that can go into makeup and actually perform the makeup to the next level—and I've been very lucky so far, that's been the case—it really helps sell the whole character.

"CHRIS-CROSSED" *Original air date November 23, 2003*
WRITTEN BY CAMERON LITVACK | DIRECTED BY JOEL J. FEIGENBAUM

Chris's future comes back to haunt him when he finds his fiancée, Bianca, in Piper's office at P3. He is soon in both emotional and physical pain, as Bianca reaches into his chest to take his powers from him. Piper walks in on this scene and blows up the intruder—she thinks. But Bianca is a Phoenix—one of a family of very elite, very powerful, and very deadly assassin witches, who re-form after being vanquished by anything but a specific potion. She was hired to bring Chris back and will not leave empty-handed.

Bianca had actually helped Chris return to the past. Her love for him had changed her, and she truly hoped that their plan to prevent Wyatt from turning evil would make their world a better place. She had plotted with Chris to get the Book of Shadows, which held the spell to send the Whitelighter back in time, and she drew the Triquetra on the wall of the attic, creating the spot for the time portal. But while Chris has been in the past, Future Wyatt has somehow managed to turn Bianca back to her evil roots, and he dispatched her to return Chris before he can undo history as they know it.

Chris fights going back until he is made to choose between leaving willingly or watching Bianca destroy the Power of Three. Before

Bianca says the new spell that will open a portal and take them from the present to the future (the one used previously from the Book of Shadows only worked from the future to the past), Chris is forced to confess that he is actually only half-Whitelighter . . . and half-witch . . . leaving the sisters even more confused about his role in their lives.

Bianca and Chris step out of the portal into the attic of the future Manor, where they are met by Wyatt's demon flunkies. Wyatt dismisses the demons, saying that the powerless Chris is no threat. But what Wyatt doesn't know is that Chris left a clue for the Charmed Ones when he left their time. He'd been complaining about a squeaky floorboard in the attic, and as he is about to return to the future, Chris tells the sisters to make sure to have Leo fix the loose board. They understand that Chris means he will wind up in the future attic. They write a spell and stash it under the squeaky piece of floor. Bianca shows her true colors and her lingering love for Chris when she interrupts Wyatt's telekinetic beating of the (half) Whitelighter long enough for him to find the spell under the board. He chants it, regains his powers, and charges at Wyatt. Unfortunately, just about this time, Wyatt shakes off Bianca and sends her flying across the room, where she is mortally wounded. Now, more than ever, Chris is determined to go back to the past and change his and Bianca's future. He finds his original spell in the Book of Shadows and rips it out as he says it so that no one can follow him. The young half witch, half Whitelighter lands back in the attic of the present-day Charmed Ones, where everyone is truly happy to see him. As he passes Wyatt in his playpen, it's hard to believe that the adorable and innocent baby will grow up to be the menace that Chris knows and hates.

"We need to try out this whole Power of Two thing, learn how to be flexible, right?"

PAIGE MATTHEWS

"Hey, future girl!"

PIPER HALLIWELL

"If I can't save you, I swear by God, I'll stop you."

CHRIS PERRY

BEHIND THE SCENES

PETER CHOMSKY (PRODUCER): This is one of my favorites. It was really cool because we got to go into the future and find Future Chris. To do that there was so much involved—between taking shots that we shot at the studio and then painting in the Golden Gate Bridge in the background to make it feel like we're in San Francisco. We did the kind of effects that I like to feel when you're viewing them, you don't even realize it's a visual effect.

I liked the look I got to do taking the film and giving it a futuristic look for some of the scenes where Chris is in the future. We radically changed the overall look of the film and I got to really get creative and do things that many shows wouldn't even try to put on the air. It was a totally cool blown-out look that was really unique, and it was really fun doing that.

PAUL STAHELI (PRODUCTION DESIGNER): If you notice, oftentimes when you go to the future, generally speaking, all forecasts—in people's minds—are sort of like everything's gone to total hell.

There's anarchy and there's chaos. Now, I don't know how long that's been going. I don't know if people in the 1850s thought that in the 1950s that anarchy would be reigning supreme, but that's what people seem to accept. So you modernize a few of the props and tear up most everything else. It's sort of like *Lord of the Flies*: When order ceases, chaos begins. Not much creativity is happening. So we obviously took that approach, because demons were reigning supreme at that point.

For budgetary reasons you couldn't do much in terms of creating the new modern house or the new modern this or redesigning. We're not like *Mission Impossible* that has an unlimited budget [NOTE: *Mission Impossible III* was filming on the lot at the time of the interview]. No TV shows are like that.

I don't like dealing with the future, because you can't really predict with any degree of accuracy. I've lived long enough to know. I've looked back at what was being predicted when I was young, certainly hasn't come to pass. When I was young, everybody was worried about what the hell we were going to do with all that free time we were going to have. And the forty-hour workweek sure isn't a concept anymore. It's gotten longer. When I was a kid, everybody was saying, "When you grow up, you'll probably only have to work thirty hours a week."

"WITCHSTOCK"

Original air date January 11, 2004

WRITTEN BY DANIEL CERONE | DIRECTED BY JAMES A. CONTNER

Paige puts on a pair of Grams's old go-go boots and suddenly finds herself in 1967, during the Summer of Love. She also finds a much younger version of Grams, who is still married to her first husband, Allen Halliwell, and who is the textbook definition of a flower child. Paige knows she can't spill the beans about who she is or where she's from. She's desperate to get back to her own time, but her magic doesn't work. Despite her circumstances, Paige soon finds herself bonding with Penny, rejoicing in meeting her mortal grandfather, and reveling in the preparations taking place in the Manor for a magical "be-in."

Meanwhile, back at the present-day Manor, Phoebe, Piper, Leo, and Chris are battling a green slime demon with no name. The demon feeds on magic, so the usual solutions aren't an option. Chris notes that it *was* defeated in the future, but it took the Power of Three. Having no idea where Paige is, or how to find her, the sisters summon Grams. After berating them about living separately, she explains that she had cast a "Return to Owner" spell on a lot of her clothes that year. She knows exactly where Paige is—and it is a critical point in Penny's life and the Charmed Ones' history. During her hippie period, Penny didn't believe in fighting, but her mind was quickly changed when she discovered Allen killed by her best friend, Robin. Allen's death at the hand of someone Penny thought she knew and trusted hardened the Halliwell matriarch into the tough broad her granddaughters came to know and love.

Grams gives Piper and Phoebe other items she enchanted during that time, and they join Paige back in 1967. They need to get their sister and get out so as not to interfere with history. But things are never that easy when you're a Charmed One. A few setbacks separate Piper and Phoebe from

Paige, who is still unaware that Robin is about to kill Allen. Paige happens upon the scene and distracts Robin so that she is the one vanquished by her own energy ball. Penny does not find her husband dead by the hand of her best friend, and she remains a flower child—which also transforms the present-day Grams back into a hippie, unwilling to use force against the deadly green slime that is rapidly taking over the Manor.

Back in 1967, Paige gets caught up on family history. The sisters know that if Death means to take Allen that night, it will, so they just have to be prepared for Robin's partner in crime—a warlock named Nigel—to strike. Allen dies saving Penny and Piper from Nigel's energy ball, but the warlock blinks out just as Phoebe and Paige's potions are thrown at him. Penny is devastated by Allen's death, but not angry—so history is still changed. Having no other recourse, the sisters tell Penny who they are, hoping that they will get their demon-fighting Grams back. Nigel returns, and Penny shows her spunk, not wanting to lose her future family. She vanquishes the warlock and vows to keep fighting the good fight—although she'll work on a forgetting spell to keep the cosmic order.

The Charmed Ones reverse the "Return to Owner" spell and arrive back in the present-day Manor just as the green slime is about to win. A Power of Three spell takes care of the gloppy demon and returns the Grams they know and love from its clutches, unharmed. She *is* already dead, after all. Grams gives the sisters her approval to pursue their own lives, but she makes them promise to keep in better touch with each other.

It seems that Grams wasn't the only flower child during the Summer of Love. During her "trip," Paige encounters a long-haired, love-beaded Leo, who puts on Whitelighter light shows to impress the ladies. When Paige enters his radar, she becomes a prime target for his free love. Needless to say, the youngest Charmed One does not miss an opportunity to tease the Elder with this knowledge when she returns home to the twenty-first century.

"How many times have I told you, men are utensils—you use them, wash them, and throw them in a drawer until you need them again." **GRAMS HALLIWELL**

"My name is Leo—like the zodiac sign." **LEO WYATT DURING THE SUMMER OF LOVE**

"Welcome back to your destiny, Grams." **PAIGE MATTHEWS**

BEHIND THE SCENES

DANIELLA GSCHWENDTNER (COSTUME SUPERVISOR): That was really a fun show. It was a little bit of everything. We were quite lucky in that time that whole seventies mood was on. We found Brian's shirts in a regular store in Sherman Oaks, and they looked fabulous. All these shows are somehow a combination of stuff we buy and stuff we make or modify. It's rare that we buy something and it goes on camera just like that. There's always a little bit of tweaking. The period shows, of course, are a lot of rentals. I don't buy thrift-store stuff that much on the show because it's hard to return. It's okay for background things if you're totally sure. For the hero actors we end up going with a rental or taking an original and having it made and trying to find fabrics that match the period.

"PRINCE CHARMED" — *Original air date January 18, 2004*

WRITTEN BY HENRY ALONSO MYERS | DIRECTED BY DAVID JACKSON

Piper decides to devote her life to protecting and raising Wyatt after she finds a demon attacking her baby in his crib. But Phoebe and Paige don't want to see their sister give up on love—especially on her birthday. Phoebe has already planned an unsurprising surprise party, but Paige has trouble coming up with the perfect gift, until she encounters Piper's obstinacy about abstinence. She conjures a Mr. Right for her sister.

Piper initially rejects her gift, and the whole idea of him, but once he starts saying all the right things, she softens. With no listing for the demon that attacked Wyatt in the Book of Shadows, Piper decides to let everyone else figure it out while she spends the day with her baby and her birthday present.

Chris and Leo determine that the threat is coming from the Order, a demonic cult that had been the most powerful force for evil until their leader was vanquished. The members of the Order believe that their ruler has returned to them in the form of Wyatt, and they're determined to bring him back where he belongs.

Chris suggests that Wyatt's powers be bound so that he will not be a target, but the sisters and Leo reject the idea. Since desperate times call for desperate measures, and the Power of Three is required for the binding spell, Chris reconfigures Mr. Right's personality a bit to get him to appeal to all of the sisters. The plan works, and they are about to bind Wyatt's powers when the Order interrupts things to reclaim their leader. They first must complete his conversion from good to evil so that the baby's innate morality is reversed. Seeing good as evil and evil as his friend, Wyatt raises his protective shield. It repels his family and engulfs the demons, who then have no trouble taking their new ruler back to their temple. The blast shocks the sisters back to reality. They confront Chris, who must now tell them the truth: He came back to stop Wyatt from turning evil, not to stop a demon from hurting Wyatt. The evil that pervades the future *is* Wyatt.

The Charmed Ones can't believe that Chris wouldn't have told them this before. They fire him (again) and go to the Order's temple to retrieve Wyatt, but he still violently rejects them. Chris has his mission, though, despite how the sisters feel right now, and he orbs in. Luckily, Wyatt has never trusted Chris and has always put up his shield around the Whitelighter. So, although the baby continues to repel his family, he now lets Chris through. Chris vanquishes the demons and tells Piper to shine the light from the Order's magical scepter into Wyatt's eyes. The littlest Halliwell is turned back to the side of good. He drops his shield against them all, including Chris—signifying that although the adults may not trust him, Wyatt now does.

And before his time is up, Mr. Right convinces Piper that she can't live without love. Checking on Wyatt before going to bed, Piper finds the birthday gift that Leo has left for her. It's a charm bracelet that Patty had given to Piper many years ago—later lost by Prue and unable to be found by Phoebe, even with a spell. Maybe it is time for her to believe in love and magic again.

"I figure magic owes Piper."   **PAIGE MATTHEWS**

"Hey, buddy, don't forget who made you!"   **PHOEBE HALLIWELL**

"The evil from the future I came back to stop isn't a demon—it's Wyatt."

                                                                CHRIS PERRY

BEHIND THE SCENES

PAM SHAE (EXECUTIVE IN CHARGE OF TALENT) on casting guest actors: We get outlines, so we know what to anticipate when the final script comes out, and we keep in close contact with the writer's office and producer's office if there's any drastic changes. Then, once we get the script, we release it to breakdown services: That goes out to all of the SAG franchised agents. Then they start submitting actors.

From there, we get on the phone and start calling. Kim [Lenae Foster], my casting director, sets up sessions and pre-reads tons of people. At the same time, I meet with actors on a daily basis on generals and will forward people over to her, often that I've worked with in the past. There's a lot of crossover work.

The casting job is really releasing the breakdown, doing the pre-reads, and getting our producer sessions ready. It's just a process of reading all the characters and piecing together everybody in this ensemble cast. Sometimes ideas are changed in the room. An actor will come in and we'll go, "Oh my gosh, this one is so interesting." Whoever is in the room, Brad, or the writer, will say, "You know, I can write for this guy." We hire them and make TV history.

"USED KARMA"

Original air date January 25, 2004

WRITTEN BY JEANNINE RENSHAW | DIRECTED BY JOHN KRETCHMER

Phoebe has put off telling Jason she's a witch, but he learns the truth when he sees her and her sisters orb in after a fight with some Swarm demons. He promptly faints—not exactly the reaction Phoebe was hoping for. Richard blames it all on himself—or more exactly, his bad karma. He reasons that he is carrying around the burden of his family's decades-long feud, during which they used magic to do bad things rather than good. No one else actually believes that, but Richard is determined to cleanse himself so he can start again and make a life with Paige. Thinking he's alone in the Manor, Richard tweaks an aura-cleansing spell and tries his luck. He's not affected by the swirling energy of unfinished bad karma that it produces—but Phoebe is.

The middle Charmed One is suddenly speaking French and dressing like a tart. Her sisters realize that the famous spy Mata Hari has taken over Phoebe's body. Both of the women were leading double lives—one a secret spy, the other a secret witch—so the unfinished karma found a familiar soul in which to nest. Phoebe/Mata seeks out Jason, who is in the middle of a big merger and cannot deal with her or his emotions right now. Feeling betrayed, just as Mata Hari was betrayed by the men in her life, Phoebe/Mata takes revenge on Jason.

Lucky for Mata Hari, the Charmed Ones are fighting the Swarm demons. She makes a deal with the Swarm King to deliver the Charmed Ones if he kills Jason. Swarm demons are distant relatives

of Kazis and vampires, which means they come from a hive. To kill the hive you need to kill the king, and you need a Power of Three spell to do that. Phoebe/Mata knows her sisters will seek her out in the hive, and she will deliver them to the king. What Phoebe/Mata doesn't know is that Richard is now practicing a bit more magic than he should. He feels responsible for Phoebe's karmic "accident," so he brews a potion to reverse the spell and pretty much forces it on Jason—just in case.

Good thing, because "just in case" arrives sooner rather than later, and as Phoebe/Mata calls for the Swarm demon firing squad to unleash their energy balls at Jason, he throws the potion. It works, and the true Phoebe is back. She telekinetically reverses the energy balls toward the demons and vanquishes them—a nice little bonus of her new empathy power. Piper and Paige orb in to save their sister and vanquish the king. They chant the Power of Three spell, and it's good-bye to the Swarm demons.

Phoebe apologizes to Jason for creating a spectacle at his merger banquet and for not telling him her secret. He says he never made time to discuss things. They decide that neither one of them is at fault, but maybe they should take some time apart to work it all through. Phoebe's concerned that he may lose the merger, but Jason's not worried—he says that sadly, he's lost worse.

"I'll see if I can piece together a spell to de-karma Phoebe."   **PIPER HALLIWELL**

"Then how do you explain my sister suddenly walking around like she's in the nudie version of Les Mis?"   **PAIGE MATTHEWS**

HOLLY MARIE COMBS (PIPER): The good thing about *Charmed* is anything can be possible, and the sky's the limit when it came to hiding my pregnancy. At first we covered it up where I sat a lot with pillows in front of me and I wore a lot of ponchos and big coats and was shot in tighter shots rather than wide shots. Then shortly later, when we couldn't hide it anymore, we had to get creative and episodes like "The Legend of Sleepy Halliwell" worked until Piper's pregnancy happened, and then we fast-forwarded to several months later and I could show onscreen.

"THE LEGEND OF SLEEPY HALLIWELL"

Original air date February 8, 2004

WRITTEN BY CAMERON LITVACK I DIRECTED BY JON PARÉ

The Charmed Ones are introduced to Magic School when its door suddenly appears on the stairway of Halliwell Manor. One of the professors, Sigmund, was dispatched to find the sisters, but he has his head lopped off by the legendary Headless Horseman before he can explain why. Luckily, Sigmund's body is still in Magic School, which means he is still alive, and he can carry out his mission to bring the sisters to the school.

The girls enter Magic School with Leo and meet its founder and headmaster—and Leo's mentor—an Elder named Gideon. Gideon explains that Magic School is supposed to be protected from evil, so someone from the inside must be responsible for the Headless Horseman being there.

Gideon has called on the Charmed Ones to help save good magic and Magic School. In the process, he believes that they will also find the answers they have been seeking to their recent personal quandaries.

When Paige takes over a class at the school, she not only regains her magical footing, but some answers to her problems with Richard and *his* magic. Piper checks out the magical

preschool, where Wyatt can play with other children and still be himself, thus giving her baby the best of both his worlds—although she still wants him to be with "normal" kids. And Phoebe goes on a vision quest to answer her questions about her future.

Magic School provides guidance, but the Charmed Ones still have a ways to go to find all the answers—and it's never an easy path. Piper loses her head to the Horseman, and Paige takes it back to the Manor, along with her Advanced Magic class. The youngest Charmed One reasons that the culprit is in that class, and it will be easier to flush him or her out without all of the trappings and temptations of Magic School. Indeed, the bad seed turns out to be Zachary, a telepath, who took powers from others—fellow students, teachers, and even Piper—which gave him enough magic to conjure the Horseman and set him on his teachers. Just before he is busted, he grabs Piper's head and returns to Magic School. The two sisters who still have bodies return to the school to find Zachary, but the Horseman finds them first and their heads join Piper's on a table in the Great Hall. Phoebe does not sense evil in Zachary, only sorrow and anger, and she deduces that he did all of this to get revenge on the school and Gideon. He is your typical unhappy teenager, and when you mix that with magic, it can be toxic.

The sisters now have a solution in hand—but no hands. They summon the Headless Horseman and recite a Power of Three spell to reunite their heads with their bodies and vanquish the demon. The sisters return to the Manor and confront Zach, who admits to everything. The Charmed Ones know the burden of being a paragon of good magic. They explain that they don't always like their destiny either—but they all have to accept it. Zach returns to his family but decides that he does not want his powers bound. It may take him some time to get used to the idea of who and what he is, but Paige thinks that he will do just fine. On the other hand, she's come to the conclusion that binding Richard's magic may be just the thing to keep him—and their relationship—on the right track.

Piper decides that she'd rather keep Wyatt home with his family for the time being. No preschool—magical or otherwise. She realizes that she may have lost her head about the idea of normalizing her very special child.

And Phoebe's vision quest gives her peace of mind—along with a few new unanswered questions. She is thrilled to see Wyatt with a little brother, and herself pregnant with a daughter, living in a world without demons. When Wyatt's brother asks Aunt Phoebe for help, she comes back to reality to find Chris repeating the exact same words to her. After everything is over and Magic School is once again safe, Phoebe confronts Chris and asks if he is Wyatt's little brother. He is, he says, if he can get Piper and Leo back together in time.

"The whole biological clock thing—it's very real and echoing. Tick, tick, tick."

PHOEBE HALLIWELL

"Don't give me that look. I've still got a mouth, I could turn you into a toad."

PIPER HALLIWELL

JON PARÉ (PRODUCER/DIRECTOR): I really liked that one. I found it to be an enchanting episode. My favorite episodes on this show are the ones that are a bit enchanting.

We actually found it difficult to film the heads separated from the bodies because we didn't want to just have the shot appear that we were doing a simple visual effect by cutting off the head from the body. A lot of times when we're faced with a creative problem, the solution isn't generated by one person; it's a solution that boils to the surface as the result of a creative meeting between several people. Everybody starts giving some ideas on how they might do things, and maybe it's the combination of four or five people coming up with ideas that come up with a sixth concept that ends up being the solution.

In this case, we thought of cutting the heads in the table, but then it just looked like that's what we were doing. So then we needed to try to do different levels; put the heads on different levels. And we had to figure out, the only way to really do this was that we would take these wonderful old books, cut holes in them, put doilies around them. All of a sudden, once we started shifting the height of the heads, it started taking on a life of its own.

Then we decided to really make it work you had to have a camera shot where you started underneath that table showing, of course, that there was nothing there. You needed to pan up to reveal that there were heads there. To do that on a television budget was very difficult to do. A lot of this ends up being done by people who just think they can make it work. Where they don't have the right equipment to do it—because they can't spend hundreds of thousands of dollars setting it up the right way—so we just kind of faked it.

In this case, we had to come up with a shot where the camera man and the dolly grip had to time the pan from where they started beneath the table to coming up to the top. We did one shot with nobody there. So it was just an empty frame with a table. Then we put the girls in and he had to feel what it was like to do that pan. And he did the same pan that way. Now, if the pan was off a little bit left, right, or center, the shot wouldn't work. So it was done by touch. But again, once we started putting people in the table to experiment, to do a test, to see what it would look like, we just all started laughing because it started working.

What always happens in these episodes, particularly on this show, is it takes on a life of its own. You see the magic before your eyes. You chuckle. You laugh. Sometimes you drop a tear, depending on the situation. It was really enjoyable to do that show.

Then we had to find a way to get a horse to attack in the Manor. It was really tricky to do because the Manor floor was linoleum, and here's a horse that's going to have all these problems slipping and sliding on the linoleum. So we had a, I forget the material that they put down, but it's something that the horse can grab onto. At the same time they had to put on different horseshoes so the horse wouldn't slide. And it was several confined rooms, so it was really difficult to do.

Again, a group of heads got together and figured out, how do we do this? What's the shot? How does this all work? And together it came out pretty good. When the horse attacked in the house, we believed the horse was in the house attacking, because it was.

NOON ORSATTI (STUNT COORDINATOR): That was another very, very fun episode. I got to use people—wranglers and cowboys—that you just don't get to see very often on a witch show. Those guys were fantastic. It was Rex Peterson and Mike Boyle. Those guys brought in the right horse, and we had to treat the floor correctly, because the horse had a lot of running to do and these are slippery floors. A lot of times we put down flooring that the horse could adhere to, so that we could do the rearing and the running and the dodging between the people. That was a big one. That was one of those where we had to brainstorm quite a bit.

We had Rex as the Headless Horseman. He rode the horse in a green stocking hood with very low visibility. He pulled it off every time, though. He was amazing. He really did a good job.

"I DREAM OF PHOEBE"
Original air date February 15, 2004

WRITTEN BY CURTIS KHEEL | DIRECTED BY JOHN KRETCHMER

Phoebe is tricked by a genie into thinking that she is helping her fight a demon, but it turns out the more vicious demon is the genie herself. Jinny, the genie, asks Phoebe to vanquish the demon, Bosk, who has imprisoned her. She and Chris find Bosk's desert cave, and moments later Bosk flies

in on his magic carpet and finds them. He drops Jinny's bottle in the ensuing fight and flies out before he is vanquished. When Phoebe picks up the bottle, she becomes Jinny's new master.

Jinny tells the Charmed Ones that Bosk is looking for the lost city of Zanbar. Before being swallowed by the desert, Zanbar was the seat of evil power. Once Bosk finds the site, he will use his last wish to bring it back into being, and there will be no stopping him. If Phoebe will wish Jinny free, she will not be able to grant his last wish and Zanbar will remain lost. Phoebe doesn't take the bait, but when Bosk attacks the Manor she has no choice and wishes Jinny free. Jinny escapes her bottle, but she is not a genie—she is a demon. She vanquishes Bosk and takes off on his magic carpet. Chris picks up the genie bottle and finds Phoebe inside.

Turns out there is a warning on the bottle that says an ancient sorcerer condemned a demon into the bottle, and whoever tries to set her free will take her place—hence, Genie Phoebe.

Jinny returns to the Manor for the inevitable fight for power and the bottle. Paige manages to contain Jinny in a crystal cage after Richard telekinetically moves her away from the bottle. He picks it up (with Phoebe still inside) and vanishes back to his house. Richard wishes Phoebe free, causing him to now take her place in the bottle. Jinny eventually breaks the force field of the crystal cage and tracks the bottle to Richard's house. She shimmers there and picks up the bottle, making her Richard's master. Jinny orders him to kill the Charmed Ones—and he must obey. She returns to the desert, with her bottle, just as her demon underlings have found Zanbar. Jinny wishes Richard to resurrect the city and again, he must obey. But back in San Francisco, Phoebe and Paige's spirits are still hanging around Richard's house, thanks to Leo's love and his Whitelighter abilities to rescue Piper before she completely crosses over to the other side—and if one Charmed One lives, the other two cannot move on, because Jinny's wish encompassed all three sisters. The ghosts of Phoebe and Paige go after Jinny. Phoebe possesses the demon's body and wishes Richard free, causing Jinny to be trapped in the bottle again. Richard picks it up and wishes for the Charmed Ones to be alive, and then wishes Zanbar be buried again. The bottle returns home with Chris, who then asks Leo to dispose of it.

During the entire genie saga, Chris is frantic to get his parents back together. If they don't reunite in the next few weeks, he will never be born. Phoebe agrees to help him, but it has to be on her terms, because Piper and Leo have been through so much.

And while Piper and Leo need to find each other again, Paige and Richard must part. He can't be around magic and lead a normal life, and she needs magic to fulfill her destiny, so there will be no happy ending for them.

"You can't just pop in from the future and play with people's lives because your big brother picked on you."
PHOEBE HALLIWELL

"If we don't do something soon, I could end up half fireman instead of half Whitelighter."
CHRIS PERRY

BEHIND THE SCENES

ALYSSA MILANO (PHOEBE) on dressing up in intricate costumes: They're just uncomfortable. It would be fun to do on any Halloween night, but not when you're walking around all day with a blond wig that's weighing your neck down and you're sore the next day. It's just uncomfortable more than anything. And you feel silly. But I look at it as an acting exercise. It's very humbling, to feel so ridiculously silly but portray and convey a sense of confidence. It's really been a lesson in feeling good on the inside, and that will come out in your acting. Some of those outfits, I'm telling you. I would look in the mirror and go, "Oh my God."

"THE COURTSHIP OF WYATT'S FATHER"

Original air date February 22, 2004

WRITTEN BY BRAD KERN | DIRECTED BY JOEL J. FEIGENBAUM

Wyatt's just turned a year old, but Chris is running out of time. If his parents don't get back together within twenty-four hours, he'll never be born. And now a Darklighter is after Leo, further jeopardizing the reunion.

The Darklighter actually winds up helping Chris, though. The family tracks the demon to an alley for what they expect to be the final showdown, and Piper blasts him before he can fire off another poison arrow at Leo. The concussion sends Piper, Leo, and the Darklighter, Damien, through a portal into the Ghostly Plane. But Darklighters can't make portals—and indeed, Damien is only a crossbow-for-hire—although he doesn't know who did the hiring. To make matters worse, good magic doesn't work in the Ghostly Plane. With their magic down, Piper says she and Leo will have to make her sisters use theirs to find them and bring them back. Leo explains that communication between planes takes practice and/or a special, intense bond. Like, say, sisterhood and the Power of Three?

As the day wears on, Chris starts to fade—literally. Phoebe and Paige have figured that Leo and Piper are in the Ghostly Plane. They retreat to the attic and say a spell to call their loved ones to cross over to them. But instead, the rapidly disappearing (and dying) Chris crosses over to the other side, where he finds Leo and Piper also in the attic. He communicates among the sisters, and Phoebe and Paige begin to formulate a plan. At the same time, Damien, who has studied his target well, has camped out across from the Ghostly Plane version of the Manor and fires at—and

hits—Leo. Piper now needs to find that portal even faster and get them back through it to save their lives.

Piper and Leo spend the night in the alley, waiting to be rescued. They reflect that their ties to each other are long and still loving. Leo confesses that he didn't go Up There as soon as he should have not only to protect Wyatt, but because he didn't want to let go of Piper. He never stopped loving her. Piper feels the same, and they spend what could be their last night—on any plane—together.

Phoebe and Paige get a little help in portals from Gideon, and they vanquish Damien just as he's about to finish off both Piper and Leo. Chris reappears—whole and apparently in good health—so Piper's sisters know what happened. Leo is healed by Gideon and finally makes his good-byes. He painfully leaves his family and takes his place among the Elders. Phoebe and Paige break the news to Piper that she's pregnant and—more shocking—that Chris is her son. Her first reaction is disbelief, but she quickly embraces the good news.

And the power behind the Darklighter attacks is finally revealed to be Gideon. Although he's a force of good magic, Gideon says the Elders made a mistake allowing Wyatt to be born—concentrating so much power in one being—and the child must be destroyed for the greater good.

"He was a really good boy and only made Mommy freeze the room once."

PIPER HALLIWELL

"It has to happen today or I don't happen."

CHRIS PERRY

BEHIND THE SCENES

HOLLY MARIE COMBS (PIPER): Like any couple, Piper and Leo went from the liking to dating to loving stage and then got married and had children. The fact that they both have supernatural powers didn't really change that. Piper and Leo are soul mates, and I think that shows through when it comes down to it, and I know the fans really like to see them together.

BRIAN KRAUSE (LEO): It's gone from me courting her to her liking me and me liking her, to getting married. You've seen our love blossom and then kind of hit the doldrums in marriage with the kids. Just like parents do. We love our kids, but it's harder to be a husband and wife. From experience I know, husbands and wives, it's a harder relationship once kids are brought along. It's just a fact. I think we've brought a bit of that into the show. Yet we've also brought the rekindling, the making up. The showing the "Yes, I love you, even though I don't show you" kind of aspect in the relationship.

    I think it's grown a lot. I know I've enjoyed it. It feels like Holly has as well. She's really a true giver. Now that she has a beautiful child, I think that her idea of marriage and understanding has grown as well. And she's grown as a person. So I think our relationship has taken on . . . there's a lot of realism there. It has a lot of depth. It's been fun to watch it grow. And sometimes it hits close to home, and then other times we just go find it. Maybe we argue here so we don't argue elsewhere.

"HYDE SCHOOL REUNION"

Original air date March 14, 2004

WRITTEN BY DAVID SIMKINS | DIRECTED BY JONATHAN WEST

An inadvertent spell, and intense emotions from seeing her old classmates at their high school reunion, turn Phoebe back into a teenage delinquent. Once she reverts—and realizes that this time around she has powers—Phoebe purposely casts a spell to return the others at the party back to their teenage mentality. She reunites with her old gang to cause some trouble, but one of them is missing. The ringleader, Rick, is in jail for robbing a liquor store, and things just aren't the same without him. So Phoebe says a spell to glamour her ex-boyfriend Todd, their friend Ramona, and herself, and visit the prison as Rick's "lawyers." Rick really is a bad seed, though, and once he sees that magic really exists, he uses Phoebe to commit more crimes. She has to make him appear to

be a guard so that he can break out of jail, and then he forces her to drive him to a point where he is going to hold up an armored truck.

Somewhere in between the jail break and the holdup, Phoebe's sense of right and wrong returns, and so does her normal adult state. Her sisters can finally find her, but when they call her back to the Manor, she demands that they return her to Rick, because he's put Ramona in danger. The desperate Rick then blackmails her into saying a spell to get the drivers out of the armored truck. When Rick enters the truck to get the money, Phoebe saves the drivers and chants another spell to make Rick think he's hearing the police on his tail. They vamoose, and she brings him to the Manor. Paige checks out all the commotion and hears Rick demand that Phoebe give him another face. Once the middle Charmed One gets the info on where he stashed Ramona, she confers with her sisters as to how best to deal with the criminal.

Paige recites a spell to make Rick look like Chris—who's being chased by Scabber demons. The Scabbers shimmer in and, thinking they've found Chris, vanquish Rick with their toxic yellow goo. Although it's hard for Phoebe to accept what she's done, she knows that Rick wasn't the guy she knew in high school anymore, just as she's no longer the rebellious teenager. After Phoebe reverses the spell she put on her reunion, no one remembers anything.

Meanwhile, Piper calls on her father, Victor, to see if he can find out why Chris is being so cold to her. It turns out that Chris and Victor are great buddies in the future, and the Whitelighter opens up to his grandfather. He explains that Piper will die when he's fourteen, and if he avoids getting close to her now, he won't feel as close later when she's gone. Victor suggests that may be all the more reason to get close to her now. Chris knows in his heart that his grandfather is right, and when he shows his true affection for Piper, she's thrilled. Besides, his coming back may have already changed that part of the future.

"He was dying and I was crying and it's all very complicated."   **PIPER HALLIWELL**

"I kill demons every day, think I'm afraid of you?"   **PHOEBE HALLIWELL**

BEHIND THE SCENES

NANETTE NEW (DEPARTMENT HEAD KEY MAKEUP ARTIST): I think the personality and the beauty of these girls and their acting ability . . . they're just fun. I don't see too many people being able to pull this sort of a show off. The demons and the . . . you know, it's pretty dark at times. And they seem to keep it really fun. I find myself watching them in the rehearsals and watching them shoot. I just can't believe that they do it. I'm following the script wondering, how are they going to do that? And they do it. They do it every time. And it's wonderful. The show is fun. Oh my God, it's so much fun.

DANIELLA GSCHWENDTNER (COSTUME SUPERVISOR): We try to fit the costumes very early, because when I know what the girls are wearing, I can go through the line and hold colors together. Even though you don't always manage; there is sometimes a closeness that I would prefer not to have. But, you know, you get one of them maybe late and you have to go with it.

When we get the girls three or four days before the show starts, there's a lot you can do. You can move a change around and make sure they're not in the same colors or go back to one of them and change it. When I set up their lines, I try to prevent as much overlap as I can, but you can't always. I think the name of the game is the sooner you can get it figured out, the better. It allows time to accessorize. I really try to take the time to put belts with everything and the right jewelry. Just really spend a little extra time on the accessories. Sometimes when you wait too long with the fitting, you don't have the time to do that. I think those little things do make a difference.

"SPIN CITY"

Original air date April 18, 2004

WRITTEN BY DOUG E. JONES & ANDY REASER | DIRECTED BY MEL DAMSKI

Chris is infected by a Spider demon so that he will help her trap her next victim: Piper. Spider demons emerge every hundred years to capture and feed off the most powerful magical being they can detect. And, with Piper carrying baby Chris, she is doubly magical, which is irresistible to the Spider demon.

The poison from the infection slowly transforms Chris into a Spider demon. Although he fights giving his mother over to the demon, he is ultimately unable to resist the evil that is overtaking him. But this is not a family that easily gives up one of their own.

With Chris temporarily on the wrong side of things, and Piper trapped in the Spider demon's cocoon, Phoebe and Paige turn to Leo for help. Phoebe tells Leo that Chris is his son, and after the initial shock, the Elder fights even harder to take back his child. Chris orbs Piper's cocoon to the

Spider demon's lair, and his family follows, armed with the potion to vanquish the demon as well as an antidote to cure Chris. The lair is impenetrable, but the two remaining Charmed Ones manage to lure the Spider demon out—with the help of some magical friends (more about them in a minute). When the sisters get ready to hurl the potion, the demon reverts to her eight-legged state, whereupon an ogre simply steps on her and kills her. The webs she had spun to encase Piper disintegrate, and the eldest Charmed One is met by her Elder husband. Leo orbs her out of the lair to the safety of her sisters.

But Chris is still infected, and he's one angry spider. He spins another impenetrable web that locks his father back in the cave, and he works over Leo as he works on his issues. Outside, Piper drinks the antidote, reasoning that it will cure baby Chris, and therefore, big Chris. She's right, but even in his normal state, Chris is so angry at Leo that he continues to pummel him.

Determined to find out why Chris hates him so much, Leo chooses to remain with his family and not return Up There. Gideon chastises him about shirking his responsibilities to the other Elders, but Leo is resolute. He packs Piper and Wyatt off to Magic School to keep them safe until Chris is born, and he vows to keep trying to make things right with his younger son.

And what about those aforementioned magical creatures? A wicked witch has been cursing them. A tall leprechaun, a cuddly ogre, and a wood nymph who looks more like a longshoreman are just some of those who turn to Paige for help. She devises a spell to vanquish the wicked witch, which restores the magical creatures to normal. They return the favor when the Charmed Ones need help with the Spider demon.

Meanwhile, Phoebe has done the math, and if she's going to have the little girl she saw in her vision quest, she's got to find the daddy soon. Alas, speed dating her way through half the men in San Francisco yields no results as yet.

"Well, you'll be happy to know you're a boy." **PIPER HALLIWELL**

"Bug spray. We shoulda used bug spray." **PAIGE MATTHEWS**

BEHIND THE SCENES

DREW FULLER (CHRIS): It was a strained relationship from the beginning [with Leo]. Chris was carrying so many demons . . . bad choice of words. Because he was carrying so many issues from his growing up, and inevitably, when he sees his father again, those issues are still there because it's still his father. Whatever time period it is. I did play a lot of animosity toward Leo. The case was that Leo was never there for me growing up. He was always off fighting Wyatt. I was always the second son. I had all this animosity toward (a) my brother and (b) my father. Not so much animosity for my mom. I was scared and didn't want to get close to her; now she's going to leave soon. So I was really alienated. And had a lot of emotional frustration just pent up.

I loved her, but at the same time knowing that she was going to pass away, how close do you really want to get to them? Do you want to feel all that pain again? Because Chris had worked so hard to get over that, to close that chapter. To come back and see his mom, beautiful and young, he wants to be close to her but he can't. He spent ten years of his life sealing that door to the pain.

"CRIMES AND WITCH-DEMEANORS" *Original air date April 25, 2004*
WRITTEN BY HENRY ALONSO MYERS | DIRECTED BY JOHN KRETCHMER

Phoebe forces a premonition, and the consequences bring back the Cleaners, whose changes to the events result in Darryl winding up on death row. This is not acceptable to the Charmed Ones, and they demand a hearing with the Tribunal—a council made up of Elders and demons to monitor magic and make sure that no one finds out about its use—no matter the cost. Gideon acts as their "attorney," and to their surprise the opposing counsel is Barbas, the Demon of Fear. The sisters had vanquished him to the fires of hell, but Barbas has been granted a temporary leave of absence to "prosecute" the case. He manages to change the focus of the trial from the Charmed Ones challenging the actions of the Cleaners to challenging the Charmed Ones themselves.

The ordeal takes place in a chamber in a black limbo, where the faces of the Tribunal float above the participants. In the center is the enchanted Circle of Truth, which reads thoughts and shows what needs to be seen. In it the sisters can see Darryl in prison. The Tribunal has accelerated time, so they have but a few hours to make their case and save his life. They also see instances when they've exposed magic—but they argue that they have always managed to clean up things on their own.

While Phoebe and Paige are in the chamber, the very pregnant Piper is safe at Magic School. Leo and Chris are dispatched to find out how this all came about, and they must put aside their differences to save their family. They discover that Barbas was working with phantasms—demons who can travel back and forth from hell to Earth. He used them to set up Phoebe and Paige so that he could cut a deal with the Tribunal to try the case. And, if he wins, he gets a "get out of hell free" card.

The Tribunal brings Piper to the court to hand down its verdict: The Charmed Ones can keep their magic, but Darryl must die to protect the exposure. The sisters say that if Darryl dies, they will give up their powers. Barbas is reveling in his luck when Leo and Chris orb in with Inspector Sheridan—who just happened to be in the right place at the right time to tape the vanquish of the phantasm that started the whole thing. They throw her onto the Circle of Truth, and another phantasm emerges from the police inspector and admits that it was working for Barbas. The Tribunal reverses its decision and Darryl is saved at the last minute.

Barbas argues that the Charmed Ones are still a threat to the exposure of magic—particularly Phoebe, who has been forcing her premonitions. The Tribunal agrees and strips the middle sister of her active powers. She will be able to earn them back if all the sisters are more careful. Phoebe acknowledges that she has been at fault and accepts the decision.

Their work done, the Tribunal leaves. The Charmed Ones orb out, but Barbas and Gideon remain in the chamber. The Demon of Fear reasons that he did just enough to win his case, because he hasn't been sent back to purgatory. He then taunts Gideon, saying that he knows the Elder's greatest fear—that the Charmed Ones will somehow find out that he is the one who is after Wyatt.

"Do we even get along in the future?"	**PAIGE MATTHEWS**
"We called for justice, not the Demon of Fear."	**PHOEBE HALLIWELL**

BEHIND THE SCENES

NANCY SOLOMON (SCRIPT SUPERVISOR): We had one episode with the floating heads, "Crimes and Witch-demeanors." That was a tricky one because we had so many looks. We had two heads on one side, two heads on the other. With that whole council thing happening, there were a lot of things that we had to match with effects. We had several scenes in that room. We had movement of a lot of people. We would block shoot it and make sure everything was matching between our characters and the heads, because those were all separate entities that we shot. We had to make sure that the good people and the bad people were looking in the correct directions. For every scene it was something different, because there were people crossing. So we had to make sure they were looking camera left to right, then they were looking right to left. And we had holograms happening in the middle.

"A WRONG DAY'S JOURNEY INTO RIGHT"

Original air date May 2, 2004

WRITTEN BY CAMERON LITVACK | DIRECTED BY DEREK JOHANSEN

With Piper safely tucked away at Magic School and Phoebe having no active powers, Paige has been doing all the magical chores, and it's exhausting being the only functioning Charmed One. Not having time to go out and find a Mr. Right to help her relieve her stress, Paige conjures one. And, just as Piper's Mr. Right was perfect for her, Paige's is the ideal man for the weary young witch. What Paige doesn't realize is that she got a two-for-one sale at the cauldron. In addition to her angelic Mr. Right, there is a demonic "Mr. Wrong," aka Vincent, running around the Underworld. But

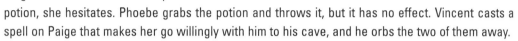

because Paige made him, Vincent is sparing Innocents and vanquishing other demons. Or rather, he hires blond bombshells clad in black leather—known as Demonatrixes—to use their deadly throwing stars to do it for him.

Vincent is the reflection of Paige's dark side, complete with Paige's knowledge and powers. He loves her and appeals to her desire to be free, independent, and able to use her magic without fear of consequences. When Paige has the chance to vanquish him with a potion, she hesitates. Phoebe grabs the potion and throws it, but it has no effect. Vincent casts a spell on Paige that makes her go willingly with him to his cave, and he orbs the two of them away.

Leo figures that the vanquishing potion didn't work because for one thing, Vincent's not real, and for another, Paige made her Mr. Right—and by extension, Mr. Wrong—invincible, so that nothing would take them away from her before their time was up. Phoebe whips up a potion and tries it out on Mr. Right. If he can be made real, so can Vincent—and that will make him susceptible to the vanquishing potion. It works, not only giving the former figment of Paige's imagination life, but also giving back Phoebe some of her self-confidence, by proving that she can still be an effective and good witch without active powers.

Phoebe heads to the Underworld undercover as a Demonatrix. She finds Paige and Vincent (named, by the way, for Paige's first love—a boy who promised her the world), and also Piper, whom Paige has orbed there from Magic School. Getting rid of one sister would be the first step in dark Paige's dark journey to her coveted freedom. Thankfully, Phoebe saves both of her sisters. They have no potion, but the middle Halliwell gets Paige away from Victor and tells her older sister to blow up the demon. And just like that, he's demon dust, because as Phoebe correctly surmised, when Mr. Right became real, so did Vincent. With the dark influence gone, Paige snaps out of the spell and returns to her sisters and her senses. She sends Mr. Right out into the world to face life and all it has to offer.

As if two conjured men weren't enough of a problem, Chris winds up in jail. And, after almost dying because of the Charmed Ones (again), Darryl has no desire to help them. Leo needs Chris's help to track Vincent, and when he uncharacteristically voices contempt for the rules, and genuine concern for his second-born, Chris's barriers begin to break down. Father and son aren't reconciled yet, but they're getting closer.

"C'mon, I'm pregnant, not stupid." **PIPER HALLIWELL**

"A demon that drives a Porsche? That's different." **PHOEBE HALLIWELL**

NANCY SOLOMON (SCRIPT SUPERVISOR): Every eight days it changes. It's not so much my job changes, it's the energy that changes. It can shift very dramatically sometimes. The energy shifts every eight days with a new director. What each director pulls from me is different. Some directors will pull from me differently than others. You have to be a chameleon. You have to be able to adapt to every situation. To be there for them and know when to hang loose a little more. I'm always making sure their show looks great; that continuity matches everywhere. Sometimes people will pull more. They'll ask more questions of me, or whatever. Sometimes less.

"WITCH WARS"

Original air date May 9, 2004

WRITTEN BY KRISTA VERNOFF | DIRECTED BY DAVID JACKSON

Having chased down more demons than they can count, the Charmed Ones consider the idea that maybe the threat to Wyatt is not demonic. Phoebe offers nonmagical statistics that prove someone they consider to be a friend could really be their enemy. And, Chris explains, time is running out—whatever happens to Wyatt happens before baby Chris is born. When Gideon hears this, he realizes that it may not be long until the sisters discover that he is the one trying to get rid of Wyatt. Conveniently for the Elder, two demons, Corr and Clea, have devised a demonic reality show that plays perfectly into his plans to throw the good witches off his scent.

A series of witch killings turns out to be linked to *Witch Wars*, a game show that is sweeping the Underworld. Demons face off against each other to kill a witch. The winner gets glory—and the powers of the witch he slays. The losers' powers revert to the show's "producers," Corr and Clea, who are using their popular creation to amass enough power to rule their fellow demons. But they need to attract some Upper-Level demons to accomplish this, so Gideon's offer to involve the Charmed Ones is just what they've been looking for.

The Elder arranges for the sisters to unwittingly participate in the "game." When Paige vanquishes a Brute demon, he leaves behind the power-sucking athame given to all *Witch Wars* contestants and a crystal that plays the program as it airs. The Charmed Ones consult with Leo and Chris, and they realize what's happening. It's time for this show to be cancelled.

This new development works perfectly for Gideon. He can get the sisters off his trail by making them believe that the gamemasters, Corr and Clea, are the ones who have been after Wyatt all along. Of course, the demons are more than happy to take on the witches and their family. It will not only make great television, it will give them Charmed powers when they win. Still insisting that Piper remain safe at Magic School, Phoebe and Leo orb into the "production studio" in the demons' cave. Clea is the only one there, and Leo kills her with the power-sucking athame—an unlikely deed for an Elder, and a painful act of last resort for a concerned father. He throws the athame to Phoebe, who absorbs its vast accumulated powers. They orb to the attic just in time to save Paige and Chris, who are fighting off Corr. All the powers he's gotten from the contestants have made him invincible to Paige's potions. But now all-powerful herself, Phoebe easily vanquishes the demon. She then looks right into the camera and asks, "Who's next?"

After a bit of a demon-killing rampage with her borrowed firepower, Phoebe has Paige stab her with the athame, as it's the only way to remove the powers. The family is convinced that they've destroyed the threat to Wyatt and that he will now be safe—or as safe as one can be when you're a Halliwell. Gideon is relieved that his secret is also safe, but Sigmund says he can no longer live with what the Elder is planning to do. When he says he's going to tell the Charmed Ones the truth, Gideon protects himself by killing his friend and former ally.

"We're the Charmed . . . One."   **PAIGE MATTHEWS**

"You'd think demons would've invented reality television, but somehow humans beat us to it."
                                                          CLEA

"Sacrifices must be made for the greater good."   **GIDEON**

BEHIND THE SCENES

E. DUKE VINCENT (EXECUTIVE PRODUCER): I enjoyed the year we did with Julian [McMahon]. That was very different. The audience didn't enjoy it as much as I did. It was a very dark year. And we turned it around the following year when we brought Chris back from the future. That was a much lighter year. We made a very determined effort to lighten up the show from the dark show it was the years before. And I think I enjoyed that as much as anything, because we were able to turn around a situation that we all loved in the first place. That's always a challenge. So whenever you have a challenge like that and you manage to succeed in turning it around, that I enjoyed more than anything.

JIM CONWAY (CO-EXECUTIVE PRODUCER): I think when they're big long arcs that work well, they're fantastic. There are times when we got a little too dark. The year before Cole died became oppressively dark, with the whole Cole story and the marriage and all that. I think toward the end of the Avatar thing with changing the world around and all that, that was very cool, but it ended at just the right time. When those arcs take over the storytelling, I think it becomes a little burdensome. When it's more an arc like having a baby, where it's something that doesn't completely take over the show, it's a lot better. But Brad always thinks long term for the show, because his secret is, it's character arcs that make the show work so well. But as a whole the arcs are great, because it gives the audience something they want to come back for each week. And they get very involved in those arcs.

"IT'S A BAD, BAD, BAD, BAD WORLD, PART 1"

Original air date May 16, 2004

WRITTEN BY JEANNINE RENSHAW | DIRECTED BY JON PARÉ

Chris is anxious to return home to the future before he is born in the present, and Gideon is equally as eager to bid farewell to Chris's brother, Wyatt. Working with his evil twin in a mirror universe, Gideon manipulates the Charmed Ones and their family into believing that a portal created with a Power of Three spell he has written will send Chris to the future. In reality, it is a gateway to the mirror universe, and the good Chris and Leo (who insisted on accompanying his son home) wind up in the evil world. Because the same things happen on each side of the mirror, the bad Chris and Leo step through the portal into the Charmed Ones' good universe. Every second the worlds are disturbed by one side crossing over into the other, good and evil are out of balance, and the Grand Design is at risk.

Therefore, Gideon urges Phoebe and Paige to act quickly. Since the sisters can't reason with the evil versions of Leo and Chris—and Paige has them safely trapped in a crystal cage for now—the Elder suggests that the two sisters change places with *their* evil twins. Both sets of sisters will undoubtedly be able to bring their men back home. Phoebe and Paige buy the idea, but when they step through the portal, they don't cross their counterparts, but find them waiting on the other side. Evil Gideon explains that the two worlds mirror each other when everything is in balance, but with the first switch, the balance was thrown off, and so was the mirror effect. With two Phoebes and two Paiges on one side of the mirror, all bets are off.

The two sets of sisters find trying to vanquish one another a futile attempt. They think exactly the same and fight exactly the same, so they cancel each other out. When good Phoebe and Paige can't find their Chris and Leo in any of the normal places, the middle Halliwell reasons that they have to reverse things. Evil is the norm in this universe, so the Underworld is where you'd find good. Sure enough, that's where they find their family, as well as the most powerful demon of the evil mirror world—Good Barbas, the Demon of Hope. Well, that'll take some getting used to. . . .

While all of this cross-universe pollination is happening, Piper has gone into labor—which is all part of Gideons' plan. They've isolated Piper from her family in both universes, so when she has to go to the hospital, each Piper must turn to the Elder to care for Wyatt.

But his cover is about to be blown. Good Barbas doesn't possess enough power to open the portal, but he can try to unite the Phoebes and Paiges to fight in a common cause. He brings the evil sisters to his Underworld garden by preying on their greatest hope—to reunite with their Chris

and Leo, who are still trapped on the good side of the mirror. The two sets of sisters can't fight their instincts to vanquish each other, but when Good Barbas drops the bomb that the Gideons are the ones who want to harm their respective Wyatts, family takes precedence over point of view. They work together to return the balance of good and evil so that they can vanquish their respective Elders. Without either Piper, there is still no Power of Three to reopen the portal—but the Power of Four seems to work just fine.

With evil back in its place, it's time to visit Piper in the hospital and then vanquish an Elder. But when Phoebe and Paige step outside the Manor, their world is a bit too bright and cheery—and they find that even a small indiscretion is now a capital offense. Enforcing the law, the security guard who previously issued Phoebe a parking ticket for blocking her neighbor's driveway now shoots her for her crime.

GOOD PHOEBE: *"Nice knuckles, brass?"*

EVIL PHOEBE: *"No, Tiffany's."*

"The Charmed Ones working for evil, who'd a' thunk it?"   **PAIGE MATTHEWS**

"Who do I have to kill so we can get out of here?"   **EVIL CHRIS**

BEHIND THE SCENES

BRIAN KRAUSE (LEO): I think every person has a dark or evil side. You know, you put the leather pants on me and spike my hair, you know, there it is. It was easy. Leo wears a cardigan and shaves.

The physicality of it and how we shot it was interesting. To have dialogue with myself was a trip. To bounce it off and have rhythm was a good challenge. In the whole seven and a half years I've been here I've had a chance to do some really challenging things. I don't think that on any other show—you could name them all out there—I'd be able to do the things that I had a chance to do here. So many characters: from being pregnant to being in the military. It's a bit like Scott Bakula from *Quantum Leap*. I always thought, what a great role. A guy gets to be everything. The four of us here have gotten to be everything. The girls have played everything. You get to play so many things. It's really fun. It's something that I'll always appreciate.

AUDREY STERN (DEPARTMENT HEAD KEY HAIRSTYLIST): I had so much fun doing Brian's hair. It took a while to do that. I had my assistant help me with that—twisting it piece by piece and drying it. It was such a great look for him, because he never changes really. Except now we're letting his hair go out.

At the very beginning when I came on, Spelling really had specific looks that they really wanted to try to keep, especially with the guys. Not so much with the principal girls. It's the same thing with our demons. Now [in Season Eight] we're changing the whole look of the demons. We're trying to make them sexier. Not so dark. A little more kind of street-smart demons, I guess you could say.

At that point when Brian's hair was that look at the beginning of the series, we just kept it. Then we started changing things. One time I gave him a real shaved look. They hated it. Oh my God, I heard that for days. But getting it longer is okay, because it's sexier. And they like that. That's our show too. Trying to make everything look as sexy as you can get, especially the girls.

"IT'S A BAD, BAD, BAD, BAD WORLD, PART 2"

Original air date May 16, 2004

WRITTEN BY CURTIS KHEEL | DIRECTED BY JAMES L. CONWAY

Phoebe proves easier to heal than the current situation of the world. By intervening in the Grand Design, Gideon allowed too much good to corrupt the mirror universe, and the only way to get the balance back is to allow a great evil to corrupt the other side. And who better to enlist in perpetrating a great evil than Barbas? Gideon joins forces with the Demon of Fear, saying that together they can accomplish his goal of destroying Wyatt, and in the process give Barbas back a world where evil has a chance to exist.

Phoebe and Paige have to tread lightly so as not to be maimed or killed for a minor trans-gression in this perpetually sunny new world. They were not affected by the shift because they—along with Leo and Chris—were crossing through the portal when it occurred. Not so for the unusually perky Piper, however. This suits Gideon, because Piper has the greatest influence over her siblings and can get them off his back. He has Barbas plant an image in Piper's mind that her sisters are killed by the Elders for condemning Gideon. Her greatest fear is losing her family, so she writes a spell that will protect her sisters—by making them happy, happy inhabitants of this new world, where they no longer suspect Gideon.

With the Charmed Ones out of the way, Gideon knows that Leo has probably figured out his game plan by now, and he turns his attention to his former pupil. He instructs Barbas that the way to get to Leo is to think of him as a father, not an Elder. The demon catches up with the concerned father at the hospital, where he's about to confront Piper to find out what spell she cast on her sisters. Barbas plants an illusion in Leo's mind so that he sees the grown-up, evil Wyatt—the child he could not save. This wounds him emotionally, and then Evil Wyatt makes it physical, stabbing his father with Excalibur. As the dream fades, Leo hears Chris calling for him. He orbs back to the Manor in time to find his younger son dying—the victim of Gideon's athame. The misguided Elder then orbs out with baby Wyatt.

Leo orbs back to the hospital with the news about Chris, and it jolts the sisters back to reality. Paige returns to the Manor to be with her nephew, while Phoebe stays with Piper, who is having a very difficult delivery. Leo is ready for his final showdown with Gideon, but he first orbs home to try to save Chris. But the wounds were caused by Gideon's magic, and only Gideon can heal them. Chris dies in his father's arms and then fades away, as if he'd never been there.

Meanwhile, the odd coupling of the Elder and the demon face Wyatt in Barbas's lair. Gideon is cautious, knowing the baby's abilities, but Barbas just dives in for the kill. Wyatt orbs out, and they wind up chasing the child all over the Underworld. Gideon finally lures Wyatt back by impersonating Leo's voice to call for the baby. When Wyatt orbs in, Gideon traps him in a crystal cage. He calls for Barbas and gives the demon the athame. But instead of going for Wyatt, Barbas stabs Gideon—and then morphs into Leo. The Whitelighter-turned-Elder calls for the mirror from Gideon's office, having devised his plan along with his evil counterpart. But the great evil that will restore the balance of both worlds must be perpetrated by good. Evil Leo watches as his twin slowly and painfully kills Gideon, thus eliminating him in the mirror universe as well. Knowing that the two worlds can never cross again, the Leos destroy the mirror.

The real Barbas flames in just as Leo begins his final confrontation with Gideon. Not wanting to be vanquished—or get in the middle of a standoff between Elders—he remains out of sight, and then flames back out, living to perpetuate his own evil another day.

Luckily, Leo's act turned the world back to normal. Night falls again, evil is given a chance to survive with good, and Piper's doctor snaps back to reality in time to save both mother and son. Leo brings Wyatt to the hospital to meet his new baby brother and return to the arms of his loving aunts. He and baby Chris join Piper in the recovery room—the picture of a perfect, happy (but not too happy) family—and the hospital doors magically close on another season of *Charmed*.

"This isn't the world we want Chris to be born into."　　　　　　**PHOEBE HALLIWELL**

"Looks like we didn't lose him after all."　　　　　　**PAIGE MATTHEWS**

BEHIND THE SCENES

DREW FULLER (CHRIS): That was bittersweet. I knew that that was going to be my last episode. Bitter Chris . . . Evil Chris. I didn't approach it any differently, because Chris always had so much anger anyway. They're, like, "We're making Evil Chris." I'm, like, "Chris wasn't so much evil, but he was already pissed. I've already spent those emotions." I spent them in "Spin City" where I was so angry at the end, yelling and screaming and beating up Leo. Evil Chris needed to be more Sinister Chris, in hindsight. But we watch and we learn and we realize . . . I probably would have done that differently.

ALYSSA MILANO (PHOEBE) on playing different roles on the show: That's been the fun part. Absolutely. I was thinking about that the other day. I was watching *ER*. I cannot imagine what it must be like to be on a show that's run that long that doesn't get to do the things we get to do. It must be so monotonous. We get to turn evil or whatever. It's really the fun of this. There are no boundaries.

Because we turn into so many things, you don't want to be repetitive in your choices as an actress. You want to change it up and do it differently. And that's the challenge after eight years. You've pretty much done everything. It's still fun, though.

DANIELLA GSCHWENDTNER (COSTUME SUPERVISOR): That top on Rose was one that stuck out to me. Those are the kind of outfits I love, because they're sharp looking. I think that is top fashion in a way, even though we call it demonic. I know Rose's top was Gucci. It was just fun to do that edgy look on them. Normally I stay away from black as much as I can with the girls, because the demons are always in black. But having them in black head to toe was a good look.

CLOSING THE DOOR ON SEASON SIX

On screen, the sixth season of *Charmed* ended with a death and a birth. Oddly enough, it was the death and birth of the same character: Chris. Considering that his character partly existed to ensure that he was conceived, it wasn't surprising that Drew Fuller left the series at the end of the season, since Chris could not exist as both a baby and a full-grown man in the same time line. But that didn't stop him from making visits in future episodes.

DREW FULLER (CHRIS) recalls a personal highlight from working on *Charmed*: The thing that sticks out most in my mind was when they told us there were a couple Make-A-Wish Foundation kids coming around. I had never been on a show old enough to ever entertain the possibility of having Make-A-Wish Foundation children to visit. They showed up and they were beautiful and I never experienced anything like that in my entire life. How excited they were about seeing the Book of Shadows and walking through the sets and playing with Alyssa, Holly, and Rose, and Brian, and me. They really had all these great questions for us. We weren't actors. We were *them*. One hundred percent. I was Chris.

I was just so affected. I was overwhelmed. I remember having to excuse myself. I went off into my trailer and I cried a while because they really grasped how beautiful life is. They're not sitting there feeling sorry for themselves. They're beautiful. They're happy. They're just so excited about life and being here and grateful for every little thing. It really puts things in perspective and, on another level, why every actor should cherish what they do. On so many levels we don't even have an idea, I mean, to brush the surface. I was overwhelmed. One of the most profound moments on *Charmed*.

THE *CHARMED* EPISODE TITLE PUNS

VALHALLEY OF THE DOLLS: In Norse mythology, Valhalla is the great hall where the souls of heroes who died in battle spend eternity. *Valley of the Dolls* is a book written by Jacqueline Susann. It was made into a film in 1967.

FORGET ME . . . NOT: A forget-me-not is a plant with small clusters of blue flowers.

POWER OF THREE BLONDES: Reference to the power of the Charmed Ones having passed into the hands of three fair-haired women.

LOVE'S A WITCH: A pun based on the idea that, at times, *life* (not love) can be particularly difficult.

MY THREE WITCHES: *My Three Sons* was a TV series of the 1960s and early 1970s, starring Fred MacMurray playing the widowed father of three boys.

SOUL SURVIVOR: Reference to being the lone (sole) survivor of a tragedy, though in this case, it refers to the saving of one's soul.

SWORD AND THE CITY: The TV series *Sex and the City* premiered in 1998. It was based on a series of columns in the *New York Observer* by Candace Bushnell.

LITTLE MONSTERS: A reference to particularly difficult children. Also a movie released in 1989 starring Fred Savage and Howie Mandel.

CHRIS-CROSSED: "Crisscross" means to move back and forth, through, or over. Here it refers to traveling through time.

WITCHSTOCK: The village of Woodstock, New York, lent its name to a historic rock music festival that took place in a nearby town in 1969.

PRINCE CHARMED: The character of Prince Charming appears in many fairy tales, particularly those centered around damsels in distress.

USED KARMA: This pun, based on the concept of used cars, refers to karma, which in Hinduism and Buddhism is the concept of determining a person's destiny.

THE LEGEND OF SLEEPY HALLIWELL: *The Legend of Sleepy Hollow* is a novella written by Washington Irving in the early nineteenth century. It tells the story of a schoolteacher's encounter with a headless horseman.

I DREAM OF PHOEBE: *I Dream of Jeannie* was a TV show in the 1960s starring Barbara Eden and Larry Hagman.

THE COURTSHIP OF WYATT'S FATHER: *The Courtship of Eddie's Father* was both a movie (1963) and a TV series (1969-1972). The TV show starred Bill Bixby as a widowed father with a young son.

HYDE SCHOOL REUNION: The "Hyde" in the title refers to *Dr. Jekyll and Mr. Hyde*, a book written by Robert Louis Stevenson in the late nineteenth century. It is the story of a scientist who developed an elixir that could separate the good and evil in his nature, creating a split personality and resulting in the murderous Mr. Hyde.

SPIN CITY: The original reference to this pun is that "Sin City" is a nickname for Las Vegas. However, the rhyme was also used as the title of a TV show that premiered in 1996, originally starring Michael J. Fox.

CRIMES AND WITCH-DEMEANORS: *Crimes and Misdemeanors* is a movie written and directed by Woody Allen. It was released in 1989.

A WRONG DAY'S JOURNEY INTO RIGHT: *Long Day's Journey into Night* is an auto-biographical play written by Eugene O'Neill in the early 1940s (though it was not formally staged until 1956, three years after his death).

WITCH WARS: *Star Wars* was the first of a series of movies produced by George Lucas. The original *Star Wars: A New Hope* was released in 1977.

IT'S A BAD, BAD, BAD, BAD WORLD: *It's a Mad, Mad, Mad, Mad World* is a film released in 1963, starring Spencer Tracy and an ensemble cast of comedic actors.

EPISODE GUIDE

Season Seven

INTRODUCTION

The new season of *Charmed* also came with a new workplace for the crew. After five seasons at RayArt Studios in Woodland Hills, California, the production moved onto the lot of Paramount Pictures, the only major television and movie studio still headquartered in Hollywood.

The move's effect on the show was threefold. It provided new exterior locations around the lot and on the studio's New York Street backlot. But at the same time, the production lost space by moving into smaller soundstages than the ones at RayArt. Ask anyone on the crew the most dramatic change, however, and the first thing they'll mention is the fact that most of them had lived in the neighborhood of the old studio and now had a longer drive to work.

JIM CONWAY (CO-EXECUTIVE PRODUCER): Here the studio's got a New York street, which is like downtown city streets. We used to have to cheat in front of our building in Woodland Hills' downtown streets, which we did very badly. Or had to go into the city to shoot. To save money, it's nice not to have to go get vehicles and go on location. So here part of our deal is to use the New York street once a week. So now we have exterior scenes in coffee shops, walking down the street. It opens the show up and makes the show more like it's shot in San Francisco. We've used the theater. We used the little quad area. We've used just about every square foot you could shoot. It's been great.

Being on the lot makes you feel much more legitimate than when you're shooting in warehouses. A lot of TV shows are shot in warehouses all over L.A. because they're cheaper. But you drive to work, there's nobody else around you except other warehouses. You sort of just feel like you're isolated. Now when you come to a studio, well, for me, when you get here you feel like you're in Hollywood. You have movie stars around. You get to see people from other shows. Other people that you know. So it feels good. It's a ten-minute drive to the writers. A ten-minute drive to the editing. So it's a much better situation. Except the drive in is longer.

JON PARÉ (PRODUCER): Moving to Paramount's been a great move. A little bit longer of a drive for most of us that live in the valley. But once we get here, we enter into this wonderful creative world where the sky really is the limit. We're making movies in Hollywood. It's really fabulous. Between being an AD and a production manager and a producer and director, I've been working in warehouses for twenty years. So moving back to a lot has really been a great experience. It makes you feel like you really have the ability to make movies.

As far as the show's concerned, we've found that we don't have to go on local location as much. We'll occasionally go to the house, which is ten minutes down the street. And we find that the lot has wonderful locations. Before we came here we went to several other lots to see what they had to offer. This lot just had a lot. It had all of the stage space we needed. It had these wonderful locations with New York Street. I remember taking a walk down the streets with Brad [Kern], and we just started looking at all the neat areas and all the neat shots and they just started making you think of stories. And started making you think of all the wonderful things that we could accomplish here.

Once we got here, we started, out of necessity, using areas the studio never used as shooting locations. They themselves were surprised at how creative we were being, using some of the spots we were using. We'd be walking into a building saying, "Hey, we could turn this into a bedroom." So we've been able to get really creative in a really creative environment. It was a jolt of energy for all of us.

NOON ORSATTI (STUNT COORDINATOR): For a lot of our things we used to have a lot of quick fixes at the old stage. We had little rigs that made everything so simple. Here it's different in the case that a lot of our rigging had to go way up in the air now. It's a little problematic, but we're dealing with it, figuring out new ways to do things. We've been able to utilize this New York Street out here. Some of our stunts have been able to get a little bit broader and bigger. We've had guys falling out of burning buildings. That's been a real plus.

PAUL STAHELI (PRODUCTION DESIGNER): When we moved from there to here I lost twenty thousand square feet of floor space to put sets on. What new sets we've done we've had to constrict. Make them much smaller. The crew has much less space with which to work, which is hard on them.

We do have the rest of the lot. We have the backlot and the street fifteen times [per season]. We can get it more, perhaps, but then it costs more money. And we have the grounds fifteen times during a season. Since we've come to Paramount, this time I think we're a hundred percent studio show. [In Season Seven] I think we went out six times in the whole year. Prior to coming here we ofttimes, I don't know what the average would be, but I would say the first year I think we probably averaged two to three days out, out of eight. It got progressively fewer until the last year, probably we maybe did one day every ten shooting days, we would go somewhere other than the studio. Here we can't do that. So it has closed it in more.

THE EPISODES

"A CALL TO ARMS"

Original air date September 12, 2004

WRITTEN BY BRAD KERN | DIRECTED BY JAMES L. CONWAY

Gideon's attempt on Wyatt's life is still being felt by the baby's parents two months after the fact. Piper is afraid to leave the house with her boys, and Leo is obsessed with finding Gideon's partner in crime—Barbas. He is also confused, not knowing who's good and who's bad anymore. The Demon of Fear plays right into his mind-set, prodding Leo to attack any Elder he sees. This causes the Elder Zola to warn the sisters about Leo and what consequences he may face, and also about a powerful threat looming on the horizon—one that will need every force of good in the fold.

Paige and Phoebe try to restore some sanity for a while by sending Piper and Leo to the wedding of their friend Christy. The Hindu ceremony invokes the spirits of the goddess and god who created all things to bless the union. Unfortunately, the spirits bless and then possess—Piper suddenly has six arms, and Leo's feeling more potent than he has in years. Paige consults the Book of Shadows and finds that Shakti, the Hindu goddess of creation, and Shiva, god of destruction, created all things, but if they consummate their love again, all things will be obliterated, and the universe will be reborn. Shakti and Shiva are also considered to be the ultimate lovers, so getting their current incarnations to keep their hands off each other is no easy task.

Paige channels Leo's renewed potency back into his quest to destroy Barbas. But unknown to the Charmed Ones, there is another being in the mix. A disembodied Creature has been speaking to both Leo and Barbas—and apparently no one else—and encouraging them to continue their fight. Barbas goes after baby Chris, knowing it will send Leo over the edge, so that he can goad him into distrusting all Elders. The demon's plan is realized when Leo kills Zola.

Paige finds a spell to remove the Hindu spirits from her family. Then, armed with a potion, she and Phoebe find Barbas in his lair and vanquish him—hopefully for the last time. But despite the destruction of Barbas, Leo is shattered by having now killed two Elders. The Creature taunts him that all the deaths, Barbas included, do not end his pain of feeling betrayed. Leo rails at the Creature and asks what it wants. "We want you. . . ."

During all of this, Phoebe feels that she is doing her readers a disservice by not giving them the best advice. Elise tells her to take a sabbatical and hires a ghostwriter for "Ask Phoebe"—a man named Leslie St. Claire. At first Phoebe is against it, but after reading his first column, she warms up to the idea—and to him.

The Elders have decided to close Magic School, since Gideon is no longer there to run it. However, Paige vows to fight to keep the school open for the next generation of magic.

Back in the real world, Sheridan is on the Charmed Ones' case about what happened to Chris, and Darryl is still not helping the sisters out. They all catch a break when an angry (and possessed) Leo throws Sheridan across the room. She is knocked out and forgets everything—at least for now.

"Bright side? At least we know that Piper and Leo still have the hots for each other."

PHOEBE HALLIWELL

"Expecting a girl, weren't you? Yeah, so were my folks, that's how I got the name."

LESLIE ST. CLAIRE

BEHIND THE SCENES

JIM CONWAY (CO-EXECUTIVE PRODUCER/DIRECTOR): When we shot it—because all those arms were basically added later—it wasn't too complicated to shoot. We had planned out what we were going to do. But when I saw it edited, all those scenes were flat because none of the effects were in it. So I wouldn't let anybody see it until we had enough temp effects in to bring those scenes to life, because when you see her without arms there's just nothing going on.

You suddenly see her with all the arms and all the charm comes into the scenes. So that was fun. That was a lot of work and that was really expensive, but that was really fun. I was worried about it. A lot of times I'll read a script and I'll say, "How are we ever going to do this and make it work?" We usually find a way.

STEPHEN LEBED (VISUAL EFFECTS SUPERVISOR): That was one of the few times when I actually got a call from the writers earlier on—even before we started that season—and they said, "This is what we're planning on doing. So think about it." That was a heads-up episode. Luckily, because it was the first one of the season, we had a little more time than we normally would.

Holly was fantastic. All of the girls are always fantastic. We always put them through hell. But Holly was really good and very patient, because we had to attach tracking marks on her and we had to have her constantly be aware that she had four more arms underneath her arms. She had to play it as if extra mass was there. And she did a really great job.

"THE BARE WITCH PROJECT"

Original air date September 19, 2004

WRITTEN BY JEANNINE RENSHAW | DIRECTED BY JOHN KRETCHMER

Battles of many types ensue as Paige faces off with the Elders to keep Magic School open, and Leo faces inner—and actual—demons. Phoebe bristles at a café owner who won't let Piper breastfeed baby Chris, and also squares off against Leslie, who she thinks is ruining her column. And Piper just wants Leo to be a father to their sons; she needs help, as she is currently the only breadwinner for the entire family. Everything somehow converges when a Magic School student named Duncan accidentally conjures Lady Godiva—still on her horse—from a history book. Along for the ride is Lord Dyson, an evil land baron, and apparently also a Repressor demon. Dyson feeds on the repressed feelings of others to gain strength. The sisters observe that he probably never made the history books—or the Book of Shadows—because Godiva's totally unrepressed ride starved him into oblivion. Unfortunately, there's plenty for him to devour in twenty-first-century San Francisco, and Dyson soon becomes more powerful than even he'd ever imagined.

The Charmed Ones need to send Lady Godiva and Lord Dyson back to the eleventh century so she can complete her historic ride and history will not be changed. But after the two are dispatched, it's obvious that something still has somehow gone terribly wrong. Everything is gray, quiet and, well, repressed. The sisters determine that since a much more powerful Dyson was returned than the one who originally existed, he must have killed Lady Godiva before she could make her statement, thus changing history. The only way to fix things is to get them both back, which is easier said than done in a world where magic isn't allowed to exist.

But this is a world that hasn't met the Charmed Ones. Paige finds the former Magic School students hiding out in an alley, doing "tricks" as opposed to true magic. She persuades Duncan to come to the deserted school to conjure Lady Godiva and Lord Dyson again. Unfortunately, once he does, it's apparent that Piper has been repressing her feelings toward Leo, and Dyson greedily feeds off of them. It looks like Dyson just may win, but Phoebe gets an idea to let Dyson feed on all of Leo's pent-up emotions. The repressed rage overloads the demon and he spectacularly explodes. Since Dyson no longer exists, Godiva can safely return to her time, make her ride, and keep history intact.

Magic School will also stay intact. After Paige convinces the Elders that the students need the school and magic needs its next generation properly educated, they agree to keep Magic School open—as long as the youngest Charmed One proves she can keep it running.

And, even a thousand years after Lady Godiva, Phoebe decides that sometimes the only way to make a point is to ride naked in the street. She takes on the café owner by donning a long, blond wig and crusading atop a majestic white steed—and makes a little history of her own.

*"Thank you for showing us you're more than a box of chocolates."***PHOEBE HALLIWELL**

"Please tell me you weren't vanquishing demons with the children?" **PIPER HALLIWELL**

BEHIND THE SCENES

AUDREY STERN (DEPARTMENT HEAD KEY HAIRSTYLIST): The hunt for that wig! That was a good one. You can't get something that long. They just don't have things like that anymore. I had to add three pieces together. I had to start out with one lace wig, then I had another piece under that to add extensions, and then I added another with these things that are actually tied onto the other wig as well. It's just continually growing and growing and growing until I got it to the length that I wanted. It was a little heavy on the girls.

Alyssa, I do anything to her and she's a dream. Everything fits on her like it was meant to be. Everything works on her. Every color works on her. Every piece works on her. She's my dream actress to work with. It was so much fun doing that.

"CHEAPER BY THE COVEN" *Original air date September 26, 2004*
WRITTEN BY MARK WILDING | DIRECTED BY DEREK JOHANSEN

Paige is determined to have a Wiccaning ceremony for baby Chris, despite Piper's decision to have as little as possible to do with magic. The youngest Charmed One summons family both mortal (Victor) and magical (Grams) so that Piper can't continue to refuse. This leaves Wyatt feeling a bit left out, so he continually picks on his baby brother. Grams uses an old spell she wrote and extracts the sibling rivalry from her great-grandsons. But instead of just disappearing, the jealousy finds the next closest set of siblings and turns the sisters into bickering adolescents. Not good on any given day, but especially dangerous with a masked demon after Wyatt.

Leo orbs with the boys to the safety of Magic School, but somehow the demon manages to attack. Leo protects his older son and a battle of dueling lightning bolts ensues, during which the demon is unmasked—and he looks just like Leo. Unable to agree on anything, Victor and Grams call in a neutral third party: Patty. The girls' mother agrees with Victor that Leo is not a danger to Wyatt, and that the giggly Charmed Ones should be returned to their adult selves. Finding no ally among any of her family, Grams dissipates in a huff.

Wyatt is taken by the demon when he doesn't raise his shield to protect himself. Patty and Victor think their grandson may be mirroring Piper's behavior after their divorce. Little Piper had night terrors, and the doctor believed that it was her subconscious way of blaming herself for her parents' split. They suggest that Wyatt may be creating demons of his own, and because he is so powerful, those demons actually come to life whenever he feels conflict. Leo confirms the theory, having seen it all in the demonic seer's pool. Wyatt has made Leo the bad guy because he feels it is his fault that his father killed Gideon. Leo and Piper find their firstborn in the cave where Gideon was vanquished, and Leo assures him that his family is what keeps him from falling apart. Wyatt understands his father's love for him, and demon Leo fades away.

Piper now accepts that she cannot avoid magic in her sons' lives, so she and her sisters call Grams back for the Wiccaning. The Halliwell matriarch is still annoyed, but she summons the ancestors together to bless their newest family member.

During the whole "The Charmed Ones: The Teenage Years" ordeal, Phoebe was honored with a Reader's Choice Award for one of her columns. Truth be told, it was one that Leslie wrote, but the adolescent Phoebe is determined to pick up the trophy herself. When Leslie has to bail her out during the award ceremony, the unguarded Phoebe lets slip some of her true feelings for her handsome ghostwriter. And it seems that he feels the same way.

"Wyatt, where did you orb your little brother?"   **PAIGE MATTHEWS**

"C'mon, dear, time to grow up."   **PENNY "GRAMS" HALLIWELL**

BEHIND THE SCENES

PAM SHAE (EXECUTIVE IN CHARGE OF TALENT) on the casting of as-yet-untried dramatic actor Nick Lachey: It did work. None of us knew at this point. He obviously was the hot guy at that time, and we needed somebody to play opposite Alyssa.

What we like to do a lot of times is do the *Moonlighting* relationship with our girls because it is wonderful, the energy you get back and forth. Until you actually see the actor doing other shows, you don't always know if it's in them. You can kind of tell persona-wise just from the sketch shows he had done with Jessica [Simpson], a little bit about his personality. He's obviously talented. He was a natural. We were so extremely blessed in that sense.

We did six episodes with him. Out of that show he got an overall deal at Fox and was highly recognized at that point. He really, really serviced exactly what we needed in a character at that time. The girls loved him and it was a fun character. He had a good time.

ALYSSA MILANO (PHOEBE): I had an amazing time with Nick Lachey. What a nice guy. The kind of guy that would invite our crewmembers over for *Monday Night Football*. Just awesome. Fun to be around. Really sweet. The whole nine yards.

"CHARRRMED" *Original air date October 3, 2004*

WRITTEN BY CAMERON LITVACK | DIRECTED BY MEL DAMSKI

Piper urges Leo to contact the other Elders, hoping that it will help her husband on his road to recovery. He discovers that several Whitelighters have recently lost track of their charges, and when he puts the Charmed Ones on the case, they soon learn that the witches have been victims of pirates!

Needless to say, there's nothing about pirates in the Book of Shadows, but lucky for Phoebe, Leslie turns out to be an expert on buccaneers. Piper and Phoebe track down the pirate cove and are greeted by Captain Black Jack Cutting, who has been "in a place beyond time and space" with his crew for nearly three hundred years. He's come to San Francisco because the Charmed Ones are the only ones who can get him the treasure he desires: the Golden Chalice that will bring forth the Fountain of Youth.

Piper and Phoebe are forced to acquiesce to the captain's wishes to save Paige's life. Impulsively wanting to save an Innocent, the youngest Charmed One had earlier encountered Cutting, whereupon she was sliced by a cursed athame that's causing her to age rapidly. The captain took the athame from a witch after she had cursed it—and him—for tricking her into giving him immortality. He killed the witch, but he, and all who sailed with him, were already sentenced to forever live in limbo. The pirate says that once Piper and Phoebe bring him the chalice, they will be free to leave and save Paige.

But once Cutting drinks from the fountain and has his youth restored, he immediately commands his crew to kill the sisters—thus breaking his word to them. Phoebe knows her pirate lore and declares parlay—which says that if a captain breaks his oath, the crew has the right to mutiny. Tied to their captain by the curse, and weary of their fate, Cutting's crew gladly run their leader through. In mere moments they are pirate dust. Piper and Phoebe take the remainder of the youth elixir to Paige, who returns to her old—make that young—self.

As if fighting off pirates isn't enough, Inspector Sheridan is still on the Charmed Ones' case. She is soon taken out of action when a federal agent named Brody shoots her with a tranquilizer dark. The sisters are grateful for the reprieve even if Brody's motives are less than obvious, at least for now.

And Phoebe and Leslie finally express their true feelings for each other.

"So, go play nice with the other Elders."　　　　　**PIPER HALLIWELL**

"I'm so sorry I don't speak pirate . . . matey."　　　**PAIGE MATTHEWS**

BEHIND THE SCENES

Among the sets for *Charmed* there is a generic cave set that can be re-dressed and reused for a variety of purposes. **PRODUCTION DESIGNER PAUL STAHELI describes how he approaches the design for the cave set with each new use:** Generally speaking, it's in the dressing. It's in the concept. The cave really just provides a background. In one instance it lended itself to pirates. The concept was, "Let's suppose that we were wherever pirates are and this was some kind of a cave next to the seashore." What the pirates had done was drag in pieces of ship and make it like a home or make it like living quarters. So that was that concept. At that point the cave just defines your space.

I would say in our show if you're in the cave you're in evil town . . . the Underworld. The cave fits whoever that happens to be the personification of evil this time around. In this case, they manifest themselves as pirates. In another one the leader manifests himself as an alchemist. So we in essence take the cave as a background and I'll draw up some alchemy kind of things, furniture and structures, and then the set dresser, Robin [Royce], will come in and alchemy it up with the tubes and the test tubes and the gold and all the stuff you have in alchemy.

Sometimes you don't have anything. Then you just scratch your head. We put rocks in. We'll just nasty it up. I don't know how many barrels of bones we've got around here. I mean they're all phony bones, but bones nonetheless. Incidentally, phony bones are more expensive than real bones. You can get real skeletons a lot cheaper than you can get a plastic skeleton.

"STYX FEET UNDER"　　　　　*Original air date October 10, 2004*
WRITTEN BY HENRY ALONSO MYERS | DIRECTED BY CHRISTOPHER LEITCH

Paige casts a protection spell on an Innocent, named Arthur. It doesn't prevent him from being mortally wounded by his half-demon relative, Sirk, but it shields Arthur's life essence, so that he is stuck between life and death and his soul cannot move on. This upsets the cosmic balance, which brings the Angel of Death to Halliwell Manor to find out why he can't collect the man's soul. Not only has this screwed up Death's day, but because Arthur is the first name on his list, it's preventing the rest of the souls on the angel's list from moving on, further disrupting the Grand Design, as the list must be followed in order.

Death is a neutral party, but he has a job to do, so he accepts Sirk's advice and exercises his power to reverse the protection spell causing both Arthur's body and soul to naturally expire. The names after Arthur's may now move up the list, but the delay has caused a backlog of work for Death—and since the Charmed Ones created the mess, they'll have to help him clean it up. Only problem is, to help souls move on, you have to be dead too, so the angel kills Piper. Like Arthur, her body is now lifeless, but her soul remains vital—and at the mercy of the Angel of Death. If she does the job he requires of her, the angel will return her soul, and her body will reanimate as if nothing happened.

Meanwhile, Sirk should have become a full demon upon Arthur's death, but his state hasn't changed, indicating that there is still one more human link. Sirk knows that it has to have something to do with Arthur's wife, Harriet. The Charmed Ones come to the same conclusion when Sirk's name doesn't appear on Piper's list. If he had become a full-fledged demon, his human soul would have died and Piper would have been dispatched to collect it. If Sirk is still part demon there is still one human relative alive.

Phoebe and Paige beat Sirk to Harriet and save the Innocent and her unborn child, but by doing so, they change circumstances which then change the Angel of Death's list. Harriet's name disappears from the top slot and is replaced—by Phoebe's!

Piper refuses to take her sister, but Death argues that the Grand Design is bigger than one life. Phoebe comes to this realization herself, and she helps Paige and Leo devise a plan to get Sirk. But when the showdown occurs, the half demon whirls and kills Paige instead of Phoebe, again changing circumstances, which then changes the list.

A devastated Phoebe cradles her dead sister and gets a premonition of Sirk attacking Harriet again. Her willingness to sacrifice herself for the greater good has earned Phoebe back one of her powers! Leo and Phoebe orb in, just in time to save Harriet and vanquish Sirk with a potion. Death comes for his human soul, but he is not on the list. Phoebe and Leo offer the angel a deal: one name not on the list for one that is—Paige. Since this will keep everything in balance, Death reluctantly agrees. He also releases Piper from her servitude, and she wakes up—in the morgue—where she finds the enigmatic Agent Brody waiting for her. He says he will cover up the story but will soon need her magical help with something greater.

"Stop yelling at Death."   **PAIGE MATTHEWS**

"Leo, relax. Piper's been dead before."   **PHOEBE HALLIWELL**

BEHIND THE SCENES

EXECUTIVE PRODUCER AARON SPELLING had the following to say about the men of *Charmed*: Brian Krause, Dorian Gregory, Julian McMahon, Drew Fuller... All of these terrific actors have come to us and brought wonderful talents to play off of our leading ladies. These gentlemen have been a wonderful blessing and just added to the magic of *Charmed*. They are all true stars in their own right.

The guest stars are just another fine example of this show being *Charmed*. From Billy Zane to Oded Fehr to Kerr Smith to Nick Lachey, Jason Lewis and Ivan Sergei, they've all wanted to do the show, and I think the quality of high-caliber talent this show attracts is a tribute to the long-term creativity the show has continued to bring to audiences over the years.

PAM SHAE (EXECUTIVE IN CHARGE OF TALENT) on casting recurring male guest stars on a female-driven show: It's always subjective. It's certainly a case-by-case. Some look at it that they want to reinvent themselves on a brand-new show, so you have that realm of what their interests are, and some see it as a really fun avenue to do. They're fans of the show, so it's sort of a foregone conclusion.

That particular role, the guys that play opposite our girls—the prominent guys in our series—have really had such huge amounts of attention. The flip side of that is agents would say, "Well, it's the girls' show. I don't want to put my actor on that show because they're not going to be as profiled." But it's quite the opposite. It is very much a collaborative series in general. The guys are just as prominent and really have a strong role with that.

"ONCE IN A BLUE MOON"

Original air date October 17, 2004

WRITTEN BY ERICA MESSER & DEBRA J. FISHER | DIRECTED BY JOHN KRETCHMER

It's a good thing that two blue moons in one year occur only every fifty years. The lunar oddity turns the Charmed Ones into hellhounds who attack Whitelighters—and apparently any paragon of good. But that's the least of their problems. The Elders are growing increasingly suspicious of Leo and exceedingly concerned about the great threat that is ever closer on the horizon.

Apparently, even Agent Brody knows about this looming menace. Concerned that he may be a demon or worse, Piper dispatches Paige to learn more about the fed. He is indeed a mere mortal, but with extensive knowledge about witches—and the dangerous beings that are about to surface. Brody tells Paige that they were in power in ancient times, but something made them disappear. They need power to come back and have amassed enough to be on the brink. Paige now realizes that they've been after Leo for his Elder's powers because not only are they strong, they can then be used against the other Elders.

The floating Creature head that has been haunting Leo reappears and is joined by two others in a Possessor demon's lair. They re-form into three human figures dressed all in black, and send a powerful Possessor demon to "occupy" Leo so that he will kill the Elders congregated at Magic School. The sisters throw a potion at the possessed Leo, but the Elders, who are running for their lives, don't see the separation. They don't have much time to argue that Leo has crossed over to evil, however, because as the final blue moon rises, the sisters transform. The Elders stop the hellhounds with lightning bolts and must wait until morning for a resolution.

The Charmed Ones argue that this great power that is advancing has set up Leo so that the Elders won't trust him, and they set out to prove their point. When they kill the Possessor demon, they see the floating Creature head and know that they are right—and that, thankfully, Leo wasn't going crazy. The Elders exonerate Leo, but he tells Piper that he's not ready to resume a normal life at the Manor. Whatever that Creature represents is still trying to get him to go over to its side, and that puts his family in too much danger.

And, as life goes on elsewhere even during a blue moon, it's time for Leslie to leave. It is a bittersweet parting for both Phoebe and Les, but the middle Charmed One is ready to go back to work—and grateful to her handsome ghostwriter for helping her to not be afraid of love anymore.

"All we have to do is make it to morning without eating anyone, and we'll be fine."

PIPER HALLIWELL

"You think we should put some snacks in the cage?"

PAIGE MATTHEWS

BEHIND THE SCENES

STEPHEN LEBED (VISUAL EFFECTS SUPERVISOR): Unfortunately, when that particular episode came down, it was at a time in our production schedule when we had no time at all to deliver the episode. That was directed by John Kretchmer. He and I had gone through step-by-step all the shots [of the hellhounds]. In this case we knew we had to go in with a very specific idea that we weren't going to deviate from. Unlike the dragon episode, where at the end we ended with more shots, because of the limited turnaround time we had to make sure that the shots we were doing were the only shots we were going to do. I believe we ended up with twenty-eight shots of the hellhounds at the end.

That worked out really great because ultimately we only had five days to turn around all those shots. My guys did an amazing effort, not only modeling the creatures, but also matching the lighting and the animating to them. It's always tough. You're always trying to put as much quality into the work as you can, but you're always up against the wire. At some point you have to just kind of push the shot forward and just get it out the door.

[Producer] Peter Chomsky helped us in that because some of the shots, again, we wish we could have had more time to make them better. But he went through in color correction and color timing and darkened out the shots. He played around with the shots in such a way so that basically they integrated into the show better than we had the time to do. He helped make the sequence work as a whole. We were happy with the end results, considering the limitations we had.

"SOMEONE TO WITCH OVER ME" *Original air date October 31, 2004*

WRITTEN BY ROB WRIGHT | DIRECTED BY JON PARÉ

It appears that demons are just as anxious as the Elders about the gathering storm of power. A Celerity demon, Sarpedon, creates a series of violent explosions and other disasters around town. His intention is to draw out the victims' guardian angels in an amulet so that their combined powers will help him fight the approaching threat. He scores a big hit acquiring Paige's guardian angel and decides that if he can also get Piper's and Phoebe's, he will have enough strength to fight whatever is coming.

Meanwhile, Piper thinks that if Leo goes on a vision quest, he may be able to slay his inner demons so that he can come back to his family and help them fight the actual demons. The Elder is first met by Chris, who acts as his guide. He reminds his father that he died fighting evil and was reborn as a Whitelighter so that he could continue that fight. Good is what Leo has always been about—it's what brought him to Piper and created his family—and he just needs to believe in it again.

It seems that Leo has finally made peace with himself as he wakes up from the vision quest. But the floating Creature head disrupts his platonic state and returns him to his pursuit. In Leo's dreamlike state, the Creature is seen in his actual state, and he is one of the men dressed in black who had previously appeared to the Possessor demon. He says he is an Avatar, and that he will lead Leo to the truth—beyond good and evil and their incessant battles. The Avatar shows Leo that if the battles continue as they currently exist, there will be nothing but destruction at the end. But, he says, there can be Utopia, where all the battles are behind them. The Avatars need Leo to join them to create this Utopia—all *he* needs is the courage to change.

Leo still believes that good and evil are necessary to maintain a balance, but his belief is soon put to the test. He wakes up from this last part of his vision quest to find that the Celerity demon has struck. Phoebe holds the demon's amulet, which left him vulnerable to Piper's blast, but Sarpedon managed to kill both sisters before he was vanquished. The Avatar returns to Leo and says that if the Elder joins him and his kind, they can save the sisters—and eventually everyone. Leo is left with no choice and accepts the powers of an Avatar. He can now heal the dead and brings his family back to life. Outwardly, Leo seems as if he's on the road to recovery, but he now has a new secret to keep.

Paige gets closer to Agent Kyle Brody as they work together to find out more about the Avatars, their looming threat, and how Brody can destroy them.

"We're not Brody's Angels."   **PHOEBE HALLIWELL**

"You guys look great for being recently deceased."   **PAIGE MATTHEWS**

BEHIND THE SCENES

JON PARÉ (PRODUCER/DIRECTOR): I had a great time working with our stunt coordinator, who in this case was also our second unit director. We both put ourselves in the same spot. There was so much for him to do and there was so much regarding action that if I was handling the A side of an action scene and he was handling the B side—meaning I was dealing with the actors reacting and he was dealing with the guy jumping out the building—we really had to understand where the other was going so that there was synchronicity in what we were doing.

   We did a lot of talking. We did a lot of communicating. A lot of times we weren't able to be specific with shots and angles, but because we weren't just talking, because we were communicating about the premise and the theme of the story, we ended up getting all the right footage. So that when we put it together, it made sense. It was heading toward where we wanted it to go. So it was really a lot of fun. It was a wonderful experience in that way.

NOON ORSATTI (STUNT COORDINATOR): Two buildings in one episode. Believe it or not, they let me direct second unit on that. The stunt was nothing I had done before. I knew that it was possible, given the locations that we have. I knew for a fact that we were going to get it accomplished. But this first gag, I wanted to hire a guy that was comfortable with fire and heights. There's not too many. Coincidentally, Mark Chadwick—the guy I hired to do the gag who got cast in the part as well—just won this year the Taurus stunt award for best fire gag in a film. So I knew I had the right guy doing the gag.

   Then I just had to come up with the rig that would make it safe. We did it all in one big master shot, which was challenging, but it still went without a hitch. Between the work of the visual effects guys and myself, it was actually simpler than it probably would come across. JP directed that episode. He mapped it out really well.

RANDY CABRAL (SPECIAL EFFECTS COORDINATOR): That was a lot of fun. I came off the roof with a jib arm and had a cable going to the stunt guy. It was rigged to pulleys that went to a building across the street with a counterbalance. So I could actually have him swing from the window, hit the ladder, the ladder falls, and I had control of him and then he could ride the ladder all the way down to the ground. At the same time the explosion was coming out the window.

   It was kind of fun because the fire department's right across the street from us. They really didn't know us when we first got here. When I said what I wanted to do—I wanted to blow out a window with a big fireball, have a guy hanging off the side of the building and have the fire escape come down—they looked at me, like, "You want to what?" The last time they had a big explosion like that on the lot the guy burnt part of the building when part of the mortar landed on another building. So they were all concerned about that. The buildings look like brick, but they're all just wood and fiberglass.

We designed the shot so that on the inside we built these big fireboxes so that we could contain the fire to the exterior of the building. On the exterior and on the sills and everything we used fire cloth and drywall so that the flames couldn't . . . well, we blackened the building a *little* bit.

We had real firemen in the scene and used old fire equipment that we rented. We had real firemen who knew how to handle the hoses. The guys squirt the hoses up and over the building. They direct their water away from the open windows so they don't interfere with the fire. That's not something you can just give an extra.

The second building fall was one of those deals where it's all line-of-sight-type gags. You have to be right there, right on top of it. The same type of deal as the fire; we had a jib arm over the top of the building. That was a good forty-five-foot fall. We put a cable on a guy. We had pretty much one shot at it.

He went through real glass. That was a real tempered glass window. As he hit that window, I had squibs on the glass so that when you see him hit that glass, it breaks on impact. If you're half a second too late, you really rap the stunt guy and he bounces off the glass. If you're too early, then it looks like the glass breaks before he hits it. Those shots are really the hardest ones. So we put a couple cameras on that. We had the up camera, in that shot, just in case you do screw up. If you're a little too early or a little too late, at least you have another camera angle on it. That's your Hail Mary. But the other camera angles, it was right on. It was a beautiful shot. We got everything out of it that we wanted.

"CHARMED NOIR"
Original air date November 11, 2004

WRITTEN BY CURTIS KHEEL | DIRECTED BY MICHAEL GROSSMAN

Paige and Brody are literally sucked into a 1930s murder mystery that takes place in an unfinished novel found at the Magic School library. The Mullen brothers had been students at the school about twenty years ago and were writing a book, *Crossed, Double-Crossed*, when Dan Mullen was found dead. Since Eddie Mullen disappeared at the same time, everyone assumed he killed his brother.

But Eddie is not only innocent of the murder, he's stuck in the narrative—and he can't get out until he finishes it. Quickly casing the situation, Paige and Brody—or as they're known in the story, Lana and the Fed—meet the less-than ethical cops, the gangsters, and Eddie, who hasn't aged in twenty years. In fact, he's shocked to learn how much time has gone by, and he thinks that his brother was killed by the crooked cops just yesterday because Dan wouldn't tell them the whereabouts of the Burmese Falcon. The same fate awaits Lana and the Fed if they can't come up with the bird.

Luckily, when Paige's sisters don't find her at Magic School, they do find the book. Phoebe gets a premonition off of it, and when she sees what happened to Paige and Brody, knows not to open the tome. Piper and Phoebe take the book back to the Manor, where, unseen by the sisters, the Avatars help Leo remove the spell so that now anyone can open the book without consequences. They notice that the story is being written as they watch. Phoebe adds in a sentence, and it becomes part of the book. But, when she tries to change the plot line, she can't. Piper reasons that they can add incidentals, but Eddie must truly become the hero to write his, Paige, and Brody's escape.

In the meantime, Phoebe keeps them as safe as she can by adding clues, which Paige fully understands. Eventually they can show Eddie that the gangsters he thought were on his side were really the ones who killed Dan, and the young witch finally writes his heroic ending. He retrieves the Burmese Falcon and smashes it on the ground, sending Paige, a mortally wounded Brody, and himself to the Manor. Leo heals Brody, Eddie is reunited with his family, and the cover of *Crossed, Double-Crossed* now says "written by the Mullen Brothers and the Halliwell Sisters." With the book completed, it is now safe for anyone to read.

Love, as well as mystery, is in the air. Their shared adventure to the 1930s has brought Paige and Brody much closer. And now that he feels the collective power of the Avatars, Leo tries to rekindle his relationship with Piper— although she's a bit skeptical of his sudden turnaround.

"Oh yeah, don't worry, magical things happen to us all the time . . . but this is the first time in black-and-white." **PAIGE MATTHEWS**

"Of all the books in all the libraries in all the world, you gotta get sucked into this one?"

EDDIE MULLEN

BEHIND THE SCENES

ROSE MCGOWAN (PAIGE): I think everything came together on that one. We had a great director, Michael Grossman, who goes between film and TV. He also pulled in favors. He knew a lot of these kind of tough-looking guys that play mafioso types all the time. So he called in favors and they just came in just as Mafia guys with no lines because they liked him so much.

We had amazing cars! We had Joe Kennedy Senior's—I wish I could remember which make of car it was, but there were only two of them made. I think it was he and then one of the Vanderbilts that owned them. He and Gloria Swanson—when they were having their affair—they had trysts in the back of it. It was, obviously, an old-style limo. But amazing. And the accoutrements inside it and all the details.

I'm an old movie buff and I think I'm kind of a bit out of time myself. So that was heaven for me. Everything. And Kerr [Smith, Agent Brody]! The script came together on that one. Just everything worked.

NANETTE NEW (DEPARTMENT HEAD KEY MAKEUP ARTIST: I did my research. It was all about the thirties and forties. I went back to the twenties. Rose is . . . her era . . . she really has a look of the thirties and forties. I went into the twenties because they were just really embarking on a new look in the late twenties coming into the early thirties. The eyebrows were getting a little bit more natural. They were still narrow; not quite Clara Bow. So we did a lot of research on that.

Of course, when it comes right down to it, Rose is going to have the final say, but she's very respectful when you do your homework. I thought that that episode was really wonderfully done in every department. The wardrobe was sensational. Rose pulled it off perfectly because she is of that era . . . her body language . . . all of it. She reminded me of Jessica Rabbit. I just looked at her and went, "Woo, you're sexy."

When I looked at her for that makeup, I thought sexy. We need to do something really sexy, but yet we had to keep it very, very natural. She looked really natural. When I look at her sometimes I think of Ava Gardner, and I did an Ava Gardner eye on her. And sort of Vivian Leigh. She reminds me of those two women. Add a little Marilyn to that and you've got a great recipe. So I went for that look.

DANIELLA GSCHWENDTNER (COSTUME SUPERVISOR): That outfit was fabulous. It was an evening gown from the time period that we modified and made shorter. We did the rhinestoning and all that. I must confess there was a lot of learning in it. For me, a lot of these things, this is the first time I'm doing it. You talk to people who give you guidelines and you're aware of certain concepts and all that. The really interesting thing right now is watching the shows to see how things actually look on camera in comparison to real life. When it's more your responsibility, you watch totally different. Before I just was, like, "Oh yeah, it looks beautiful." But now you just dissect it more. Things look so different under the lights.

"Charmed Noir" was so much fun because it did look so real. That was a big achievement. You try to do that on every show, to make it as authentic. But not everything always looks good. But that show just looked fabulous the way it just came together.

PETER CHOMSKY (PRODUCER): The episode was originally shot in color. Then I went in with our color timer and we took the color out and added contrast and gave it a look. It was a show that had a specific look in mind when we read the script, so there were certain angles—camera angles, film noir camera angles—and ways in which it was shot that sold that whole era.

We just went in and took out the color and did some transitions where it was color and then all of a sudden the color was sucked out of it when they first orbed in and things like that. We played around with that and some of the transitions.

I also worked very closely with our composer on that episode, J. Peter Robinson. He went out and hired ten or twelve musicians and did a really amazing supercustom score for that show. And I love it. It's one of my favorite episodes.

"THERE'S SOMETHING ABOUT LEO"

Original air date November 21, 2004

WRITTEN BY NATALIE ANTOCI & SCOTT LIPSEY | DIRECTED BY DEREK JOHANSEN

Piper knows that despite being kind and loving of late, Leo's keeping something from her—and she's not happy about it. Leo's angry that he has to keep her in the dark, and his frustration is making him unwittingly reverse time. Avatars Alpha and Beta explain to Leo that emotional control is the first discipline of an Avatar. Without it, their powers can become a danger to others and to themselves. Additionally, every time Leo rewinds time, it weakens the collective Avatar power, and they need to be at full strength to bring about Utopia.

Leo says that Piper will understand, but the Avatars are skeptical. They know they will need the Power of Three to join their forces, but they say the sisters must come to "the truth" in their own time and in their own way. The loving husband makes a good argument, however, and Alpha relents. Leo breaks the news to Piper . . . who immediately tells Phoebe and Paige . . . who tell Brody . . . and all hell breaks loose.

Brody is a man possessed. He believes the Avatars killed his parents, so now it's time for payback, starting with the one Avatar he can find—Leo. The battle ensues, and Leo blasts the federal agent with a lightning bolt, causing Brody to drop a potion bottle. It is the last of a potion that he found at the scene of his parents' death—and it is fatal to Avatars. The bottle bursts, emanating black smoke that immediately finds its mark. Brody is dead and Leo lies dying when Alpha and Beta freeze time. Leo now understands that they were right—although Piper was receptive to a world without demons, she will have to learn about it on her own. The Avatars rewind time to just before Leo confessed to Piper, and everyone is alive, well, and clueless again.

During all of this drama, two rival demon gangs are vying for the same turf. One gang had set up the other to take the fall. But when time is reversed, Leo knows all of this before it happens, so he and Piper can vanquish both gangs and save their Innocent.

Totally unaware of everything else that's going on, Morris makes his way back to the Charmed Ones and even asks for a little magical help to find out what happened to Inspector Sheridan. He's convinced that something's not quite right—and that Brody is responsible.

"Oh you know, the gathering storm, looming threat—that would be Leo."

PIPER HALLIWELL

"We are not going to let you kill Leo."

PHOEBE HALLIWELL

NOON ORSATTI (STUNT COORDINATOR) on working with the recurring guest actors: What I like about it personally is I get to get a nice, new, fresh face in there. That's always nice. That's the beauty of show business: never doing the same thing ever twice. Even in the same take it can vary so greatly. Seeing a nice, new face. Having a new guy to double.

We've had several guys that have martial arts backgrounds as our new leading guy, our new love interest. You utilize what they can do. I'm going back to Kerr Smith. This is a guy that—along with being a great, supernice guy—he really wanted to do a lot of his things.

We had a scene in the Manor where he's got Phoebe hostage at gunpoint. We needed to ratchet him, and the shot that they designed was such that I really couldn't throw a double in there at any point. We had to use Kerr. So here I was, going to Kerr and being nervous about it. "Kerr, what do you think?" And his response was, "Oh, man, put me on that wire. I want to do this." So we do that . . . in one shot. The very first take was a ten. It really was an unbelievable shot. There were so many different elements going on. So then we had another one for him to do and I'm ready to hire another stunt guy to come in and he's, like, "No way! I'm doing that."

"WITCHNESS PROTECTION"   *Original air date November 28, 2004*

WRITTEN BY JEANNINE RENSHAW | DIRECTED BY DAVID JACKSON

The Avatars intercept a message the demonic Seer, Kira, sends to the Elders and find their way to convince the Charmed Ones to join their cause. The Seer has decided she wants to go "good" and offers the Elders a deal—she'll sell out her fellow demons if they'll make her human. Acting on orders from the Avatars, Leo rescues the Seer and stashes her at Halliwell Manor for safekeeping. Naturally, this doesn't sit too well with the sisters, since they're used to blowing up demons in their house, not entertaining them, but Kira provokes their interest when she says she also has information about the Avatars.

The sisters are still skeptical about the unknown powerful beings, and Brody is still out for their blood, so Kira combines her power of premonition with Phoebe's to show them the truth. Phoebe sees a Utopian world beyond good and evil, where her nephews and daughter don't have to fight demons, and she becomes convinced that maybe the Avatars aren't evil after all. Maybe, in fact, Kyle Brody is the enemy for wanting to destroy them. This, of course, doesn't sit well with Paige, who believes that her new boyfriend's take on the Avatars is correct and breaks with her sisters over it. Piper is still on the fence, even after Leo's forced to confess that he is now an Avatar because he believes in that new world.

Unfortunately, during her psychic hookup with Kira, Phoebe not only saw Utopia, but Kira's vanquish at the hands of a demon named Zankou. The Underworld has been a bickering mess of factions unable to come up with a unified plan to counter Kira's defection from their ranks. After several of their number are vanquished challenging the Charmed Ones' protection of the Seer, they decide they have no choice but to release Zankou—a demon so powerful he had been banished by The Source. Zankou kills demon, witch, or Innocent without remorse, and then takes the powers of his victim. While Phoebe and Leo are at Magic School getting the spell to turn Kira human, Zankou acquires the powers of a shape-shifter and heads for Halliwell Manor. He arrives in the form of Phoebe, but quickly shows his true self and vanquishes Kira, just as he had in Phoebe's vision. The loss of another (not so) Innocent, and the promise of a world without demons, spurs Piper to request a meeting with the Avatars.

While the sisters are protecting Kira and Zankou is making his return, Darryl is still convinced that Brody has something to do with Sheridan's disappearance. There are no records of her being transferred, as the fed claims, and all evidence that the inspector existed has been cleared away. Darryl comes to Phoebe again for some magical help, and luckily, there's a powerful Seer on the premises these days. Kira tracks Sheridan to a mental hospital, where the cop is still in a coma after being shot by Brody with that tranquilizer dart several weeks ago. This, coupled with the new idea that the Avatars may be a force of good, adds to Piper and Phoebe's distrust of Brody—and their fears for their sister's safety.

"Is this how you went from psycho crazy guy to happy, happy guy—because you became an Avatar?"
PIPER HALLIWELL

"I know, I wouldn't actually have a soul, but I could live with that."
KIRA, THE DEMONIC SEER

"It's good to be back."
ZANKOU

BEHIND THE SCENES

PAM SHAE (EXECUTIVE IN CHARGE OF TALENT) talks about the difficulties of managing episodes with a number of notable guest stars (in this case, Kerr Smith [Brody], Charisma Carpenter [Kira], and Oded Fehr [Zankou]): It was numerous phone calls back and forth to the WB to figure out just how we were going to structure these deals. And certainly getting creative approval from them. What we like on our side, they may not necessarily respond to. So it's a back-and-forth situation.

These three particular actors were very much in good favor with the WB. I felt that they were extremely strong and powerful actors, which is what we absolutely have to have on this show. It was extremely challenging to keep up with our girls that know their roles inside and out and are so very, very strong. You have to have it be seamless when you are putting together your guest cast. It's got to be like they were a part of the show from the beginning. That was extremely challenging.

E. DUKE VINCENT (EXECUTIVE PRODUCER): I enjoyed bringing back Charisma Carpenter, because Charisma did that show with us when she was a kid, *Malibu Shores*. It was one of her first jobs. So it was fun bringing her back.

"ORDINARY WITCHES" *Original air date January 16, 2005*

WRITTEN BY MARK WILDING | DIRECTED BY JONATHAN WEST

Piper has heard the Avatars' pitch, but she's still not convinced. It's one thing to save the world from evil every week, but it's another to change it—just because you can. Phoebe switches powers with her sister so that Piper can see the Utopia for herself, but as usual in situations like these, something goes horribly wrong. The girls are attacked by Zankou just as their free-floating powers hover overhead, sending the powers out the window and into two unsuspecting mortals who happen to be nearby.

The newly empowered people are at first frightened by their abilities, but then decide that they will use them for personal gain. Phoebe and Piper's warnings go unheeded, and the now powerless Charmed Two must find a way to get their powers back before magic is exposed. Phoebe helps the man who got her premonitions see what she wanted Piper to see, and afterward he agrees to return the power to its rightful owner so that she can help make that world happen. Unfortunately, when everyone returns to the Manor to make the switch, Zankou is waiting for them. He thought he'd leveled the playing field when he revealed to the Elders that Leo had "switched sides" and

is now an Avatar. But repeated attacks by his former associates can't kill the newly powerful being. Zankou retreats when he realizes that Leo is still alive and the Avatars are stronger than he anticipated—which, he says, is bad news for both good and evil. He flames out to devise a new plan, leaving Piper and Phoebe to fight another day. Piper now gets onboard the Avatar Express, after seeing how someone who doesn't battle evil daily was so changed by just one short glimpse of what could be.

So two of the three Charmed Ones are ready to follow the Avatars, but what of Paige—and Brody, who has made it his mission in life to destroy the powerful force? Kyle must see for himself that the Avatars were not responsible for his parents' deaths, so Paige accompanies him on a trip back in time. Brody's desire to change the events of his life is overwhelming, but Paige convinces him that he must just watch and not act on what he sees. And what he sees is that it was demons who killed his parents—not Avatars. The demons were after the Avatar-killing potion to stop the gathering power from creating a demon-free world. All of the potion bottles were destroyed in the attack, however, leaving the demons to wait for the inevitable fight. Or so they think. When grown-up Kyle comforts little Kyle after his parents are killed, he spots one bottle still intact. Before his time traveling, Brody had tried to kill Leo (again) with the vial he'd been safely keeping for the last twenty-four years. But Alpha and Beta stepped in, prevented the attack, and took the potion. Although he now knows the truth about his parents' murders, Kyle still doesn't trust the Avatars completely, and he takes that last bottle as insurance. Paige, however, has no reason to doubt the Avatars' word or Phoebe's vision, and after seeing the havoc wreaked by Zankou, joins her sisters in the quest for a demon-free Utopia.

"Your boyfriend tried to kill my husband."   **PIPER HALLIWELL**

"Zankou. How do they come up with these names?"   **PHOEBE HALLIWELL**

BEHIND THE SCENES

STEPHEN LEBED (VISUAL EFFECTS SUPERVISOR) discusses working with the Golden Gate Bridge set that appears throughout the series: The Golden Gate Bridge sequences are an interesting challenge. It's essentially the notion of a virtual set that you hear bandied about all over production today, because we only have a few set pieces and we're shooting our actors in front of a green screen. Trying to play the whole scene in front of a green screen is tough, because it's often our actresses talking to somebody, so we have wind blowing through their hair and we always have to have fine hairs against the green screen. Those are always issues that we have to deal with. It's a real tough challenge for the compositors to take the footage and put it in there and get rid of any telltale signs that may look like it's a composite.

At the same time, it's tough for directors because they don't have the freedom to shoot the shots they would anywhere else. We're using footage that we've obtained from that vantage point on the Golden Gate Bridge. There are only so many angles we have, so we try to repurpose and reuse them. Our directors have been really creative in terms of slicing and using those shots so it doesn't feel like we're using the same shot over and over again. It's been a real challenge to make those work. Especially since it was never intended to be a location we were constantly going back to. It was originally intended just to be seen once. And suddenly, episode after episode, it kept coming back. As each director came in and saw what the previous director had done, they wanted to put their own little spin on it. So it became a real challenge.

PAUL STAHELI (PRODUCTION DESIGNER): The two requirements are, first off you have your spatial requirement. We don't have any space. Number two, then how do you show the Golden Gate Bridge? Well, obviously, you can only show a tiny little piece of it. If you show more than a tiny little piece of it then the audience is going to know that you're not there.

I used to go back and forth across the Golden Gate Bridge every day when I lived in the Bay Area, so I know the color and I know the basic construction. The assumption was when they go to the Golden Gate Bridge, they're standing on a cross section up near the top on those towers. So you do a little piece of the tower and a little piece of the floor and then they pop in the CGI [computer generated images] of the city in the background. Then you have to shoot that very tight.

BRIAN KRAUSE (LEO): When we first did it, it was just the green screen without an actual wood-built piece of set, which they eventually built. Now when you look down you see orange. So that helps you believe a little more. If you're in the scene with somebody, you eventually forget you're on it. Even if you're standing on the bridge, you would forget you're on the bridge eventually. Except the wind would be howling and you'd be yelling to talk to each other, which we never really did. We just go into the scene and it just became a little hideaway. We try to make it sort of that attitude up there.

"EXTREME MAKEOVER: WORLD EDITION"

Original air date January 23, 2005

WRITTEN BY CAMERON LITVACK | DIRECTED BY LEVAR BURTON

Time is running out for Zankou. To create Utopia, as many demons as possible must be vanquished to reduce the possibility of conflict seeping in. Zankou has thus far eluded the Charmed Ones, but his ranks are rapidly thinning. To save his kind, and keep the balance of good and evil in the world, Zankou recruits Agent Brody to join his fight. Although Kyle now knows that the Avatars didn't kill his parents, the fed is still not a big fan of the men and women in black. He's not eager to work with a demon, but Zankou leaves him little choice.

The Avatars will now deal only with the Charmed Ones, so Zankou's plan is to go through the sisters to weaken the collective. He gives Brody a crystal that causes paranoia in witches. Kyle doesn't want to use it, but when Paige is adamant about implementing the change, he reluctantly follows Zankou's wishes. By the time they bring about Utopia, the three witches have many doubts—but they do not stop the process.

The sisters chant a spell while combining the Avatars' magic with the Power of Three, and the whole world falls asleep. It will only be for a few hours—time enough to erase a mind-set of the duality of good and evil and to allow the original design imprinted in people's hearts to take over. The Charmed Ones are kept awake to vanquish any straggler demons that will not have gone to sleep with everyone else.

Brody is also still awake, being shielded by Zankou in his Underworld lair as part of the demon's plan to foil the Avatars. Playing on Paige's growing apprehension, Zankou maneuvers the youngest Charmed One, Brody, and Beta to meet in Kyle's apartment so that Brody can use the Avatar-vanquishing potion that he found at the scene of his parents' death. Kyle breaks the paranoia crystal, returning Paige to her normal emotional state, and then faces off with the Avatar. When Beta sees the potion in Brody's hand, she blasts him. As he falls, so does the vial. It shatters and spews black smoke, killing Beta instantly. Paige is inconsolable and angry at Alpha and Gamma, who come to collect their fallen comrade. They say that they can't heal Brody or reverse time to save one of their own, because they have come too far to go back now.

With the sisters now emotional and volatile, the Avatars put them to sleep with the rest of the world. Beta's death weakened them, and they do not have enough collective power left to fight both Zankou and the Charmed Ones.

Everyone wakes up to a sunny new day. The sisters are thrilled to have their demon-fighting days behind them and are ready to lead a normal life. They are sad about Kyle's death, but not angry. In fact, Paige insists that he's gone on to a better place, and her sisters agree. Leo is the only one who seems to think that this is a strange, and not entirely brave, new world. And Zankou's counting on those feelings to enlist the Avatar to help him change things back to the way they were before.

"I'm a little antsy, Phoebe's nostalgic, and you're scared—that's how we do things."

PIPER HALLIWELL

"How much advice can a world with no conflict need?"

PHOEBE HALLIWELL

"I did not sign up for this experiment so you could play God."

PAIGE MATTHEWS

BEHIND THE SCENES

NANCY SOLOMON (SCRIPT SUPERVISOR): We kind of have a loose atmosphere here on the set. But it's good. You have to keep it fun. We're coming here every day. You don't want to keep it bitter or anything. We have a lot of fun here. It's great. We had some new directors last year. We had Levar Burton, which was awesome. He came in with full energy. And we're both Aquarians. We bounced off each other like two molecules.

"CHARMAGEDDON"

Original air date January 30, 2005

WRITTEN BY HENRY ALONSO MYERS | DIRECTED BY JOHN KRETCHMER

The Avatars are pleased with their work, but they have much to do to maintain their new world order. There are those who still cause conflict, and when that conflict passes a certain threshold, it is not acceptable. The troublemaker is "removed" by the Avatars, who monitor everything from their star chamber. When Leo witnesses this absolute power over everyone's destiny, it confirms the doubts he had formed upon seeing the creation of Utopia. And that's just what Zankou is waiting for. He offers Leo an uneasy and unlikely alliance that the Avatar reluctantly accepts.

Unfortunately, it's not as simple to get the Charmed Ones on board. They are happy to be demon free, and, like everyone else, they are under the influence of the Avatars' mind control. Zankou suggests that the sisters may need to face another great loss to fully understand the evils of the world they've helped create, and Leo realizes that the demon may just be right. Knowing that the Avatars will see his actions from their star chamber, Leo faces off with Zankou and his demons. The conflict he creates causes his "removal," but before he's taken, he cautions Phoebe not to let the Avatars make her forget the pain of losing him. He tells her to go to the Book of Shadows and remember all the losses she's suffered throughout her life, and then go to Zankou.

Piper copes very well with the death of her husband, but Phoebe has a gnawing uneasiness about everything. She hears Leo's words echo in her head and begins to experience the pain of his death. When she touches the Book of Shadows, her visions of people she's lost over the last seven years jolts her back to reality. Phoebe makes her sisters face their pain too, and the Charmed Ones are back—and ready to meet Zankou.

Understandably wary of working with a demon, the sisters nonetheless accept Zankou's reasoning that combining the forces of good and evil is the only way to defeat the Avatars. The ancient tomb in which Zankou has been hiding contains hieroglyphs of the previous incarnation of the Avatars, and how they were defeated thousands of years ago. Included within the symbols is the formula for the deadly potion that Brody had found. Armed with freshly brewed vials, the witches and Zankou enter the star chamber and demand that the world be returned to the way it was. The Avatars proclaim that the Charmed Ones are not ready for Utopia, and they agree to use what remains of their power to rewind time to when the new world order began. Leo will be alive, but Kyle will not.

A bright light again washes over the world, and when everyone wakes up, conflict abounds— and it is music to the Charmed Ones' ears. Zankou bids farewell, but it is no doubt only a temporary exit. Leo is indeed alive, well, and sure that he will be punished by the Elders for siding with the Avatars. And speaking of Elders, they have made Kyle a Whitelighter as a reward for his unselfish act of trying to stop the Avatars and save the world.

"Well, when I'm not mixing vanquishing potions all the time, I tend to get a lot more done."   **PIPER HALLIWELL**

"I have to fix a mistake. I love you."   **LEO WYATT**

"It's good to be back. Warts and all."   **PHOEBE HALLIWELL**

BEHIND THE SCENES

BRIAN KRAUSE (LEO): Playing the whole mistrust of Chris's character was interesting, and then the spin of finding out that he was my son was also interesting. The fact that Holly had a baby helped with that. It was the one place to take my character. I think that Leo didn't want to believe it. He wasn't able to keep his children away from the demonic world well into the future with a grown son. Chris is still dealing with the life and death of his parents and himself. I think it was hard for Leo to take. So he really wanted to change that future and protect his son as well, yet Chris was his own man. I think that was the dynamic he was trying to go for.

I think that's why when the Avatars came along after that, Leo fell into the idea that he could change and further his son's life. If I could control the world, I can have my son live a full life. I think that was part of the lure of the Avatars; to not only help his wife, his family, his sisters, but to keep the Halliwell name going as long as possible. I think that was his goal with the Avatars and the whole year.

"CARPE DEMON"   *Original air date February 13, 2005*
WRITTEN BY CURTIS KHEEL | DIRECTED BY STUART GILLARD

The Charmed Ones return to their lives disappointed that they will never know the serene world that was promised by the Avatars, and it takes a handsome, charming, and somewhat snarky ex-demon named Drake to snap them out of their respective funks. When Paige has an opening for a professor at Magic School, Drake rides in on his motorcycle, ready, willing, and able to handle the job. He discounts the sisters' fears of employing a demon—ex or otherwise—explaining that he has never harmed an Innocent. And, although he still has his powers, Drake can't use them, or they will revert to the sorcerer who made him human and consign the ex-demon to an eternity in a fiery purgatory.

When the Charmed Ones still resist, he argues that the problem isn't him—it's them. The experience with the Avatars has shaken them to their core—Paige has lost faith in herself, Phoebe has been disheartened by the fight, and Piper has closed down her heart because she's petrified that it will be broken again. Drake decides that the sisters need a hero, and Robin Hood is the man for the job. The overly dramatic demon becomes the swashbuckling savior of Sherwood Forest, but

things go a bit wonky when the sorcerer picks that particular moment to shimmer in and cast a spell. The sorcerer hopes to cause Drake's inner demon to emerge and use his powers. But Drake's current inner being is Robin Hood, so rather than affirming his evil essence, he now truly becomes the altruistic Robin.

Our hero makes quick work of tracking down a modern-day "Prince John" and coerces the man into making financial reparations. But the ever-determined sorcerer casts a spell on the Innocent so that he will defy Robin's commands. The rage that rises up in Robin taps into Drake's demonic instincts, and the sorcerer finally succeeds in prodding his prey to use his powers. The powers transfer to the sorcerer, and Drake reverts to his normal self just in time to go up (or down) in flames. The Charmed Ones now have a new Innocent to save—Drake.

The sisters reason that if they can vanquish the sorcerer, all of his magic will be reversed, thus freeing Drake. They outsmart the sorcerer, who thinks he's setting a trap for them. A Power of Three spell vanquishes him in flames, which then spit Drake back out of the fiery destiny to which he had been consigned.

The sisters have to admit that despite his somewhat unconventional methods, Drake has put them back on track. Paige once again trusts her instincts, and Piper is no longer afraid to be open to love and the possible loss that may result. Phoebe's jaunt with Robin Hood reminds her how good it feels to help people and make a difference in their lives. It also reminds her that romance is alive and well if you'll just embrace it. Drake is made a temporary visiting lecturer at Magic School—temporary, because his deal to become human lasts only a year. He's got two weeks left to live, and he intends to make the most of every day.

"Phoebe, how many times have I told you not to play dress-up with the demons?"
PIPER HALLIWELL

"That's because since the day I was hatched, I've been reading books, and they taught me about feelings, human feelings."
DRAKE

PAM SHAE (EXECUTIVE IN CHARGE OF TALENT): From the very first episode of the series, over the years Brad would say, "I need a Billy Zane character." Just sort of what he brought; all the levels that he brought to his roles was what we were looking for week after week after week. Then last year it just so happened that Billy was with my agent and I would call regularly to see if he was available. Billy was another actor that just always worked. And she goes, "You know what, I think we can make this work." And it just clicked. I got him on the phone with Brad and it just transpired. He did a very, very nice arc for us in an extremely difficult role that required so much talent. All the levels. Billy Zane played Billy Zane very, very well. So that was really wonderful.

ALYSSA MILANO (PHOEBE): Billy Zane was really fun because he is so eccentric. It doesn't stop when the camera stops rolling. So there's an energy there that's very infectious. I was happy working with him and I thought that the work we did together was really strong. But he is definitely zany: Billy Zany.

TODD TUCKER (SPECIAL EFFECTS MAKEUP): One of the makeup applications [in this episode] that was actually a lot of fun was we did Billy Zane as Cyrano de Bergerac. It was just kind of fun because it wasn't a huge makeup. It was a fake nose and a beard and mustache. But it was also a character makeup, where I went in and tried to take his features and just, with color, try to take it to the point where it felt you weren't looking at Billy, but you were actually looking at this historical character.

It was a little bit of a challenge because I wasn't able to cover more of his face, with the nose being right in the middle of his face and making sure that looked real. Obviously, having a long nose like that is kind of a bizarre look anyways. So that was a little bit of a challenge just to make sure that it didn't come off silly. It's something that could be cheesy if it's not done right.

Usually with these makeups I try to keep them as real as possible, or at least organic, so that even with my creatures and all that it feels like it could exist. In another world, obviously, but there's a certain . . . kind of like *The Lord of the Rings* characters, where it feels like it could be in history. Like these things may have existed at some point. As opposed to something that is so fantasy that no one could identify with it. To do a subtle makeup like that, and like the ugly makeup on Suzanne [Krull in "Freaky Phoebe"], those are challenging, because there's not as much to play with. You have to make it work as a more subtle makeup.

"SHOW GHOULS"

Original air date February 20, 2005

WRITTEN BY ERICA MESSER & DEBRA J. FISHER, & ROB WRIGHT I DIRECTED BY MEL DAMSKI

Darryl enlists the aid of the Charmed Ones when his old friend and mentor, Mike, appears to be possessed by a spirit. Phoebe, Paige, and Drake figure out that the construction site near Mike's job as a security guard used to be the location of Cabaret Fantome. The nightclub was full of people when a fire broke out there more than a hundred years ago, trapping and killing all inside. Drake says Mike is probably possessed by one of the lost souls. When souls die a violent death together, the good ones can't move on because the bad ones are holding them back—and vice versa. Drake has a spell to

go back to find out what happened, but there's a catch: You have to die to make the trip. Luckily, the spell will send Phoebe and Drake back to 2005, and to life, when the fire starts and the souls become lost—hopefully with information to help the Innocents to finally move on. Drake can't wait to revisit 1899, but Phoebe is a bit more reticent. However, her sense of responsibility and Drake's irrepressible charm ultimately win out.

What unfolds is a century-old story about a nightclub owner named Count Roget, who made a deal with a demon. Roget is the only one who is aware that the fire is played out night after night in an endless loop. He is also the only one who sees Phoebe and Drake enter the scene, and he now knows he has a way out of the constant nightmare. Having gotten the lay of the land on their first trip to Cabaret Fantome, Phoebe and Drake go back to try to stop the count before he can make the deal with the demon. But by the time they arrive, the demon is long gone. Roget shoots Drake and takes their place at the portal back to twenty-first-century Halliwell Manor. When Count Roget wakes up in Drake's body, Piper and Leo are not initially aware of the switch. But when he shows no concern for a still lifeless Phoebe, they figure out what happened. Unfortunately, Drake's body is impervious to Piper's blast, and Roget is gone before they can do anything else.

Meanwhile, Phoebe and Drake are trapped in the Cabaret Fantome fire, with Drake dying from his gunshot wound. Phoebe finds a Tarot configuration for "escape from the ordinary" in a fortune-teller's book, but Drake has nowhere to go, since Roget is in his body. He stays at the club, knowing that Phoebe will find a way to free him. She makes her escape and wakes up at the Manor, where Piper has brewed a potion to separate Count Roget from Drake's body.

Phoebe has a good idea where to find the count, and when she throws the potion, his spirit rises up from Drake's body and then descends to where it should have gone a hundred years ago. The other souls are now free and move on to their final destinies. Drake finds his way back to his body, grateful to be alive—even if it's only for one more week.

Inspired by his trip to Cabaret Fantome, Drake works up his own act, and Piper books him for a one-night-only engagement at P3.

Piper and Leo had missed the first part of the ordeal because they had taken the boys on a whirlwind world tour. Worried about the punishment the Elders will exact on Leo, perfectionist Piper wanted to control every moment they still had together. She realizes that in the end, there's nothing she can do, but Leo is grateful to his wife for trying to distract him from his uncertain fate.

PIPER: *"Wait a minute, what's my middle name?"*
PHOEBE: *"Uhhh, Shirley?"*
PIPER: *"Hah! That's my girl!"*

BEHIND THE SCENES

JIM CONWAY (CO-EXECUTIVE PRODUCER): "Show Ghouls" was a big, big show with the fire in the old theater. That big fire scene ended up being incredibly expensive and tough to do. Everyone's in that very expensive wardrobe. We had to create that set. We had to have two or three days of shooting in there and two or three days of second unit shooting in there to do all the fire and the falling and all that. That was one of those that if you don't do right, it looks really cheesy. So we had to spend the money. That was one of our most expensive episodes ever. But you had to do it right or it was going to look just bad, bad, bad.

AUDREY STERN (DEPARTMENT HEAD KEY HAIRSTYLIST): One of my favorites was when they went back to the eighteen nineties. That was like . . . I had research books. I had four different hairdressers that were helping me. Alyssa had different pieces that she wore. And we had feathers in her hair. And Billy had his wigs. It was really fun to do that. And all the girls and everybody inside that saloon was just perfect. Absolutely perfect.

"THE SEVEN YEAR WITCH"

Original air date April 10, 2005

WRITTEN BY JEANNINE RENSHAW | DIRECTED BY MICHAEL GROSSMAN

Leo finally learns his fate for becoming an Avatar. The Elders say that they understand how Gideon's betrayal could lead to Leo's actions, but they still don't excuse the fact that he defied his former colleagues. They see Leo being caught between two worlds—one with Piper and the boys, and one with the Elders. They believe that the only solution is to test him to see where he belongs, so the Elders strip Leo of his powers and his memory and relocate him. They believe Leo's heart will

guide him to his true destiny, either his family or the greater good. Whichever one he chooses will be his ultimate fate, and he will have to give up the other part of his life forever.

Meanwhile, Piper goes into a coma after being struck by a Thorn demon. She is caught in a cosmic void between life and death, where she finds an unlikely ally—Cole. He says he's there to help her, but Piper's mistrust of her former brother-in-law/demon/Source of All Evil runs deep. When the eldest Charmed One becomes frustrated that neither her sisters nor Drake can see or hear her, her only option appears to be listening to what Cole has to offer.

After a fair amount of bickering, Piper finally gets Cole to admit that he has an ulterior motive for his actions: He wants to insure that Phoebe never gives up on love. Cole says he's come to Piper for help because she and Leo have the real deal. If Piper gets Leo to reject the Elders and return to her, Phoebe will have something to believe in again, and Cole will feel less guilty about his past actions. The bad news is, Piper will have to die—or almost die—for the psychic shock to be great enough for Leo to sense her. Not knowing who he is has broken their normal bond. Drastic times call for drastic measures, so Piper re-enters her body and hopes that she can create her desired destiny.

Needless to say, Phoebe and Paige have not accepted the Elders' game plan, and they have tracked down Leo with the help of Darryl and the San Francisco police force. But by the time they find their brother-in-law, the Elder Odin has convinced him to join his cause. Odin has not played fair, and has exploited Leo's confusion, but once the former Elder unknowingly commits to his old calling, there's no turning back. He is orbed Up There with no memory of his wife or his family.

Piper takes a turn for the worse. Paige and Phoebe orb to the Golden Gate Bridge and demand that Odin bring Leo to see them. Phoebe vehemently argues for her sister's life and for true love. When Piper calls out for her husband with her last gasps, he is able to hear her. He walks over the edge of the bridge and literally falls from grace. Without Odin's maneuvering, Leo's heart makes his decision: to become a mortal and live out his days with his family.

Paige orbs them all home to find that Wyatt has healed his mother, and Leo and Piper settle in to finally have the normal life they've always wanted.

Leo is starting anew, but Drake must make his final farewell. His year is up, but he has no regrets. He bids a loving good-bye to Phoebe, who thanks him for helping her move on with her life but also wonders how he happened to appear at just the right moment to give her exactly what she needed. "What's magic without a little mystery?" Drake answers, but after Phoebe leaves, Cole shows up. We find that he was behind everything. He set up the deal with the sorcerer so that Drake could experience humanity and put romance and hope back into Phoebe's life. Drake thanks The ex-Source, and as his dead body turns to dust, his soul ascends to the heavens. Resigned to his loveless eternity, but pleased that Phoebe will not face the same fate, Cole dematerializes.

"Oh no, am I dead again?"   **PIPER HALLIWELL**

"You always were the smart one."   **COLE TURNER**

"Think of me when you dance."   **DRAKE**

BEHIND THE SCENES

JIM CONWAY (CO-EXECUTIVE PRODUCER): That was great for Julian to come back. Brad asked him, and normally somebody like that wouldn't come back. But Julian loved the experience so much, loved us so much, that he said he would. We only had him for one day. Eleven pages. It was a long day. That was special.

E. DUKE VINCENT (EXECUTIVE PRODUCER): Bless his heart, we thanked him a lot for that. Julian really had not established himself too well when we first took him on. He recognized that. So when he became a big star on *Nip/Tuck*, a lot of guys would have said, "I'm not going to come back and do an episode. I'm the star of my own show." But not Julian. He said, "I'll do it. I'll come back and do it." And he was terrific.

"SCRY HARD"   *Original air date April 17, 2005*
WRITTEN BY ANDY REASER & DOUG E. JONES | DIRECTED BY DEREK JOHANSEN

Leo doesn't know what to do with himself now that he has no powers and has to accept Piper's protection. To keep busy, he cleans and straightens everything in the Manor, unearthing in the process a wonderful dollhouse that is an exact replica of the Halliwell ancestral home.

Domestic tranquility is interrupted by a crescent-wielding demon named Craven, who grazes Leo before evading Piper's blast and shimmering out. He leaves behind his bladed weapon, making it easy for the sisters to track him. Little do they know that the whole thing is a setup by Zankou, who has returned to battle the Charmed Ones for control of the Spiritual Nexus and the Ultimate Power of the Shadow within it. Zankou's plan is to draw the sisters out of the Manor, so that Craven can enter it and search for the Nexus. But Piper and Leo stay behind with the boys, while Phoebe and Paige go demon hunting. Craven and his minions are surprised to find that they are not alone and start defending themselves against Piper's blasts. She vanquishes most of the intruders, but Leo is severely wounded by Craven's latest crescent. Wyatt witnesses his father's pain and decides to keep his parents safe by shrinking them and

putting them in the dollhouse, which he then magically seals. No one can hurt them inside, but they can't get out, either.

When Phoebe and Paige can't find Piper and Leo anywhere, Paige orbs the boys to Magic School. She returns with her sister to find Zankou, Craven, and his followers now inhabiting their house. Zankou throws the two sisters out and becomes intoxicated with his success in having breached the hallowed Halliwell Manor. Nothing will stop him now. When the Nexus is found in the basement, Zankou recites the spell to call for the Shadow, but it does not enter him. Zankou reasons that good must still be somewhere in the house.

The search is on for Piper and Leo, who have discovered a way out of the dollhouse and made it to the Book of Shadows. They send a message to Phoebe and Paige at Magic School just before Zankou puts them in a box like two pet mice. Phoebe and Paige orb back to the attic and convince Zankou that he needs the Power of Three—full-size—to help him join with the Shadow. Leo knows that Zankou won't succeed and tells Piper to go along with her sisters' plan. The Charmed Ones recite the spell to call for the Shadow, and when it emerges, it is confused by paragons of both good and evil being present. So it enters the only neutral being it can find—the mortal Leo. The former Elder is restored to his normal size as he bursts out of the box and shatters it, his eyes black from the entity within him. He makes quick work of the lesser demons and repeatedly blasts Zankou, who is smart enough to know that it is better to live to fight another day and flames out. The sisters recite the spell to return the Shadow to the Nexus, and Leo is back to his old mortal self.

With Paige frustrated with the rigors of running Magic School and anxious to spread her wings, Piper and Phoebe decide that Leo's extensive knowledge of all things magical makes him the perfect man for the job. He gratefully accepts the position of headmaster, and Paige can't orb out fast enough.

"I guess I didn't expect normal to be so hard."   **LEO WYATT**

"Hope you guys got a discount on all that leather."   **PHOEBE HALLIWELL**

"I'm insulted. You didn't think I warrant the Power of Three?"   **ZANKOU**

BEHIND THE SCENES

NANCY SOLOMON (SCRIPT SUPERVISOR): Luckily our Wyatts have grown up and they've gotten much better. They come by a lot more and they just visit with us. They've gotten a lot more comfortable with us. We never shoot them now with the demons in the same room. One time we had Wyatt looking at this big, huge, ugly demon with one eye. He was actually looking at me. So I was standing there, pretending, in a very monotone voice, not scary, to get the reactions that we needed from him. If we need them to laugh, they always laugh with me. Or whatever. He would work off of me.

MARIA SIMMONS (MOTHER OF KRISTOPHER AND JASON SIMMONS, THE TWINS WHO PLAY WYATT): Only one time, they did something with a demon there and Kristopher freaked out. After that, it was a while before he wanted to go inside again. So it's good that they separate them. They do two different parts, the demons and the kids.

I'd been letting them watch the show, and the last time they asked, "What is that demon doing there?" And now they're asking me, "Are there demons there?" So now that they're understanding more, but not quite to the point that they know what is going on really, I'm thinking that I'm not going to be able to let them watch the show yet.

ALYSSA MILANO (PHOEBE): I am so protective. Absolutely. It's really important to me that the kids don't have to see the demons. I remember when I was doing *Commando* when I was eleven, and there was that scene in the beginning of the movie where the whole cabin gets shot up with guns and Arnold picks me up and throws me into the cabin. I had nightmares for a good couple of months after that. So, yeah, those things are really important. And our crew is so unbelievably gracious and fabulous. They're all pretty protective. It's not just me.

"LITTLE BOX OF HORRORS"   *Original air date April 24, 2005*

WRITTEN BY CAMERON LITVACK | DIRECTED BY JON PARÉ

The legendary Pandora's Box is protected from generation to generation by magical beings called Guardians. It is the job of the current Guardian to train her successor so that if evil strikes, the box will automatically find its new protector. Unfortunately, a shape-shifting demon named Katya kills the box's current Guardian before her successor has been educated.

The Charmed Ones become involved when Katya needs help identifying the new Guardian. She shape-shifts into the former keeper of the box and fools the sisters into finding the box. It is in the dorm room of a college student, appropriately named Hope, who has no idea that she's magical—and has no desire to embrace her fate. Although Katya manages to get Pandora's Box, only the Guardian can open it, so when Hope rejects the sisters' offer to guide her through her magical destiny, the demon steps in. She tries to con the teenager into doing her bidding, and when that doesn't work, she threatens to kill Hope's best friend if she doesn't open the box. Hope saves her friend, Darcy, and unleashes the ills, too naive to realize that the demon will now kill them both anyway. Katya is about to strike with one of her deadly sai daggers, but Hope throws her across the cave with her new and impressively forceful powers. Piper and Phoebe orb in, and Katya disappears with the now-empty box. She then tries to fool the sisters and Hope again by shape-shifting into Darcy, but when they get back to the Manor, Phoebe realizes that there is something strange about Darcy's behavior.

Pulling a little con of their own, the Charmed Ones have Paige glamour into Hope so that when "Darcy" takes "Hope" back to the Underworld, the teenager becomes a powerful good witch with more than enough experience to vanquish the demon. Paige meets the real Darcy and orbs the teenager and the box back to the Manor, where Hope opens it and calls for all its ills to return. Once they are safely back inside, she shuts the latch and begins to understand and accept her destiny.

Speaking of destiny, Paige missed much of this latest race to save the world because she has apparently come into her Whitelighter powers. After what happened to Leo, Paige wants no part of the Elders. But Leo urges her to give it one try before rejecting her calling. Paige has to admit that once the experience is over, she feels good about it and herself. The Elder Sandra suggests that her Whitelighter side—something that she does not share with her sisters—may be the separate identity for which Paige has been recently searching.

Meanwhile, Piper and Leo contend with a very magical toddler who has hit the terrible twos. They have differing opinions on how to handle a child who orbs at will, but eventually they agree that they will have to teach Wyatt when, and where, to use his powers.

"Wyatt! Time out means no magic!"   **PIPER HALLIWELL**

"You'd think there'd be something about Pandora's Box in a place called Magic School."
                                                                            PHOEBE HALLIWELL

BEHIND THE SCENES

KEN MILLER (EXECUTIVE IN CHARGE OF POSTPRODUCTION): I really like keeping [music] scores fresh. I like two composers on a show. I usually will assign two composers, or bring two composers to an executive producer and tell him this is who I like. My background is, music was my education. I can usually tell who is a real orchestrator or arranger. That's who I'm looking for.

Charmed is a very difficult show scorewise. You can have thirty-two minutes of score per show. That's a lot to write in seven days. Every time the girls throw a fireball or something like that, you gotta hit it. You gotta stick it. I go to the playbacks of all the shows and I'm not averse to changing a tune if I have to. The two composers in now, J. Peter Robinson and Jay Gruska, have been on the show a long time. They are very orchestral and do a great job. They alternate shows.

It is a very debilitating show to write from a scoring standpoint, because there is so much score. And you need to embellish a lot of the hits of dialogue and special effects. I like having two composers on because it keeps the scores fresh. It keeps a competitive spirit alive. Some shows don't require that. But this show does because it's a hard show to score. The fantasy element lends itself to a wider range of orchestration. Composing is about starts and stops. That's what it really comes down to. Most composers don't like a lot of starts and stops, but this show demands it.

"FREAKY PHOEBE"

Original air date May 1, 2005

WRITTEN BY MARK WILDING | DIRECTED BY MICHAEL GROSSMAN

The latest demon to challenge Zankou as ruler of the Underworld is a soul swapper named Imara. The hideous-looking woman plans to vanquish Zankou's chief lieutenants, thus making him vulnerable to her ultimate attack. Since Zankou's loyalists are masquerading "up top" as mere mortals, Imara needs a body that will not arouse suspicion. And what magical bodies are better than the Charmed Ones?

Imara's minions first go after Piper at P3, but the eldest Charmed One's active powers prove too difficult to overcome. Paige is equally unapproachable, dealing with her new Whitelighter abilities, so Imara targets Phoebe. The middle Halliwell is presently angry and preoccupied with very human affairs at the *Bay Mirror*, and Imara's henchmen easily overcome her in an elevator on her way to work. She soon finds herself locked in both an Underworld cage and the demon's grotesque body. On the other end of the soul swap, Imara zealously embraces all the advantages her new, beautiful appearance affords her.

Piper is peripherally aware that something is not quite right with her sister, but Imara is pretty convincing. The demon is an expert on the Charmed Ones, having broken into Zankou's lair and read all the research he'd compiled on the witches. Finding the demon that attacked her at P3 is foremost on Piper's mind, so when "Phoebe" is suddenly gung ho, she accepts the help. But since Imara sent those demons after Piper, she has no intention of vanquishing her minions. She feigns premonitions that lead to Zankou's followers instead, and she manages to vanquish two of them before things start to unravel.

"Phoebe" points to Imara as the demon they've been hunting and leads them to her cave. When the sisters vanquish "Imara," a white spirit rises, signifying good rather than evil. "Phoebe" is happy to tell Piper and Paige that they've just killed their sister.

Luckily, Phoebe's spirit is a bit too determined to move on just yet. The Charmed Ones are reunited thanks to Paige's new charge, whose powers help the sisters swap back the souls. Imara's spirit has no body left to enter, so she descends to the demonic wasteland.

Paige was initially nervous about her new path as a Whitelighter, and she had problems getting through to her charge. But, never one to walk away from a challenge, Paige perseveres, and with a little guidance from Leo, she begins to truly enjoy her calling.

With demons and charges out of the way, the only thing the Charmed Ones now have to worry about is Inspector Sheridan. Brody used his new Whitelighter powers to bring her out of a coma, and he erased her memory so that she wouldn't pursue the sisters again. But experiencing similar events can trigger the past, and "Phoebe's" vanquishes of Zankou's demons have left no trace of the seemingly mortal men. Piper and "Phoebe" were seen at both crime scenes, arousing Sheridan's suspicions and her doubts about the sisters.

"You've been a Whitelighter for sixty years and toast is all you've got?"

PAIGE MATTHEWS

"That was Phoebe's soul, we just killed your sister."

IMARA, AKA "PHOEBE"

BEHIND THE SCENES

TODD TUCKER (SPECIAL EFFECTS MAKEUP): For Imara we did a prosthetic nose, which gave her a look of a broken, bumpy nose. Right off the bat, that took her to a much more ugly place. We also did some dentures that messed her teeth up and made her look like she had snaggly teeth. And then I also did fake eyebrows to busy up the eyebrows to make her feel a little bit more manly. And then we gave her, also, a giant mole with hair coming out of it. Just to take her to that point where it was just yuck. Suzanne [Krull] was great. She's a very pretty girl to start off. So to take her to that point was fun. And she's a great actress, too, so when she got into it, she just embraced the ugliness.

STUNT COORDINATOR NOON ORSATTI discusses the staging of the attack on Phoebe in the elevator in the *Bay Mirror* building: That was a particularly small set. My regular stunt double for Alyssa was missing in action because she was pregnant. So I got another girl who happened to be a world champion kick-boxer. She was a good gymnast and all that. So we started working around her abilities. She was really good. It was one of those where I got in there and I had my thoughts and then I bounced it off everybody else; all the combatants, all the stunt people who are involved. Some coordinators like to keep it all in themselves, but I find that the collective head is better than a singular head.

"IMAGINARY FIENDS"

Original air date May 8, 2005

WRITTEN BY HENRY ALONSO MYERS | DIRECTED BY JONATHAN WEST

Wyatt appears to have developed an imaginary friend when he continually talks to himself at pre-school, but in reality he is interacting with a demon named Vicus, who preys on children, turning them down the path of evil. Vicus has made sure that only Wyatt can see him, so that he can gain the toddler's trust. Once he curses Wyatt's favorite teddy bear, Wuvey, the child will incrementally grow more and more evil. If he can add Wyatt's immense magical power to his collective, Vicus will be a force to be reckoned with in the Underworld.

Paige notes that every time Wyatt's preschool calls, a demon assaults the Manor, and she thinks that somehow Wyatt is causing these attacks. Since he is only two, and won't talk at home, Piper is unable to communicate with her son. She casts a spell to talk to the "inner Wyatt," but it winds up bringing the grown-up Wyatt from the future. He is good and loving, and thrilled to have a chance to revisit his past. But he tells his mother that he can't remember anything unusual happening at this point in his life. He heads up to his room to have a talk with his younger self and sees Vicus talking to the child. Since only Wyatt can see Vicus, the demon reasons that the adult he saw is the grown-up version of his prey. Vicus succeeds in getting little Wyatt to trust him and to hand over Wuvey, and Future Wyatt turns from good to evil right in front of his family's eyes.

Grown up, very evil, and very powerful, Future Wyatt black orbs to Vicus's cave, determined not to let his family change his future. Phoebe and Paige orb in, and Wyatt allows them to vanquish Vicus. But when that doesn't reverse the demon's curse, the sisters are at a loss. Wyatt explains that it is because he's not under a spell, but—unaware of the cursed teddy bear's effect on his life—has made the choice to be evil of his own volition. He then has Vicus's followers detain his aunts long enough to confront his parents and kidnap the younger version of himself. Wyatt tries to get the Book of Shadows as well, but it repels him now because he is evil.

The Charmed Ones regroup at the Manor and know that Wyatt will again try to get the Book so he can take toddler Wyatt back to the future, where it will be impossible for his family to turn him good. Leo offers himself as bait with the Book, having faith that his son will not hurt him. His love and trust in Wyatt pay off, and Evil Wyatt cannot bring himself to kill his father. Leo gains little Wyatt's trust and gets the toddler to give him Wuvey. Trust was the magic ingredient in Vicus's curse, and once Leo touches the bear, the curse is removed. Future Wyatt once again becomes good, but he is confused and unaware of what happened.

The family is happy yet tearful as they send grown-up Wyatt back to the future. As he disappears in a swirl of white, little Wyatt says "good-bye" to his future self.

"Do I ever have a life in the future?"   **PAIGE MATTHEWS**

"Let's go talk to me."   **FUTURE WYATT HALLIWELL**

"I can't just sit here and let my son corrupt himself."   **PIPER HALLIWELL**

AARON SPELLING (EXECUTIVE PRODUCER): Family is such an important aspect of all the shows we do, whether it's a traditional nuclear family like the show we did called *Family* or where a group of close friends endure high school, college, and finally, on to adult life like *90210*. Family in any sense is such a backbone of everything in life; and in television, we have art imitating life, while we entertain as well.

JONATHAN LEVIN (CONSULTING PRODUCER/PRESIDENT OF SPELLING ENTERTAINMENT): Over time we have told the stories of the changing personal lives of our characters and watched their relationships grow closer. The show is now as much about family as it is about fighting evil.

"DEATH BECOMES THEM"

Original air date May 15, 2005

WRITTEN BY CURTIS KHEEL | DIRECTED BY JOHN KRETCHMER

Zankou returns to launch into his Ultimate Battle with the Charmed Ones. His first goal is to get the Book of Shadows so that he can control the Manor and the Nexus. He knows that the Book is linked to the sisters, so he plans to weaken them, and by doing so, weaken the Book's defenses.

The powerful demon targets Innocents who will particularly rattle the sisters. He also raises a few lost Innocents from the dead to accomplish his goal. Zankou uses his power to bring the

corpses back to "life" and then employs the services of a demonic alchemist who can control the undead. After a few hauntings, Phoebe begins to fall into his trap, but luckily, her sisters maintain more faith in themselves and their powers and put together the pieces of the puzzle.

The Charmed Ones know they won't find Zankou, but they hope to get the alchemist to talk. When they orb to his graveyard lair, they find not only the demon, but many more undead former Innocents who accuse the witches of betraying them. The sisters experience renewed guilt and remorse as well as abject fear as the alchemist commands his zombies to accuse and attack them. Potions and spells are useless as the undead throw their fallen heroes around the chamber like rag dolls. Piper knows the only way to stop the assault is to kill the zombies again. She feels bad enough about losing them once and doesn't want to be responsible for their ultimate demise, but the alchemist has left her no choice—it's her sisters' lives or theirs. Piper blasts the zombies one by one until nothing remains but dust. The alchemist is stunned by the brutal behavior of a Charmed One and says that Zankou led him to believe that they would never act in such a manner. "I lied," Zankou admits, just before he blows up his henchman.

The sisters are stunned and confused by the demon turning on a lieutenant, but they soon understand Zankou's objective. The alchemist served as a disconcerting distraction that made the Charmed Ones emotionally and physically vulnerable, which weakened their link to the Book of Shadows. He also kept them preoccupied so that Zankou could plunder his prize. For when the sisters return home, they go to the attic and find their family legacy gone. Zankou has succeeded in taking the Book and is now ready to begin his final assault on the Charmed Ones.

In the mortal world, Darryl is put in a difficult position as dead bodies go missing and the Halliwells are once again tied to the cases. Inspector Sheridan grows more and more suspicious of the sisters and threatens that if Darryl is not with her, he's against her, and she'll take him down with her suspects. To make matters worse, Shelia Morris has had enough of her husband being in magical harm's way and gives him an ultimatum—our family or theirs.

"I'm starting to think there's only one demon who could be responsible for this."

PAIGE MATTHEWS

"I wouldn't mess with them if I were you."

DARRYL MORRIS

"Now the fun really begins."

ZANKOU

BEHIND THE SCENES

JON PARÉ (PRODUCER): I think we've got a great group of people who've been making TV and movies for a long time. When Brad sends us down a script that's challenging, rather than freezing anybody up, it makes everybody start putting their heads together to come up with a creative solution. At the end of the day, it becomes a very satisfying experience to come up with a creative solution to a technological problem because you beat it. You figured it out. And then when you get somebody to look at it and they respond to it in an emotional way— whether they're laughing or crying—you feel like you've been successful communicating.

At the end of the day, we're making television where we're communicating, and we just happen to be communicating a really fun thing here. Ultimately it's the battle of good winning over evil, and we get to demonstrate it in all these really interesting ways, whether we're coming up with headless horsemen or people taking journeys. It's hard to figure out how to do something that everybody has an image of in their own minds, but you can't really lay it out on paper. It's really hard to try to execute that in a visual style.

"SOMETHING WICCA THIS WAY GOES . . . ?"

Original air date May 22, 2005

TELEPLAY BY BRAD KERN | STORY BY BRAD KERN & ROB WRIGHT
DIRECTED BY JAMES L. CONWAY

On the run from Zankou, the Charmed Ones take shelter in the protection of Magic School. With the Book of Shadows firmly in his grasp, the powerful demon and his minions flame into the Halliwell home and prepare to take over the Nexus. Since Zankou now controls the Book and the Manor, there is no good present to conflict with his evil, and the Ultimate Power easily finds its way into the demon. It also easily finds its way back out when a well-timed spell from the sisters expels the Shadow back into its home. They know that it will be much harder to expel Zankou from *their* home, however.

Fortunately, the sisters are now as familiar with their enemy as he is with them. They offer themselves as bait to distract Zankou from his ultimate goal of possessing the Nexus. No demon has ever been able to resist the opportunity to defeat the Charmed Ones, and Zankou is so close he can taste victory. He also knows that he can't fully access the Book of Shadows without the sisters'

powers, and by taking them from the witches, he will solve two problems at once. Zankou's counsel, Kahn, cautions his leader to stick to his original game plan, arguing that once he has the Nexus, he can easily kill the Charmed Ones. But Zankou cannot pass up the challenge to fight the sisters on more equal footing—and that's exactly what they're counting on.

Attempts to get the Book leave Piper and Phoebe powerless, not to mention a little worse for wear from having battled Zankou. But a little pep talk from Leo reawakens the famous Halliwell determination. The Elders tell the sisters that there is a spell in the Book of

Shadows to destroy the Nexus. It was placed there in the event that evil ever took over the powerful source of magic. Once again relegated to do the Elders' dirty work, the Charmed Ones accept their responsibility—but vow that if they're going down, they're taking Zankou with them. With their fate certain, but their confidence renewed, the sisters plan for their final battle.

One thing they couldn't plan for though, is the phalanx of law enforcement personnel that surrounds their home. Inspector Sheridan had called for Homeland Security again, bringing an Agent Keyes, who is determined to expose the sisters' magic. Sheridan still believes there is a much more human and criminal element to the unsolved mysteries in the Halliwell file, but she encounters the truth when she is killed by one of Zankou's energy balls. The loss of the inspector mobilizes the various law enforcement organizations to close in. Darryl is about to leave on his family vacation when Leo gets word to him about what's happening, and Shelia agrees to let him help this one last time.

The Charmed Ones make all the necessary final arrangements for their lives. The boys are left in the loving custody of their grandfather, Victor, and Leo is somewhere safe, now that Magic School has finally been breached by Zankou. The Book of Shadows again recognizes its rightful owners, who are back to their confident, kick-ass selves, and they get the spell they need. Zankou finds the sisters at the edge of the Nexus and promptly throws them across the room. He chants the spell to take the Nexus into himself—which is just what the Charmed Ones were waiting for. Zankou turns to them with his black eyes of ultimate evil, and they say the spell to destroy the Nexus. Since it is now inside of Zankou, he is destroyed along with it—as well as everything else in the room.

The police outside witness the massive explosion and cautiously enter the Manor. There is no trace of anyone left.

And that's exactly the way it's supposed to be. When Leo returns to his house, three strangers take him aside and glamour into his family. Thanks to Prue teaching Leo how to astral project, and his passing on the knowledge to the sisters, they were never really in the basement with Zankou. Their astral projections blew up the Nexus, while the real Charmed Ones watched it all looking like nothing more than curious bystanders. With the Underworld, the mortal world, and the Elders thinking they're dead, they will be free to live their lives. They give Leo a new persona too, and as a devastated Darryl walks out the front door of the Manor, the four strangers pass by. When one gives him a familiar smile, he understands that good magic has again prevailed. And with that, the door to the Manor magically closes.

"You can't take them head-on, it doesn't work—demons die."　　　　**ZANKOU**

"Never say never—not in this family."　　　　**PHOEBE HALLIWELL**

BEHIND THE SCENES

JIM CONWAY (CO-EXECUTIVE PRODUCER/DIRECTOR) on filming the final episode of Season Seven without knowing if the show would return for an eighth year: I was directing the *series* finale. In my mind I felt that we were not coming back. I believe in being a realist and never being too much of an optimist. With television the way it was and the network the way it was, with a new person at the helm and they had a lot of pilots, I just assumed we were going to be canceled. Brad felt the same way. We had hopes that we would get picked up, but we had to work with the assumption that we were being canceled. So to be fair to the fans, we had to provide a series finale.

All during the shooting of it I felt like since it would be the series finale that it was the last time I would be on this set, it was the last time I'll be in that set. The last time we do this or that.

Everybody did. The final day of shooting with the girls was very emotional. The last thing I shot was a close-up of each of them on the green screen. After each close-up we said, "Ladies and gentlemen, that's it for the season for Alyssa Milano," and everybody clapped and she would get emotional. And then the same for Holly. And those two could come to the wrap party and were able to come and were there. But Rose was going out of the country. So as we did her final thing, she went back with a video camera and prerecorded a little thing to play at the wrap party. Which was nice. And she got a little emotional.

So, for everyone, it was a wonderful, emotional, cathartic thing. It was great. And at the wrap party we had a DVD of all the crew people, a gag reel, but we still didn't know. So the only thing sort of hanging over it was, "Do we have jobs next year?"

CLOSING THE DOOR ON SEASON SEVEN

Jim Conway wasn't the only person wondering if he was out of a job at the end of Season Seven. The cast and crew ended filming that year not knowing if the show was going to be picked up for an eighth season. Though that's not entirely unusual in Hollywood, it was different for a series that had always received its pickup order well before the production wrapped for the season.

Charmed was still one of the most popular series on the WB, but as any television show gets older, costs increase and the network starts questioning if those rising costs are offset by the amount of income they receive. Then the network has to look at the new slate of shows for the following season and determine if they can fill the hole left by the absence of an older show. Unfortunately, due to the lead time it takes to get the final episodes of a season on the air, the *Charmed* cast and crew said good-bye that year not knowing if they'd ever work together again.

HOLLY MARIE COMBS (PIPER): That was something that I was kind of in denial about, in a good way. Because, you know, I remember we were shooting our last shot with the three of us together, and one of the producers is rolling a video camera and I'm, like, "Okay, that's not a good sign! He thinks we're dead in the water!" You know, like, "Oh, this is our last shot!"

And then one of my favorite directors, Mel Damski—who we used a lot and have for years—came by to say good-bye and watch the last shot from another show he was doing. I saw him walk through the door and I went, "Oh God, yeah, now you're going to show up? You've never shown up at any other season wrap that we've had." I was, like, "We're dead in the water! You're killing us!" And he's, like, "Oh God, don't say that!"

The girls were very emotional, and we did our last shot and everybody started clapping, and the girls just started bawling. And I, for some reason, wasn't crying. I was just, "Nope." You know what, for some reason I had some feeling that it wasn't the end. And it could have been straight denial, but it worked for me at the time. We owe it to the fans to do it right and so, in a way, we have the luxury of being able to do that here, and we have the responsibility of tying it up in a way that will make everybody kind of happy. So we'll see. It's bittersweet, definitely.

RANDY CABRAL (VISUAL EFFECTS SUPERVISOR): It really was like the last show. The girls were saying good-bye. That was like the defining moment. It was, like, "Holy cow, this maybe really *is* it." Up to that point you're working to that apex, so you're not really thinking about it, until that last day. It was like the last day of high school.

NANCY SOLOMON (SCRIPT SUPERVISOR): We're sitting here wondering, "Are they going to pick us up? Are they not going to pick us up?" So as a crew we're wondering if we should start networking. Start looking for another job to go to. Do we sit and wait? My predicament was that. We wrapped on April 17, and for that next month we were in this whole, "What do we do? Do we pay bills off? Do we not pay the bills off?" It was kind of a crazy month.

PAUL STAHELI (PRODUCTION DESIGNER): That's the nature of this business. Every job you just never know. When I was teaching at Oregon State and other places as well I would tell the students if you're going into show business and think it's a leaner job than perhaps your parents—you know, they go to work wherever they go to work, if it's an investment brokerage or a steel mill or whatever. It's not that. You have good years and you have bad years and that's the way it works. It's less so in this town if you are decent and you get established. But there will be bad years. So this show's been a bit of a luxury—up till this year I knew I was coming back the next year. So it has been a luxury.

THE *CHARMED* EPISODE TITLE PUNS

A CALL TO ARMS: Generally speaking, a call to arms is a battle cry announcing that it is time to take up weapons to defend oneself.

THE BARE WITCH PROJECT: *The Blair Witch Project* is a hugely successful low-budget horror film released in 1999.

CHEAPER BY THE COVEN: *Cheaper by the Dozen* is a film released in 1950 about a rather large family, based on the book of the same name. It was recently remade (with a sequel even) starring Steve Martin.

CHARRRMED!: A riff on the fact that pirates are typically portrayed as liking to say "Arrrrgh!"

STYX FEET UNDER: "Six feet under" refers to the depth at which the dead are traditionally buried in cemeteries. It is also the name of a TV series that premiered in 2001. In Greek mythology, Styx is the name of the river leading to the underworld, Hades.

ONCE IN A BLUE MOON: A blue moon refers to the second full moon to appear in one month. Since this is a rare occurrence, the phrase "once in a blue moon" is generally used to describe something that is also rare.

SOMEONE TO WITCH OVER ME: "Someone to Watch Over Me" is a classic song by George and Ira Gershwin.

CHARMED NOIR: The term "film noir" refers to a film style emphasizing the use of darkness, light, and shadow; it is usually associated with crime movies. "Noir" is also associated with hardboiled crime fiction.

THERE'S SOMETHING ABOUT LEO: *There's Something About Mary* is a film starring Ben Stiller and Cameron Diaz (1998).

WITCHNESS PROTECTION: The United States Federal Witness Protection Program provides for the relocation of any witnesses of crimes whose lives would be in jeopardy if they testify.

ORDINARY WITCHES: *Ordinary People* is a novel by Judith Guest published in 1976. The book was made into a film in 1980, starring Donald Sutherland, Mary Tyler Moore, and Timothy Hutton.

EXTREME MAKEOVER: WORLD EDITION: *Extreme Makeover: Home Edition* is a home makeover show that premiered in 2003. It aired opposite *Charmed* in most American television markets.

CHARMAGEDDON: "Armageddon" is a biblical reference to the battle between good and evil that is predicted to mark the end of the world.

CARPE DEMON: *Carpe diem* is Latin for "seize the day." The phrase was popularized by the 1989 film *Dead Poets Society*.

SHOW GHOULS: *Showgirls* is a film released in 1995, starring Elizabeth Berkley.

THE SEVEN YEAR WITCH: *The Seven Year Itch* is a 1955 film starring Marilyn Monroe. It was adapted from the 1952 Broadway play of the same name. (Note: The episode title is a nod to the fact that this is the one hundred fiftieth episode of *Charmed*, which takes place in the seventh year of the series.)

SCRY HARD: *Die Hard* is the name of a series of action movies starring Bruce Willis.

LITTLE BOX OF HORRORS: *Little Shop of Horrors* is a Broadway musical about a man-eating plant, which debuted in 1982. The play was based on the famous 1960 B-movie classic of the same name, starring Jack Nicholson.

FREAKY PHOEBE: *Freaky Friday* is a film released in 1976 starring Barbara Harris and Jodie Foster. It was recently remade (2003) with Jamie Lee Curtis and Lindsay Lohan.

IMAGINARY FIENDS: Young children often have playmates who exist only in their imaginations, making them imaginary friends.

DEATH BECOMES THEM: *Death Becomes Her* is a 1992 film starring Meryl Streep, Goldie Hawn, and Bruce Willis.

SOMETHING WICCA THIS WAY GOES . . . ?: "Something wicked this way comes" is a line from Shakespeare's *Hamlet.* The quote has been used in various forms in pop culture over the years. Most notably, it is the title of a 1962 Ray Bradbury novel that was made into a film in 1983. (Note: As the producers believed this could have been the final episode of the series, the title—and the question mark at the end of it—was chosen to mirror the first *Charmed* episode: "Something Wicca This Way Comes.")

EPISODE GUIDE

Season Eight

INTRODUCTION

The WB did pick up *Charmed* for the eighth, and eventually final, season shortly before the network announced its 2005–06 schedule. After weeks of uncertainty the producers happily started making their calls to let everyone know they'd be back, while Alyssa Milano was the one to spread the good news to the fans via her website. Though everyone was thrilled that the series would return, they could not ignore that certain requirements imposed by the network would present new challenges to the production. The main challenge came in the form of a considerably smaller budget for the eighth season. Almost every area of the show was affected by the budget cuts, as all the departments were forced to tighten their belts. Onscreen, this was seen in a variety of subtle changes; it had major repercussions on the set and the cast as well.

At the end of the seventh season, the Charmed Ones effectively left their lives and their home in search of a new beginning. Unfortunately, with no budget for new sets, the producers were forced to come up with a believable way to adjust the story so they could return the characters to that home and that existing set. The new budget also meant that Dorian Gregory would not return for the final season. Though the character, Inspector Darryl Morris, did have a resolution of sorts in the seventh season finale, Dorian was a close friend to the production and an integral part of the success of the series. The loss was hard on everyone, especially considering the important role his character played as the lone mortal in the magical universe. But that was not the only difficult news when it came to cast changes, as the network made it clear that they could afford Brian Krause (Leo) for only part of the season. The departure after the tenth episode of Brian, arguably the most popular cast member among the entire staff, would be especially sad for the entire crew, bringing Rose McGowan to tears during her interview for this book. But the party celebrating his departure at the end of "Vaya Con Leos" wasn't so much a good-bye party as a "See You Later" party. Brian would be back for the last two episodes of the season to bring a final resolution to Piper and Leo's story.

While the network was subtracting, it also insisted on additions, in the form of a new character that eventually became Billie Jenkins. Knowing that Holly, Alyssa, and Rose's contracts all expired at the end of the eighth season, the WB was looking for ways to continue the series or spin it off focusing on the new character. Kaley Cuoco, fresh off the sitcom *8 Simple Rules,* was hired to fill that role and, possibly in conjunction with one of the original actresses, take the show in a new direction. Unfortunately, after the WB merged with UPN, it was determined that the resulting network would have no room on its schedule for the Charmed Ones or their recent charge. However, this final eighth season did give the production the chance to wrap up story lines the way they had envisioned.

COMING BACK FOR THE FINAL SEASON . . .

ALYSSA MILANO (PHOEBE): I think, from reading my message boards, the fans were almost more concerned about the show not coming back than I was. Because I think when you're actually in the situation, you sort of have control of it. Even though it's not a controllable situation, you still understand what your life is going to be like without it. I know that the fans that post on my message boards were crazy, crazy, crazy concerned. So it was important for me to get the news out to them before a press release was out, just because I didn't want them to have to wait anymore. That was silly. If I knew, I thought they should know. They're the reasons we're still on, anyway.

    The great thing about Safesearching.com is having that connection with my fans that has become incredibly personal and important to me and to them. It's a nice relationship and nice balance to have. I feel like the fans took care of us in the beginning of the show. No matter where we were moved to, no matter what time slot, they always found us. Now it's sort of our turn to take care of them. Part of the reason I felt it was so important to come back for an eighth year was to tie up all the loose ends in the story lines.

NOON ORSATTI (STUNT COORDINATOR): It was a summer of crossing your fingers and hoping that it was going to get new legs or at least get picked up for one last season. It was to the point that I was offered two features and a big TV show that were going to start right at about the same time we would go if *Charmed* got picked up. I actually bit the bullet, took my chances on this, and it literally—the day I turned down that TV show, just crossing my fingers—on the same day I got the call that [Season Eight] was going to happen.

ROGER MONTESANO (PROP MASTER): We all had the feeling that we weren't coming back because of all the vibes around here. Our producer, JP [Jon Paré], just told us to store everything. "Don't take anything or destroy anything. Just put it away." So we stored everything. And then I got the call to come back, so it was kind of nice. We just kept everything. Most of my stuff is rental, like all the weapons and all that kind of stuff. So all that, naturally, goes back. But the other stuff—the potion table, the bottles, the candles and stuff—all went into storage.

BRINGING IN A NEW CHARACTER . . .

PAM SHAE (EXECUTIVE IN CHARGE OF TALENT): That was an interesting process, because for the first time, we were really concentrating on going younger for one of our series leads. We wanted somebody that was going to be noteworthy, that would be somebody attractive to the WB, and obviously somebody very, very good at their craft because it was going to be a very demanding character.

I did a master list of all of the gals in that age range. There are not that many, because they're either working or doing features or already on features. So it's a limited group that we have to pull from. *8 Simple Rules* was just finishing, and Kaley was somebody that I had on my list. I adored her. The WB hooked me up with her and I brought her in. Kaley really popped. She came into my office, and I brought Brad Kern down and she lit up the room. She was bouncing off the walls. Told us amazing stories and really won the job in the room. It was sort of a foregone conclusion at that point. The character needed to be somebody that was spunky and very, very confident, but a little unsure of her skills. At this point she was still trying to learn what her abilities were. Kaley just was amazing from the get-go.

KALEY CUOCO (BILLIE): I think they just wanted a blonde on the show. I had a meeting with Brad Kern, and it was a great meeting. We got along so well and then that day they called and were, like, "Yes or no?" And then that week I was going to a gallery shoot with the girls. It was really fast. There was no time for me to be nervous about it. The second I met them, when I went to the gallery shoot, the first person I met was Holly. Then I walked into the makeup room and Alyssa was so cute. She was surrounded by all these people. And I walked in. I was ready to throw up. I was so nervous. *So* nervous. And she came over and gave me the biggest hug and kiss, and was, like, "Kaley! I'm so happy you're here!" And she was giving me kisses. Then Rose came in. It was really nice.

JIM CONWAY (CO-EXECUTIVE PRODUCER): Kaley's been fabulous. Her character addition is great for two things: One, it spices up all the scenes because you've got a new character that's thrust into them, who's got to sort of relearn everything our girls have learned and make the mistakes that they made. And now we have a character we can dress up in weird outfits, because our girls are a little sick of that. The other thing you have is a new actress who brings her own energy—and it's a lot of energy—to the scenes, which lifts all of our girls' energies. They've been doing it for eight years, and sometimes they get a little bored with the scenes. But when you get somebody in there that's new and isn't bored, they bring that freshness that is infectious to everybody else. So it's lifted up, I think, the show for everyone.

THE EPISODES

"STILL CHARMED & KICKING"   *Original air date September 25, 2005*
WRITTEN BY BRAD KERN | DIRECTED BY JAMES L. CONWAY

The Charmed Ones need to lay low so as not to arouse suspicion that they—and Leo—may not actually be dead. Their continual change of appearance has Wyatt and Chris upset and their father, Victor, confused. So Phoebe says a spell. To the outside world, they will look like the strangers they've each chosen as a persona, but to family, they will look like themselves. One last quick *poof* in the cauldron, and their identities are magically—and legally—changed. From now on, they will use as little magic as possible to avoid detection by demons or Elders.

The sisters approach their new lease on life with their typical demeanor. Phoebe is upbeat and ready for new adventures, including—if a premonition is to be believed—marriage to a hunky guy who used to see her in the elevator at the *Bay Mirror*. Piper is hesitant to embrace change but has always dreamed of a demon-free life, so she gradually accepts the new developments and even learns to like them. Things are harder for Paige, whose whole life has revolved around magic and who can't escape her Whitelighter half, which keeps jingling in her head. She summons Grams for advice, and the Halliwell matriarch tells her that although she doesn't approve of the girls' decision, they'll have to live with it. She is not happy with what her granddaughters have done with their legacy, but since it's a done deal, she urges Paige to go out and enjoy herself. Although she tries, the jingling doesn't stop, and Paige can't ignore it any longer. Since the sisters have cloaked themselves from the Elders, Leo says that the cry for help must be coming from a new charge.

That new charge turns out to be a young witch who dresses like a movie femme fatale and thinks nothing of exposing magic. The first time she attempts to vanquish a demon, she's psyched—it's her first demon—and she doesn't really know the drill, so he shimmers out before she can finish the job.

She nails him later at the Manor, when he tries to claim the house by attempting to kill Victor (who had been staying there with the boys to keep up pretenses). With a flip and a telekinetic flourish of her deadly athame, the mystery witch is gone, leaving the Charmed Ones curious—and worried that their cover has been blown.

The sisters figure that the demon, Haas, who survived the assault, will come after Victor again. When Haas shows up at Victor's condo, the mortal is saved by Wyatt, who vanquishes Haas's henchmen. The child allows the powerful demon to live so that he can tell the rest of the Underworld what they will face if they make any further attempts on the Halliwell family. Haas flames out, and Victor and Wyatt morph into Phoebe and Piper, who hope that their ruse worked. But Haas doubts that a small boy would have that much power and is convinced that the Charmed Ones are still alive. All he has to do now is prove it.

Haas isn't the only one who thinks the rumors of the Halliwells' demise is greatly exaggerated. Agent Keyes is still around, still looking to expose magic and convinced that the sisters and Leo are alive and in hiding. He packs up his operation to make it look like he's giving up, but he leaves a young agent, Murphy, behind to keep tabs on everything.

PIPER: *"You can't pick up a guy at a funeral."*
PHOEBE: *"Why not? It's my funeral."*

"Hey, if you don't want my advice, don't conjure me next time."

PENNY "GRAMS" HALLIWELL

BEHIND THE SCENES

NANCY SOLOMON (SCRIPT SUPERVISOR): Lately the scenes with Wyatt have been pretty good. The boys have been laughing a lot. It's cute because they're actually doing their gestures now, because the parents have been working with them. Seeing them doing the little gestures has been adorable.

MARIA SIMMONS (MOTHER OF KRISTOPHER AND JASON SIMMONS, THE TWINS WHO PLAY WYATT): The first episode of this season, I saw them actually do something! Where Kristopher was throwing the spell. We practiced that two weeks. We were throwing spells at everything in the house. But seeing them doing it on TV . . . he was enjoying it. When they started this season, the first two days were awful, because I guess they forgot because it was three months. Their dad had to talk to them, but after that everything was fine.

JIM CONWAY (CO-EXECUTIVE PRODUCER/DIRECTOR): At the end where we've got Wyatt—who isn't really Wyatt, it's actually Piper—controlling all the fireballs and doing all that. Well, he wouldn't work that day. So we have close-ups of him that were shot later with nothing around him, doing some stuff, and then we put him on a green screen and somebody ran around on the other side of the green screen and his arms were following. You cut it all together and it looks great, because he moves his hands and the fireball moves that way.

And then his face, there's something about these boys' faces, they are so full of expression. But the expression can work for any emotion. They look at something and they're supposed to be interested, they look interested. They're supposed to be sad, they look sad. It's an amazing thing. They have such big, expressive faces and eyes that it works for so many things for us. And they're sweet kids. Great parents.

"MALICE IN WONDERLAND" *Original air date October 2, 2005*
WRITTEN BY BRAD KERN | DIRECTED BY MEL DAMSKI

The Charmed Ones are still adjusting to being their alter egos, the Bennett cousins—Jenny (Piper), Julie (Phoebe), and Jo (Paige)—and the fact that they don't have to fight evil on a daily basis. Making things more difficult is the jingling Paige still hears in her head from her new charge and the demon, Haas. Convinced the sisters are alive, he is determined to flush them out. It all ties together when Haas and fellow demon Black Heart use an *Alice in Wonderland* theme to lure teenage Innocents. Haas knows that the sisters won't be able to resist trying to stop him to save Innocents.

What he didn't count on, though, was Billie—the young mystery witch—who is self-taught after recently discovering her considerable powers. In contrast to the Charmed Ones, who have created disguises to avoid magic, the pretty, blond college student decides to affect the black-haired, black-garbed persona to fight evil. Although Billie thinks she's got every-thing under control, her inner witch is a bit more nervous about her new calling and unconsciously keeps calling her Whitelighter for help. When Paige answers the call and interrupts her latest demon battle, the young witch is steamed. A witch-to-witch smackdown ensues, during which Paige begins to discover the identity of this mystery witch.

Paige lays down the magical law to Billie, but at the same time can't help but be impressed with her knowledge and abilities. She tells the teenager to stay put in her dorm room while she and her sisters—uh, cousins—handle the situation. The Charmed Ones determine that the demon responsible for the kidnappings and subsequent catatonic state of the Innocents is sending them a message. Phoebe explains that *Alice in Wonderland* is the perfect ploy, because the story is all about the loss of innocence, the need for escape, and the search for identity. Sound familiar to anyone named Jenny, Julie, or Jo?

Much like the Charmed Ones, Billie rarely does what she's told when fighting evil is involved. Having been attacked by the mystery witch twice, Haas is convinced that she is one of the sisters in disguise, and that the Whitelighter who came to her rescue is another. Black Heart and Haas kidnap Billie and put her through their mind games, but just as she's getting to the point of no return, Black Heart is vanquished. Billie is thrown out of the spell and sees the Charmed Ones vanquish Haas. Having done a bit of research after Paige's slip of the tongue, Billie is impressed to learn that the sisters are as good as their reputation. She swears to keep mum about the fact that they're alive and says that she will help them fight demons if they agree to teach her everything they know in return.

While Billie was dealing with Haas and Black Heart, the Charmed Ones were dealing with their "normal" lives. Paige flirts with the idea of becoming a cop, but finds that she likes flirting with a certain cop more. Piper feels she has no identity now that she has a new identity, but Leo reassures her that she is important and loved even without magic. And Phoebe, trying to read where signs might lead her, finds that they point to a relationship with the handsome and charming Dex and a return to writing "Ask Phoebe," since Julie seems to have the same gifts as her cousin when it comes to giving advice.

"For all you know, I could have saved the world, like, a hundred times over."

JO BENNETT, AKA PAIGE MATTHEWS

"I can't believe this, you guys really are the Charmed Ones."   **BILLIE JENKINS**

BEHIND THE SCENES

AARON SPELLING (EXECUTIVE PRODUCER): When a series runs for such a long time as *Charmed* has, it's the natural progression to introduce new characters to support our three main leads. While our three lovely stars primarily carry the show, these supporting characters enhance the show and help move the story lines along.

E. DUKE VINCENT (EXECUTIVE PRODUCER): Kaley, she's cute as a button, that girl. She is. I really love her. She's fantastic. Apparently the format of this show is a format that the audience loves. Well, we can't keep going on with these three girls, obviously, because these three girls are not going to want to do this forever. I mean, Alyssa's got a motion picture career she wants to go to. Whether she'll have a success or not, I don't know. I think she will. Rose has done a lot of features. Holly, I don't know what Holly wants to do. Now she's gotten married. She's got a child. It's a little bit different. So we brought Kaley in. I think she's doing very well.

KALEY CUOCO (BILLIE): I loved coming onto the show because it's been on for so many years and they have their core audience that's been with them for years. It's a well-established show. They know what they're doing. They're not trying to prove anything to anyone. It was a really easy place for me to join. To just get in there and not be overpowered or overpowering to them. It was just kind of a nice addition, I think.

"RUN, PIPER, RUN"

Original air date October 9, 2005

WRITTEN BY CAMERON LITVACK | DIRECTED BY DEREK JOHANSEN

In an effort to make a new life to go with her new look, Piper agrees to a meeting set up by her father with a corporate headhunter. Everything goes well and the man is ready to recommend "Jenny" for a high-level position, until her security check sends up an alert. It seems that the person whose image Piper assumed is wanted for murder!

Phoebe and Paige do a little investigating and find that the woman with Piper's borrowed identity is Maya Holmes, a local model who is accused of killing her photographer boyfriend. While Piper waits for her sisters to find the real Maya so they can swap her in the jail cell, she gets a visit from a vain and arrogant assistant district attorney named Walter Nance. His conversation leads Piper to realize that Nance had been dating Maya and that he killed the photographer because he was angry that the beautiful blonde left him for a younger man. His threats leave no doubt that Nance will now kill Maya, too. Piper knows that the woman is not only innocent, but an Innocent.

Nance gets Maya released from jail and believes he kills her. He doesn't know that Piper and Paige are tracking their Innocent and have saved her life. The question now is, how to bring Nance to justice?

The answer comes from Billie, who has been studying magic with Paige. The young witch's presence fills needs in the Charmed Ones' lives on many levels. In Billie they have a bright, eager pupil to whom they can impart their knowledge and experience, and also someone who will fight demons while they are "dead," so they don't have to feel guilty about the evil that continues to run rampant. Tutoring the teenager gives Paige a purpose and keeps her connected to magic.

Billie suggests that the sisters take a page from Barbas's book—strike such fear in Nance's heart that he is forced to confess. Maya tells the witches that the one thing the arrogant attorney fears the most is growing old. When they make him see himself as a hundred-year-old man, he is appropriately spooked. He falls to his certain death, but Piper freezes him a few feet from the pavement and gives him the chance to confess—or die.

With Nance behind bars, Maya's name is cleared, but Piper needs to find a new identity. Although she needs a new look, she decides to stick with everything else, because she's pretty happy with the life she's been living.

During all the Nance baiting and trapping, Phoebe is trying to figure out how to save Dex's art show from the earthquake she saw in a premonition. The middle Charmed One worries that if his life's work is ruined, she may never get her man. But it turns out that Phoebe wasn't supposed to stop the show, she was supposed

to be there for it, for as the earth begins to move, Dex grabs hold of Phoebe to protect her. She has her "moment" where love begins to bloom, and her future, like most of Dex's sculpture, remains intact.

"Oh, honey, orange is so not your color."   **PAIGE MATTHEWS**

"We don't usually vanquish humans."   **PIPER HALLIWELL**

BEHIND THE SCENES

NANETTE NEW (DEPARTMENT HEAD KEY MAKEUP ARTIST): And now we have Kaley. Talk about fun. She's so beautiful. She has been so wonderful. I love doing her makeup, and it's so fun because she's nineteen and she's just this really fun little witch. So we get to do all kinds of wonderful makeups on her. I can take her over the top. With the other girls we stay into the beauty makeup, but with Kaley I can go over the top with her. She loves the liner and the dark eyes. We kid a lot with her. She's really light and fun. She's been a great energy on the show. She really has.

One of the things I do see is, it is so magical with Kaley. The energy is shifting into a different place. We have all kinds of places we can go with it, with her mother and father, finding her sister. . . . A new fresh energy is great.

NOON ORSATTI (STUNT COORDINATOR): We brought in a new stunt person for Kaley. It's actually a girl that I've sort of weaned into the business. She was a world-class gymnast. She was on the United States trampoline team. And we have seen some more gymnastics on the show now. She comes from a good martial arts background. Her name is Nicole Surels. I actually introduced her to her husband, another stunt guy who doubled Julian McMahon for us. Kind of keeping it all in the family. She's a great girl with unbelievable talent. And she is strikingly close in appearance to Kaley.

The eighth season is going to be an exciting one because we have been able to explore our new character's abilities and had some really great stunts. We've been hitting people with cars, more battling, more intricate battling, more trickery with this new girl. Kaley's great because she's such a gamer. She wants to learn. She's hard-core. It's fresh.

"DESPERATE HOUSEWITCHES"   *Original air date October 16, 2005*
WRITTEN BY JEANNINE RENSHAW | DIRECTED BY JON PARÉ

The seemingly perfect mother of one of Wyatt's preschool classmates gets under Piper's skin. What the Charmed One doesn't know is that a Possessor demon literally has done the same to the unsuspecting mortal. Believing that the sisters are dead, the Possessor targets Mandi, so that she can gain Wyatt's trust by acting like a loving and nurturing mother. She also encourages him to use magic, further endearing herself to the toddler. It's all part of the Possessor's plan to use Wyatt to resurrect The Source and once again turn the child and his immense powers toward Evil.

While Piper endures the condescending comments of Mandi and the other mothers, Leo continues Billie's education in magic. She has more of an interest in the nunchaks she's tele-kinetically twirling than the books he encourages her to read, but the idea of Magic School intrigues the young witch, and she's anxious to visit the historic institution. Leo and Piper veto the idea, as it could risk exposing them to magical elements both good and bad. But Billie is about as impatient as her three magical mentors and concocts a potion that takes her and Leo to the school. The former headmaster is confused to see demons populating the hallowed halls, and he worries that their access to all the information stored there could destroy good magic. He says they need to go back to the Manor and alert the sisters, but Billie didn't bring a return potion. As they search for the book with a spell to transport them, they are busted by two demons, and Billie puts that nunchak practice to good use. Leo and Billie assume the downed demons' positions (and their clothes) and infiltrate Demon Central. They are about to return home when Mandi materializes, with Wyatt in tow. Something is very wrong, and Leo is not about to leave his son in this situation. He sends Billie back to update the Charmed Ones, while he stays on the scene to watch over Wyatt.

With the toddler's innocent help, Mandi conjures The Source. As the ultimate evil approaches the child, Leo speaks out—and is found out. In the interim, Wyatt had orbed to his father, who now takes him to a safe place as the Charmed Ones arrive. Knowing that The Source was conjured by the Possessor, and is therefore tied to her existence, the sisters vanquish the lesser demon. The Source follows her fiery demise—gone for good this time.

Piper wants to leave the obnoxious and unconscious Mandi with the demons at Magic School, but her sisters insist she be returned home. When Piper and Leo see Mandi at Wyatt's preschool play, she's lost some of her perky perfection, leading them to believe that on some level the desperate housewife knows something strange happened.

Meanwhile, Paige is concerned that Dex is playing Phoebe and that her sister is pinning her hopes on a misguided premonition. When she sees Dex with a beautiful brunette, her worst fears are confirmed. A badly botched undercover operation incurs Phoebe's wrath, but as a result, Paige learns that Dex truly cares for her sister.

"Please tell me there's a demon somewhere, because I really need to blow something up."
PIPER HALLIWELL

"I didn't realize I had to learn how to vanquish vanquished demons." **BILLIE JENKINS**

MARIA SIMMONS (MOTHER OF KRISTOPHER AND JASON SIMMONS, THE TWINS WHO PLAY WYATT): I loved the costumes, but I think the pumpkin was kind of hot, because five minutes and they wanted to take it off. But it was so cute. And the other kids, too. It was such a great show for them. It's good for the kids, too. Because even when the other kids of the people that work here come in, they feel more comfortable. They like to see other kids their age.

HOLLY MARIE COMBS (PIPER) on how motherhood has affected her acting: I definitely think that there's a little bit more method in my acting these days. It's like when I read the last scene of "Desperate Housewitches," when Wyatt is doing his school play. I actually started getting a little teary-eyed when I was reading it, because I realized that I was going to have that experience myself, and I was, like, "Oh my God." It's just hard to… you know you want them to grow up and be happy and be on their own and be individuals, but at the same time you're, like, "Please don't grow up! That's my baby!" So I realized the moment Finley started walking—at nine and a half months, by the way, which was horrifying—that as soon as he started walking, he was walking away from me. It's like they take those first few steps away from you, and you're, like, "Kill me. Kill me now."

JON PARÉ (PRODUCER/DIRECTOR): When I got the script for "Desperate Housewitches," it was a different type of show for me to do because there wasn't a lot of action. There wasn't a lot of visual effects. There were a lot of kids. There were *a lot* of kids. It was about actors. It was about people. It was about relationships. And that's harder for me to do, because that's not where a lot of my experience has been. I tried to study hard. I tried to work hard on it. And it was a very rewarding experience to do scenes that pushed the story forward because of the actors' performances, as opposed to an action sequence or a visual effects sequence. The characters were pushing the story forward. As a result of that, the scenes would flow and they would evolve.

Sometimes when you're doing stunts and visual effects, there's a lot of stop and start with the scenes, because you always have to stop to put in the magic or stop to put in the stunt. When you're dealing with performance-driven pieces, the scenes are able to evolve all to themselves. All of a sudden you see somebody do something and there's magic to that process as well. It was really rewarding for me, because at the end of the show I felt the sentiment of this sister, in this case Piper, and her love for her child when her child was up onstage. I understood that because of my own experience with my own children. And when I saw that look in her, I knew that she understood the same thing. And it was really rewarding. It really made a lot of sense. I could tell it held a spot in her heart too, because she just had a child. It's a special time for her, too.

"REWITCHED"

Original air date October 23, 2005

WRITTEN BY ROB WRIGHT | DIRECTED BY JOHN KRETCHMER

Billie's anxiety to stop studying and get into the fight begins to chip away at the Charmed Ones' satisfaction with their new lives. Defying Paige's orders to just observe a demon and not engage him, Billie attracts the interest of an Upper-Level fiend named Antosis, and also Homeland Security Agent Murphy. Murphy's been following Billie to get a lead on the Halliwells, and he's about to strike pay dirt.

But first, the Bennett cousins have a lot to do. Julie, aka Phoebe, is supposed to go to Napa with Dex, but thanks to a wayward spell from Billie, winds up marrying him instead! Jamie—Piper's new identity since the whole Jenny-wanted-for-murder thing—is holding a speed dating night at P3, and she's coerced Jo, otherwise known as Paige, into participating. When the sisters admonish Billie for casting the spell on Phoebe and Dex, she makes a good argument that maybe this was truly Phoebe's premonition and her fate. Although initially stunned by the events, Phoebe has to agree with Billie's logic. She also begins to have a newfound respect for the young witch's talents and her commitment to picking up the baton that she and her sisters have dropped.

Meanwhile, Piper has managed to make speed dating cool, and the club is back on track. So is Paige, who meets a great guy. But when he tells Jo how beautiful she is, Paige decides that she doesn't want an alter ego any longer. She returns to the Manor to find Phoebe having similar regrets—Dex is married to Julie, after all. Phoebe has also come to terms with the fact that they can no longer ignore their destiny. Paige agrees, and the Charmed Ones are two-thirds of the way back to being resurrected.

Oddly enough, it's Agent Murphy who convinces Piper that it's time to return to her old life. He doesn't realize he's talking to one of the most powerful witches in existence when he chides Jamie

about letting the bad guys win, but he knows there's a connection somewhere. The sisters reverse the secret identity spell and easily vanquish Antosis. The only thing left to do now is to rise from the dead.

Agent Murphy had promised Jamie that unlike Agent Keyes, he would not arrest, pursue, or harm the sisters in any way. He just wants good to triumph over evil, and he just wants the Charmed Ones' help again, so they go to him and offer it. Initially overwhelmed by the reality of the supernatural things he'd suspected, Agent Murphy accepts the offer and provides a cover story.

Everything is back to normal, or as normal

as it gets for the Charmed Ones, but Phoebe still has a husband to deal with. Like most of San Francisco, Dex has seen the press conference held by Agent Murphy and knows that Phoebe is really alive, but he's puzzled when she comes to see him. She decides the easiest way to explain everything is just to show him, so Phoebe morphs into Julie, but before she can say anything, Dex faints.

"He can't prove you're alive. You don't even look like you."   **BILLIE JENKINS**

"I miss me."   **PHOEBE HALLIWELL**

"Everyone's gonna freak out because technically, we're still dead."   **PAIGE MATTHEWS**

BEHIND THE SCENES

JIM CONWAY (CO-EXECUTIVE PRODUCER): I think the fact that Julian launched off of *Charmed* really helps the young male guys get interested in the show. I think it helped us to get Nick Lachey because of Julian's success. Nick got a lot of attention off of *Charmed* when he was on it, because it was his first acting job. I think that helped us get Kerr. And now we've got Ivan Sergei [Henry Mitchell] on the show. So I think it's a great place for these guys, who are available to be seen by their audience. Because their audience is primarily young women, and it's a great place for them to get noticed. We got great ratings at the beginning of last season with Nick. I think he really helped us. And we had Jason Lewis [Dex Lawson] at the beginning of the year. He was great. A terrific guy. So it's fun for the show to have these really attractive guys do these arcs with the girls, and it's fun for the girls because they keep getting different interesting boyfriends, and that's always good.

"KILL BILLIE: VOL. 1"   *Original air date October 30, 2005*
WRITTEN BY ELIZABETH HUNTER | DIRECTED BY MICHAEL GROSSMAN

The Charmed Ones return to their "normal" lives just in time for Halloween, and the early trick-or-treaters at their door are the unrelenting members of the press, anxious to get the scoop on the sisters' undercover operation for Homeland Security. Piper tries turning some of them into rats, but even that doesn't seem to deter them. Paige says that the only way to get them off the story is to prove there is no story, but that may be a bit difficult with Billie determined to vanquish a demon.

Wanting to prove her abilities, Billie takes on the Dogon, a demon who has been killing other demons to obtain their powers so that he may be feared enough to rule the Underworld. She has a plan and she has potions, but when she faces off with him at Magic School, the young witch freezes. His appearance causes her flashback to the night her sister, Christy, was kidnapped. Billie hears the thunder and sees the lightning and the mocking grin of a jack-o'-lantern that preceded the demon with a flowing black cape and taloned fingers who dragged her sister from the safety of her bed—and the memory paralyzes her.

Determined to not let it happen again, Billie returns to the Manor and goes to the Book of Shadows. She recites a spell to erase her memories, and with renewed confidence seeks out the Dogon again. She successfully launches her vanquishing potion at him, but he telekinetically diverts it to his henchman, who explodes into flames. A battle ensues, and Billie finally manages to seriously wound the powerful demon. He flames back to Magic School to regroup and form a plan.

When Paige finds the Book open to the memory-erasing spell, she orbs to Billie's dorm just in time to orb the young witch out before the Dogon can finish her off. The sisters brew more Dogon-vanquishing potion as they confront Billie about what's going on. As she recounts the story again, she realizes that the Dogon is not the demon who took Christy—but that doesn't mean that he doesn't need to be stopped. The Dogon shimmers into the Halliwell attic with a score to settle and takes Billie back to Magic School. Luckily, she grabs some of the vanquishing potions from Piper's hand before shimmering out, and she finally finishes off her nemesis. The Dogon explodes in a fiery mass, but Billie's nightmares won't be as easily conquered.

And neither will Phoebe's heart. After Dex asks some serious questions about their relationship, she comes to the conclusion that it all happened too fast and too magically. Neither one of them knows their true feelings for each other, since premonitions, spells, and an assumed identity were central to the entire affair. Phoebe and Dex decide to take things slowly and see where they lead.

All that's left to deal with is that pesky press. Paige consults the Elders, who confirm her first instincts—if there's no story to tell, they'll just go away. And indeed, when Paige opens up the Manor to them, all they find is a somber Phoebe and Piper and Leo in the middle of a very ordinary and very loud marital dispute. The reporters slink away in search of their next big scoop.

"You can fight demons but you're afraid of pumpkins?"   **PIPER HALLIWELL**

"Piper, you cannot blow up the entire media."   **PAIGE MATTHEWS**

BEHIND THE SCENES

TODD TUCKER (SPECIAL EFFECTS MAKEUP): When we first started conceptualizing the Dogon, he was supposed to be kind of a Phantom of the Opera meets Darth Vader. That was what was in the script. So I wanted to be very careful, because you can very easily design something and then once you actually make it, it comes off very cheesy. So you have to be careful that what you make feels original and has some meat behind it so that your beasts and your demons don't feel weak. With that character we wanted to create a half face mask, and right off the bat I didn't want it to just look like the Phantom. So I changed the color of it. I changed the design and made it feel more like an Aztec kind of sculptured look as opposed to a smooth porcelain look like the Phantom was.

Originally the idea was that because he has a cape he's got bird qualities about him. So we talked about one of his hands being diseased and looking like a bird's talon hand. And then we designed it, and I was a little concerned because we weren't really doing anything else on him except for the side of his face. I was a little concerned that it would look odd that you have a monstrous hand but everything else feels somewhat normal. So we built it and we checked it out and it was exactly that. It looked odd. It didn't match. We all knew it right when we saw it. We were, like, "This just doesn't work. How am I going to fix this?"

What we did was, we actually made a couple changes in the wardrobe. His wardrobe felt a little bit light, and I wanted him to feel thicker and a little bit more aggressive. So we gave him a thicker cape and we beefed up his clothes so he felt a little bit more solid. Then we decided his creature hand was so out of place that instead what we did was we put finger extensions on him and diseased up his hand. So that what happened is the mask that was covering his face was covering a diseased face so that to have a diseased hand that looks just more creepy as opposed to monstrous. It all tied in. So we quickly made the change and then he shot the next day. We had to turn around and come up with a fix-it very quickly. But we did and everyone seemed to be very happy. It actually gave him more mobility with his hands, too, because he wasn't wearing a giant glove; it was just finger extensions. So he was able to get more motion and movement out of his performance.

"THE LOST PICTURE SHOW"   *Original air date November 6, 2005*
WRITTEN BY DOUG E. JONES & ANDY REASER I DIRECTED BY JONATHAN WEST

Paige isn't exactly welcoming when her father, Sam, orbs into the Manor. It's been three years since she saved his life and he hasn't kept in touch, so she's openly hostile to the Whitelighter when he asks for help with a charge named Jonathan David Williams. Known as JD, the man was a future Whitelighter who suddenly vanished in 1955. He reappeared just as abruptly that morning—and he hasn't aged a day!

It's obvious that a demon is behind everything, and as neither of her sisters is available, Paige reluctantly teams up with Sam to solve the mystery. They enlist the help of Agent Murphy, and armed with JD's explanation of what he remembers, father and daughter track down a demon named Vaklav, who feeds off of the emotional pain of others. He maintains his supply of Innocents by taking their picture with his special camera, which traps his victims as an image in a demonic montage. Vaklav then lives off the anguish of the family members who have lost their loved one. When there is no one left to grieve, Vaklav frees the Innocent to make room for another in the photo, and then kills them before they can know what happened. But JD escapes the demon's fireball, and now Vaklav has to contend with Paige and Sam.

When they find Vaklav's photo shop, Sam can feel the pain of the trapped Innocents—all future Whitelighters. Father and daughter argue over their use of their powers, their legacy, and their relationship, and after Paige storms out, Vaklav appears. He snaps Sam's picture, trapping him in the collage, and offers to trade the Whitelighter for JD. The sisters are now all on the case and, of course, won't bargain with a demon, but JD offers to accept the deal. He's out of his time and place, with no loved ones left, and wants to repay Sam for turning his life around.

Vaklav promptly kills JD and has no intention of freeing Sam because, even if she won't admit it, Paige truly loves her father. When she comes to that realization, her sisters suggest that all she has to do is call for Sam as her father, not simply as Sam, and he will have the power to orb to her. The power of love is indeed strong, and Sam materializes, along with the other Innocents who were trapped in the picture. They are quickly followed by Vaklav, but the Charmed Ones are expecting him. Piper blasts his fireball back at him and knocks him squarely on his butt, allowing Paige to grab his magic camera and snap a picture, trapping Vaklav inside for eternity.

Paige and Sam acknowledge that they'll have to work on their relationship, and they part with the promise to try. Piper and Leo also make a promise—to try to listen to each other and understand each other's problems. After a soothsayer switches their bodies, the charmed couple continues to ignore their issues, until Phoebe gives them some sage advice.

And as for Phoebe, her premonition of her future daughter still haunts her, so she considers artificial insemination. But the middle Charmed One soon realizes that she wants the whole deal—a loving husband with whom she can create a family and live happily ever after.

"How did I wind up the only sane one here?"   **PAIGE MATTHEWS**

"You guys have forgotten how great you are together."   **PHOEBE HALLIWELL**

BEHIND THE SCENES

JONATHAN WEST (DIRECTOR OF PHOTOGRAPHY/DIRECTOR): There are so many aspects to think about when shooting a TV series, *Charmed* or otherwise. With an eight-day filming schedule, communication is a key factor. Meetings are fast and compact. A lot of information goes out and has to be acted upon . . . in every department . . . set design and construction, costume, makeup, set lighting, camera gear, visual effects, special effects . . . all end up on a piece of film which is ultimately my responsibility. To translate the collective visions of writers, producers, directors, actors into photographic images that help to tell a story every week is quite a task.

The DP [director of photography] experience adds a strong visual repertoire to my preparation when I'm directing. Working with many directors over the years was both intimidating and encouraging when I started directing in 1994. I wanted to be perceived as an actor's director too, not just a person who knew where to put the camera. I had done some acting in my twenties . . . all theater. I'd also been part of a two-year workshop sponsored by the TV Academy for nondirecting members in 1991. Brad Kern gave me the okay to direct during my first year on *Charmed*. I will have directed six episodes during my tenure on the show. I love directing and I'm truly happy being able to do both jobs. It stimulates a different part of the brain, I'm sure. I can never give up DP work . . . I'd miss it terribly. Although, when I direct, the DP work is performed by camera operator Kris Krosskove.

STEPHEN LEBED (VISUAL EFFECTS SUPERVISOR): We're probably working with three-fourths of the budget we had the previous season. Brad's done a really good job of writing the episodes in such a way that we're doing less and less; we're relying less heavily on the effects in order to carry the show. That's been a great help. Because of budget constraints on effects, it affects a lot of things. I find that I don't have as much freedom to plan things a certain way because of issues of overtime or just general production issues. So it's forced me to be more creative in terms of how to adhere to what the writers want while working with an even tighter and even smaller budget. For me this season's been particularly fun, because when you have less to work with it just forces you to pull out the stops. It really forces the creativity. In the end I think it's paid off. Now it feels like the effects counts are slowly starting to creep up again. I think what's happened is, as the writers see that we're able to accomplish what they've set, they set the bar a little higher and force us to do a little bit more.

PETER CHOMSKY (PRODUCER): When the show started, a big visual effects episode was, like, thirty-five shots. With technology advancing and our show growing, Brad has written more and more visual effects into the show. Last year we were averaging probably about 140 visual effects an episode. Three of the last five episodes, we had in the neighborhood of two hundred effects shots per episode. It was huge. This year, with the budgets being pulled back, it's been addressed in story so that there are less fight sequences and less visual effects, and a bit more character and story being told. So we're averaging probably about eighty to a hundred visual effects an episode.

We just did an episode that probably has about fifty visual effects. It's got a really tight turnaround. So that's a really light show now. With the artists that we have and the way we're able to turn over the shots—they know what to do—they get it turned around. It's not easy. I'm delivering a show for this Sunday. Today's the first day of the mix—it's a Wednesday—we'll be putting in some visual effects today and finish the color timing. Tomorrow will be my second and last day of the mix, and I'll finish the show and make delivery tapes Thursday night and deliver Friday. It airs Saturday in Canada. It airs Sunday night here. That's just the way it is.

"BATTLE OF THE HEXES"

Original air date November 13, 2005

WRITTEN BY JEANNINE RENSHAW | DIRECTED BY LEVAR BURTON

While helping Agent Murphy with some cold case files, Billie naively puts on Hippolyta's belt (the Golden Belt of Gaea) and is transformed into a superhero, complete with super powers. Her first magical metamorphosis freaks Billie, especially since she knows how this story ends. Hippolyta was a powerful Greek queen who wanted to create a world where men and women were equals, and she was butchered by Hercules for her efforts. The thought of such a messy demise makes her angry and triggers her new powers, which accidentally turn Leo invisible. The growing power of the belt also begins to affect other women around her, so a solution is necessary—and fast.

Adding to Billie's problems is a demon named Zira, who is tired of doing the bidding of her male superiors. When she is alerted to the fact that the belt's powers have been activated, she angles to control them to her advantage. Zira cannot wear the belt, as its immense power would immediately kill someone evil, but, she can manipulate Billie to do her bidding—and she does, once the belt's strength overtakes the young witch's better judgment. It is now just a matter of time before that belt will consume Billie and kill her.

Once Billie has left the Manor, Piper and Phoebe are no longer under the spell of her enchanted accessory and mobilize to rescue their young protégée. Leo—made visible again per Piper's request—says that there's a book at Magic School with a spell that will remove the belt. Now all they have to do is find a way to get into Magic School under the wary and watchful eyes of Zira and Super Billie.

Piper comes up with a plan and makes Leo invisible again so that he can go undetected while he looks for the book. She and her sisters follow him, and they arrive just as Billie has vanquished the male demons for her new best friend, Zira. When Leo locates the spell, Paige calls for the book and reads it, and the belt drops off of Billie. She returns to normal and Paige orbs the artifact onto Zira, who explodes, taking Hippolyta's belt with her. Piper makes Leo visible again and points out that Billie was saved by men and women working together—just as Hippolyta wanted them to.

Before she was called to save Billie, Paige had to attend to her new charge, a young man named Speed, who is destined to become a Whitelighter—if he can stay out of trouble. Unfortunately, trouble follows Speed, as does his parole officer, a rather gruff but oddly charming man named Henry Mitchell. Henry and Paige both want the same thing for Speed—to keep him on the straight and narrow—but they have very different approaches to solving the problem. In the end, Paige's faith in Speed trumps Henry's cynicism, and the two find that they work well as a team—in more ways than one.

And Piper is having trouble finding a band to play at P3, so she's forced to turn to Leo's chauvinistic buddy Smitty for help. She's grateful that Smitty books Liz Phair, but she vows to never deal with the man ever again.

"Who are we, Charlie's witches?"   **PAIGE MATTHEWS**

"I've been turned into a mermaid, a mummy, a genie—okay, trust me, I know these things."   **PHOEBE HALLIWELL**

BEHIND THE SCENES

CELEST RAY (MUSIC COORDINATOR): The song with Liz Phair is "Somebody's Miracle." Brad Kern selected that song off her brand-new album, because he really wanted to underpin the fact that relationships that we have are something that we work on and that we need to feel that our marriages are precious and that counterpart that we've selected in our life is a miracle in our life. It was the culmination in that episode to Leo and Piper arguing and having issues and the fact that women and men have different parts to them, but at the end of the day, there's that special miracle you have with somebody. So that song was specially selected for that reason.

KEN MILLER (EXECUTIVE IN CHARGE OF POSTPRODUCTION): If we can do something thematic from the song's perspective to help tell the story, we're going to look for it. God bless Aaron [Spelling]. In the old days we always had a montage at the beginning of our shows. We'd show the streets of *90210* or *Melrose* and play a song. Aaron never liked credits over dialogue. I really respect him for that. Unfortunately, the networks really want the shows to get going now, so we can't do those like we used to. But that was kind of the advent of creating montages and using music to carry the opening of the show and get people involved. We're always looking thematically for songs that can be reflective of what's happening on the show, if we're fortunate enough to find that.

"HULKUS POCUS"

Original air date November 20, 2005

WRITTEN BY LIZ SAGAL I DIRECTED BY JOEL J. FEIGENBAUM

Agent Murphy wants the Charmed Ones to bring him a Krychek demon. But when Piper and Paige go after it, they find a much bigger and stronger, not to mention uglier, version of what they were expecting. Unable to overpower the normally low-level demon, they question Murphy about its mutant state, but he's not talking. The sisters get a better idea of what's going on after another hulked-out demon infects Billie with the virus that's overtaking the magical world—good and evil creatures alike.

Billie will soon die if the sisters don't get answers, so they go back to Murphy, and Piper threatens to blow him up unless he tells them the truth. The virus is a result of some failed government experiment involving the Krychek. Since the human patient (Patient X) involved had no adverse effects, the sisters reason that his blood will provide an antidote. But there are no records left from the project except Patient X's ID badge, and that's been wiped of any information. Piper says that even if they combine their powers, they won't have enough time to save Billie, but Phoebe suggests if they increase their powers, they might. So the sisters infect themselves from Billie's wound, and the Hulked Ones' superscrying quickly finds Patient X. He cooperates, and the sisters, Billie, and the rest of the magical world are saved from certain death.

During all this drama, Paige agrees to help Henry with a sweet baby named Ramon. The parole officer needs to find Ramon's father before Social Services takes the infant, and although Paige doesn't "do babies," she is sympathetic to the situation. When Billie hulks out and furniture begins to fly at the Manor, Paige uses a little magical assistance to speed up the governmental red tape, and Ramon is soon safe in his father's arms. Some questions arise about Paige's methods, but Henry doesn't pursue them, allowing the woman he describes as "beautiful, with a great smile and a little wacky," to have her secrets. Just one more reason for the Charmed One to want to spend more time with this strong, caring, and (conveniently) handsome man.

And when the day began, Phoebe had decided that her premonitions were no longer reliable and resolved to give up on her powers. But the experience of almost losing Billie makes her embrace her magic once again. She even begins to believe her premonitions when she sees the vision of herself with her little girl again. Her future self reassures her that it will all be real, although the timetable may have altered a bit. Phoebe is once again hopeful, because she knows if you can't trust yourself, who can you trust?

"Why are all these demons running around on steroids?"   **PIPER HALLIWELL**

"Cliff Notes version? We hulked up, kicked some butt, and saved the world."
                                                            PHOEBE HALLIWELL

BEHIND THE SCENES

RANDY CABRAL (SPECIAL EFFECTS COORDINATOR), who coincidentally worked on the original *Incredible Hulk* television series: We've got some bodybuilders on this show too, so that's kind of a fun deal. They're hulking out in a little bit different way. It's not something like before on the original *Hulk*, where you'd have to twist a tire iron or do something to go through the metamorphosis to show that anger sent him to. This is a spell. But it's still fun. There's a lot of fun things that we're having fun with. That's basically what today is. We're going to go in there and bust up some more balsa-wood furniture—have our Hulk come in—and we've got cables on tables for flipping and flying.

My guys are the best in the world. We've been together since we started. In fact, Vinnie [Borgese], who works for me . . . we worked for Vinnie's dad, Mike, on the original *Hulk*. We worked for him on *Jaws 2, Jaws 3*. He was the big Universal coordinator over there. We've been together for almost thirty years. Everybody has their own talents. I've got really good guys, so I know what they can do. Everybody trusts everybody. It's not like there's a newbie or somebody that you can't trust. We've done so much breakaway and so many things that we know exactly what to do.

TODD TUCKER (SPECIAL EFFECTS MAKEUP): Today I'm playing a creature called the Krychek demon, and it's supposed to be a big, giant, hulkish creature that one of the actors transforms into because of a scratch they get and they become diseased. We have all three of the girls changing into these creatures also, and Billie. We have stunt girls that are playing the parts once they Hulk up, and they were the perfect body type. We've got really sexy, toned, muscular girls that once we put them in makeup, it's supposed to be a hulked-up version, monstrous version of our lead characters.

We have the girls in a full-face prosthetic, and then we did body makeup to make their muscles and the definition stand out more. They look great. When they first started trying to cast these characters, I asked them to bring in big girls. The first group of girls that came in, when I said big, I meant muscular and toned. The first group of girls that came in were tall and thin. I was, like, "Oh, boy. This is not going to work." Luckily, all of a sudden they brought in three girls that could not have been more perfect. They had acting background and they were totally into the prosthetics, especially for this episode. It really came together nicely.

"VAYA CON LEOS"

Original air date November 27, 2005

WRITTEN BY CAMERON LITVACK | DIRECTED BY JANICE COOKE LEONARD

Everything is going well for the Charmed Ones—they've been "demon light," Piper and Leo have settled into a loving and easygoing relationship again, and everyone's healthy and happy. So Piper knows that something will surely come along to screw things up, but even she didn't think that something would be the Angel of Death—and that he would be coming for Leo. To hide her husband from Death, Piper casts a spell that goes a little awry and turns every man in San Francisco into the image of her husband. It's not perfect, but it will confuse Death until she and Paige can come up with a better plan.

Meanwhile, Phoebe is helping Billie, who has found the demon who kidnapped her sister, Christy, fifteen years ago. She's just about to get him to talk, when he's wounded and taken by a demon bounty hunter named Burke. When she goes to Burke's cave, she finds that he keeps his "trophies" in ice chambers—frozen, but not dead. He's about to put Billie on ice too, when Phoebe shoots him with his own crossbow, but her sisters call a lost witch and she's drawn away before she can finish him off, allowing Billie to escape.

Piper and Paige have summoned their sister because they need the Power of Three. Despite their best efforts, Death found Leo, but although he is mortally wounded, he was not killed immediately, and Piper knows there must be a reason for this. But Death can't tell her, nor can an Elder or an Avatar she summons. So she and her sisters use the Power of Three to call for the one power who can give them the answers they need: the Angel of Destiny. Piper says she knows that there is some Grand Design that she cannot change, but she pleads with the angel to consider that there may be a way to satisfy the plan without Leo having to die. The angel is initially resolute, but the sisters make a good argument, so she gives them some insight into why such

drastic measures have been taken. The Charmed Ones are destined to fight one more battle—one that they may not see coming, and one that they may not survive. Losing Leo will motivate them to fight, and without the determination instilled by that pain, they may not prevail. But after meeting the sisters and seeing their resolution, the angel agrees to listen to options.

Phoebe remembers Burke's cave and the ice chambers. After the sisters convince Billie that they need Burke more than she does right now, the Angel of Destiny brings a healed Leo to the cave. He is confused, but Piper asks him to trust her—and of course, he does. Tearful good-byes are said, and Burke moves his series of crystals to freeze Leo. The angel promises to return him if, and when, the sisters succeed. The sisters orb out to await their fate, and the higher powers that control Burke vanquish him.

As Piper fights not to lose her love, Paige begins to realize that she may have found hers. After a misunderstanding over the check from a lunch date, Paige and Henry start to open up about their feelings for each other.

"I've been given a death sentence by the one guy who means it."　　　　　　**LEO WYATT**

"I have to lose you to save you. It's just our screwed-up destiny, and you kinda got caught in the middle."　　　　　　**PIPER HALLIWELL**

BEHIND THE SCENES

ROSE MCGOWAN (PAIGE): I guess Paige is unemployed again. It just makes me laugh. I'm, like, Piper must be making a hell of a lot of money to keep us all in these new fancy clothes all the time. That club that was in danger in the beginning of the season must have a big reserve, because the other day I'm on a coffee date and I had to plop down twenty dollars. And I'm, like, well, when does Piper get back? Do I have an allowance? I think we're actually friends with the Harry Potter people and I just hit up Gringott's bank. We've refied the Manor forty million times. We have to because it keeps getting blown up.

DANIELLA GSCHWENDTNER (COSTUME DESIGNER): Leo was another one where the wardrobe just changed a lot [over the years]. We just wanted to make him a little bit younger and more edgy. It all works together. He looks so good. And he's more into the clothes this year, I feel. I don't know why that is. Maybe he's just more excited about his clothes. He's doing a lot of things that he wouldn't have done in the past.

This episode, him being so many different characters, I think we had a total of about thirty different outfits that we ended up having for him. It was an intense day, not so much for me, but for Chic [Gennarelli], who takes care of the guys. They had, like, literally a change every five minutes. I had two extra people just to deal with that. You need somebody to help dress and somebody to keep track of the pieces and continuity. And Chic had to keep track of it all.

JIM CONWAY (CO-EXECUTIVE PRODUCER) on the evolution of characters: They have to keep growing. Once you get somebody where you think they belong, you've got to get them out of there. The real miracle has been the ongoing up-and-down relationship of Piper and Leo. Because those relationships work best when there's something that's not quite right. So it's been that way from the beginning. And now as we're coming to the point where Brian is going to leave for a while, we finally get the marriage and the relationship in the perfect place. So just when it's perfect, you're freaking out because he's taken away.

BRIAN KRAUSE (LEO): When I found out I was only going to be in half the season this year, it was a bit of a blow, a bit of a shock. But I didn't even really know if we were going to be picked up for the whole season. When I found out, it had just happened. That was my pickup. I was a bit indifferent about it. Then as I started to think, you know, all good things. Being done when I'm done leaves me open to break out into different pilots. It's good timing. And before the holidays. Who has a month off or two months off before Christmas? Probably ask everybody around here, would they take two months off? The difference for me is I don't know what I'll be doing in January and February.

Fortunately for me, being on the show for so long, I've been lucky to save. I'll be all right for a while. It's a whole change of life. My dad worked in the same place for thirty-two years and retired. Here I am doing one fourth of it. I couldn't imagine what he went through leaving there. What a change of pace it must be.

I've made a lot of good friends here. It's going to be different waking up next week. It may not settle in for a while. It'll be nice to have that time to let it settle in before I go back out into the workforce. It's hard to think I'm not going to see friends. It's easy to get emotional about that aspect of it; not being here every day to have the conversations that I have. They're my family. It's kind of like breaking up.

"MR. & MRS. WITCH" *Original air date January 8, 2006*
WRITTEN BY ROB WRIGHT | DIRECTED BY JAMES L. CONWAY

Billie's got a new theory about Christy's kidnapping, but she's not about to share it with her visiting parents. She's not too crazy about the people she describes as a robot dad and a wallflower mom, and who she thinks never bothered to search for her sister. She's also got a new power developing, but no one is aware of it until Billie confronts her parents about Christy and calls them assassins—and promptly turns them into exactly that. Phoebe speculates that Billie may have the power of projection—the ability of a witch to turn people and things into whatever comes to mind without a spell or a potion. It's pretty powerful and obviously needs some honing to be used more effectively. Unfortunately, Billie can't just project her parents back to their former selves, because she needs to be in the same emotional state as she was when she transformed them in the first place. Plus, the hired guns are moving all over town and she can't even pin them down.

The new personalities of Billie's parents are the perfect solution for a couple of demons ready to grab a foothold in the business world. It was thought that baby Dalvos had been kidnapped (like Christy, except Christy never returned), but he had actually been switched at birth by his demonic nanny, Nanta. All that stands in their way of taking over Dalvos's very powerful family business is his cousin, Grant, and that's where the assassins—and the Charmed Ones—come in. Billie and the sisters figure out that something is up and save Grant from Mr. Jenkins's bullet, only to have Dalvos finish the deed and blame Mr. and Mrs. Jenkins for the murder. Nanta doesn't like "loose ends," so she hires the assassin couple to unwittingly finish each other off, but the Charmed Ones call them to the Manor with a spell before they can accomplish their

assignments. By now Billie has learned that her parents never stopped looking for Christy. She confronts them again, feeling both angry and sorrowful, and her heightened emotional state returns her parents to normal.

All that's left is to clear their names, and after Piper morphs into Dalvos and confesses everything, they are free to go. Mrs. Jenkins tells Billie that she knows her daughters are both witches—just like their grandmother—and leaves her Christy's diary to help her find her sister. She says that maybe her younger daughter will have better luck deciphering the last entry—a drawing of an elaborate, if ominous, occult symbol—clearly created by a hand far older and wiser than the kidnapped young witch who kept the diary.

During all the confusion with Billie's parents, Piper is making a video diary of everyday life for Leo, and that's just one more thing distracting Phoebe from finishing her column. She's having an unusually difficult time with a letter from a reader with a sibling issue. Phoebe eventually discerns the answer that is right for her reader, and also for herself: Sometimes a person can rely too much on a sibling for their emotional needs, and they just have to move out to move on.

And Paige and Henry are starting to open up to each other more as they realize that they've both found someone very special.

"Your parents jumped me. That's the last time I invite them to dinner." **PIPER HALLIWELL**

"Wait, the demon has a nanny?"   **PHOEBE HALLIWELL**

BEHIND THE SCENES

ROGER MONTESANO (PROP MASTER): There are special props sometimes that have to be made. It called for in the script that there was a briefcase that we see them carrying in and there's a mini-recorder and lipstick tube and a few other little things that I had to make into a gun. So we talked it over with the producers and stuff and Brad Kern said, "Well, just kind of get creative and come up with something." So instead of the lipstick tube I got eyeliner, which is a little longer. I made that a barrel, so I put that at the end, coming out. The shop that I was working with made a trigger that would come out when you press a button on the micro-cassette recorder. In the back where the batteries are is where we put the bullets. So they take the bullets out and pop it in where the cassette would be and then they have the gun.

"PAYBACK'S A WITCH"

Original air date January 15, 2006

WRITTEN BY BRAD KERN | DIRECTED BY MEL DAMSKI

Wyatt's third birthday party is just about to begin when Piper hears Billie torturing a Possessor demon named Rohtul in the attic. The younger witch is systematically capturing demons and grilling them for information about her sister, Christy. Piper will not tolerate demons and party guests in the house at the same time, and as the two women argue, Rohtul shimmers out, vowing to get revenge on Billie.

In the meantime, Phoebe plays with Wyatt to try to better understand why the little guy has been misbehaving. She enchants his favorite teddy bear, Wuvey, and makes him talk, hoping to get her nephew to do the same. But instead, it gives him a magical idea and he turns the action figures that he's playing with into full-size, living and breathing humans—just in time for the party guests to arrive. Luckily, Phoebe passes them off as entertainment for the party guests, and no one's the wiser.

Paige is missing the party because she and Henry are being held hostage in a bank after Henry's parolee, Nick, is turned down for a loan. Billie becomes trapped there too, having gone to Paige for help with her demon dilemma. Nick wavers back and forth a few times and is just about to give himself up when Rohtul returns for his avowed revenge. He possesses Nick's body and continues the drama, so that a wounded Henry will not get the medical attention he needs in time. Paige cannot bear the thought of losing Henry, but Rohtul knows she won't orb him and expose magic. The Charmed One's emotions are on overload, and as she holds her hands over Henry's gunshot wound to stem the bleeding, they suddenly emit a healing glow. Stunned by Paige's full-fledged Whitelighter powers, Rohtul says he'll shoot and kill Henry anyway. Surprised by her new abilities, but having no time to lose, Paige tells Billie to throw the potion the young witch had been making from odd items in the hostages' belongings. A smoke bomb erupts, during which the two witches glamour into each other. Rohtul grabs "Billie," who is the one he wanted all along, and leaves, ending the crisis.

He takes her to Magic School, where she vanquishes Rohtul's fellow demons by orbing their energy balls back at them. "Billie" grabs the Possessor's leg and orbs with him to the Manor, where Piper and Phoebe are waiting with potions to separate him from Nick. "Billie" glamours back into Paige, and the real teenage Billie joins the sisters, who allow her the honor of throwing the potion to vanquish Rohtul.

Billie tells Piper and Phoebe how Paige healed Henry, and they all tease her about how strong her feelings must be for the guy if they could manifest a new power. Paige tries to laugh it off, but she is forced to finally acknowledge how special Henry has become to her.

After the party and the demon vanquishing is over, Piper sits down with Wyatt. Phoebe had overheard the life-size action figures talking and realized that they were speaking Wyatt's feelings—and that the toddler feels responsible for his father's disappearance. Piper explains to her son that what Leo is doing is very brave and that his absence is no one's fault—it just is. She knows it's hard to understand, but she assures Wyatt that she is doing everything she can to reunite their family. Wyatt trusts his mother's promise and blinks his toys back to their normal size.

PHOEBE: *"You've got to admit, the army guy is kinda cute."*
PIPER: *"Forget it, Phoebe. He's not anatomically correct."*

BEHIND THE SCENES

DANIELLA GSCHWENDTNER (COSTUME DESIGNER): [Former *Charmed* Costume Designer] Eilish and I worked so closely together for so long that it doesn't feel like she had a look and I have a look. It was such a collaboration with the girls and their personalities and their characters and how they see themselves going through the script. And then, maybe, our ideas and all that mixed together always created the look anyways.

You try to keep it interesting and find, within each look, something that is exciting still, and new and fresh. We changed the look a tiny little bit over the years. I think Holly dresses a lot hipper now, without losing the fact that she's really very classic and still very elegant, but with a little bit more of an edge, which I think is beautiful on her. Rose is a tiny little bit more elegant than she used to be. We took her up into more sophisticated, even. Alyssa looks beautiful in everything, basically.

We don't run after every fashion fad so that it looks dated two years later. We look for something that will hold up over time and be beautiful in five years still, because it's not trendy—more classic and timeless and beautiful; things that are a bit more one-of-a-kind, which is a little easier this year because we're not doing as many stunts. So I can go a little bit more one-of-a-kind things than we used to in the past. That helps too.

"REPO MANOR"
Original air date January 22, 2006

WRITTEN BY DOUG E. JONES | DIRECTED BY DEREK JOHANSEN

Piper is preoccupied with looking in the Book of Shadows for demonic seers, oracles, and wizards who may be able to tell them who the sisters will have to fight to win Leo back. It's also a way of not having to face the fact that Phoebe is moving to her new condo. Paige is bravely facing her future, however, determined to tell Henry that she's a witch—if she can make sure he has a good day to put him in the right frame of mind.

While the Charmed Ones are each doing their own thing, a demon named Savard is ready to unleash demon doppelgangers of the sisters. The women have been training for years and have infused their blood with that of the sisters, perfecting the witches' powers, so that they can vanquish the Slave King that has kept their demonic race in servitude for centuries. The vanquish requires the Power of Three, which is unfortunate, because even though Pilar, Phoenix, and Patra can look and act like the Charmed Ones, they have not yet been able to harness their combined power. One by one, Savard picks off the Charmed Ones and replaces them with his demon doubles, who find that once they are in the Manor, they can finally create their demonic version of the Power of Three. The real sisters are sent to the dollhouse, which Savard has stolen and stashed in his cave. The teeny, tiny Charmed Ones are powerless to fight the big, bad demon, as their magic has shrunk with their actual size.

The demon doubles are brewing the Slave King vanquishing potion when they are interrupted by Billie, who has been using Phoebe's room as her "Operation Christy" headquarters. They are cruel to the teenager, and "Paige" orbs her out of the Manor, along with any hope that Billie will know what's happening and save the real sisters. The demons vanquish their Slave King and return to find that the doll-size Charmed Ones have managed to do the same to Savard. But the real witches are still going to be toast if they don't harness some extra firepower. They reason that if they can get the demons to act like demons, they can no longer channel the Power of Three, so the sisters taunt their captors. As the three demons form fireballs, the Charmed power reverts to its rightful owners and Paige is able to orb them in the dollhouse back to the Manor, where they find the confused, but relieved, Billie. They tell the young witch to find the power-switching spell in the Book, and she recites it as the demons shimmer in. By replacing "powers" with "bodies," Billie switches the Charmed Ones with the demons. The three would-be Charmed Ones are now trapped in the dollhouse, and the full-size and full-powered Piper promptly blows them up.

Piper and Phoebe agree that moving on is the best thing for the younger Halliwell, but they both reserve the right to be sad about it, at least for a little while.

And, after calling on some friendly magical creatures to insure the luckiest, most inspired day ever for Henry, Paige breaks the news to him about her magic. Although he seems a little stunned at first, Henry assures Paige that he's not afraid of her powers—or her.

"Welcome to the dollhouse. We're trapped, and even worse than that, we're really, really small."
PHOEBE HALLIWELL

"You wanted to live like us, now I guess you get to die like us."
PAIGE MATTHEWS

JONATHAN LEVIN (CONSULTING PRODUCER/PRESIDENT OF SPELLING ENTERTAINMENT) on _Charmed_ becoming the longest-running television series with female leads (surpassing _Laverne & Shirley_ with this episode): Our actresses have done exceptional work over the years, and it's a fitting title to reward them with for all of their talents. It's a milestone of which all of us associated with the show can be proud.

JON PARÉ (PRODUCER): I'll go out and direct an episode twice a season, and the rest of the time I get to come in here and sit in my warm office and sign bills and break down scripts in the comfort of this environment. But those girls, every day, they show up. They're there at six thirty and they stay till eight or nine. And they're there. And the next day they're there again. They've really been the backbone to this. They've kept this whole thing moving forward, and you really have to respect their work standard. That they've been able to still show up and still be fresh. They're still moving forward.

I saw Holly Monday on a show that I did that she was big in. I came in Monday and she had a big smile on her face. And I'm thinking it's so neat that we still get excited about doing good work. Fortunately for me, she was very happy with her work, she was happy with the show, she was happy with how the story turned out.

After eight seasons we still get excited about doing it right. And that's really special. And it's going to make it very difficult at the end of the season to think that that gift is going to be taken away from us. It's been a gift. It's been a blessing for all of us to be able to show up, to be able to drink coffee in the mornings and coffee at night and spend our days together.

"12 ANGRY ZEN"   _Original air date February 12, 2006_
WRITTEN BY CAMERON LITVACK | DIRECTED BY JON PARÉ

Piper and Billie are magically divining for a sign about the final battle and find a Chinese character in their cauldron. The character leads them to a laundry and an enigmatic man named Lo Pan, who takes them through a tapestry in the back of the store that leads to a secret, sacred garden. They arrive too late to stop a gang of demons, led by the fiend Novak, from killing Rooster, one of the twelve Chinese Zodiacs who guard the Buddha's mystical staff. Although he cannot take the staff, Novak has weakened the Zodiacs, as it is the first time one has been killed before he was able to pass the staff to the next recipient, thus ensuring the eternal cycle. Piper is not too pleased about being given the task of guarding the sacred object until the ceremony at midnight.

The eldest Charmed One returns to the Manor to get some help from her sisters while Billie remains in the hidden garden, where Lo Pan helps her master her new power of projection. He trains her to use it to look for her sister, but rather than the adult Christy, she finds the young Christy, who was recently kidnapped. Locked in a cave, Christy hears her demon captors whispering but does not understand what they are saying. She doesn't know how to escape or that she is a witch with powers. Billie notices a necklace with the same symbol that was written in Christy's diary, and the little girl tells her that her captors gave it to her. When demons threaten the two sisters, Billie calls for Lo Pan to bring them back to the garden, but he brings back only Billie. He tells her that she has seen the path and must now find the adult Christy on her own.

Meanwhile, the sacred staff has caused all kinds of problems for the Charmed Ones. Eventually Novak finds his way to the sisters and takes the staff. Knowing that the one who controls the object also projects his emotions and desires onto others with it, Novak spreads his evil to the sisters and dispatches them to the sacred garden to kill Lo Pan. Lo Pan tells Billie to use her power of projection to see the sisters as she wants to see them—the good witches that they truly are. The young witch restores her mentors to their rightful state, and they follow Novak to Magic School. Paige orbs the staff from him, and with all four witches holding the powerful instrument, Billie vanquishes Novak and his fellow demons with her new power.

Piper is left with the staff again, and when midnight arrives, she brings it to the Sacred Garden for the ceremony. For his heroic efforts and devotion to the Zodiacs, Lo Pan has been made the new Rooster. The staff is passed to Dog, and the eternal cycle is once again safe.

Henry can't comprehend why Paige doesn't use her magic to fix the major problems of the world. Under the influence of Piper's recent obsessions being projected by the sacred staff, Paige orbs Henry around the world to try to make him understand. Once things settle back to what passes for normal for the Charmed Ones, he tells her that he now sees how she uses her powers to make the world a better place. The two then admit that they are falling in love with each other.

And Billie returns to the cave in which she found the young Christy. She cautiously opens the door and calls out for her sister.

"So, I take it you guys heard about Chicken?" **PIPER HALLIWELL**

"No big deal, you guys were just trying to kill me, but I changed your minds." **BILLIE JENKINS**

BEHIND THE SCENES

PAM SHAE (EXECUTIVE IN CHARGE OF TALENT): In eight years we have hired, certainly, thousands of actors. You're hoping that when you open a new script that you've got a window that somebody is available. What I'm finding now is that TV obviously has changed, because there is so much programming: independent films, all the cable networks. There's just a lot of scripted TV, even though reality has taken a dent. We go to check on actors to book and they're not available for the dates we need them. I may have a huge guest star that I need for the run of the week and maybe I can't have them a day or two because they're finishing some other show. There have been scheduling issues. It's just the volume of people we've hired over the years.

"THE LAST TEMPTATION OF CHRISTY"

Original air date February 19, 2006

TELEPLAY BY LIZ SAGAL | STORY BY RICK MUIRRAGUI
DIRECTED BY JOHN KRETCHMER

Billie finds Christy in the cave and brings her to live at Halliwell Manor, unaware that her sister is a pawn of evil. Initially (and understandably) withdrawn, Christy hears voices that tell her that demons are about to attack. The Scather demons that had held Christy captive are low-level demons who do not have telepathic powers, so the Charmed Ones reason that a higher power must be communicating with Christy—or she is calling them. They arrive, as Christy predicted, and she scares them off by setting the sitting room couch on fire. The sisters now know that the older Jenkins is not only a telepath, but a firestarter as well.

Christy is telepathically called again and sets Billie on fire before allowing the Scathers to take her. The Halliwells save Billie, who relates that her sister talked back to the voices this time, saying that she did not want to be the key to the Ultimate Power. Billie is confused and upset, but when she hears Christy calling to her, she begs the Charmed Ones to let her go because the young witch trusts her sister. The Halliwells say a spell and send Billie to the Underworld cave, where the Scathers are holding Christy. They start to attack Billie, but Christy seems to be in a trance and doesn't move. Billie pleads with her sister to use her powers for good, so they can work together and end Christy's ordeal forever. Christy reacts to her sister's love and determination and forms a gigantic fireball that Billie then telekinetically hurls at the demons, vanquishing them. They return to the Manor, and Christy says that she hurt Billie only because she was being controlled by the demons. Billie believes her and promises that she will never let anyone hurt her sister again.

Although Christy is safe for now, the Charmed Ones are aware that she is either the willing, or unwilling, key to whatever power that is their adversary for the predicted Ultimate Battle. The all-powerful Triad takes up residence at Magic School, pleased that they have maneuvered Christy just where they want her to prepare for that final fight.

Throughout the Christy dilemma, Piper literally runs into her old boyfriend, fireman Greg, and although he's still loving and adorable, she remains true to Leo, knowing that she will see him again soon.

Paige keeps getting distracted from the Christy problem by a witch named Sir Simon Marks, who literally pops into the Manor declaring he intends to make Paige his bride. Forty oracles, sooth-sayers, and a couple of wizards have predicted that the powerful good magic of the Halliwell and Marks families will be joined, and since Simon "requires" that his wife be half-Whitelighter, Paige is the lucky winner. The determined Brit quickly gets under Paige's—and Henry's—skin, and finally, the handsome parole officer endures demonic fireballs and a magical duel to prove his love for his lady. Paige orbs Simon back across the pond, confirming that Henry is her one and only guy. Seeing how someone might swoop in and take Paige from him, Henry proposes to her—at "their spot" on top of the Golden Gate Bridge—and she happily accepts.

"She's your sister. There's no stronger bond than that." **PHOEBE HALLIWELL**

"You just want some trophy witch so you can be some power couple." **HENRY MITCHELL**

BEHIND THE SCENES

KALEY CUOCO (BILLIE): The first few weeks I was very light and I thought, "This is great. I'll work, like, two days a week." Now I work almost every day. I had the day off yesterday and it was great, but I work almost every day now. I was, like, "One day a week—this is amazing! I want to be on this job for, like, ten years. I love it." Now they're, like, "You're going to be here at six tomorrow." I'm, like, "What are you talking about, I was just here." Now I'm getting used to it.

This show, it's all about sisters. I love it. That's what I like about it. It's about women. There aren't a lot of shows that are about that. Strong women. It's their show. Mostly the men are always overpowering the women. I like girls that kick butt. I love stuff like that. It's like *Charlie's Angels* a little bit. I love being here. I love the girls.

"ENGAGED AND CONFUSED"   *Original air date February 26, 2006*
WRITTEN BY JEANNINE RENSHAW | DIRECTED BY STUART GILLARD

Piper is busily planning an engagement party for Paige and Henry, while Phoebe and Billie work on Christy's social skills. The older Jenkins sister still carefully hides the fact that she is an agent of the Triad, although the Halliwells worry what exactly it means that she is the key to the Ultimate Power.

Meanwhile, a demon named Xar, who has been excommunicated by the Triad, is looking for a little revenge. He also knows that if the Triad gains power again, it will be hell for every demon, especially him, so Xar contrives to have the only entity powerful enough to defeat the Triad—the Charmed Ones—do so. When the sisters learn that the Triad is back, they assume that this is the final battle predicted by the Angel of Destiny. Both the witches and the demons depend on their full complement of three members to maintain their strength, so the adversaries know if they can eliminate just one of their opposite number, they can triumph.

The showdown takes place in Magic School, where the Triad has been hunkered down. After Paige orbs in with her sisters, Phoebe distracts one of the Triad, splitting him off from his fellow demons. As one Triad demon launches a superpowered fireball, Piper freezes him and his weapon. Paige orbs his fellow demon in the path of the fireball and Piper unfreezes the action, so that one Triad member vanquishes another. The fearsome threesome is weakened by the loss, and Piper is able to blast the second one until she vanquishes him. Returning to his brothers, the third Triad demon sees that he is defeated and descends into the Underworld. The sisters have won, but Leo is not returned, signifying that this was not the Ultimate Power that they are destined to meet.

The remaining Triad demon visits Christy and tells her that she needs to stay the course and fulfill her destiny. To do that, she has to "save" Billie from good so that they can unite to form the Ultimate Power and defeat the Charmed Ones.

A handsome Cupid named Coop causes a major distraction for Phoebe while she prepares to battle the Triad. The Elders are trying to make amends for screwing up the middle Charmed One's love life these last eight years, and they have made Phoebe the Cupid's one and only charge so that she can find true love and have the family she's always wanted—and envisioned. Phoebe is really not interested, but Coop is persistent, and it's clear that he will not leave without finishing his mission.

And the happy couple—Paige and Henry—are squabbling over stupid little things like toothpaste when it's time to take on the Triad. Not wanting to have Henry's last memory of her be an argument, Paige tells him of their battle plans and how much she truly loves him. Henry makes her promise that when they win, she will marry him as soon as possible, turning the engagement party into a wedding. After a little magical assistance, Piper and Phoebe are beautiful and proud bridesmaids, and Paige is simply radiant as she and Henry pledge their love and devotion to each other.

"I don't know, I'm making this up as I go."   **PIPER HALLIWELL**

"Don't you have someone else's love life to meddle in?"   **PHOEBE HALLIWELL**

ROSE MCGOWAN (PAIGE) on the pending wedding of her character: Someone did tell me I was getting married, which is very funny because if I do, of course my perverse side wants to find one of those hideous Bon Jovi–era wedding gowns with the giant puffy sleeves and the horrible headdress with something hanging down my forehead. I don't think they'd let me get away with that. I'd have bridesmaids with hideous electric blue gowns. I can always ask. No. Paige would go with a more simple, more refined look.

"GENERATION HEX"   *Original air date April 16, 2006*
WRITTEN BY ROB WRIGHT | DIRECTED BY MICHAEL GROSSMAN

Piper throws Paige a bon voyage breakfast, and everyone promises the newlyweds a demon-free honeymoon. Christy isn't in as celebratory a mood, however, since she is finding it harder than she thought to break Billie's ties to the Charmed Ones. When former Magic School students, one of whom has seen her commiserating with demons, show up at the Manor looking for Leo's help, things get even more complicated.

The students are on the run from unvanquishable Noxon demons. After being killed, they regenerate, which was why Leo used them as illustrations and target practice for his students. Once demons took over Magic School, the Noxons were freed and started looking for a little target practice of their own. With Leo gone, Piper vows to help her husband's former students, but it's not so easy to vanquish the unvanquishable—even for a Charmed One.

While Piper is preoccupied with the Noxons, Billie finally convinces Christy to see their parents, and when they are reunited, some of the vulnerable little girl returns to the hardened adult. Sensing that he could lose all that he's worked for, the remaining Triad, Candor, reminds his charge of her duty and her destiny. Tired of being controlled by the demon, she sets him on fire, but he is still too powerful to be harmed. He explains that she will have the power to destroy him only when she leaves behind the ties that bind.

Candor decides to insure that those ties are broken beyond repair. He sends the Noxons to kill Mr. and Mrs. Jenkins so that Christy cannot consider going back. She angrily confronts the Triad, and this time she is able to kill him. He dies knowing that his heinous act will bring Billie closer to Christy as her only remaining family, and that Christy has reached a point of no return where embracing good is no longer an option.

After killing Mr. and Mrs. Jenkins, one of the Noxons heads to the Manor, still bent on getting revenge. Leo's students have come up with a plan to kill the demon, but Piper is reluctant to allow them to use themselves as bait. She looks for a sign from Leo as to what he would do, and Wyatt tells her he would take the chance. Piper trusts that her husband taught his students well, and that her son is as wise as his father. As the Noxon is vanquished, the students banish him to the Astral Plane—where time stops and he cannot move forward—so that he will now live in a state of perpetual vanquish, unable to escape.

Meanwhile, Coop the Cupid takes Phoebe on a tour of her past relationships to find out why she has such a strong energy field around her heart that's keeping her from being able to love again. After seeing how events unfolded with Dex, Drake, Cole, and even the warlock Anton from Phoebe's past life, he begins to understand. Coop encourages his Charmed One to focus on what the beginning of love feels like, and he uses his magic ring to remind her of Jason and Leslie. When she remembers those emotions, Phoebe is able to break down her barrier and open her heart to possibilities again.

"You were held captive by demons for fifteen years, you can handle fifteen minutes with Mom and Dad."
BILLIE JENKINS

"You can't run from love, Phoebe, you know that."
COOP

BEHIND THE SCENES

JONATHAN LEVIN (CONSULTING PRODUCER/PRESIDENT OF SPELLING ENTERTAINMENT): The consistently good ratings in the key demographics over all of the different time periods the show has aired is a tribute to the loyal audience and the never-ending creativity the series has kept up over the eight years on the air.

E. DUKE VINCENT (EXECUTIVE PRODUCER): Winding down through now into the eighth year, the challenge always is, how do you come up with something new? Every story that you'll ever see has already been done fifteen times. You can go back to Aeschylus and find the stories we're doing today. Shakespeare did them better than anybody. We're still doing them. But the real trick is to come up with a fresh way of doing it.

Now, how do you come up with a fresh way of doing a love story? There's been four thousand love stories. So that's a challenge. And then if you do it the way we try to do it, to put a backdrop in, it's a real challenge. And Brad [Kern] handles that challenge as well as anybody. So that's what I enjoy. I enjoy the challenges; how do we figure out how to do something differently and make the audience think they really haven't seen it before? They have. They've seen it four thousand times. But it's just a little bit different twist. That's true of any series. It's especially true of this series, because it's a unique type of backdrop.

"THE TORN IDENTITY"

Original air date April 23, 2006

WRITTEN BY ANDY REASER | DIRECTED BY LEVAR BURTON

Billie and Christy have only each other now, which makes it easier for the elder Jenkins to finally break her sister away from the Charmed Ones. Piper realizes that the Noxon demons had to have been acting on orders to kill Mr. and Mrs. Jenkins, and she wants to know who gave them. Paige locates the surviving Noxon, Pator, in the Underworld, but Christy shows up just as the sisters are about to leave. She says she wants revenge for her parents' death, but what she can't tell the sisters is that she also wants to make sure that the Noxon doesn't tell any tales. Although Piper and Paige tell her to remain at the Manor, Christy hitches a ride on their orb. The sisters just want to grill the Noxon a bit, but Christy starts to recite the spell to send him to the Astral Plane, so Piper reflexively blasts her to make her stop. The Noxon gets away, and Christy gets her leverage to finally draw Billie to her side.

Piper feels awful about what she did, and although she understands Christy's need for revenge, she doesn't understand why she seems to constantly work at cross-purposes. The two sets of sisters divide when Christy convinces Billie that the Charmed Ones act only for themselves, and that they have been using their young protégée just to get what they want. The Halliwells don't know why Christy thinks they're on opposite sides and why she twists everything around—but it is soon painfully clear.

Deciding they can trust no one but themselves, the Jenkins sisters want the Noxon demon dead. They do a little telepathic eavesdropping on the Charmed Ones to find him, and they follow the Halliwells to the Underworld. Billie uses her powers to amplify her sister's, and together the Jenkins sisters explode the unvanquishable Noxon in a ball of fire. They throw down a potion and are transported back to Magic School, and the Charmed Ones know they have just witnessed the Ultimate Power.

When she's not fighting demons, Paige is fighting with herself for not telling Henry what's bothering her. She loves her new husband with all her heart, but she is afraid of losing her own identity to their union. Desperate for a solution, Paige calls on Coop for help, and he makes her communicate with Henry by literally putting her inside his head. Paige is forced to finally talk to Henry about her issues, and he tells her that he loves her just the way she is and doesn't want her to change. But maybe marriage will help her find something new, and together they can make each other stronger. Paige's fears are assuaged, and the newlyweds are back on track—once Coop separates them into two bodies again.

And speaking of the Cupid, he sets Phoebe up with a coworker from the *Bay Mirror,* but as he makes his pitch, Coop realizes that he's in love with the beautiful Charmed One himself.

PAIGE: *"Okay, they just vanquished a demon that can't be vanquished."*
PHOEBE: *"What does that mean?"*
PIPER: *"I think that means we just found the Ultimate Power."*

BEHIND THE SCENES

RANDY CABRAL (SPECIAL EFFECTS SUPERVISOR): If you sit down and start breaking gags out, and I have a tendency to do that when I watch it the first time, it's, like, "Oh, that didn't work." I have a tendency not to watch it for the show value. I want to see how this gag went, how that went. What's really funny is when you look at them, like Season Five or Season Six, and you look back at them and you say, "Oh my God, that was a lot of work. That was a lot of work." And it really paid off. It really did.

I crack up at all the crazy stuff we've done on this TV show. I used to look at *The Lucy Show* and the classics and think that was a lot. And I think of this show in the same way. The girls are so great. They have been mermaids, they have been frozen, we have turned them into clay dolls. They've been troupers all the way through.

"THE JUNG AND THE RESTLESS"   *Original air date April 30, 2006*
WRITTEN BY CAMERON LITVACK | DIRECTED BY DEREK JOHANSEN

The battle lines are drawn, but the impending war is clear only to Piper and Christy. Phoebe and Billie are still trying to understand the other's feelings, and Paige is on the fence—and busy with a new marriage and a new charge. To convince her sister that the Charmed Ones have given up their responsibility of serving the greater good, Christy has Billie send the sisters to Dreamworld. She tells Billie that everything in Dreamworld has meaning—no matter how bizarre. Everything the Halliwells dream will be a manifestation of who they truly are—together and separately—which will show Billie that her former friends are now merely selfish and self-serving. Christy gives Billie a red crystal so that she can escape Dreamworld whenever she wants, but the sisters will have to find their inner truths to be able to wake up.

Billie wanders through the Charmed Ones' dreams, but her interpretation of what she sees is not the same as the sisters' intent. She sees Paige forsaking her charge to pursue finding herself, Phoebe ignoring her gifts to create a family, and Piper disregarding everything else in her life until she gets Leo back. And with Christy twisting right and wrong, Billie sees all of these as irresponsible acts, with the Charmed Ones using their powers only for their own personal gain.

Piper and Phoebe work through their dreams and emerge on their own, but Paige is interrupted in her journey by a call from her new charge, Mikelle, who has been taken by a Darklighter. Paige forces Billie to take her out of Dreamworld and orbs to the future Whitelighter, where she is promptly shot with two Darklighter arrows. Mikelle dies before her eyes, and knowing she doesn't have long either, Paige sends a ghostly message to Piper for help. The two Charmed Ones find their sister and vanquish the Darklighter, but there is nothing they can do for Paige. They need a Whitelighter to heal the wounds, and find one in the very recently deceased Mikelle, who is quickly given her wings so that she can save her former protector.

When Paige recovers, she considers that maybe Billie is right after all—maybe they have become too selfish. She was supposed to save Mikelle, but her charge wound up saving her instead. However, Phoebe says they're not selfish, just human. That doesn't make them bad people or bad witches, except in Christy's warped view of the world, the one into which she has now completely drawn Billie. All three Charmed Ones are finally in agreement: They will have to fight Billie and Christy—and hope that they win.

Phoebe's Dreamworld experience opens her eyes to something more than the inevitable battle with the Ultimate Power. She realizes that she is in love with Coop but tries to rationalize that he was just her subconscious symbol for love. There's no point in considering a relationship with him, because the rules forbid a Cupid to marry his charge.

"They can't be trying to kill us, otherwise we wouldn't be dreaming, we'd be dead."

PIPER HALLIWELL

"Well, apparently we're going to have to stop them—before they stop us."

PHOEBE HALLIWELL

BEHIND THE SCENES

AUDREY STERN (DEPARTMENT HEAD KEY HAIRSTYLIST): Watching people get married. Watching people go through different relationships. Watching babies being born. Watching just the changes of everybody. It's so close. I have never been in such a close-knit workplace. I will always remember this.

Also, having a hair and makeup trailer of such great people to work with. It's not always like that. The vanity department is hard. Everybody's artistic, and when it comes to art, everybody's got their own opinion and everybody had their own ideas. And it's wonderful. That's what makes art. Letting everybody just express themselves.

Nono [Nannette New] and I are such a great team. We just collaborate, and it's so easy. We both get it. And it's not always like that. In this business it's very competitive. I'm not in the place of my life for competition.

NOON ORSATTI (STUNT COORDINATOR): I want to thank everybody that's made it possible for the show to go so long. It's something, the producers pulling together this crew. This crew works together like no other crew I've ever seen. The actresses, for putting up with us and at the same time us putting up with them. It just has a really good, good feel to it.

"GONE WITH THE WITCHES"

Original air date May 7, 2006

WRITTEN BY JEANNINE RENSHAW | DIRECTED BY JONATHAN WEST

Christy has managed to sway Billie to join her and leave the Charmed Ones, but she still cannot convince her sister that her former mentors need to be annihilated, so she calls in some help. Dumain is Christy's teacher, confidant, and friend, the one who showed her the "way" and molded her into the warped little witch she is today. She's hoping that he can persuade Billie to see things their way. Dumain is also the one who went to the Triad fifteen years ago with the plan to bring down the Charmed Ones—even before the sisters knew they were the Charmed Ones.

He continues his upside-down litany that the Halliwells are evil, and he proves his point to Billie by showing her the future, where Wyatt is the evil and absolute ruler of the magical world. He doesn't bother to explain that this future has been avoided thanks to Chris's intervention and the Charmed Ones changing their family legacy. Dumain indicates that this is what the sisters' unchecked power will lead to, and that only she and Christy have the ability to stop it. It is their duty and their destiny. This gives Billie some serious pause, but she still cannot bring herself to kill the sisters.

Meanwhile, the Halliwells sense a sudden and great source of energy emanating from Magic School, but they have no idea that it is the Triad re-forming. Their search leads them to an empty black room, but they are chased by demons before they can find out anything further. Knowing it's too dangerous to return to Magic School themselves, the sisters call on friendly magical creatures to do some snooping for them. Little do they realize that this gives Dumain the opening he needs to finally convince Billie that killing the Charmed Ones is the only solution.

After the leprechauns are attacked by demons and saved by Billie and Christy, Dumain uses the Charmed Ones' past to turn all good magical creatures against them. Looking through the book Billie has compiled about her knowledge of the Charmed Ones, he casts spells on the Halliwells so that they will be possessed by their current obsessions. Dumain then sets demons on the rest of the magical world, and when the Charmed Ones are no help, the creatures fear that they have truly been forsaken. This, coupled with the peek at the future she received, convinces Billie that Christy and Dumain are right—the sisters have gone over to the side of evil and must be destroyed. The Jenkins sisters confront the Halliwells at the Manor and once again use a giant fireball as their weapon of mass destruction. With the magical creatures, and now Billie, firmly against them, the Charmed Ones have nowhere to turn. They grab the Book of Shadows and orb out, winding up in the only place that will accept them—the Underworld.

Before Phoebe was forced to orb for her life, she and Coop finally admitted that they loved each other. But since it is forbidden for a Cupid to love his charge, it's just one more problem for the Charmed One to overcome—assuming she stays alive to try.

"I'm beginning to think that the Ultimate Power's power is to drive us crazy."

PHOEBE HALLIWELL

"I don't know who has gotten to you, but contrary to popular belief, we are still the good guys."

PAIGE MATTHEWS

BEHIND THE SCENES

ROGER MONTESANO (PROP MASTER): I've been on *Charmed* eight years. Worked on the original *Love Boat* for ten years and *Full House* for eight years. Now hopefully I'll do another show, ah, I don't want to go too much longer, but I'd like to go another two or three years. Then I'd be able to call it quits. Forty-three years doing this. I started set dressing and worked up to props and then prop master. Did a lot of movies of the week and a lot of stuff for Aaron Spelling Productions. It's a good company to work for. It's been a great eight years. I didn't think the show would last this long, but it's been a great show. Everybody on the show has been very nice. And I've had some good times.

"KILL BILLIE: VOL. 2"   *Original air date May 14, 2006*

WRITTEN BY BRAD KERN | DIRECTED BY JON PARÉ

It's kill or be killed for the Charmed Ones, and hanging around the Underworld is not increasing their odds of coming out on top. They stealthily orb back to the attic of the Manor to brew vanquishing potions with which to confront Billie and Christy, first dropping off the Book of Shadows at Phoebe's loft for safekeeping. Armed and ready as they'll ever be, the sisters descend the staircase, where they find Billie and Christy wielding the same potions. All five vials collide in midair, causing a spectacular fireball. Piper, Phoebe, and Paige are blasted back into the conservatory and out the doors, while Billie and Christy are slammed into, and through, the banisters on the stairs. Piper is down, and Christy is hurt, but they can all retreat to their respective corners to fight another day.

Regrouping at Phoebe's loft, the Charmed Ones are visited by unlikely allies—two demons named Nomed and Zohar. Nomed wants to stop the Triad, and the sisters are his only hope. The demon offers to find out what the other side is planning, if the sisters agree to vanquish the Triad once and for all. They're a bit confused, believing that they've already accomplished this, but Nomed explains that the Triad has the ability to resurrect—first as spirits, and then in total—because they are evil incarnate, and evil never truly dies. Needless to say, even in such dire circumstances, the sisters are not anxious to trust a demon, but when Piper sees a vision of Leo, she is prepared to accept any offers that will help her reunite with her husband.

Phoebe is momentarily distracted by Coop, who is happy to see she is still alive. But it is a distraction she can't afford right now, because she must focus everything on the fight. As much as she loves her Cupid and doesn't want to hurt him, she also doesn't want him drawn into the battle. Phoebe is anguished by the fact that she must simply dismiss Coop, but it is better to wound him emotionally than physically right now. With luck, he will accept her apology and her love if she can make it back to him.

Meanwhile, at Magic School, the Triad is not too pleased with Dumain's charges. They've failed to kill the Charmed Ones—twice—and now it's time for the Triad to take over. They tell Dumain to have the Jenkins sisters call for the Hollow, so that its infinite source of power will give them the boost they need to triumph. The Triad doesn't care that the Hollow is contained and guarded by both good and evil because it will cause whoever ingests it to consume all power, be driven insane, and eventually die. A world without any powerful witches has been the Triad's goal all along. They will need

Charmed power to call for the Hollow, so Dumain coaxes Wyatt—who has been staying with his brother at his grandfather's—to help Aunt Billie "help" his mommy.

Nomed hears the plan for the Hollow and tells the Charmed Ones that they must get it first. The five witches call for it simultaneously, and it splits and goes into each of them. Possessed by raw power, Billie and Christy take Wyatt's protective shield, but Chris is beginning to manifest his powers and orbs his brother back to safety as Dumain wisely shimmers out. On the other side of town, the possessed Charmed Ones vanquish Zohar as they absorb his power to throw fireballs, while Nomed narrowly escapes.

The Halliwells then go gunning for the Triad. The hubris of the evil trio causes them to believe they can withstand the magic that is about to hit them, but the power of the Hollow, combined with the Power of Three, proves them wrong. The Triad is finally gone, never to resurrect again.

The Ultimate Battle begins in the Manor, with none of the witches knowing that either side possesses the Hollow. The megapowers collide and cause a cataclysmic explosion. As the famed house blows up, the Hollow is released from the witches and streams back into its rightful place—hopefully, never to be released again. When the smoke clears, Piper is still standing, devastated to find that Phoebe and Paige are dead. Billie stirs, but she cannot find Christy anywhere. The Angel of Destiny returns Leo, who doesn't know what's happened since he left, so he can't understand why he finds Piper angrily attacking Billie. He stops his wife from killing her former charge, allowing the young witch to escape. Sirens sound and questions will soon be asked, and with nothing left for them at their home any longer, Leo leads Piper away to their uncertain future.

"The battle is over—though not as I expected." **ANGEL OF DESTINY**

BEHIND THE SCENES

BRIAN KRAUSE (LEO): Changing our identity last year and being able to step away, thinking that we had done it—which I guess in a way could have been a series finale last year. I'm so glad it wasn't, because it just wasn't the right way to wrap up seven years of getting to know these characters and how far we've grown with all of them and everything that they've gone through. It just wasn't a great way to wrap it up. I'm so happy for Brad as the head writer that he could still expand his story and take a whole season, this season, to wrap up all the characters. Take them to the places where he really sees them going. I think it's great to let the writer fully conclude his whole vision.

ROSE MCGOWAN (PAIGE): I did a movie called *Phantoms* a long time ago, and I'd only done a couple of independent films before that and it was my first big-budget movie, and I did it because Peter O'Toole was in it. Coming from this little indy world and all of a sudden doing this big-budget thing with special effects and "Oh, that'll be so exciting." Holy Jesus, it's boring. I called it my Thousand Faces of Fear. Here I am, reacting scared again to something that's not there. It was tedious and boring and it was quite hard.

That's why *Charmed* is good, because a scene like that is broken up by other things . . . like some other human beings. That was just constantly things that weren't there. So, never say never, but I would really prefer not to do something with giant special effects monsters that don't exist.

"FOREVER CHARMED"

Original air date May 21, 2006

WRITTEN BY BRAD KERN | DIRECTED BY JAMES L. CONWAY

Relatives past, present, and future are needed to save the Halliwell family and its legacy. Piper borrows Coop's magic ring to take her and Leo into the past so she can save her sisters from dying. They aim for Phoebe, but the ring isn't practical, it's emotional—and they wind up finding Patty, who has just likely conceived her youngest daughter. They decide to next pick up Grams, hoping the family of powerful witches can replicate the Power of Three.

Aiming for the Halliwell matriarch, Piper, Leo, and Patty wind up in the future where Piper is the Grams. She and Grandpa Leo are fully expecting to see their younger selves, because they know they were there fifty years earlier. The older couple advises their younger selves how to better use the ring, and this time they indeed find the right Grams. She's a little shaken to see her daughter come back from the dead and her granddaughter a grown woman, but she's soon her old self, and the three witches combine their powers to take them to the Manor just as the Ultimate Battle begins.

At the same time, Dumain coaches Billie to use her power of projection. Having no one left to turn to, Billie seeks the counsel of the demon, but once she learns his true nature and sees his obsession with bringing back the Triad, she understands that both she and Christy had been manipulated. Billie will not do his bidding, but she wants her sister alive, so she finally succeeds and arrives just before Piper. This time, as the five sisters launch their hyped-up powers at each other, Piper, Patty, and Grams recite a spell to remove the Hollow from all of the witches. Without the magical steroids, there is no explosion—just confusion. Billie and Piper blur into their past selves as Time catches up with itself, creating a new present where Phoebe, Paige, and Christy are still alive. But

since the Ultimate Battle does not take place, the Angel of Destiny comes to take Leo again, which means that things will not end here.

The five Halliwells figure that there must be some way their combined power can defeat the Jenkins sisters, but their planning is put on hold when Future Wyatt and Chris show up because Wyatt no longer has powers. A spell to take them to the cause has brought the boys there. Piper realizes that Christy and Billie must have stolen little Wyatt's powers when they were infected by the Hollow—and that they used the toddler's Charmed magic to call for the entity. That just makes her even more angry, which makes Billie's returning to the Manor even more dangerous. But now that the young witch knows the truth, she pleads with the Charmed Ones to forgive her and let her help them vanquish the Triad—again—because Christy and Dumain have just figured out how to get them back.

The sisters will need Coop's ring to take them to the past again, but he doesn't come when Phoebe calls. Future Wyatt and Chris know that this means something is very wrong, and not wanting to give away too much, they just say that Phoebe and Coop's love is not, and will not be, forbidden, so all Phoebe has to do is think of her Cupid and he will appear. When he does, he's worse for having fought off Dumain, who has taken his ring so that the demon can go back and warn the Triad that the Charmed Ones are coming. The real Ultimate Battle is about to begin.

Still hoping to save her sister, Billie projects them to the Triad's black room, where they find Christy and the demons, including both past and present Dumain. But the Triad are still only spirits, and the evil threesome is easily vanquished by the Charmed Ones' potions. Piper blasts both Dumains to the Wasteland, leaving only Christy to face the good witches. Paige calls for Coop's ring to make sure no one does any unscheduled time traveling, and Billie issues one last plea to her sister to join her and use their powers for good. But Christy's been programmed to fight to the death. She creates a fireball with her powers and aims it at the Charmed Ones, but Billie reflexively gestures and telekinetically sends it back at her sister, incinerating her. The young witch can only sob uncontrollably after having to kill the sister she gave up everything to save.

Coop's ring returns the Charmed Ones back to the Manor, where family past, present, and future have gathered. The only one missing is Leo, who is promptly returned by the Angel of Destiny, as this is the way the battle was supposed to end. Four generations share hugs and steal a few precious moments from the natural progression of time before they all must return to their rightful destinies.

Winning the Ultimate Battle puts an end to the Charmed Ones' battles with demons. Whether it is a reward for a job well done, or simply the fact that the only demons left wouldn't dare challenge them, is unknown. What is known is that at some point evil will resurface to challenge good again, and when it does, it will face the next generation of Halliwells. In the meantime, the sisters will continue to record their family history in the Book of Shadows. And someday, when Old Piper and Leo remember the Ultimate Battle, they will also reflect on the peace of its aftermath, when Phoebe did indeed marry Coop and have that lovely little girl from her vision with him—along

ook of
hadows
-1693-

with two more girls that she didn't foresee. The demon-free life allowed Paige and Henry to be the parents of twin girls and a boy, while Paige continued to train the next generation of witches and Whitelighters. And their own long lives together included a daughter named Melinda, a restaurant for chef Piper, and a return to teaching at the reclaimed Magic School for Leo, until it was time to retire.

In a Manor full of love and memories, surrounded by children and grandchildren, the door once again closes as Piper concludes, "And though we certainly had our struggles and heartaches over the years, we're a family of survivors and we will always be, which is why we've truly been Charmed."

BEHIND THE SCENES

HOLLY MARIE COMBS (PIPER): In getting older, just like the character, we've both definitely evolved. Piper has gone from a rather nervous middle sister and peacekeeper between the other two sisters, to the capable oldest sister who got married and is raising two young sons virtually by herself, since her husband Leo was out of the picture for a while.

ALYSSA MILANO (PHOEBE): So, you sort of look back and in my life, when I started I was twenty-four years old. I was a puppy. I have done so much growth and so much personal growth and had so many incredible things awakened inside of me, goals have shifted and priorities have moved. I think it's the same thing that Phoebe went through. I give our writers credit for not fighting those things, because they could have certainly made me a thirty-two-year-old free spirit. But with my growth I think it was important for them to stay true to what was happening in my life and translate it.

It's exciting. It's an exciting time. Yeah, it'll be sad, obviously, to say good-bye to everyone and to sort of lay Phoebe to rest. I'll miss my crew members horribly. But I like new beginnings. It'll be an interesting time. I'm not scared.

CLOSING THE DOOR ON *CHARMED*

And so, *Charmed* ended with a considerable bang, but with also a quiet whimper. For each of the eight seasons, the series has ended with a door—usually the front door to the Manor—closing out the season. Though story requirements necessitated that the characters end the sixth season in the hospital with Chris's birth, the producers still managed to close a pair of hospital doors to fill that need. And in the end, the series would end just as it had begun. . . .

BRAD KERN (EXECUTIVE PRODUCER): It ended the pilot. Prue telekinetically closes the door at the end of the pilot. At the end of the first season, Connie [series creator Constance M. Burge] and I were working out the last episode, and we just kind of looked at each other and said, "Well, why don't we just close the door like we did at the end of the pilot?" And we did that, and it became something where, "Well, we just have to keep doing that." Which is why I always felt badly that we couldn't figure out how to do it in Season Six. It was just brutal. We had some doors closing, though.

There was no question in my mind that the last shot of the series would always be the door closing. The trick, though, was how to be able to do that without being able to go out to the Manor, because we can't afford to go off the lot. But we figured out a way.

We'll close the door on the series. I think that's appropriate, because it's for the loyal fans who can appreciate the little nod to them; that we're aware that that's how we say good-bye at the end of every season. But I'm hoping that this show ends with the audience not feeling like we've said good-bye. That's why I named the episode "Forever Charmed." So hopefully, it's forever *Charmed*.

THE *CHARMED* EPISODE TITLE PUNS

STILL CHARMED AND KICKING: "Alive and kicking" is a phrase used to refer to something that is lively. There are several anecdotal explanations for the origin of the phrase, one of which refers to the time during a woman's pregnancy when she starts feeling the baby kick.

MALICE IN WONDERLAND: *Alice in Wonderland* is the abbreviated title of the classic children's book by Lewis Carroll, *Alice's Adventures in Wonderland*.

RUN, PIPER, RUN: *Run, Lola, Run* is the English name for the German film *Lola Rennt* (1998).

DESPERATE HOUSEWITCHES: *Desperate Housewives* is a popular nighttime soap opera created by Marc Cherry that premiered in 2004.

REWITCHED: *Bewitched* is a classic sitcom starring Elizabeth Montgomery that premiered in 1964.

KILL BILLIE: VOL. 1: *Kill Bill: Vol. 1* is the first of two films written and directed by Quentin Tarantino and starring Uma Thurman.

THE LOST PICTURE SHOW: *The Last Picture Show* is a film released in 1971, based on the Larry McMurtry novel of the same name.

BATTLE OF THE HEXES: "Battle of the sexes" is a figurative phrase referring to the differences between men and women that often find them in conflict.

HULKUS POCUS: "Hocus-pocus" is a phrase often used by magicians to showcase a trick. It is possible that the phrase originated from the Latin *Hoc est corpus* ("this is my body"). The Hulk is the titular character in the comic book series *The Incredible Hulk,* published by Marvel Comics. The character has spun off into cartoons, movies, and a popular TV series (1978-1982).

VAYA CON LEOS: *Vaya con dios* is a Spanish phrase meaning "go with God" (or "may God be with you").

MR. & MRS. WITCH: *Mr. & Mrs. Smith* (2005) is a film starring Brad Pitt and Angelina Jolie.

PAYBACK'S A WITCH: A play on words with a similar-sounding phrase regarding the concept that revenge can be cruel.

REPO MANOR: *Repo Man* is the title of a comedy/sci-fi film released in 1984.

12 ANGRY ZEN: *12 Angry Men* is a 1957 film based on a TV play of the same name that aired in 1954. Zen is a notable school of Buddhism.

THE LAST TEMPTATION OF CHRISTY: *The Last Temptation of Christ* (1988) is a Martin Scorsese film based on the novel by Nikos Kazantzakis.

ENGAGED AND CONFUSED: *Dazed and Confused* is a film released in 1993.

GENERATION HEX: "Generation X" is a term used to describe the generation of people, primarily in the Western world, born in the 1960s and 1970s. Though the term had been in existence for decades, it was popularized in the early 1990s.

THE TORN IDENTITY: *The Bourne Identity* is a 2002 film based on a book by Robert Ludlum.

THE JUNG AND THE RESTLESS: Carl Jung was a psychiatrist credited with the development of analytical psychology. *The Young and the Restless* is a daytime soap opera that premiered in 1973.

GONE WITH THE WITCHES: *Gone with the Wind* is a classic film released in 1939, based on the book by Margaret Mitchell.

KILL BILLIE: VOL. 2: *Kill Bill: Vol. 2* is the second of two films written and directed by Quentin Tarantino and starring Uma Thurman.

FOREVER CHARMED: Is Executive Producer Brad Kern's promise to the fans that the *Charmed* universe will live on after the end of the series.

Behind the Scenes

THE CAST

HOLLY MARIE COMBS   *as Piper Halliwell*

Holly Marie Combs began her career working in commercials and print advertising when she was ten and was cast in her first movie role, *Sweet Hearts Dance*, by age thirteen. Her breakthrough role, however, came at age eighteen, when she was cast in the critically acclaimed television drama *Picket Fences*.

During the eight years that *Charmed* was in production, Holly continued working outside the series in TV and film, appearing as herself in the film *Ocean's Eleven* and in the ABC Family telefilm *See Jane Date* (along with Charisma Carpenter, who later played Kira the Seer on *Charmed*). The sole cast member from the original *Charmed* pilot to work throughout the entire series (Alyssa Milano appeared in scenes reshot from the original pilot), Holly became a producer during the show's fourth season. However, she experienced much larger changes in her life outside the show.

HOLLY MARIE COMBS: Working on a show for eight years, for the majority of my twenties . . . I've grown up here. I met my husband here and I had my child here. Focusing on the relationships between the family and the girls' romantic relationships is always the fun stuff for me, and it's stuff I find more interesting to play. But don't get me wrong—I still love doing the stunts and I love doing all the stuff that's exciting. And that's what's great about the show, is that you can do so many different things in one day.

Our crew is great, and we have a lot of fun, and it's an easy show to make. Even though it's technically difficult, it's easy to be here and it's easy to make, because doing this kind of stuff, you end up spending a large portion of your life here, and it's got to be the first place you want to be.

Alyssa Milano began her career in 1980 at age eight with the national touring company of *Annie*. She first garnered worldwide attention playing the role of Sam in the hit series *Who's the Boss?* Literally growing up onscreen, Alyssa has starred in numerous films and television series. She first joined the Spelling Entertainment family when she starred for two years on *Melrose Place*. Like Holly, Alyssa also became a producer on *Charmed* during the fourth season.

Outside of her work on the show, Alyssa has been an outspoken Internet advocate, creating the search engine Safesearching.com as a safe haven for Internet users that provides family-friendly websites. She has also found a deeper interest in charity work in recent years and has been appointed a national ambassador for UNICEF.

ALYSSA MILANO: The first time that my career made sense to me was when I realized . . . I was in South Africa for three months and I realized that I could not ignore this humanitarian pull that I had. It was such a great way to exercise that there, because they've suffered so much social and political struggle that they didn't care that I was a celebrity. It was sort of just doing whatever I can to help people. It was the first time I realized, I think, why I was so blessed to have the career that I have. It finally made sense to me. It's a big part of my life and a big part of my happiness to do that.

Even if I wasn't an actress, I think I'd be doing some sort of service work. But it becomes more powerful because when you're a celebrity you hopefully have a bigger voice to effect positive change and to empower people to want to make changes within themselves. That's the thing that I think is almost most important about doing this at the age that I'm at now. I think that most actresses wait until their own kids are grown before they start going on these missions and doing stuff. But for me it really was so important to be able to, perhaps, inspire a younger generation of future humanitarians.

Rose McGowan made her television debut on *Charmed* following a short, but notable, movie career highlighted with independent film work. One of six children, Rose was born and raised in Italy and spent her childhood traveling throughout Europe. Her family eventually returned to the United States and settled in Seattle, where she attended high school. On a trip to Los Angeles, she was cast in the film *The Doom Generation*, which garnered her a Best Newcomer nomination at the Independent Spirit Awards. That same year she also appeared in the box office hit *Scream*.

Rose joined *Charmed* in its fourth season, following the departure of Shannen Doherty. She continued to work outside the show, most notably starring as Ann-Margret in the CBS mini-series *Elvis*. The outspoken actress doesn't take herself too seriously, though she is quite committed to her work. Like her costars, she was offered a producer title after several years on the series. She turned it down due simply to lack of interest . . . and since there was no additional money attached to the title.

ROSE McGOWAN: I told Kaley [Cuoco], in the beginning when I started . . . and for a while after . . . and occasionally still . . . I would feel like such an idiot when I had to do strange things or speak in a strange, foreign sort of language or invented words with demons, et cetera, et cetera. I could tell Kaley was feeling very self-conscious about it too when she got here. I was, "Just go with it. Trust me." Because I was almost embarrassed to do it in front of the crew or something. And it's, believe me, they're old hands at this. They don't even notice. It's completely normal that you're talking to a leprechaun.

BRIAN KRAUSE *as Leo Wyatt*

Brian Krause's acting career has straddled movies and television for years. His first starring role in film was in *Return to the Blue Lagoon*, and he had a lead in the Stephen King film *Sleepwalkers*. He's appeared in numerous television series, such as *Walker, Texas Ranger*, and had a regular role on the long-running daytime drama *Another World*. Behind the scenes, Brian has shared a writing credit on the *Charmed* episode "Sense and Sense Ability." And he has written, directed, produced, and starred in the independent film *The Mission*.

Almost every season of *Charmed*, Brian feared it would be his last because story lines kept dictating that his character, Leo, end the year in some kind of jeopardy. But the decision to end his run on the series was more monetary than story driven when the network told the producers that there was no room for him in the budget for the full final season. Understanding the nature of network television, Brian did come back for the first half of the season and returned for the final episodes. Though he was gone for only a part of the year, the entire production felt the loss of his presence over those ten episodes.

BRIAN KRAUSE: We're one big dysfunctional family. Who are the parents around here? We can't find them. They left us alone here in this house and it's a big party. We kind of all watch over each other. I've never been a part of anything like it. I've played on sports teams for four years at a time. It's still not what we have here on a personal level. I'd love to go through something like this again. Of course I'd love to bring everybody here with me.

DREW FULLER *as Chris Perry Halliwell*

Drew Fuller began modeling in his teens and quickly started working on top accounts. His print work naturally evolved into commercials and then series television. His first notable role was on the WB series *Black Sash*. Though the series was short-lived, he impressed WB executives enough with his work to suggest him for the role of the mysterious Whitelighter from the future, Chris.

Drew joined *Charmed* for the final episodes of the fifth season and became a regular character during the sixth season. Though the full identity of his character was unknown to Drew at the start, once he entered the sixth season he sat down with Executive Producer Brad Kern and learned possible directions his character could take. Though Brad did not speak in specifics, he gave Drew much insight into how to play his character. Though his story was complete by the end of the sixth season, Drew did return for "Someone to Witch Over Me" in the seventh season, and he appeared in the show's finale, "Forever Charmed."

DREW FULLER on going back to *Charmed*: I missed it. I love work. Period. I love working every single day. When you're not on a television show and you're focusing on films, there will be months and months and months of dry spells. Whereas on a show you might have a couple days off, but there's that job to wake up to every morning. I loved it. I missed it. I thought it was a great little thing to see them. It was cool.

KALEY CUOCO · *as Billie Jenkins*

Kaley Cuoco started working as a model and commercial actress at the age of six. She has appeared on stage, screen, and television, guest starring on such series as *Ellen* and *My So-Called Life*. Her breakout role was in the sitcom *8 Simple Rules*, for which she won a Teen Choice Award for Breakthrough Actress of 2003. Among her large body of work for such a young woman is the ABC Family TV movie *Crimes of Fashion*. As if she weren't already busy enough, she has also guest cohosted the talk show *The View* on several occasions.

Kaley joined *Charmed* in the eighth season with the intention that she—in conjunction with one or more of the existing cast—could continue the series or spin it off to another show. With the transition of the WB into the new network, the CW, that plan changed, and she closed out the series with the rest of the cast. Never one to rest on her laurels, Kaley had a new pilot lined up before the series ended filming.

KALEY CUOCO: I feel like I've been here for eight years because of everyone. It's just been amazing. We all love each other. From hair and makeup to the girls and the directors, it's just been really cool. It's very rare to be able to get along with everyone so well. Especially girls. It can be very difficult. That's the thing, though. It's not like you're doing a pilot with four girls. That can get a little icky. They've been here for eight years. They're, like, "We're over it. We don't care anymore."

I love when I have scenes with all the girls, because I never really get to work with them because we all do different things. That's something that's changed for me from a sitcom to a one-hour show. I don't see everyone every day. Maybe I'll work with Rose or whoever on a Friday and I won't see her for another week. And then I'll do a whole episode with her. On a sitcom, you're with everyone every day. So it's kind of almost better, because you don't get annoyed with each other. You get excited to see someone.

DORIAN GREGORY *as Inspector Darryl Morris*

Dorian Gregory began his work on *Charmed* as a recurring character, moved to a regular cast member, and returned to recurring status over the first seven years of the show. He has made numerous guest spots on a variety of television series over the years. He has also served hosting duties for a number of media events and radio shows, with his most notable hosting work on the long-running dance series *Soul Train* as well as the short-lived talk show *The Other Half*.

Dorian has type one (or juvenile) diabetes and is a national spokesman for the American Diabetes Association. Unfortunately, Dorian was unavailable at the time the interviews for *The Book of Three, Volume 2* were conducted. However, Executive Producer Brad Kern had the following to say about the actor:

BRAD KERN: I had every intention of bringing Dorian back this year, even though I wrapped up his story line last year and it felt like he had gone through enough with the demons and the girls that he deserved to move on with his life. So if that was to be the end of the series, I wanted Dorian's character also to feel like he got to have a life beyond *Charmed*.

I had hoped to bring him back this year because I love the guy. He's a friend and he's just meant so much to the show. When you do a show about magic, you're always looking for the reality to offset the magic, so the magic doesn't look like a cartoon. Obviously the sisters and their real issues—the loss, the love—that's been a reality to balance out the magic that we've used and taken advantage of. But Dorian's character being a policeman—having to deal with the pressures of having to cover for the girls and their wacky magic—he has always been an important rock to the show. And we've missed that rock this year, because we haven't had the police presence. We haven't had the real nonmagical everyday character that's been in the show. I've missed that. But there were just too many things to tie up and too many things that needed to be accomplished. There really wasn't an organic way to get him back into the show, which I'm sorry we couldn't do that.

The Executive Producers

Aaron Spelling passed away a month after the *Charmed* finale aired. The most prolific producer in television history, he excelled at developing series that he proudly considered "mind candy," while still managing to bring quality entertainment to the masses with shows like *Family* and the TV movie *And The Band Played On.* We were very lucky to have had the chance to speak with Mr. Spelling for both volumes of the *Book of Three.* He was a warm and friendly man that we found, fittingly, to be utterly charming.

With over 4,500 hours of television programming under his belt, Aaron Spelling is listed in *The Guinness Book of World Records* as the most productive television producer of all time. His incredible list of successful TV series spans decades, including such popular shows as *The Mod Squad*, *Starsky and Hutch*, *Family*, *The Love Boat*, *Fantasy Island*, *Dynasty*, *Beverly Hills 90210*, and *Melrose Place*. His prolific company has also produced such popular films as *Mr. Mom*, *The Usual Suspects*, and *Soapdish*.

With *Charmed* running eight seasons and *7th Heaven* lasting ten, Spelling Entertainment produced the two longest-running series on the now defunct network, the WB. As for longevity, Mr. Spelling himself has received numerous lifetime achievement awards from a variety of organizations. In March 2005 he was also honored with the first ever Pioneer Achievement Award from the TV Land Awards.

AARON SPELLING: We're honored that *Charmed* is the longest-running series in television history to feature all female leads. These are three sisters who happen to be good witches, and not three good witches who happen to be sisters. That helps keep the relationship between the sisters realistic and very honest. I thank Holly, Alyssa, and Rose, Brad Kern and the rest of the cast and crew for their passion and commitment to keep this series fresh, which is a tribute to its longevity. Our audience of young women really looks up to our ladies, and it's something of which we're all proud.

As I learned working with the great Bette Davis, the eyes are windows to the soul, not mirrors but windows, and with Holly, Alyssa, and Rose, I saw eyes that are windows. Watching these gorgeous girls continue to charm audiences and us over the years has been truly wonderful and remarkable. I've seen them grow lovelier every day and become even more talented actresses.

E. DUKE VINCENT

A former naval aviator, E. Duke Vincent signed a contract with RKO General and Seven Arts in New York City to write and produce seven one-hour documentaries called *Man in Space* in 1963, bringing him into the entertainment industry. From there he met up with the executive producers of *The Dick Van Dyke Show* and worked with them on their next series, *Good Morning, World*. The following year he became producer/head writer of *Gomer Pyle, U.S.M.C.* and continued to work in television and movies over the next decade.

Mr. Vincent joined with Aaron Spelling in 1977 and has coproduced a huge list of television series, miniseries, and movies. He recently published his first novel, *Mafia Summer*, which is loosely based on his life growing up in the Hell's Kitchen section of New York.

E. DUKE VINCENT: [The relationship between Aaron and me] worked great for twenty-eight years. We had a couple hits along the way. People ask me all the time—most marriages in Hollywood don't last twenty-eight months—they ask me, "What is it?"

I think we work because we are so totally completely different people. Aaron was born in Dallas, Texas, from the other side of the tracks, from a Jewish family. He became an actor, who made it then as a writer and then as a producer. He will not get on an airplane. He will not fly. He won't play golf. He plays tennis. I, on the other hand, was born in Hell's Kitchen, New York City. I'm Sicilian. Catholic. I flew with the navy for ten years. I was a navy pilot. I do play golf. And I don't play tennis. So if you go right straight down the line we are totally opposite in every single way. But I think because of that, we get along beautifully.

Everything I don't know, he does. Everything he doesn't know, I do. We complement each other. If we were both exactly the same, why would we need each other? So the balance is there. We have a lot of fun together . . . a lot of fun and laughs.

Closing the Door on CHARMED with

EXECUTIVE PRODUCER BRAD KERN

Brad Kern burst into the entertainment industry when his student film, *Weekend Prisoner*, garnered awards in more than twenty international film festivals. His first professional writing job was on the romantic comedy/mystery TV series, *Remington Steele*. He was also on the writing staff of the critically acclaimed series *Hill Street Blues*; he served as supervising producer on *The Adventures of Brisco County Jr.* and as co-executive producer on another romantic comedy, *Lois & Clark: The New Adventures of Superman*. Prior to *Charmed* he was executive producer on the award-winning drama *New York Undercover*.

In addition to serving as executive producer and show runner for *Charmed*, Brad directed the fourth-season finale, "Witch Way Now." During the run of the series, he also worked on a pilot for the WB for a series about a mermaid. The inspiration for this potential series was the fifth-season opener of *Charmed*, "A Witch's Tail." Unfortunately, the network ultimately decided not to pick up the series.

Brad was generous enough to sit down with the authors of *The Book of Three, Volume 2* twice during the final season to discuss his work on *Charmed*—in the middle of the season and after he finished writing the last episode. Here's what he had to say.

BOOK OF THREE: *How did your approach to writing Charmed change over the course of eight seasons?*

BRAD KERN: I think evolution is the key to the success of the show. In the first year or two we were just throwing out episodes, trying to figure out what the series could be and what individual episodes could be. You kind of stumble across a few little character arcs, but more often you're trying to figure out how to make an episode. Part of the legs of the series are that we began to take a longer view of the season. And then even a longer view of two seasons and three seasons. It kind of began to take a life of its own. I think that it created its own momentum. It brought in new characters, which brought in fresh dynamics for our stars to play off. And the love and loss of those characters would create openings for other new characters to challenge the dynamics.

Luck is the number one reason we're still here. And a loyal audience is number two. But if there's a creative reason, I think it's that we've begun to take advantage of the life the show itself has taken and the characters have taken on and tried to evolve it. It's a longer view. We look at the bigger season arcs and know that we've got our core audience that doesn't just want to see an episode. They want to be rewarded for a season-long investment of their precious time. We try to honor the prior season's investment of their time as much as possible as we work on each new season.

It kind of has its own momentum now. As a writer, it feels like we've got so much under our belts now. A lot of people always ask, "How do you come up with ideas? Isn't it hard?" The characters are alive and they're growing and they're having children and they're breaking up with guys and they're fighting demons and getting jobs and losing sisters. It creates a path; a journey that seems to imply where to go next. That, with a little bit of imagination, and we've got another season.

How do you go about planning out a season?

It all has to be organic. If the sisters are real women, and their backstory—meaning all the years that precede the year that we're talking about—matters, then we have to play off of that. So we have a natural starting point. Then we deal with the question of where can we see it going for the season. Though at the beginning of the season I don't say, "*This* is exactly where we're going to end up." I have an idea about where we're going to end up, but I want to be open to discovery.

The success of the show seems to be creatively about being aware of its natural evolution. I want to be aware of the natural evolution of the season I'm embarking upon. So we kind of divide the season into three chapters. If a story is divided naturally into a beginning, middle, and end with every episode, then we look at the season as having a beginning, a middle, and an end. At the beginning of the season we have an idea. We know where we're starting, because it's where we ended [last season]. We talk about where we want to end up, and then we really focus on the first third of the season. So that the first third—the first six or seven episodes—tells its own story as the setup for the next two acts, if you will, of the season.

Each episode has its own story, but where that episode falls in the respective seven-episode run plays into the beginning, middle, and end of the season. As we work through the season, we discover new ideas and let the characters take us new places, which might adjust, ultimately, where we end up.

And with those many episodes you tend to have several stories within each episode. How do you handle writing so many stories within episodes, within a season?

The challenge really becomes, "Okay, when we cut from one sister's story to the next sister's story, to another sister's story and back to the first sister's story, were they equally balanced? Did we care enough about each one as we did the other?" That's the biggest challenge. Because there's plenty of stories to play if they're real characters, real sisters, real women. We can come up with where we want to take them every episode. But are all the stories as interesting as each other's story? Otherwise, when it cuts to the next story, you're going, "Oh, it's not really interesting" and you flip the channel. So I think the balance is the hardest part.

Nowadays, in the eighth season, we've got more than three stories. We've got Kaley and you also have the demon story. So sometimes we've got four or five stories. It's always daunting, I can tell you. Every time we erase that damn [story] board and are just looking at a big, blank whiteboard, I always take a deep breath and say a silent prayer because, "Here we go. How are we going to do this one?" And you just start building the building blocks and watching it come together. And then erase it again and do it again.

How did you approach the season arc for Season Six? Was Chris always intended to be Piper and Leo's second child?

At the end of Season Five, Piper and Leo were separated. Part of the job I have as show runner is to look at the big picture. I'm always hoping that there will be another season. No matter how many seasons we have, my job is always to see if I can get one more season out of the show. Having had a lot of experience with romantic comedies on television and how difficult it is to stretch them out without, on one hand, upsetting the audience because they're not getting enough of what they want in the romantic comedy, meaning Piper and Leo. Or on the other hand, giving them too much and they're bored. Knowing that we were separating Piper and Leo, I knew the audience wouldn't like that for very long. At the same time we had to separate them, because they couldn't just be happily married and everything's going to be hunky-dory, because then there's no inner conflict to play. Then their story's kind of soft.

We had the plan to bring Chris in as the future Whitelighter. As I said earlier, things can evolve and change over the course of the season, and we're open to it, but it was originally the idea that he would turn out to be Wyatt's younger brother from the future. And if it didn't work out that way, then he'd be somebody else. But that was the plan. It was timed so I wanted to have a big reveal for the audience about two-thirds of the way through the season: February sweeps. I always look to that mark because that's the second part of the three-act structure for the season. I knew I wanted a big surprise for the audience. And I knew that Piper and Leo would probably have to get back together by then, otherwise the audience would probably give up on the show. But I didn't have to make that decision yet [at the beginning of the season]. It was my hope that he would turn out to be the future son.

When Holly called—actually, Alyssa called. Holly was afraid to call because she thought I'd be mad. Alyssa was in the trailer and she called for Holly and said, "Holly thinks you're going to be mad, so I'm calling to say that she's pregnant!" I was, like, "Why would I be mad? That's fabulous. Are you kidding?" But it just worked out. Because I thought, this is perfect. Then it became really fun because now we realized we weren't faking a baby. It was going to be a real baby. The challenge then became, "Now we have to get Piper and Leo back together a little bit quicker than we thought we wanted to, because she's going to start showing." And that became the big challenge, how to tie all that in. We ended up with a lot of fun episodes because of that.

Considering Holly was showing before the character was pregnant, how did you deal with that? Episodes like "The Legend of Sleepy Halliwell" come to mind.

That was tricky. It was one of the reasons why we chopped off her head. One thing I've learned to do on *Charmed*—because there are so many challenges, whether it's what the girls may or may not want or what the network wants or what we've done before or what haven't we done—is to try to look at everything as a creative challenge, not as a problem. So we couldn't show Piper pregnant, because she hadn't gotten back together with Leo yet. It was, like, "Okay, let's just look at this as a challenge."

I can't remember who thought of it, but it was, like, "Well, let's just chop off her head." And then it was, "Okay, how can we chop off her head and have it be funny and cute?" Because it is *Charmed*. So she didn't have her body for most of the show, and we bought another episode as far as not having to see her showing.

With the idea for your overall arc set, how did you approach the start of the season?

The year before, we started out with mermaids, and that was a pretty—no pun intended—splashy premiere. So how do you top that? I'm not sure that we did top that with Valhalla, because you can't top Alyssa Milano with green scales on her and a tail. So the challenge the network had thrown this gauntlet down to me was, "Okay, what do you want to do for a premiere for Season Six that's going to match the mermaid show?" And I said, "It's not possible."

A little bit of trivia is that what I had originally pitched turned out to be the eighth episode, "Sword and the City." I had pitched basically the Excalibur story line for the two-hour premiere. The network executive at the time didn't really like the Excalibur idea. He was pretty much against it. It's a subjective thing. Everybody has their reasons.

But I snuck it into episode eight and it became one of our best episodes. It was a fun episode, and I wanted it to be the premiere. I think it would have been a better premiere because I wanted to play the Piper/Leo relationship with King Arthur, Sir Lancelot, and Lady Guinevere. I wanted to have that kind of triangle with the bad guy between them, and we'd get to see that Sir Lancelot would have been Leo and that Piper . . . they really did love each other.

Valhalla turned out to be a good episode. It was pretty challenging to create Valhalla on a television budget and television schedule. It was big to accomplish, and I think Jim Conway did a great job directing it. But I always liked that for the production value.

What do you consider some of the highlights of Season Six?

Bringing in Wyatt's powers was fun with "Forget Me . . . Not." Bringing in a dragon. That was a hard episode to think about and to work out because it took a lot of thinking to not have it fall apart. Those are the kinds of things you have to do early in the season when you have more lead time.

There were a lot of the stories I liked. I loved doing the Romeo and Juliet story; the Capulets and Montagues in "Love's a Witch." I really loved "Sword and the City," obviously. I thought Holly did a great job. And she was pregnant during that episode. There was a scene, actually . . . we had just found out she was pregnant and in that story she's supposed to get impaled by the sword in the stomach. And we were, like, "That's not going to look right." So we changed that.

I thought "Little Monsters" was a terrific episode, because we got to deal with using the demon story to play the age-old question of, is nature or nurture more important in a child's upbringing? Sometimes those are my favorite stories, when we're able to use the demons or the evils of the week to be able to play some of those age-old questions.

Because Paige was adopted, she's pro-nurture. And of course, Holly's character, Piper, just had a baby and she's pro-nature. The great thing about doing a show like that is that it helps differentiate the characters, which is really important. One of the things I'm most proud of on the show is that the three sisters are three different people. They're not the same. They're not interchangeable. Even in the dialogue, you can't switch them around. So they each have legitimate points of view. There's nothing wrong with Paige's point of view in that episode. There's nothing wrong with Piper's point of view in that episode. No one's wrong.

At the end of the episode, they both kind of begin to see each other's side. We kind of make the point that it's both nature and nurture by having them both start off the episode with their natural perspective points of views that put them in conflict. Then we end the episode coming to the conclusion that it's both, which is where we wanted it anyway. To me as a writer and dealing with the girls, that's the best part of the show.

Obviously, "Chris-Crossed" was a . . . it seems like every episode ten that we do is a great episode. Not coincidental, because usually episode ten becomes the last episode we air before the Christmas break. And sometimes we're off the air for six or seven weeks. So what we try to do—and we have the last three or four years—is we try to make episode ten more of a cliffhanger. So we hold the audience so they want to come back after a long break and too much Christmas cheer, to want to pick up where we left off. That's why ten is going to be big. "Chris-Crossed" was exactly that, because we really got to go to the future and learn why Chris came from the future and the surprise of all surprises that Wyatt is evil in the future. That's the future that his little brother has come back to try to change.

Prior to that episode, it seems like many people assumed that Chris was actually Wyatt come back from the future.

I check the boards every once in a while just to see if the fans have taken the bait. And you want them to, because that's my job—to entertain them. They had it hook, line, and sinker. I like keeping the audience looking at one thing so that it's really a magic act. It's a shell game. So they're not thinking that it could be Wyatt's younger brother. It was perfect. I think it made the audience feel that much more rewarded when they realized it was the younger brother. And then how do you get Mom and Dad together to conceive in time? Which became the next three or four episodes.

Getting a glimpse of the future was great. And getting a glimpse of what was at stake, which I think became the undercurrent for the rest of the season. This was what Chris had to do and it wasn't just fun and games trying to get his mom and dad together. He had to get them onboard to be able to stop what they thought was the ultimate good in Gideon from inadvertently turning Wyatt evil in the future.

As for other episodes, "The Legend of Sleepy Halliwell" was a terrific episode and a very difficult show to make look good. If you're going to start chopping heads off and be funny, that's a challenge. I just think that turned out to be a great episode. And it introduced Magic School to the show, which became a template and a set piece that opened up another avenue for us for stories. Which ultimately Paige took over and Leo took over and now in the eighth season evil has taken it over. It was just one set in one episode and before you know it you're going, "Maybe we can use this again." And now, two years later, it's another staple of our show.

"I Dream of Phoebe." Phoebe playing *I Dream of Jeannie*. She had a great line in that one. She says, "Why am I always the one that's stuck with the bad wig?" Which cracked us up. She actually did the ad-lib on that. We didn't write "bad wig" because that really is breaking the fourth wall. It was "bad hairdo," but she changed it to bad wig and it was actually funnier.

"The Courtship of Wyatt's Father" was really the touching story about getting Piper and Leo back together again and finding out that they really, truly did love each other. That was kind of cool. And she was very pregnant at the time. The season jumped between episodes sixteen and seventeen because February sweeps ended with episode sixteen and we were off the air for four or five weeks, which became a three-month change for Piper.

The next challenge became, "Okay, we've successfully, creatively gotten Chris conceived, and now Piper can organically be pregnant, but now the actress is pregnant too and entering her third trimester. She can't do the hours. She can't do the stunts." So the challenge became, "How do we keep Piper alive in the show but not really have her available to us?" So that became the rest of the season. We started to get her more and more out of the show and work our way up to the conclusion. And we wanted a worthy conclusion to the season, because we had started off with such a bang.

I think the challenge became for us on a big season with a big opening and a big reveal, was what's the big end? We knew we were coming back for a seventh season when we were designing the end of Season Six. So part of what I was doing was thinking about what we could play off of next season in Season Seven. One of the things that I wanted to do was I wanted to rock the girls. That's something I wanted to do. What haven't we done yet? We got through Season Six. Saved Chris. Saved Wyatt. And stopped Gideon so that we could make the future world good and have a hopeful future for Wyatt after this tumultuous year. But I also wanted to do something to help set up Season Seven by rocking the girls' world.

This is the big reward for the real loyal audience. We try to connect from the first season to where we're at now. The Elders didn't want Piper and Leo together in Seasons One or Two. Gideon became the reason why six years later. Because the power that could be created by the union of those two magical beings would be so powerful that it could be corrupted by evil, and the universe shouldn't have anybody that powerful. Now we're talking about a little one-year-old child, which is the great part about it. But we've got to get a glimpse of the future to see what Gideon was talking about. So we could intellectually understand his concern and why this child had to be eliminated. It's still Piper and Leo's child, and you can't just go around killing our kids even if it is to save the world.

It's the old question of, if you knew Hitler as a baby was going to do that, what would you have done to that baby? And that's kind of the launching point we were working off of with Gideon in saving Wyatt, saving the future, getting rid of Gideon. It allowed me to start Season Seven with having Leo—who all of his lives has always been about good—betrayed by good. And therefore, not sure what good and bad means anymore. That would set up another full set of moral dilemmas and a whole season arc.

And how did you go about setting up that story arc for Season Seven?

I think that the show is always about good and evil and the eternal battle. We felt like we had done so much of the good versus evil fighting we weren't sure—in our never-ending desire to come up with new material—how we were going to play the good-versus-evil battle freshly in Season Seven versus the prior six years and one hundred thirty-four episodes. That's a lot of episodes to play good versus evil. So we took Leo's story and the plan was—because he was the ultimate in good, he was an Elder—to watch his mentor betray him and kill his son because [Gideon] thought that was for the greater good. We wanted to rock Leo's moral foundation. We wanted to make somebody who was always a freedom fighter—always believed in the greater good—and we wanted to rock him to his core. And that's what the beginning of Season Seven was all about: What happens when the greatest good becomes unsure about whether good is really that good anymore?

That left him vulnerable to a new approach, which is how we worked our way towards the Avatars. Endeavoring to come up with something other than just good versus evil battling all the time, we came up with a third option. We'd test the age-old duality of good versus evil and have someone come in and say, "Okay, we've been watching you guys fight—good and evil—for eons and it doesn't really work. It never ends. What if we talked about power? What if we came up with Utopia?"

Leo became the key to that, because his moral foundation was rocked. They went to him first. They felt like if they could turn him, he would then help them turn the girls and have them be open to this new way. So that really was the whole point of betraying Leo at the end of Season Six and having him be open to a new way. To allow us to touch on different story-arcing issues.

[Ultimately,] the characters had to recognize that good and evil is the way it's set up, and we've just got to go with it. There is no such thing as a perfect world. Without bad, good doesn't have meaning. We've made the point on the show that without death, life doesn't have meaning. Accepting that death is a natural part of life is, I think, an interesting message that we've been able to throw at the show over the years.

From an objective point of view, I don't think the Avatars story line worked as well as I would have liked it to. I think it got a little more serious and intellectual than I probably would have liked it to have gotten, which is why we ended it a little bit earlier than we had planned on.

The seventh season also saw the production move from your original soundstages in Woodland Hills to the Paramount Picture lot. How did that move affect the show?

At the end of Season Six, everybody was tired. We had been working in a warehouse in the San Fernando Valley for five years. It's very isolated out there. There was only *Charmed* to live and breathe. One of the major changes that I was able to help make was to move the show, in the seventh season, onto the Paramount lot. I remember saying, to anybody who would listen to me, that, "If you want an eighth year we need to get to the Paramount lot in the seventh year. If you don't want an eighth year, then let's just go to Van Nuys. Let's just get a small little industrial building and let's just say, "Okay, we've got our seven-year run."

In order to give new life to the show and to give new energy to the girls, we needed to give them something else to look at and have lives outside of the daily workings of the show. We can do that here. At least as important is to have access to the [New York street] backlot, because we were stuck with one street in the Valley that we always had to use. So after a while, the show looks kind of the same every week. And the people here at Paramount were great about making it work for us financially.

I think it had as much to do with us coming back for one more year as anything else. The fresh look of the show and the freshness it gave all of us involved on a daily basis. And the show looked bigger. Even though it was smaller financially, even though we didn't have as much money, even in the seventh season.

Charmed has always attracted big-name guest stars, but at the beginning of Season Seven you added untrained dramatic actor Nick Lachey to the cast for a recurring role [Leslie St. Claire]. At the time, some people believed it was simply stunt casting. How did you feel about it?

I had the same reaction. I was like, "Oh, great. Stunt casting. One for ratings." But the guy could act *and* he cared about acting. That was the other thing. He really wanted to do a good job. He wanted to learn, and each episode on his six-episode arc I gave him a little bit more to play as an actor to see if he could do it. And he was always able to do it. Then I'd give him a little more. A little more comedy. A little more emotion. A little more to see if he could reveal the pain. He really wanted to learn how to do that. I think the guy has a huge acting career if he wants it.

And we're told that you were especially excited to have Billy Zane appear later in the season [as Drake].

Billy Zane was a great highlight for me. He's just colorful. He's so energetic. He's wild. He's wacky. The show is wild and wacky and Billy Zane is wild and wacky. To bring in a character that would reflect the feel of the whole show in one human being was why I always wanted Billy Zane. I let it be known that I liked Billy for years. And finally we got him.

He and I had dinner, and it was one of those dinners where I thought it would last about an hour and a half and then four hours later we both closed the joint. When I walked out of there, I thought, "This guy's amazing." And he got into what we were doing on *Charmed*. He'd seen the show enough to say, "I really like the magical world that you guys play in. I really enjoy the bigger issues that are beneath the surface of the wild and wackiness." And he wanted to be a part of that.

At the time, he was only getting cast for bad guy roles. What I had pitched to him was a demon. But he said, "That's what I always get cast as." So he and I talked at length about different ways to approach his character, and we came up with a reformed demon, which was kind of where he was at in his career too at the time. Because he's a star. He doesn't have to be a bad guy. He's a lead. So that's how Billy Zane became part of the show. And we've been friends ever since.

He brought an enormous amount of energy. Part of my job, I feel, over the years has been to keep infusing the show with energy. That's the first thing that goes away, understandably, after twelve-hour days, five days a week, year in and year out. Where do we get new energy? Julian McMahon brought in a ton of new energy. Rose brought in a ton of new energy. Billy Zane brought in energy. Nick Lachey brought in energy. Kaley Cuoco brings in energy. That's kind of what I'm always looking for. Where can I throw more energy into the show to keep the girls energetic? Because they're working hard. And it's understandable that they're going to be tired. So where's the new fresh material going to come from?

Which is a natural lead-in to discuss the fact that the seventh season also included your one hundred fiftieth episode, a huge milestone in television production.

I was awestruck by it. I remember doing the hundredth episode and being amazed at the big party. We had the press from around the world coming. And it was a hundred episodes and "My gosh, how did we make it that far?" I remember somebody had a speech saying, "Well, we'll see you again at the hundred and fiftieth episode." And we all laughed at that. That was two and a half seasons later.

I never thought I'd be part of a show that I'd been on for a hundred and fifty episodes. But now I can cut to here, twenty-eight episodes beyond that, and say I can't believe I've been on a show for eight years. Every milestone has blown us all away. It certainly has blown me away. In this day and age of television, it's really remarkable to be part of a show that hits so many milestones. I'm hyperaware and feel blessed by each one of them.

What do you consider some of the highlights of Season Seven?

I like "Styx Feet Under." I wouldn't say that's probably a favorite for a lot of people, but I think there was some real depth to that show. We brought the Angel of Death back in the show. He kind of brought in the feeling that death gives life meaning. In this culture we don't talk about death very much. It's, like, people die and they're buried and we move on. I think that's a sadness because, for all the reasons I wanted to do "Styx Feet Under" was to have the Angel of Death, of all people, tell us that death gives life meaning. If there wasn't a deadline, we wouldn't appreciate this moment. So I personally liked that one a lot.

"Once in a Blue Moon" was fun for us because, what happens to all three witches on their period at the same time? And I think the truth is, they all were. All the actresses were. Of all things to happen. It's well known that women, when they work together, cycle together, oftentimes. If we're doing a show about women and we're doing a show about sisters and that's a natural aspect of life, it seemed like a fun thing to do. Not to make fun of it, because it's a real thing that happens. What happens when it's three women who have powers? That was kind of a fun show in that way.

Of course, "Charmed Noir" was a special show because we were able to do something that really epitomizes what *Charmed* can do versus almost what any other show on television can do. We can have a character swallowed up in a Damon Runyon novel or go into a film noir and have everything be black-and-white. When do you get to do that on television? And Rose did an amazing job on that show.

Then, being able to remake the world [in "Extreme Makeover: World Edition"]. I remember telling the writers if we're going to make the story line work, we actually have to produce a show that remakes the world. They all thought I was nuts. And I kind of thought I was nuts. But the production people involved did an amazing job selling us changing the world and then changing it back again.

Those issues . . . we talked about the building blocks of the show that help balance out the magic that keep it from becoming a cartoon and the issues that we touch upon. When we bring in death, that's hyperreality. That helps to keep the show from feeling like it's just a silly magic show. When we deal with the issues of changing the world and do we have the right to use our powers for that? Those issues help ground the wackiness of the show. I think that unique balance is what we sought to try to preserve year in and year out. And with that show in particular, I think productionwise we absolutely pulled it off.

I think the girls did a great job dealing with the inner conflicts of "Do we have the right to do this?" I think that putting them in those kinds of situations on and off over the course of the series has been rewarding for me, too. People don't really talk about that part of the show that much, but it's a fundamental part of the show. It's what keeps the show from looking like it's just *Bewitched*. There's nothing wrong with that, but that was a half-hour show. What do we do for an hour every week? And that's also a different time. We're dealing with different issues now. With the Internet and mass media, we're all aware of so much more, and I think we have to be aware of that when we're writing the show.

Then we get to the Billy Zany episodes and the hundred and fiftieth episode. . . .

And on to the end of the season. But at the time you weren't sure if it was going to be the end of the season or the end of the series. How difficult was it wrapping up the season not knowing if you were coming back?

It was really frustrating. But I didn't blame the network, because they had the prerogative to hold their decision until the end. It was a new regime that had taken over the network, and they didn't have the same affinity for the people involved—for the show—that the old regime had had since the beginning. It was unsettling, because we weren't sure what they thought and how they felt about *Charmed*. And it was unsettling because it felt like after so many years we needed to end the show properly, but we didn't think we were going to be able to have that opportunity. So it was very difficult to chart out what the shows should be and almost impossible to build towards a conclusion when we always felt like we were a week away from finding out one way or the other.

On top of that, I was doing a pilot in Miami and my workload was just so over the top that it was really hard to do both projects. Considering one of the projects I still wasn't sure if it was going to be a season finale or a series finale. So I actually wrote the last episode in a hotel room in Miami over Easter weekend in two and a half days, because that's where I was shooting my pilot. We waited as long as we could to find out one way or the other from the network and we never did get to hear. So I ended up having to do what I call a hybrid, which was neither here nor there. It wasn't, obviously, a season finale. It wasn't really a series finale. But I wanted to put something in that show that made the audience feel like there was a period on the end of the sentence if that was to be the last sentence.

I wasn't satisfied on the level I'm satisfied now with the series finale that we're doing, because I was holding back. I had to leave elements in that show and design a show that would allow me to get out of it because I might have to get out of it. Ultimately, thankfully, that's what happened. But that kept me from being able to write the series finale the way I would have written the series finale, which is the way I've done it now.

How did you find out the show was coming back?

I was actually at the San Diego Wild Animal Park with my five-year-old, and we were feeding a giraffe when my cell phone rang. It was the president of the studio saying, "They want you back." Naturally the cell phone is dropping in and out. And I'm saying, "What do you mean they want us back? Is it thirteen episodes?" "No, no, they want you back for a full twenty-two." Which was a big surprise. I thought the most we would ever get would be thirteen. The next surprise after that was when the president told me they want hundreds of thousands of dollars out of the budget on a weekly basis. So my first reaction didn't last very long. "Oh, great, we're coming back" then became the monumental task of "Okay, they've given us this twenty-two episode pickup, but they've come up with a budget that doesn't look like it can be met, which means we might actually have to say no to the pickup."

So over the next several days—and my wife will never forgive me for this—we're in a hotel room and I'm on a phone trying to figure out where this money is coming from to be able to piece together what the eighth season could be, given the budget that they were willing to pick up the show for. So there wasn't much joy because quickly I realized a lot was going to have to be cut from the show and it was going to hurt. I gave up some of my salary. The network mandated that we wouldn't be able to afford Brian for more than ten episodes, no matter what. We couldn't go off the lot this year. We'd have to stay on the lot. We couldn't afford to go anywhere. We couldn't build new sets. We did build, ultimately, Phoebe's loft. But that wasn't a very expensive set to build.

Here I had a situation where all the characters had died, yet they had to stay in the sets that we had already built: P3 and the Manor, the cave, and the backlot, which we could only use a certain amount of days because that's expensive too. It really became almost reverse engineering the show into what we had and what we could afford. That, I think, a lot of fans don't realize—nor should they—was a huge albatross and mitigating factor on us creatively. "Okay, we got the show picked up. We figured out how to make it work on this incredibly tight budget. But now what do we do? We're stuck with dead characters that have to live in the sets that they shouldn't be living in anymore." So that was really hard. And even once we got them out of that predicament, after episode five, they still had to stay in their lives. How do characters grow? How do we have them go into new directions when they can't go into new places? The budget was a huge factor this year, obviously, and a lot of choices were made.

It became part of the creative process. I told everybody involved, "Look, we can complain about it. We can resist it. But it's the reality, so let's make it part of the creative process. Let's just make it a creative challenge. How do we make it work given what we've been given? It's a Rubik's cube. Let's solve it."

But you were able to make some changes within the existing sets, like having Magic School taken over by demons.

It was that point when I realized we could make it work. I didn't want to have demons in the cave for twenty-two more episodes. I hate that. I forget where the idea came from, but when somebody said, "Why don't we make Magic School the bastion of evil?" It was, like, "Oh my gosh, that's great." Then we had a place to put them as well as the cave. That made me begin to feel like, "Wait a minute, maybe we can make this work." And it also gave us new material, because now suddenly evil has access to all the great magical notes. That puts our characters, and good, at a greater disadvantage than they've ever been, which is a great place to start the last season.

You also brought Kaley Cuoco in for the eighth season. What did that addition bring to the series?

New dynamics. New energy. And, again, always looking for new ways to help shake up the girls so that they're playing something they haven't played before, or at least variations on a theme. If Alyssa, Holly, and Rose aren't going to be interested or justifiably engaged in what they're doing, then there's no show. So bringing Kaley's character in . . . first of all, it was a network mandate. The new regime was looking for a chance to create new characters to possibly go on to a ninth season or to do a spin-off. No one ever really discussed exactly what the elements could be, but the network felt very strongly that separate from all the budget cuts—and this is an important thing that a lot of people don't realize—the budget cuts were one aspect of what the network insisted upon buying the show for. In addition to those budget cuts, they wanted us to pay for Kaley.

Some people think that Brian left so that we could afford Kaley, and that's not true. Brian was a casualty of the budget cutback that was forced upon us when the show got picked back up. But the network made it very clear that in addition to those budget cutbacks—whatever that number was—they insisted that we spend a certain dollar amount more to bring in characters that could possibly help in some combination of existing cast to spin off the series. So we had the budget cutbacks and they made us add cast to the show after the budget cutbacks. That was really hard.

Kaley, though, was a blessing. Out of these arguments that we had with the network—"I can't believe you're making us do this. We can't squeeze out any more blood. Now you want us to add"—we get Kaley, and it worked out great for us. We had a new young witch who brought in a new danger and created a new, overarching story line for the season that has become very compelling as far as I'm concerned. Kaley's character has also helped take some of the workload off the girls, too. I couldn't ask them to work five days a week, fourteen hours a day, week in and week out in the eighth year. That's just not fair. I wouldn't do that to them. So Kaley's character served the purpose as well.

How did you come up with the arc for what would become the final season?

This was my thinking at the beginning of the season: I had to break down the season into three sections again. Because the first section was, "How do I get out of the series finale that we basically wrote?" So that's the first six or seven episodes. Then once we got through the first third of the season, I was hoping that Billie's story line would begin to rise to the surface a little bit more and take hold and she would become, in essence, a fourth sister. I was hoping that that would happen during the time that we would have to lose Leo. Because I knew we'd be losing Leo after episode ten. That was nonnegotiable.

We were forced to say good-bye to him then, although I kept writing the show as though we were getting him back. That was the biggest leap of faith I've ever taken in my life creatively. Because I did not know if I was going to get him back. I just felt like I would wine him, I would dine him. It's nothing he didn't want to do. He wanted to come back. My fear was that—he's a terrific actor—he would get on a movie, get on a series, and be gone. He always said, "I'll come back if I'm available." But I just couldn't imagine ending the series without Piper and Leo back together again somehow.

I thought, one of two things is going to happen. I'm going to succeed in getting Brian back because I'm writing it as though I'm going to get Brian back. Or I'm going to fail at getting Brian back, in which case I better go into the witness relocation program, because people are going to want to kill me. But I had to take the leap of faith that we're going to get him back. And I was so relieved when we were finally able to make it work out with him to get him back.

That was the middle third of the season, bringing Kaley's character up into the level—not quite to the level—of the three. The new little sister, in essence, that they brought into their fold completely when we lost Brian. Then the last third of the season would be . . . the ending of the series, for me, was always going to be about sisters. If it starts out about sisters, the ending battle had to be sisters versus sisters. So to bring in Kaley's demonically raised sister and have Marnette Paterson's character—who is another terrific addition to the show—turn Billie away from the girls, sets up the final battle.

Part of what I was looking at this time last year was, "How am I going to end the series on a bigger battle then we've ever had?" We've had The Source. We've had the Avatars. We've had goddesses. And also, given this incredibly small budget, I have to be able to produce anything. So it became clear to me that we were going to do sisters versus sisters on some level. And that became the beginning, middle, and end arc too.

What are some of your highlights of the season?

Just surviving "Still Charmed and Kicking" was a favorite memory, because that was a scary episode to write and conceive because, again, "How do we get out of a series finale that was written?"

"Rewitched" was a terrific episode, I think, which also brought the girls back to life and freed us from the constraints of having to pretend like they were dead. And I really enjoyed playing the conundrum that I imagine freedom fighters feel when they want to retire. They've been doing this great thing at their own sacrifice, but when they quit, how do they feel when they see bad things happen all the time but they're retired? They've stopped working. They don't have to do that anymore. I don't happen to have the honor of being a freedom fighter, but the characters have been. And for them to be free, finally getting what they always wanted, but to see demons taking advantage of the void that was left . . . how do you stop that? How do you get what you deserve, which is a life, at the same time how do you ignore all the terrible things that are happening out there? That's where Kaley's character came into the show. For them it became someone they could actually train to help them do some of the heavy lifting. So "Rewitched" really was all that for me.

"Kill Billie: Volume One," I think, was a really terrific episode . . . a very emotional, very powerful episode. Michael Grossman did a great job directing it. It was an important episode, because it really had to elevate Kaley's character so that she was somebody that could hold her own scenes separate from the girls from that point forward, otherwise the design wasn't going to work. If we were building toward some kind of a possible spin-off—and at the time the network was still in place and they still wanted that—Kaley's character was obviously in some combination what we were all looking for to try to help keep the show going. So it was an important episode on that level to be able to sell that she could hold her own. And she did.

"Vaya Con Leos," of course, was a very powerful episode, as episodes ten tend to be. They tend to be our cliffhangers. And it worked out that way for this one as well. That was such a bittersweet episode, to lose Brian's character. That began the anxiety for me of, "Do I choose to keep thinking in terms he's coming back and have Piper fighting to get him back, or do I try to find some other way to deal with the loss of his character?" And I could just never come up with that other way. I didn't think that the fans would ever forgive us. I thought that I'm just going to go to Las Vegas and gamble everything that I've got that we're going to get him back and that Piper's going to get Leo back. That kind of set Piper's attitude for the rest of the season. She's going to get her husband back. Her children are going to have their father back. And then all I had to do was come up with a way to get the actor back.

That was a tough episode. It was just hard. We were letting go of a regular character and we didn't want to do that. But he was gracious, and he understood that one of the reasons why the show could stay on the air was because he would be willing to leave. He didn't have to come back for the ten episodes. He could have said, "No. The contract is twenty-two or nothing." So the fans need to be very grateful to Brian for being willing to say, "I get it. If ten episodes is all the network will pay for, and that gives the audience twenty-two more episodes, then that's the sacrifice I'll make." And God bless him for doing that.

One of the challenges after episode ten was how not to play the next twelve episodes dark and gloomy. We'd just lost Brian Krause's character. Leo was gone. How do we try to bring some of the lightness and the fun back to the show in eleven and twelve? They were kind of designed to be a little more modular episodes; not really serialized as much. And then we would start building toward bringing Billie and Christy together and then leading up toward the finale.

Holly and I talked about this, and the writers and I talked about this. We decided to play the conundrum of the problem of a missing-in-action soldier. I mean, killed in action, as horrible as that is, there's closure there. At least the family can mourn and begin the process of rebuilding their lives. Missing in action seems to be almost worse. You can't really mourn because you're not really sure if he may walk back in the door. And that's what we decided we wanted to play with Piper's character. Her sisters were understandably concerned about that, because, "How do you tell her to move on?" It looked pretty serious. Even though there was a technicality that he could come back, was Piper looking at it with rose-colored glasses? (No pun intended.) So that was something we wanted to play, and, I think, we've played successfully.

Holly did a great job of believing. If the show was a leap of faith . . . if magic is a leap of faith, then her belief that he was going to come back—and my hope as the producer that he was going to be able to literally come back—were all leaps of faith. I think that's what we were all hanging our hats on. And I think that's part of what has made *Charmed* so successful and so rewarding to me. There have been so many leaps of faith that we've taken that have just worked out for us.

I enjoyed doing "Payback's a Witch," because I don't think anybody's actually landed a helicopter on the backlot of Paramount. It wasn't actually until we were filming that episode and I was there watching the helicopter lower onto the lot that I realized that the backlot was built to 80 percent scale. And the helicopter wasn't. The helicopter was a real helicopter. So suddenly this big helicopter is landing on what I realized then was a smaller street with smaller buildings than what's normally out there. We were all a little nervous about that, because you don't mess around with helicopters. The history of helicopters in film and television is not pretty. We wanted to make sure that wasn't going to be our legacy. So there was some anxiety there. But it was a fun episode because it really stood alone.

How did you feel about bringing Billie's sister into the series?

I think it worked very well. It was hard to bring a human being into the show to be the "ultimate threat." We've seen some of the most dastardly demons our production people could possibly imagine coming and attacking over the years. So bringing an attractive woman as a human being to be—in conjunction with her sister—the ultimate threat was challenging to pull off. And I think that we pulled it off pretty well. I have no regrets about it. I think at the end of the day their emotional threat was everything I hoped it would be to Piper, Phoebe, and Paige. Their physical threat, I'm not sure ranks up there with The Source, Balthazar, or the Demon of Fear, because, again, they're human beings. They're sisters. So we traded off some of the physical threat, I think, in exchange we got the great emotional threat. And I think that worked out in that way as well as I had hoped it would.

This time, you knew you were leading up to the series finale and there would be no spin-off. How did you approach ending the show for good?

Once Christy turned Billie, the last four episodes really become serialized. Even though they're individual episodes as we always do on *Charmed*, knowing that we were doing a series finale—as opposed to last year—it really felt like we could then begin to put into the dialogue some of the reflections of the whole run. Like in episode nineteen, I know they talk about, "Do we have the right to live normal lives? Are we being selfish to even think like that? After eight years of doing this, is this something we have the right to expect?" Raising those issues are series-ending issues.

The last four episodes really work toward the ending. And the last two are a two-parter. With "Kill Billie: Volume Two" we really do the pyrotechnics. We do the big bang. We do all the production value. The big explosions happen in episode twenty-one. And terrible things happen, of course, which then leads to the "To Be Continued" and follow through into the last episode, "Forever Charmed," which I always looked at as putting Humpty Dumpty back together again.

Again, looking back on it, "What's the one thing we haven't done yet? Let's blow the Manor so it looks like World War II." And sisters die because of it. And Piper, who has been on a mission all year to get Leo back, to get her family back, and get their lives back, continues that process in the last episode. Messing with the past and the future, putting Humpty Dumpty back together again. Along the way, she gets Leo back, she loses him, and she gets him back again. So it's really a fun episode, trying to bring in all the characters and tie up all the loose ends.

What we try to do in the last episode is to honor the legacy of *Charmed*, because that's what a family is. A family isn't just the people who are alive in this moment, it's the people that were alive before and the people that will be alive afterward. And that's the legacy of all families and certainly the legacy of *Charmed*.

What was it like writing that last page?

It was a very intense script to write, because of all the reasons you can imagine. There was so much pressure. So many expectations. By the time I got to the last page I felt like I had accomplished everything I wanted to accomplish.

At the end of every script you write, "Fade Out. End of Episode." Every year, I write, "Fade Out. End of Episode. End of Season." This was the first time I ever wrote, "Fade Out. End of Series." Writing those last three words, which is the last thing I will have ever written on *Charmed*—"End of Series"—I just stopped and looked at my monitor and looked at those three words and felt instantly nostalgic. Instantly reflective. Instantly blessed. It was a swirl of emotions.

Before I was ready to turn in the script, I just kept looking at the computer screen and saw "End of Series." I just kept looking at it and asking myself, "Did I do everything I possibly could do in this script as far as I'm concerned, to be worthy of the end of the series?" And I felt very good about that, I must admit. I felt like I had accomplished the feeling I wanted to leave the audience with, which is that the good feelings continue. That *Charmed* continues. Obviously, it's up to the fans to decide if they agree or not with me. But that's how I felt. And that's how I wanted to feel.